SKYVIEW
LORD OF THE WILLS

M. SHEEHAN

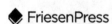 FriesenPress

Suite 300 - 990 Fort St
Victoria, BC, V8V 3K2
Canada

www.friesenpress.com

ISBN
978-1-5255-7606-5 (Hardcover)
78-1-5255-7607-2 (Paperback)
978-1-5255-7608-9 (eBook)

1. Fiction, Fantasy, Action & Adventure

Distributed to the trade by The Ingram Book Company

CONTENTS

CHARACTER REFERENCE

WARD LINE

William Ward • 1296

Peter Ward • 1328
Gareth Ward • 1390
Hildwulf Ward • 1492
Aldred Ward • 1598
Dinadan Ward • 1699
Faramond Ward • 1797
Henry Ward • 1892
James Ward • 1912
John Ward • 1942

Bill Ward • 1968   *Ernest Ward • 1971*
William Ward • 1996

WASSEMOET LINE

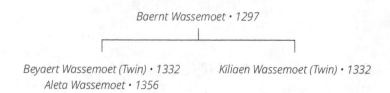

Baernt Wassemoet · 1297

Beyaert Wassemoet (Twin) · 1332   Kiliaen Wassemoet (Twin) · 1332
Aleta Wassemoet · 1356

THE WAR OF THE TWIN BEARS · 1358

Jochem Wassemoet · 1397
Goedert Wassemoet · 1494
Danckaert Wassemoet · 1590
Maer Wassemoet · 1692
Hiddie Wassemoet · 1787
Berend Wassemoet · 1887
Adelaert Wassemoet · 1911
Hanneken Wassemoet · 1932

Stijn Wassemoet · 1951   Coen Wassemoet · 1953   Joost Wassemoet · 1955

Haven Wassemoet (Ftwin) · 1977   Thijs (Thees) (Mtwin) · 1977
Nikher Wassemoet · 2000   Famke Wassemoet · 1999

DEL VERDIER LINE

Huc del Verdier · 1288

Alize del Verdier · 1392
Audric del Verdier · 1409

Hilaire del Verdier · 1458   Ghislain del Verdier · 1461

THE NOVARA EXODUS · 1494

White Pillar	Black Pillar
Aymon del Verdier · 1595	Raoul del Verdier · 1585
Lohier del Verdier · 1702	Alixandre del Verdier · 1696
Heraut del Verdier · 1794	Loeis del Verdier · 1794
Estiene del Verdier · 1888	Severin del Verdier · 1886
Audric del Verdier · 1915	Nathaly del Verdier · 1905
Odilon del Verdier · 1939	Tremeur del Verdier · 1923
Colville del Verdier · 1962	Didina del Verdier · 1946
Nael del Verdier · 1995	Varocher del Verdier · 1973
	Florian del Verdier · 1997

VON STEINACH LINE

Bligger von Steinach • 1291

Enderl von Steinach • 1399
Kelby von Steinach • 1478

Lothar von Steinach • 1500　　　*Lütolf von Steinach • 1502*

THE SPANISH ROAD · 1565

White Pillar	**Black Pillar**
Gawin von Steinach • 1607	*Volkmar von Steinach • 1592*
Hanno von Steinach • 1686	*Felke von Steinach • 1691*
Serilda von Steinach • 1792	*Giselher von Steinach • 1782*
Avicus von Steinach • 1893	*Holger von Steinach • 1892*
Elfriede von Steinach • 1924	*Hilda von Steinach • 1911*
Theobold von Steinach • 1945	*Hagan von Steinach • 1936*
Hauke von Steinach • 1970	*Clovis von Steinach • 1962*
Dieter von Steinach • 1997	*Adolar von Steinach • 1990*

KADANĚ LINE

Hynek Kadaně • 1293

Kristan Kadaně • 1389
Katarzyna Kadaně • 1580

Svinimir Kadaně • 1601   Redimir Kadaně • 1598

THE BOHEMIAN REVOLT • 1618

White Pillar	**Black Pillar**
Olīgŭ Kadaně • 1684	Strom Kadaně • 1703
Reina Kadaně • 1807	Basai Kadaně • 1792
Tyesca Kadaně • 1877	Ladislav Kadaně • 1889
Rehor Kadaně • 1908	Damek Kadaně • 1968
Ludomir Kadaně • 1953	
Kalene Kadaně • 1975	
Bodhi Kadaně • 2001	Veleslav Kadaně • 1994
	Spytihněv Kadaně • 1995

O'SULLIVAN LINE

Finghin O'Sullivan • 1298

Dónall O'Sullivan • 1397
Diarmuid O'Sullivan • 1493
Alsún O'Sullivan • 1590
Isidore O'Sullivan • 1697
Turlough O'Sullivan • 1802
Rian O'Sullivan • 1825

Ruairí O'Sullivan • 1844   *Clár O'Sullivan • 1847*

EMBERS OF IRISH ATROCITIES • 1885

White Pillar
Liadán O'Sullivan • 1893
Tiarnán O'Sullivan • 1922
Olly O'Sullivan • 1952
Cillian (KIL-ee-an) O'Sullivan • 1973

Aoife (EE-fa) O'Sullivan • 1995

Eoghan O'Sullivan • 1997

Black Pillar
Oisin (O-sheen) O'Sullivan • 1895
Éibhear (eh-VIR) O'Sullivan • 1919
Senan O'Sullivan • 1942
Feargal O'Sullivan • 1969

Ciara (KEE-ar-a) O'Sullivan • 1993

Finian O'Sullivan • 1994

THESS LINE

Eleutherios Thess · 1292

Gelasia Thess · 1405
Spiro Thess · 1491
Damianos Thess · 1588
Callistus Thess · 1696
Pyrros Thess · 1790
Phaedrus Thess · 1886
Nikolaos Thess · 1908

Kaethe Thess · 1938   *Nereus Thess · 1941*   *Vassilios Thess · 1951*

THE DIAMOND WAR · 1999

White Pillar
Helios Thess · 1968
Apollinaris Thess · 1989

Black Pillar
Archelaus Thess · 1974
Dareios Thess · 1999

LOSADA LINE

Alvero Losada • 1285

Falcona Losada • 1403
Cristóbal Losada • 1502
Goncalo Losada • 1606
Nicolao Losada • 1706
Terceiro Losada • 1789

Venacio Losada • 1902

Nemesio Losada • 1933   *Porfio Losada • 1937*   *Dael Losada • 1939*

The ultimate realization is that if one holds the world's knowledge, then one can shape its reality. You only need to see what others choose to ignore. There's a very simple explanation to the history of this world and how we ended up here, a simplicity to all our triumphs and our malice. The truth to every major event, war, plague, famine, economic collapse, revolt, conspiracy is, well…simple. To bring this truth to light, first you must look at reality not as fact but as designed, as if somebody is shaping it, and then you will see that everything has gone as planned.

William didn't set out to rule the world—the Spaniard did. The very idea of it never crossed his mind, but events seven hundred years in the making unfolded exactly as designed, which paved the way for the greatest of all feats. But as you will see, it ended up being quite brief, because as we all know, the world has a will of its own and is the greatest rebel of all!

CHAPTER 1
A VERY OLD RELATIVE

The company William worked for, The Interlaken Beer Company, was having a party to celebrate seven hundred years of business. William had been working there in the summers since high school, when his father, Bill, offered him a student job. After graduating from college, he'd secured a full-time position with the company and had been working there for just over a year.

The party was quite the spectacle. Seven hundred years was an insane amount of time for a company to be around. After about an hour or so of mingling, all but the stage lights were dimmed, and the CEO, Jim Parkins, got up to speak.

"Good evening, friends. This is a wonderful night, and I'm honoured and delighted to be the CEO for this monumental achievement. As you know, we're celebrating seven hundred years of successful business! From our humble beginnings as a brewery to our investments in various industries such as hotels, aerospace, oil and gas, renewables, health, and space exploration, we have always strived to be the best at whatever we do.

And it's all thanks to you, our loyal, devoted, hard-working team. Here's to another seven hundred years!"

Jim raised his glass, looked into the eyes of as many employees as he could, and said, "Cheers! Enjoy your party."

Throughout the evening, William talked with many of his co-workers. He was popular and treated well for his age. Although his father had helped him get the job, William was well qualified for it in his own right. In the background, a short film about the history of the company was playing on a loop, but the sound was off due to the music and dancing. In the middle of a conversation with Freddie, his research partner and friend, something on the screen caught William's eye.

"William? William? Wakey wakey" said Freddie. "Are you okay?"

William was staring at the screen. "Sorry, Freddie, I could have sworn I saw my name as a founding member of Interlaken, the original name of the company."

"That's odd. Well, William Ward is a common name, or maybe he's a very old relative. Has your dad ever mentioned him?"

Freddie had experienced a different up bringing than William…let's just say it was a little rougher, and he left when he was eighteen. His father had tried to push him into being a policeman, but Freddie hated guns and violence and didn't want to be around them all day.

"Not that I remember. I'm going to find him and ask. It would be cool if our family had been part of the company when it started," William said, thoroughly intrigued.

William walked away before Freddie could say anything and went searching for his father. He spotted him on the balcony, enjoying the warm California air and talking with Ethan Ronald, the chairman of the board of directors. Ethan and William's dad were friends who golfed together and socialized in each other's homes, so William felt comfortable approaching them. William looked out at the ocean and politely waited for a break in the conversation. The water always put a smile on his face.

"Dad, did you know there was a William Ward who founded the original company back in 1318? Are we related to him in any way?"

"No, but the Ward name was quite common back then," replied Bill unconvincingly.

"Are you sure, Bill?" Ethan quickly asked with a disappointed look.

The film was playing on random TVs throughout the room, and just after Bill gave Ethan a dirty look, they both looked at the window, where the film was being reflected. It had started over and began with a scene in modern-day Interlaken with a painting of eight men standing around barrels surrounded by mountains. The word *annui*, was engraved in the barrels. The film then dramatically zoomed in on each founder. William was third to the left.

With Ethan, Bill, and William staring at the reflection in the window, each member's portrait popped up with their name and place of birth: Alvero Losada from Montesa, Spain; Huc del Verdier from Le Verdier, France; William Ward from London, England; who looked exactly like Bill; Finghin O'Sullivan from Cork, Ireland; Baernt Wassemoet from Alkmaar, Netherlands; Bligger von Steinach from Colonge, Germany; Hynek Kadaně from Kadan, Bohemia; and finally Eleutherios Thess from Thessalonica, Greece.

The paintings were of the men in there later years, likely when the company had found success. William's dad was now forty-eight and looked just like William Ward in the painting. William had seen pictures of Bill when he was twenty-two, and he was startled to see how much William looked like the younger version of his dad. *We must be related*, William thought. *Same name, similar look.*

William began to feel connected, and this was the moment his life started to change. He'd seen all those portraits before near the main boardroom, but there had only been seven of them. No William Ward I.

Bill just stared, unable to justify the resemblance and looking for words to shed doubt, but only unintelligible sounds came out: "Err…umm…I think…"

"Yes, William, you are related," said Ethan.

"That's enough, Ethan. Don't fill his head with this nonsense…it's too vague," said Bill sharply.

"I think William is mature enough to know the possibilities. He has done all you've asked his whole life, he's just like you, safe, and predictable. That's why he's such a great researcher. Let him be curious for once, at least before he gets married and starts a family."

"What are you talking about, Ethan? William asked, feeling confused. Suddenly the party seemed far away. William couldn't hear the music anymore, and he was already feeling different.

Bill gave Ethan another sharp look and walked away, frustrated. Ethan pulled William close and excitedly started to tell him the epic myth of William Ward I.

"He was an adventurer, and from what we can tell, a bit of a wanderer. They all must have been to end up in Interlaken that long ago. He was born in England in 1296. We don't know what he or the rest of the founders were chasing, or fleeing, but together they discovered that adding hops to beer dramatically increased the taste. They were the first group of people to mass produce and distribute that now- famous beer across Europe and, eventually, the world."

William's eye's lit up as the sense of adventure began to stir within him.

"That's the spirit that founded this company and still lives on to this day—perfect beer and adventure."

Bill was beginning to cool down. He'd wanted to keep the secrets and history of William Ward I away from William as long as he could, for he knew William would eventually get the letter. He wanted William to first establish security, safety, an education, and hopefully a family before being introduced to the long line of failure and pain. Bill sat in the distance but within view of William and Ethan.

"For decades, the company was run by the eight gentlemen. It first expanded along the trade routes that brought them to Interlaken and then back to their home countries. Then it spread across Europe. Through the founders' travels and adventures, they amassed expansive knowledge of trade routes, different languages, local customs, who to pay off, and who to avoid. The main company was always run out of Interlaken and grew to be one of the largest companies in Europe. William had a son named Peter, and around mid fourteenth century, he suddenly sold his portion of the company to the remaining seven founders. He was found dead one day later. In William Ward I's will, he stated that his fortune was to be left to any future Ward who could find it. As you have likely guessed, it has not been found."

"Wow, that's incredible," exclaimed William. Turning to his father who was now reluctantly making his way over, he asked, "Have you searched for it?"

"Briefly, but it was a terrible idea…worst year of my life. I lost a year with you, and let's just say your mother's patience ran quite thin. Many a Ward has gone mad, and many lives have been ruined. The money doesn't it exist. The story is not real. We made it to Interlaken and found the old guy's will, but it was very cryptic. The Will specifically stated that we weren't allowed to make a copy, and Ethan wasn't even allowed in the building, so I had to memorize as much as possible. It was filled with places and events. Our only guess was that he wanted us to experience what he did.

"We travelled to France, England, Germany, Czechia, and back to Switzerland, trying to figure out the relevance of the events to William and/or the company, but we found no connection. We ended up back where we'd started but not any closer to learning of the fortune's whereabouts. We finally tried to journey through Gotthard Pass over the Devil's Bridge, which stood out as a point of interest in the will. We even walked it; it's a fourteen-mile journey through the Swiss Alps, but we found nothing. I gave up on our quest once we reached the Tremola Aussichtspunkt, a lookout point with a view of the Tremola Valley. The great Tremola Road up the Fibbia Mountain. It romantically twisted and turned at least twenty times up the mountain like a sweet dance; you could see mountaintops for miles. All I could feel was peace, and I wished you and your mother had been with me. The view was what I imagined when I read about the Rütlischwur, named from the Rütli, a meadow above Lake Uri near Seelisberg. It's the site of the legendary oath taken at the foundation of the Old Swiss Confederacy by the three founding cantons: To me, the Rütli symbolised you, your mother, me, and my oath to the three of us. That's where I left Ethan and headed home. I felt more drawn to go home than continue on, and I was on the next flight." Bill smiled greatly at his son as he remembered finishing his part of the quest.

"I continued on," said Ethan, wearily remembering. "I made in through Gotthard Pass and over the Alps and ended up wandering through a few cities and towns in Italy. But without your father, and with no way of claiming the fortune even if I found it by chance, I slowly succumbed to the city of Siena. It was beautiful and rich with history, wine, food, women…" Ethan trailed on excitedly.

"There's a long line of fallen Wards," Bill said grimly. "Many Wards are missing, many dead. Your Uncle Ernest, my sweet brother, died in the search."

"You told me he died in a farming accident in England. You said a tractor overturned on him!" William shouted in confusion.

"No, William, he died scuba diving near Cape Verde. He was attacked by a shark while searching a three-decker ship, called the *Hartwell*, that sunk in 1787 and was full of silver. His body was ripped to shreds.

"Many generations have skipped this temptation. There's something strange about this will. In every country we found ourselves in dangerous situations; we were constantly followed, detained, imprisoned, and repeatedly questioned by either police or someone. We assumed it was other Wards, distant relatives overly obsessed with the fortune. Listen, you have a great job and a wonderful fiancée. You'll have a family soon, and you'll realize, as I did on that mountain, that your family is your true fortune."

William stood there in awe and a little impressed that his dad had made it that far. He hadn't grown up with any of these stories, so he had no idea his father had any sense of adventure.

"I can't believe you went all those places," William said. "I just don't understand why you didn't tell me; it seems like such a great story, such an amazing adventure, you could have shared with me growing up. How old was I when you went?"

"You were five, and I was twenty-four" answered Bill.

"How did you find out about it?"

"I received a letter stating I was an heir to the fortune and that the details were in his will. But I don't think there's any money; it's either been found or never really existed. I think it was more about the adventure and the travel. Maybe there was money at some point, I guess."

"I think it's real," Ethan says excitedly. "After months of searching, we found old company records, and sure enough, among a list of people receiving payouts for the year on October 1, 1357, there was a transaction for 2,500,000 fiorino d'oro to William Ward, which is about 1.25 billion dollars today."

"That is a lot of money," William replied as he looked off into the California night. "Well, to be honest, I don't really know what to make of this, plus I haven't received any letter."

"It doesn't really matter if you get a letter or not, William. You're not going. You've just started your career, and you'll lose your job. I guarantee there is no fortune. Let's not discuss this any further. Let's enjoy the party."

The conversation grew a little quieter. Bill felt better and laughed a bit as they went back into the party and enjoyed the rest of the night. Later, when William got home, he told his fiancée, Sarah, all about the fortune. She hadn't made it to the party because she was in the middle of exams and had to study. For the next few weeks, Sarah and William jokingly discussed the fortune and whether they should go after it.

Sarah had one year left of school and was planning on travelling through Europe the summer after she graduated. William hadn't planned on going with her, as he wasn't really interested in Europe. He was never much interested in anything. He only ever thought of school, work, his friends, and Sarah. He didn't have strong opinions on much, and he never cared about small things, such as what restaurant they went to, or what apartment they rented. He was extremely easy-going.

Over the next few months, William and Sarah kept their jokey attitude toward the fortune. Sarah never really took it seriously. William didn't talk as much about it with his father, as he knew his opinion, but he couldn't shake the idea of searching. He was tremendously drawn to it, like a purpose. He spent many quiet hours researching the fourteenth century and the events his dad had mentioned. Sarah grew concerned with his late nights. Even though he wasn't out often, she could sense that he was being drawn nearer to, rather than farther from, the quest. She noticed that he was becoming preoccupied and distant.

William continued to study the events of the fourteenth century, as well as some old maps. He even took an online course in the history of trade and the rise of the merchant class during medieval times. Then, of course, came the letter.

CHAPTER 2
WORDS THROUGH HISTORY

William was enjoying a morning coffee when he saw something white slide under the door.

Dear Mr. William Ward, 1996–,

You are an heir to the fortune of William Ward, 1296–1357. Instructions to claim the fortune can be found in his will, located in a private vault below the Swiss Alps in Zermatt.

William had his will drawn up in 1337 and placed it in our care to keep it safe and seek out eligible Wards throughout history. William owned 1/8 of the Interlaken Beer Company, and on October 1, 1357, he sold his portion, which included his customers, trade routes, and distribution methods, for 2,500,000 fiorino d'oro.

Sincerely
Gabriel Müller
Will Keeper

William lived in the University Heights neighbourhood of San Diego. It was a short drive to work, but after seeing the letter, William decided to walk. It was still early in the morning, dim and cold, and the sun had just begun its ascent. After reading the letter a few times, he started to walk, deep in thought. Feeling the need for a break, he grabbed a coffee from a random coffee shop, one he never would have gone into before, as it was dirty and boring. But it had coffee, and he felt...different. As he waited in line, he quietly thought to himself how excited he was to go on this adventure. His only source of stress was figuring out how to tell his dad and Sarah. Ethan, it seemed, would be supportive and would likely make sure he had a job if he failed and had to come back.

William knew he needed more info. He needed to know more about the Wards who had gone mad, the ones who had failed, the ones who went missing, the ones who died, and how they died. William grabbed his coffee and began to walk toward work, although he knew he wasn't working that day, or any day soon. His desire to seek that fortune was too great, and he knew he couldn't fight it. But he had to go to work and see his dad for the last time before he left. He also knew that he'd have to tell Sarah, who he knew would be more supportive than his parents were going to be.

As William got closer to his office, he could see it in the distance, hovering over San Diego, the glass glowing red with the sunrise. William kept his pace as he walked toward the office, enjoying his coffee and deep in thought and excitement regarding the will. He thought back to his dad's story and how Bill had stopped his quest, and he wondered if he would continue after Gotthard Pass. He revelled in the thought of that windy road and was excited to go to see it—to be there with his dad, as he once wished.

William entered the lobby with its sleek, shiny floors that flowed to the wood columns covered with carved city skylines and country borders, city names, and places and people. William said hi to security and Laura, the receptionist, and then walked around the corner and down the hall to the elevators. He first went up to the floor where the main boardroom was located, as he wanted to look at the portraits again. He wanted to see the founders and get a sense of them and of what happened so long ago. William got off the elevator, and saw Ethan.

"Ethan!" William exclaimed in surprise. "I got the letter this morning."

"Let me see it," Ethan replied.

William pulled out the letter. The paper was warm but blank, as if the words had simply fallen off. William was thinking quickly. "Oh sorry, I left it in my office. It was quite short and simple anyway, just mentioned that I'm an heir, like Dad said."

Ethan didn't seem to think anything of it. "I assume you're going?" he excitedly questioned.

"Yes, of course. I've thought about it for months, ever since the party. I didn't speak to anyone or share my thoughts because I didn't think I'd receive the letter, but deep down

I knew that If I did, I would go. I've wanted to go so badly that my work here has suffered and I haven't been able to my job effectively."

"I understand," said Ethan. "I'd go again if your father wanted to, but he's set in his ways." Ethan looked proudly at William. "What are you doing up here, though?"

"I wanted to see the founders again and study them a bit. I feel that there must be more to William Ward I leaving the company and his sudden death."

"I agree," said Ethan. "Your father and I looked deep into the records but only found the transaction. That's the only reason we went. If not for that bit of evidence, we never would have left Big Sur."

William and Ethan finished their conversation and agreed to meet up later after William had talked with Bill. In the meantime, William went into the waiting room of the corporate boardroom and studied the paintings intently. The portraits hung higher than a normal painting would, each framed in thick gold leaf lit with a brass lamp and blood-red shade. They had an eerie feeling about them, and he immediately noticed the different facial expressions. *That's truly amazing for seven-hundred-year-old paintings*, he thought. He noticed the detail in each founder's posture and expression, as if they all had something different to say or prove. Each was painted in a different environment, and he could tell that the artist had taken great care in depicting the background.

He remembered reading that the Renaissance had its origins in Italy in the late fourteenth century. The portraits were so lifelike, he felt that they could have been from the Renaissance. Maybe a famous artist painted them, and if so, there may be other works by the artist.

The first portrait he looked at was Alvero Losada from Montesa, Spain. William jotted down some notes and took pics with his phone. Alvero was tall with darkish skin; he had a squint in his eyes and seemed to be looking up into the sky, which had a few clouds but a great rayed sun. He looked strong and rugged, and you could tell he'd been well travelled and could easily defend himself if attacked. In the background was part of an old fort tower recessed into a cliff face, and beyond that were three boats headed toward the Spanish coast.

Huc del Verdier from Le Verdier, France had fairer skin and of a slighter build than Alvero. He stood proud and straight. Inlaid behind him was a map of lower France with the Occitan area embellished. There was also what William thought looked like parliament buildings and royal courts off in the distance, scattered around France.

Finghin O'Sullivan from Cork, Ireland had by far the toughest face—pale, scarred, and beaten. He had thicker brows, deep eyes, and looked as if he had weathered many punches over time. Off in the background were shadows of men. He was tall and well-built and dressed well for what looked like humble beginnings for him.

Baernt Wassemoet from Alkmaar, Netherlands had hair like a lion's mane with a matching beard and strong shoulders. He stood with his fists on his hips and puffed out his chest. He seemed even larger than Alvero and Finghin. In the background was a deep channel with axes, spears, and shields lining one side of the coast, almost like the remnants of a small battle but with no bodies or warriors. There were also faint markings that resembled roads on a map that weaved to all edges of the painting behind him.

Bligger von Steinach from Cologne, Germany had a strong jaw and a stout frame. He was a little heavier than the rest, but you could tell by his chubby, wrinkled face that he was well travelled. He was standing on barrels with a happy look on his face. The barrels and tools were stacked in an orderly fashion, and a cross section of a factory stood out in the background. Beside the factory were the faded images of patrons in a pub enjoying drinks.

Hynek Kadaně from Kadan, Bohemia had dark eyes, black hair, and sneaky look about him. *He seemed to be the shortest of the group*, William thought. He stood in a hop field with rows as far as the eye could see. In the background was a blue sky and one single cloud.

Eleutherios Thess from Thessalonica, Greece had curly hair and deep, ghostly, grey eyes. He had the most notable pose as he looked behind him in fear, but there was nothing on that side of the painting. On the other side was an image of space filled with stars that looked like constellations, and in the background was what looked like a faded ancient Greek city in its splendour.

After a about an hour or so, William began to feel tired, as if he'd taken in too much information, kind of like what happens to a computer. He slowly backed out of the room and started toward his dad's office. As he walked, he stared at the floor and tried to organize the info he'd taken in.

William gently knocked on his dad's door. "Hey, Dad, do you have a minute?"

"Of course. What do you need?"

William entered the room and sat down. "I received the letter this morning and have decided to go." William felt a huge weight lift off his back. He held up his hand in a quiet gesture. "Before you object or try to talk me out of it, I want you to know that I've been thinking about this for months— more than I should have, to be honest. Please understand that I want both. I want the adventure just as much as the money. I feel like something is pulling me to this, to the point that I don't think I could even do my job effectively if I stayed. And I don't think I'll be disappointed If I don't find anything. I feel like there's an itch in my head that needs to be scratched. As long as there's possibility, I will feel the pull."

Bill sat quietly in thought. "But it's not real!" he finally cried angrily, leering at the wall. "You must understand that this quest ruins lives; it preys on our weaknesses. William Ward I found great success in travel and adventure, and I feel he wrote this in his will to encourage future generations to follow, because he knew what life as a peasant was like."

"But there *is* money; you and Ethan saw the transaction," replied William sharply. "And he was found dead; there is mystery here. There's also this letter from Gabriel Müller. What's his connection to this?"

Bill stood up and walked over to the window, looking a little defeated. "Nobody knows what happened back then, and I don't know who Mr. Müller is. My letter was from somebody else. Yes, he was wealthy, but too much time has passed. There are just too many unknowns. We didn't find anything, absolutely nothing, not even a clue. His will was too vague to be able to intuit anything."

"I don't know how to explain this, but I need to do this. I need to try," William stated sternly.

William got up and walked over to his dad. He asked him to help him sort through the history of the Wards. William wanted to know the Wards who had gone, the ones who'd gone missing, the ones who'd died and how they died. He needed as much info as possible.

Bill reluctantly agreed to help, seeing as there was no convincing William to stay. They decided to meet up with Ethan at lunch in the waiting area of the main boardroom. In the meantime, William went to his office and cleaned out his desk. He had feeling of closure, like it was the last time he'd be there, the last time he'd be this version of himself. He took one last look out the window at the shimmering ocean, narrowing his vision as if to peer across the sea. He smiled, took a deep breath, and then finished.

William met Bill and Ethan in the waiting area by the main boardroom as planned. Ethan had catered the event so that they wouldn't waste time dawdling over which delicacy to order. The company employed a well-travelled house chef, privy to all manner of staff. He put together a nice sushi platter with all the variety one could expect from an office.

"Am I supposed to look into this? Are you trying to tell me something?" William asks Ethan jokingly.

"No, no," said Ethan, laughing. "This is more for my taste; you won't be heading to Japan any time soon. Well…I guess you might." Ethan paused. "Come to think of it, you might! I don't really know where your travels will take you. What do you make of it?"

"Not much so far, I…"

"See, this is the problem," Bill interrupted. "We simply do not have enough info. The will was too vague, so you'll just end up wandering like we did."

"Relax, Bill," said Ethan. "It was meant as a joke. The boy has chosen to go. You knew this day would come, so let's help him now—if only to speed his journey along, either back home or, if fate is on his side, to a nice fortune." Ethan rolled his hands over each other, and his eyes happily gleamed.

"Thanks, Ethan. Please, can we start with what we know of the seven men?" William pulled out his laptop, eager to take notes.

"Sure," Ethan replied "but we don't know much, just their initial roles. The company branches out quite quickly and much gets lost. There are definitely better records somewhere. The organization was quite, big even back then."

Ethan got up, took off his suit jacket, and hung it in the closet. He wondered where to start. He walked over to the portrait of Bligger and pointed up to the barrel.

"Bligger was a merchant barrel maker from Cologne, Germany. He was credited many years after his death for standardizing barrel sizes, which made it easy to reproduce and distribute to keep up with the demand at the time. Beer was being shipped to all corners of Europe by then, so the company naturally started to produce barrels for other brewers. Bligger's barrels was essentially the first side business to start up after brewing.

"Hynek was the farmer. He grew and tended the hop farms. It was rumoured that he stole the recipe and snuck it out of Bohemia. Nobody was using hops at the time, and it really increased the taste of beer. This led to increased demand across Europe. Once the barrel making business was established, the company started growing hops in other provinces, and this is where it gets vague. They funded lots of other breweries as competitors. The records become quite speculative at this time about what business they owned, where the funds were coming from, and where they'd go. We simply do not have access to them."

William typed as fast as he could, trying to keep up. Ethan continued looking at Bill for approval, as Bill wasn't helping yet. Ethan fixed his cuffs and moved down the wall to the next portrait.

"Finghin and Baernt, as you may have guessed, were the muscle in the company. If you didn't pay your bills, you got a visit from "Finny" or "the Bear," as they were aptly nicknamed. As the company grew, Finghin employed lots of muscle. Using the large mercenary and privateer market at the time, they managed all the protection along the trade routes so the cargo could safely get where it needed to go. As you might guess, the company then created their own mercenary armies and sent privateers around Europe, which added extra revenue as well as opened up armouries and weapon making. War was big business back then, so naturally they danced in it. It wasn't long before the company controlled most of the trade throughout Western Europe. One thing for sure is that they diversified quite early, keeping each company separate and only settling affairs annually in Interlaken to avoid any unwanted attention from those in power at the time.

"Eleutherios, from what we can tell, controlled the books, along with Huc. He was an astronomer and mathematician before he fled Greece. I can only assume that he and Huc structured the company to run like a modern organization, as they were the only academics among the group. Huc was a Master of Law prior to leaving France, which was his main responsibility in the group—navigating between the different regulations of each country they dealt in.

"Unfortunately, we know nothing of Alvero, as he's not mentioned in the records much, except when funds were portioned out. His share was always equal. Same goes for William; we do not know their roles. William is only mentioned when funds were portioned out and on his final transaction."

Bill stood up and walked over to Ethan, who was staring at the portraits. "We only know of William's death from the letter. We questioned the will keepers—that's what they called themselves at the time—but they gave no answers. This Gabriel Müller won't have any answers either, I suppose." Bill took a deep breath walked over to William. "So, in short, Bligger made the barrels, Hynek brewed the beer, Baernt and Finghin protected and distributed it, Eleutherios managed the money, and Huc navigated the laws of each territory."

"We can only guess that either Alvero or William was the head of the company," Ethan added. "Ultimately, there's always a leader of a company, somebody to make the tough decisions—like Jim, our CEO. He's responsible for the direction and strategy of the company."

"Maybe William and Alvero both ran it at the time but had a disagreement, and that's why William sold," William said out loud but to himself.

"And maybe Alvero had him killed and took back the money," added Bill, now seemingly participating.

"What about the will? What can you remember about it?" asked William.

"The will was a tale of his life, mainly of the places he travelled and historic events of his century," answered Bill. "He grew up in England at the beginning of the fourteenth century. At that time, England was at war with the Scots and constantly invading them. Remember the movie *Braveheart*? William, not wanting to participate, started working at an early age to ensure he had enough money to buy out his military obligations. At sixteen he started travelling and looking for a better world. He sailed to France and found work on a merchant vessel. He worked for a year seeing most ports in Europe. He eventually landed in Greece and travelled through Europe, working city to city and town to town until he made it to Interlaken, where he and the rest of these gentlemen founded the Interlaken Beer Company."

Bill handed a very old, small leather-bound notebook to William. He opened the first page to see that it plainly listed:

The First War of Scottish Independence 1296–1328
The Great Famine 1315–1317
Treaty of Edinburgh-Northampton March 17, 1328
The Second War of Scottish Independence 1332–1357
Hundred Years' War 1337–1453
The Black Death 1347–1351
Hanseatic League 1356
Treaty of Berwick 1357
Pfaffenbrief October 7, 1370

Ciompi Revolt 1378–1382
Winchester College Founded 1382
Victual Brothers 1392
Kalmar Union 1397
The Renaissance in Italy
The Peasants' Revolt of 1381

"This is the list of events in the will; this book belonged to your great-great-grandfather, Henry Ward, and it contains all his insights. He died trying to find the fortune. His body was found by hikers near the top of the Matterhorn. He was still clutching the book," Bill said sadly. "It was given in to me years after I returned. I kept thinking I might try again, but I realize I won't, so you may as well have it. I've added my notes as well, as few as they were."

"That's all we know," added Ethan. "Travelling through Europe, we couldn't figure out how anything connected. We researched and researched and thought and travelled. We learned much about historical events, but we couldn't make any connection to the company, and that's ultimately where we failed."

William leaned back in his seat feeling overwhelmed and a little defeated. The weight of the challenge was becoming apparent. He took a deep breath, remembering the one of his favourite quotations: "To reach the heights of heaven you must also reach the depths of hell." Although he never thought a quotation like that would apply to his life, quests like this were supposed to be overwhelming. That's what made them great. *It's supposed to be hard,* he thought, digging deep to find the energy to move forward. Suddenly, he got excited, remembering his letter.

"You are an heir to the fortune of William Ward, 1296–1357!" he exclaimed. "The Peasants' Revolt of 1381 and Pfaffenbreif on October 7, 1370 both happened after his death. Why have these been added by the keepers? William must have given instructions for these to be added, but why?"

"We're not sure," answered Bill. "The Hundred Years' War likely wasn't called that prior to his death, or when it ended in 1453. We found no connection between William, the company, or any of the historical events or places, unfortunately."

William excitedly continued to take notes, trying to immortalize his internal connections. Bill and Ethan could sense his excitement, briefly remembering their own when they realized little clues.

"I'm wondering about the fallen Wards you mentioned?" asked William.

"It's all in the book. Please read that part first. You may change your mind, as it's very bleak," answered Bill reluctantly.

William felt he had what he needed to start, and he didn't have the heart to read the deathly part of the book just yet. He was beginning to sense that to solve the riddle, one must move forward. He felt he needed to start to act like William Ward I and move forward—take action.

Perusing the book, he read a quote from Henry he connected with: "Success is when opportunity meets preparation." This was comforting to him.

That night he went home and told Sarah. She was unhappy with his decision. She loved William very much, but she began to question their relationship. The argument got quite heated until, reluctantly, she made him choose between her and the quest. At the same time, somewhere deep inside, she was proud of him.

He had the same feeling as with his father, who eventually relented but likely only to keep him safe in some way.

"Why do I have to choose?" he said to himself under his breath. "With Sarah or my father? Why am I always being pushed toward what's safe and normal? Am I unfit for this type of quest? He nervously wondered if he wasn't smart enough to figure it out, or strong enough to see it through. He wondered what he would do if Sarah or his father had this choice before them now. He thought he'd be supportive and encouraging; after all, Sarah was going to Europe anyway, and his father had already gone on the quest. *There must be some flaw in me that Sarah and my father see, some weakness*, he thought.

After the argument with Sarah, William slept on the couch. Late in the night he went online and looked for flights to Interlaken, but every flight he looked at booked up before he could secure a seat. *That's odd,* he thought. Soon, the only flights available were months out. Growing frustrated with every click he noticed an ad that kept popping up looking for

SHEEHAN

crew members to sail yachts over to Europe, which he thought
wasn't a bad idea, *I could start my journey at sea, just like William
did,* he happily thought. He really wanted to see that will.

Reluctantly he started reading the old book. He figured
he'd spend the next few months learning as much as possible
about the fourteenth century. The book was ominous and
intimidating. It was wrapped in old grey leather that was
faded and rough. It edges pushed out like stories trying to
escape: random words and thoughts, directions, maps, ideas,
drawings, madness. Inside the book in big letters read, "Henry
John Ward" along with his address and next of kin.

The hours grew late. William stayed up all night reading
and researching side notes, avoiding the deathly part of the
book. His internet search history looked like a tragic mess.

Late in the morning, the power flickered and briefly went
out, resetting the internet. Giving up, William closed his
laptop and decided to go to sleep. After his eyes adjusted
to the dark room, he could see the pale moonlight shining
through the bedroom window. He didn't want to sleep on the
couch, rather he wanted to spend the night with Sarah so he
sat in a comfy chair near the foot of the bed and finally got
the courage to read the end of the old Book. Sarah peacefully slept while he read the madness of Henry's travels. The
book was heavily damaged and had seen many years. Many
pages were covered with faded ink and different handwriting.
Some pages contained printing, but much of it was illegible.
William procrastinated scrolling through the book, but finally

28

he built up the courage. If this was the depths of hell that they'd reached, he needed to be a part of it. Slowly he thumbed the page until reaching a dog ear. He opened to that page and the title read, "Fallen Wards." He then fell asleep.

CHAPTER 3
NEVEAH

The next day, William awoke with his thumb still holding the place at the "Fallen Wards," but he still couldn't read it. He realized then that he needed to be on his way first before knowing what awaited him. Plus, it felt good to go against his father's advice for once. He thought of William Ward I and his plan to leave England. He'd known at an early age to be prepared, because he knew he didn't want to fight in that war. Then when opportunity presented itself, he moved forward and likely took the first vessel out of England.

"And that's what I must do. I must leave; I must start the journey," William quietly but encouragingly said to himself.

William grabbed his old book and packed lightly. He loved Sarah deeply but knew he had to go. He made his way down to the San Diego Port and found the oldest, ugliest fisherman there and asked if any ships were going through the Panama Canal.

"Ha, ha," the old fisherman laughed. "Only cargo ships go, and there ain't no crew no more. I can get you on a fishin' boat, but they come back here," the old man chuckled. "You'll need to talk with the Port Authority; they'll get you on a ship, but it won't be no cargo ship."

"What will it be then?" asked William.

"Likely a pleasure vessel. Rich folk get crews to sail their yachts to the Caribbean, but they fly because it's too dangerous for them."

"That's ridiculous," chuckled William.

"I agree. It's an interesting time we live in, that's for sure. I grew up in this port. The boats get bigger and bigger and emptier and emptier."

The old fisherman pointed to an office. "You'll find the Port Authority over there; somebody in there will help ya. Tell 'em Pete sent you."

"Thanks, I appreciate the help. I'm William, by the way."

"Yer welcome. My name's Pete—Pete Billows. Best of luck to you."

William started walking toward the office but suddenly looked back.

"Any advice, Pete? I mean, I feel like there's probably more to just getting a ship to Caribbean."

Pete got up and walked over to William. "Are you all right, son?"

"Yes, I'm fine, I've just never been on a boat before."

"Well, you'll need a few books. It's four days out to the Panama Canal, and you won't be allowed to use much boat… only the crew's quarters, which are small. Keep the talk with the other members small; don't get involved personally, and you'll be fine. They tend to create their own entertainment drama and such. The sea is meant for you and your thoughts. Long journeys make men go mad, but you should be okay for four days."

"Well, to be honest, I plan on making it to Greece."

"I recommend you find land and board different ships often. It's a safe route, but don't go straight there, especially since you look like you carry a burden. I can tell from that look in your eye, I've seen it before. You're not the first person to come here looking for such a long passage, every once in a blue moon folks come around here questioning stuff."

"Thanks, Pete. Take care." *Burden?*, William thought.

"Aye, you too," Pete reluctantly answered with a queer look in his eye.

William made his way over to the office, looking at yachts off in the distance and thinking that they looked a little lonely and seemingly a waste of money. "If I find the money, I hope to spend it more wisely," he whispered quietly to himself. "I'd sail my own boat."

William opened the door to the office and peeked inside. A well-dressed man was sitting at a desk.

"Sorry to bug you, but Pete sent me over. I'm looking for passage to the Caribbean. Are there any boats leaving today?"

The man looked at the schedule. "There's a charter going to Panama City tomorrow morning."

"Nothing going to the Caribbean?" asked William nervously.

"No, sorry, Panama is the closet available."

The Port Authority employee gave William the contact info for the charter company. William immediately called and was able to convince the crew to let him aboard as free labour for the trip. William went back to see Pete to thank him.

"I found one, Pete" said William after sneaking up on him.

"That's great! When does it leave?"

"Tomorrow morning. I've already called and convinced the crew to let me aboard."

Pete and William talked for a bit longer. Pete offered an old boat for William to stay on to "help get his sea legs." William refused and said he was going to get a hotel for the night. He knew he couldn't go back home and risk being talked out of going. Eventually, though, he gave in and thought it might be good practice to sleep on a boat, since he'd never been on a large one before.

The next morning, William had a quick breakfast with Pete and thanked him again. He then walked down the dock, feeling the cold morning air across his face and enjoying the unevenness of his steps. He made his way to Pier 13 slip 57 as per the instructions. The yacht was over 350 feet long and seemingly brand new; it grew shinier and shinier as William approached. He could see an infinity pool at the back surrounded by lounge chairs. The deck was perfectly clean and led to an indoor/outdoor saloon that was the most luxurious space William had ever seen. William was quite impressed but didn't understand how he was supposed to clean something that big. As he approached the vessel, a tall, attractive, athletic looking woman came down to greet him. She had messy hair, faint freckles across her nose, and she wore a cute long-sleeve top and lifeguard shorts.

"Hello, you must be William. I'm Nikher. Nice to meet you"

"Yes," William nervously answered, feeling a little intimidated. "Nice to meet you too." She stared intensely at him as they shook hands. The handshake lasted a little longer than normal.

"Okay then, come aboard. The captain is prepping the engine and going through final checks, and then we're to set sail to Panama City. Our job is to keep the vessel clean, and I mean clean!" Nikher said with another stare. She looked slightly disappointed, which confused William.

"The owner will be taking delivery of the vessel in the Cayman Islands. Then we have a few more stops in the Caribbean. Depending on how the owner feels, we might take it to Cape Verde."

"That's great. I thought it was just gong to Panama," William said, surprised and excited.

"Once we get through the canal, we can go wherever we want—wherever the owner wants, I mean. He'll likely change his mind, but owners typically like to cruise through the Caribbean. I'd be surprised if we make it to Cape Verde, so don't get your hopes up."

"I'm hoping to get to Greece," said William.

"I know, Pete told me. He also warned me that you've never been on a boat before, and that I need to look out for you."

Nikher smirked. "*Do not* get seasick! If you vomit on this boat, I will literally throw you overboard. Owners of yachts this expensive are very particular."

"You know Pete?" William asked in surprise.

"Yes, sir, he's a good friend. Loves his whiskey. Follow me and I'll show you to your cabin. Take off your shoes and put on these deck shoes as well as this hat; the rest of the uniform is in your cabin. Nikher playfully messed up William's hair and softly put the hat on herself, almost in a flirting way, thought William.

"I hope I get cute shorts too," William regrettably joked.

Nikher gave him another disappointed look and proceeded to escort him through the yacht, which was brand new and super clean. Some items even still had protective plastic on them. There was a large main saloon with a bar open on three sides overlooking the infinity pool. Nikher led him through a door and down a hall. There was luxury everywhere. William expected to enter a small room where he thought he'd likely have to sleep on a hammock, but Nikher smiled and opened a door that was as thick as a vault door.

"Here's your cabin. Keep it clean," she exclaimed. "Don't touch anything you can't afford to replace, especially any buttons or switches. I don't want to see fingerprints anywhere. This is the stateroom. Do you know what the master stateroom is?" she asked.

"No." William shrugged and answered.

"Well, this is where the owner sleeps. This yacht only has four staterooms, and three are already taken. You can stay here as long you promise not to touch anything."

"No problem," William said with a laugh.

"Not funny. Get settled in, put your uniform on, and get up to the helm to meet the captain."

William returned a nod of approval. He was beginning to think she didn't like him, but he didn't care. The well-decorated cabin was the width of the yacht and was walled with windows on each side, very elegant but also nautical. Thoughts of the will and the fourteenth century filled his head again.

A little while later, after getting settled, William wandered the yacht and looked for helm where he was to meet up with Nikher and the captain. Wearing the uniform, he felt a little like an imposter. He noticed that the fabric was made of an unusual material he'd never felt before.

He made his way to the helm to meet Nikher. On his way, he admired the luxury and the storage space—there seemed to be hidden compartments and doors everywhere. On the bridge he noticed that the luxury faded and it looked more like a control room with switches, buttons, screens, and computers showing graphs and codes. The captain and who William assumed to be the first mate were both tall and muscular. They were in a serious discussion with Nikher regarding the route and safe passage through to the Panama Canal.

The captain reached out his hand and gave William a strong, firm handshake. "William, I'm excited to meet you. My name is Coen, and this is my first mate, Cillian. And of course you've met Nikher."

"Yes," William politely answered.

"My friend Pete tells me you're trying to get to Greece," Coen said.

"I am," William answered, confused. *Pete must be worried about me.*

"Well, I'm sure Nikher has told you we're hoping to get you as far Cape Verde, which is a lovely journey, but we do have a few stops in the Caribbean. There are lots of nice islands and special places for you to see."

As William and Coen conversed, Cillian sat quietly and continued preparing for the voyage. It was nearing 8:00 a.m., so Captain Coen shook William's hand once more and told him to stay close to Nikher. She would be his boss for the voyage, and he'd answer to her. He revved the engines a little, and William could feel the power of the yacht.

The San Diego skyline shrunk as they rumbled past the breakwaters. William could see Pete waving on the dock, oddly smiling. The cold air William breathed in felt rich and new. His excitement was growing, and he was feeling nearer to his great relative. He couldn't wait to read the will.

The morning was quiet and cool. William had the pleasure of watching the sun rise above his old office building with the slight feeling of closure. Cillian was going about many things, pressing buttons and flipping switches.

Nikher watched William intently as Coen captained the helm. William caught her deep in thought as their eyes connected, and she waved William over.

"Now that we're off, I'd like to take a break and go over a few extreme situation precautions with Coen," she said.

"Sure," said William, a little taken aback.

Walking back through the main room past the bar and up a set of stairs, they met Coen again at the helm. Upon entering, William noticed the thickness of the doors as they slowly closed automatically with a distinct sound of relieving pressure.

Coen gave William an approving nod. "You've noticed. In here, we're waterproof, fireproof, explosion proof, and bioweapon proof. We have provisions to last a year if need be; there are also thrusters, and this helm can delve fifty feet under water. Same as our cabins. If you notice anything unusual, just jump in here or into a cabin. Controls are voice-activated, and your voice has been temporarily mapped for emergency authority. There's also mini scuba gear stored throughout the yacht. Just look for a little scuba sticker, and it will allow you to escape under water up to fifty leagues."

"Seems like overkill. Who attacks a personal yacht?" he asked nervously.

"Nobody in particular, but sometimes the owners of these yachts have enemies," answered Coen. "This could be owned by a member of a drug cartel or the Mafia, or by a soldier of fortune."

"Or an evil CEO," Nikher jokingly added.

William, satisfied that a threat was unlikely, started looking more closely at the yacht. He reimagined the many compartments as full of machine guns, rocket launchers and turrets, and snipers.

"So, William, where you from? What brings you aboard and on your way to Greece?" Cillian asked in a friendly voice. Nikher gave him a queer look.

"San Diego, but I was born in Big Sur," answered William, remembering what had happened to the letter when he tried showing it to Ethan, how the words seemingly fell off, which gave him an eerie sense to keep the adventure secret "No reason in particular for going to Greece; I have some very old relative's I'd like to visit."

"You don't look Greek," said Cillian.

"I'm really just landing in Greece, but from there I can travel around Europe by land. Where are you guys from? How did you end up in this line up of work? Seems unnecessarily dangerous."

"I'm from the Netherlands," said Nikher.

"Me too," added Coen.

"And I'm from Ireland," Cillian spoke proudly.

Time slowed a little and all could feel and awkwardness in the air after Cillian said Ireland. William paused and thought for second but smirked and dismissed any coincidence.

"It's a great line of work for those wanting to see the world," Coen added. "It's really not that dangerous…just a potential for danger."

The four days went by quickly. William kept to himself like Pete suggested and found he felt surprisingly well. Nikher still kept a close eye on him, always looking disappointed, but William did notice the odd laugh when he made his typically awkward jokes. Coen and Cillian always made him feel safe and comfortable, and they always pointed out the beautiful Baja coast when it came into view, especially as they passed through the small Mexican towns along the coast, as well a Guatemala, El Salvador, Honduras, Nicaragua, and Costa Rica. He had plenty of time to think and reflect. There wasn't much to do, as everything was already so clean and new. He continued to read the about the events of the fourteenth century, cognizant of not getting too buried in the details, as that's where he felt his father and Ethan failed. While reading the old book, he still avoided the deathly section, but he came across another quote he liked: "History is written by the victorious." William began to steer away from the details of the historical events and focus on the facts. Ethan and his father had tried to find connections to the company within the wars and treaties, but they couldn't find any. *Maybe they were written out*, he thought.

After finally reaching Panama City, Nikher, Coen, Cillian, and William went through customs. William noticed that his three companions seemed unnecessarily nervous, and they kept William within arm's length. Nikher took a deep breath as the officer scanned William's passport. William noticed that they looked at each other frequently, which made him uncomfortable.

After making it through customs, the yacht rumbled through the canal, powered through Limon Bay past Colón, and entered the Caribbean Sea. It sailed northwest along the coast, past the eastern borders of Costa Rica, Honduras, and Nicaragua, eventually steering straight north en route to the Cayman Islands.

William had been ordered to stay in his cabin for most of the trip, but Nikher called him up to the helm, where he enjoyed the view of the coast of Nicaragua. Coen was busy steering the boat, and Cillian was on the flybridge looking out. The yacht sailed past the small island of Providencia. William could hear the faint rumble of new engines. Suddenly, from around the island, two identical hundred-foot yachts approached—one from the south and one from the north side of the island. They sped toward them, drawing nearer and nearer.

"Here we go, Nikher," Cillian yelled. "Starboard side north and south. William, stay in the helm and do what Coen says."

William gave Coen a surprised look. "What's going on?" William calmly asked.

William seeing the concern in Coen's eye suddenly thought it might be one of those other Wards; distant relatives overly obsessed with the fortune, his dad cautioned about.

"I'm not sure, William. Two smaller hundred-foot yachts are in an aggressive position and driving right at us from north and south. You can see them on the monitor."

William looked at the screen and could see the boats powering directly at the front and back of them. "Who are they?" he asked. Coen didn't answer.

"*Neveah*, enable Blast Door Protocol!" Coen commanded the ship.

Nikher was standing on the aft deck, waiting for the rear-attacking boat to approach. Cillian was at the front of the boat, bouncing on the balls of his feet, almost like he was going to attack the yachts.

William gave Coen a concerned look. "What is Cillian doing?" he asked in a panic.

Coen ignored him and tried to manoeuvre the yacht away from the attacking vessels. Nikher was still on the aft deck, holding onto the rail as if she was going to jump on the attacking yacht. With the yachts closing in, Coen franticly steered the much larger and slower yacht to the northwest, hoping to avoid the imminent collision.

"What are they trying to do? What do they want?" William finally yelled, now in actual fear, as he could see it wasn't a joke.

"They're trying to sink us," said Coen calmly.

"But they'll sink too," said William.

"There will be a third boat or a plane. They want something"

"What do they want?" William was confused.

"You." answered Coen in a stern voice. "Take a look these people; look closely." Coen pointed to the security screen.

William braced himself on levers and controls and moved closer to the screen. He could see the attacking yacht within ten feet speeding toward the stern. On the bow stood an angry looking man gripping the railing and awaiting the collision. Just before the attacking yacht made contact, William watched as Nikher leaped off the aft deck and collided with the man, knocking his weapon loose. The man tried overpowering Nikher but couldn't. He swung wildly as Nikher calmly dodged and counterpunched and kicked.

Coen and William held on as the yacht swayed back and forth from the collisions. William looked at another screen and noticed that Cillian must have jumped onto the other boat as well, as he was rampaging through that boat as it violently swayed back and forth. Looking from screen to screen, William could tell that there was also lots of talking going on, almost as if they knew each other. Nikher had knocked out the angry looking man, but two other men came after her from each side of the yacht around the helm, holding on as the boat swayed in the wave. William could see that they both were holding what look like axes. He panicked and tried to get out of the security helm, but the doors wouldn't open.

"Coen, open the door. We have to help her. They're going to kill her!" William screamed in terror.

"We can't, William. Nikher and Cillian can handle themselves. Get away from the door."

"*Neveah*, open blast doors now," William commanded to the yacht, trying out his voice commands.

"You only have authorization to close, not open. You need to stay safe in here," Coen said.

"We have to go out there and help!" William screamed again

"Wait until we get clearance from Nikher. She has ordered you to stay in here," replied Coen calmly.

Just as Coen finished speaking, a flash of red steel swung from above, right between William's eyes. It smashed into the blast door and knocked William back. A man from one of the yachts had snuck on board and was wildly swinging an axe, desperately trying to get at William as he scrambled on his back in shock.

William fearfully got up and backed over to the control screens. Nikher had both men down, and William could see what looked like blueish steel blades dissolve into her forearms. Cillian had also swum around to the boat Nikher was on and was disabling the engines.

William could see Nikher and Cillian talking and then lifting the men and placing them into the berth; Nikher surprisingly carried one by herself. Back on the deck, they were pointing off into the distance.

"And that's the third ship," said Coen.

"No, there's a fourth," said William, still scared.

Coen looked panicked over this fourth ship, just as the crazy guy swung an axe and touched his ear.

"Nikky, Cilly, get back to the boat now, Coast Guard alert!"

Nikher and Cillian immediately jumped into the water and swam back. The crazy guy with the axe also noticed the Coast Guard and dropped the axe and jumped overboard. Once Nikher and Cillian were on board, Coen hammered the throttle and the yacht rumbled much louder than before. Coen pressed a button and quieted the engines, but William could still feel the power.

The yacht sped around to the east side of Providencia. William looked at the controls and could see they were going over fifty knots while crashing into waves and bouncing all around the helm. William wondered why they didn't go that fast when the two boats approached.

"What did you mean by they wanted me?" William asked, concerned.

"Its best if Nikher explains; she's your equal," replied Coen.

The helm blast door opened with a distinctive pressure-release sound. Nikher and Cillian were relaxing in the main saloon and drying off. Nikher changed into a tank-top, and William could see what looked like a blueish-grey tattoo across her forearms, elbow to pinky. It looked like old-Dutch markings. Cillian also dried off, but William couldn't see any visible tattoos on him. But he did see an opened bottle of Irish whiskey and an empty glass beside him. Nikher sat on the sofa and spotted William as he walked down the stairs.

"Are you okay?" Nikher asked William.

"Are you?" he asked, feeling confused. "I was safe behind the blast doors."

"Good, so you can take direction. I suppose you wondered what that was all about." Nikher stood and poured a glass of whisky for herself and offered William one.

"The man on the yacht that attacked the stern was Spytihněv Kadaně and some hired help. The creepy guy Cillian took care of was Archelaus Thess. Do those names sound familiar?"

"Yes, they do. Thess and Kadaně are names of two of the founders of a company I used to work for. Coen said they were after me. I don't quite understand."

"They are after you. They need you to get to Henry Ward, as he has their fortune," said Nikher.

"My great-great-grandfather Henry?" exclaimed William. "He died fifty years ago, before I was even born."

"We don't know if he's dead or alive, but he's the twentieth Ward, which means he controls the wealth," explained Cillian.

William shook his head in disbelief. "He'd be over 120 years old. Is this about the will? The lost fortune?" asked William.

"Yes, but the fortune's not lost. The clues to find it are hidden somewhere in your head. There are a lot of secrets in your head," Nikher stated frustrated.

"Believe me, there is nothing in my head. I have no idea what's going on," said William.

"What do you mean by the twentieth Ward?"

"Are we almost there?" Cillian ignored William and asked Coen who was at the helm, he touched the back of his ear and was communicating with Coen some how. William assumed the answer was yes by the nod of approval to Nikher. Nikher looked relieved then touched the back of her ear to inform Coen. "The Coast Guard is taken care of, and both boats are disabled. They won't chase us,"

William not understanding how they were talking shifted his thoughts to the fact that the owner of the yacht was not going to be happy.

"Twentieth relates to the century Henry has been entrusted with, and his heir will be the twenty-first Ward, but don't worry about it too much right now. We're almost at Grand Cayman, where we'll meet up with someone more familiar with the details who can explain the rest."

The yacht abruptly slowed down, shifted momentum, and approached Grand Cayman Island, William, Nikher, and Cillian all stood on the bow and looked at the massive, luxurious mansion they were approaching. The endless windows reflected the glimmering blue sea. There were tennis courts, huge pools with waterfalls and waterslides, and a sandy beach waterfront. The mansion itself was three storeys high with a centre structure, containing indoor and outdoor space, and two wings extending into multiple patio and lounge areas.

"Here we are, William; this is Crystal Harbour," said Nikher.

"Is this the yacht owner's house?" asked William. "He's not going to be too happy that the yacht's a little banged up."

"I don't think the owner will be too upset…he has about twenty of them," said Cillian with a laugh.

"Twenty? Wow," William whispered in awe.

The yacht slowed through a dredged laneway with not much room to spare on each side. Coen expertly steered around to the far side of the mansion, hiding *Neveah* from the sea.

"*Neveah*, enable sunken treasure," Coen said as the four of them waited on the mid level prior to exiting. William could hear water gurgling loudly, and the yacht started to submerge itself about eight feet turning the 357-foot yacht into a 99-footer with its windows de-tinted, the flybridge rolled back, and much of the bronze panelling faded to white.

As they got off the yacht and walked down the dock toward the mansion, William could see an older gentleman, who looked a lot like his father, smiling and walking briskly toward him.

"Ernest," cried William. "Is that you? I thought you were dead. What are you doing here?"

Ernest didn't say anything but gave William a big hug.

"I thought you died in England...or were eaten by a shark. I can't believe you're alive!" William stated in shock.

"Yes...yes, it's me. I'm so glad to see you, glad you made it here safely."

"Is this your house? Oh no—is this your yacht?" William pointed at the yacht and cringed a little, slightly relieved that most of the damage was hidden. "I'm so sorry, we didn't mean to damage it. We were attacked; these two crazy boats ambushed us, and Nikher and Cillian saved..."

Ernest cut William off. "Don't worry about the boat, my boy. I see you got my letter?" Ernest said with a smile.

"That was you? Is this the fortune? Did you find it?" asked William excitedly.

"Yes, part of, and no—to answer your questions in order. But let's not get too hasty. Let's have a pint, some bangers and mash, and mushy peas. I'm sick of soufflé's, feta cheese, and mutton. I had this food specially flown in. I've been very excited for you to get here; I need to get you back to your English roots. I was so happy when you decided to come—not that I had any doubt. You're a Ward!"

Ernest and William walked toward the mansion and caught up. Ernest laughed about the shark attack and repeatedly told William, "In due time, son, all in due time."

William was excited to talk with Ernest but also noticed many other people—swimming, relaxing, meditating, and exercising—all around the mansion.

After a much-needed English lunch, William and Ernest were summoned to the rooftop patio to discuss what William guessed was the Spytihněv and Archelaus attack.

"Now listen, William," Ernest said seriously. "Before we go up there, I just want to warn you that some of the things I'm going to say will be surprising. Please stay calm and don't ask any questions unless absolutely necessary." Ernest rubbed William's shoulders supportively.

"Is this about the Spytihněv and Archelaus, and why they attacked us?" William asked, eagerly trying to put things together.

"Yes, but there's way more, and I want you to be prepared for the shock of it," said Ernest as he urged William out of the dining room.

"Should I be taking notes? I'll go get my laptop."

"Umm…no, your laptop is long gone. Cell phone too, and wardrobe," said Ernest apologetically.

"What!" William said, confused. "Where did my laptop go? I've been keeping all my notes in there!" He looked defeated.

"I told Nikher to make sure they got lost when she went through immigration at the Panama Canal. Everything will be shipped back to San Diego for you. You can have them back after this is all done," Ernest said with a very proud grin on his face.

"When what's done?" William muttered after a confused pause. Ernest ignored him and urged him to the rooftop.

CHAPTER 4
THE COUNCIL OF ERNEST

The rooftop allowed for a great view of the island with its colourful architecture, surrounding cruise ships, palm trees, sunshine, and endless blue, glittering sea. In the meeting area were three large couches and two comfy chairs surrounding a fifteen-foot-long centre table that had a three-dimensional model of Central Park in it. It was exquisitely detailed with fields, ponds, baseball diamonds, skating rinks, and buildings. One small pond next to a small castle was even lit from underneath, giving it an eerie, bottomless feeling. On each couch sat four people, twelve in total, who all stood in respect as William entered. They eyed him closely. Ernest gestured for William to sit in one of the chairs facing the three couches.

Ernest did not immediately sit beside him, but William could tell that was his spot. He was nervous to meet everyone.

"Please sit, everyone," Ernest spoke gently. "As you all know, this *is* William, the twenty-first Ward. Unfortunately, William doesn't know who any of you are, aside from Nikher and Cillian, who were entrusted with the task of getting him here safely. I also know that some of you have just left the Cradle, and most of this is quite new to you, so I thought I'd use this opportunity to make clear all that I know regarding these wills and the whereabouts of the fortune. Nothing discussed here will be repeated by me or anyone in an open venue. This is the one and only time I will discuss this very brief history. Most of you by now have developed an eidetic memory; for those who have not, I recommend that you stay quiet and listen very carefully, making sure everything finds a place in your mind."

Ernest took his proud hands off William's shoulders and started to move about the rooftop. He stopped beside Nikher, who was sitting next to an equally beautiful athletic woman (*Likely her mother*, William thought) and two other gentlemen, one older and one close to William's age.

"As you all know, seven hundred years ago eight gentlemen founded the Interlaken Beer Company. One of those founders, William Ward, of whose line I'm a direct descendant, sold his portion of the company in 1357 and was found dead one day later."

As Ernest had begun to speak, the table had clouded to a solid metal state, and a well-coloured, detailed digital hologram appeared and danced over the table, giving a visual representation of his story.

"The company was very successful by that time, leaving his heirs quite wealthy. The remaining seven founders kept on at the Interlaken Beer Company (IBC), and the following year, the Baernt Wassemoet line was divided. During what is known outside of the Cradle as the War of the Twin Bears 1358…" As

Ernest spoke, the hologram froze on the image of two bears fighting over a pile of wealth, but gave no more details. "… Baernt's twin boys, Beyaert and Kiliaen, each choose different paths. Beyaert formed the Ward League along with William's son, Peter. Kiliaen chose to stay with the IBC.

During this war, the Ward League took possession of all of the Wassemoets' wealth, to be returned to the rightful heir upon completion of a final task." The hologram depicted a shrouded figure carrying off much of the wealth, with one of the bears following and the other retreating in the opposite direction.

"I will get to that task shortly. I don't know why William left the IBC, but it's speculated that he and Alvero had a falling out regarding the direction of the company. Nevertheless, we assume that the Ward League formed as a result of the War of the Twin Bears. There are, however, conflicting stories regarding what started the war, one being that Kiliaen killed William on orders from Alvero, prompting revenge from the Wards. The other claimed that William faked his own death, as he was dissatisfied with the actions of Beyaert and Kiliaen."

Ernest urged Nikher and the woman beside her to stand. "This is Nikher Wassemoet, heir to the Wassemoet fortune, along with her beautiful mother and guardian, Haven Wassemoet. It is a family line pledge to protect and aid the twenty-first Ward in the completion of his task."

William's eye's widened uncontrollably; he'd known there was something more to Nikher. His mind was racing, and he almost blurted out a question, but then he remembered that Ernest had asked him to stay calm. He took a deep breath and calmed himself, eagerly awaiting the details of the "task."

Ernest now moved his attention to the two gentlemen. "Moving ahead to the fifteenth century..." The hologram sped through numerous wars and historical events. "...and the early stages of the Italian Wars, 1494–1559. The Ward League annexed a majority of the Huc del Verdier line's wealth, after what we call the Novara Exodus 1500." The hologram illuminated two opposing armies laying down their weapons. "They forced Hilaire del Verdier, the leader at the time, to join the Ward League, which he ultimately did. This destroyed his brother, Ghislain, who continued the del Verdier line within the IBC." The hologram then froze on an image of two men, one in shambles and the other following the shrouded figure and bear. A locked vault was also depicted in an unknown location.

At this point, the two gentlemen on the couch stood up without being urged. "This is Nael del Verdier, who is heir to the del Verdier fortune, along with his father and guardian, Colville, who descends from Hilaire" The HoloTable digitally scrolled through the descendants. "And just like the Wassemoet line, they have pledged to protect and guide the twenty-first Ward," Ernest added.

Ernest moved to the next couch while the HoloTable sped history forward. "During the sixteenth century, the King of Spain linked his territories through a trade route know as the Spanish Road 1567 to transport his military; this gave way to the discovery of the Bligger von Steinach line. The Ward League acquired much of the von Steinach wealth and divided the brothers, Lothar and Lütolf." The HoloTable once again stopped on a single image, this time of two brothers agreeing to separate. Lothar stood beside the bear. A third vault appeared along with the Spanish road, illuminated in the background.

"This is Dieter, the rightful heir, along with his grandfather and guardian, Theobold, who descends from Lothar," said Ernest.

Both Dieter and Theobold stood up and gave William a bow of respect. He returned the gesture promptly with a friendly nod. Ernest continued. "The seventeenth century." Once again, the HoloTable sped through wars and events. "I'm sure you all are seeing the theme by now. In that century, the Hynek Kadaně Line joined the Ward League during the Bohemian Revolt of 1618. Their wealth is now under the control of the Ward League and is to be returned to Bodhi here." The HoloTable image depicted two teenage boys caught up in the revolt.

Ernest gingerly rubbed Bodhi's shoulders. "He is accompanied by his grandfather and guardian, Ludomir. I understand, William, that you've already met Spytihněv, who is a descendant of Redimir Kadaně, who stayed within the IBC, while his brother, Svinimir, joined the Ward League during the revolt.

"Now to the eighteenth century." Ernest walked closer to the centre table as the history raced to join him. He threw his arms up in air. "Nothing outside the Cradle happened that we are aware of. No other member joined, and no additional wealth was acquired, aside from normal business."

William's insides were now on fire; he was doing everything he could to not interrupt or ask any questions, but his mind was all over the place. He couldn't control his curiosity; he started panic and feel overwhelmed. He couldn't help it anymore.

"Excuse me, Ernest. I really apologise for interrupting, but what is the Cradle?" Apollinaris asked nervously. Ernest quickly gave Dieter a slightly disapproving look. William felt a rush of relief flow through him.

"Well, it's hard to articulate, but essentially the Cradle is what reality is, what in general everybody thinks is real or commonly believed and accepted. It's both a mental and physical place for some; it's all these events that this HoloTable is speeding through." Ernest calmly paused, searching for the proper words. He knew it was a difficult concept to grasp.

"You, William, Nael, and Bodhi," Ernest pointed to each respectfully, "were born inside the Cradle. Almost everybody is, meaning you all have a birth certificate, a country of origin, and a passport. But some are not. Nikher, Aoife, and Dieter, for example, were born outside the Cradle, which means they have no country, no formal identification. They can freely move about the world using one of many different individuals we have invented, and the world knows no difference. Take me, for example. I exited the Cradle by dying…well, faking my own death, to be exact. Now I can continue my duties as a guardian and move about the world without any trace. I'm no longer active in any database. Everybody is trackable inside the Cradle; the only way to stay completely hidden is to die or never be born." Ernest finished and then paused before starting again.

"Events are also described as being either outside or inside the Cradle." Ernest continued, catching his breath. "The War of the Twin Bears happened outside the Cradle, and you won't find it in any historical text, but it is lore among us. The Italian Wars did happen inside the Cradle, and you can read all about them; however, the Novara Exodus, which was the war within the Huc line that created the division, would be considered outside the Cradle.

"This wealth that has been accumulated over time weaves in and out of the Cradle. Inside the Cradle, reality can easily be designed; for example, most of you had a hint of a fortune, a will, a letter. Using your passport to cross a border issued a trace, which was promptly followed by unwanted attention. We knew this would happen and we were prepared for it. We designed all of this to get you here at the same time. Nikher had the idea to give some of you a brief look at what hunts you. Is that any clearer?"

"Yes, thank you, please continue," Apollinaris replied. But all could sense he was still unsure.

Ernest continued. "As already mentioned, the eighteenth century was uneventful in terms of the Ward/Alvero conflict, but the nineteenth century, however…" The HoloTable sped through time again. Ernest now moved closer to the third couch and to William, and to his chair, which he was longing to sit in. He continued but with a deepened sadness. "That century refers to the Embers of Irish Atrocities. We know that a division took place in the 1880s and members of the Finghin O'Sullivan line were added to the Ward League, along with not all but an immense amount of wealth. Much was lost during a subsequent war, which also lead to many Ward League deaths, but I won't get into that here.

"Turlough O'Sullivan, who was the leader at the time, had died and left Clár and her brother, Ruairí, as representatives prior to 1880." The HoloTable illuminated a rapid scene of deaths across the globe and then froze on a single image of a fifth vault joining the others, with Ruairí taking his place beside the shrouded figure, along with the descendants of the Bear, Huc, Bligger, and Hynek. "This beautiful young redhead is Aoife; she is the heir to the O'Sullivan fortune, and this young man, whom you've already met," Ernest jokingly smiled and playful nudged him, "is Cillian, her father and guardian, who descends from Ruairí. Ruairí joined the Ward League, but unfortunately his sister, Clár, did not. They have pledged as well to aid us, with the understanding that their fortune will be returned."

William sat with his mouth wide open. His brain was on fire connecting all these people and events. Electrons fired back and forth between his head and the pages of his old book, searching for revelations. Little fires ignited, starting to clarify what needed to be completed. But still he stayed calm, respecting Ernest's only request.

"Finally, the twentieth century." The HoloTable sped through history for the last time. "The century many of us have been involved in. What we call the Diamond War saw the Eleutherios Thess line, led by siblings Nereus, Kaethe, and Vassilios, divide; Nereus and Kaethe joined the Ward League, and Vassilios continued with the IBC. The Ward League again acquired a major portion of their fortune."

The familiar image froze, this time adding a sixth and final vault. Nereus and Vassilios were shown in mid-fight; the background depicted a defeated Vassilios, and Nereus joined with the shrouded figure and a new line of descendants. "This fine young man is Apollinaris Thess, heir and grandson to Nereus, and beside him is his father and guardian, Helios, whose line has pledged to aid the twenty-first Ward.

Ernest walked back over to William and stood beside him. "This is William Ward, the twenty-first Ward, direct descendant, father to father, future leader of the Ward League, and rightful heir to the fortune in its entirety. He is entrusted with this century, and I am his uncle and guardian. My duty within the Ward League, along with the other guardians, is to ensure succession by keeping you all safe until you come of age. The current leaders of the Ward League are the century heirs of the twentieth century, and you seven are century heirs of the twenty-first. You are tasked with destroying the current leader of the Alvero line and his heir. Doing this will free the fortune for proper disbursement. The Ward League has been secretly defending against the inhumanity of the Alvero line for seven hundred years. In attempting to destroy them, we have divided each family line and seized much of their wealth.

The Alvero line during these wars has managed to retain members of the Wassemoet, del Verdier, von Steinach, Kadaně, O'Sullivan, and Thess lines; they have evolved into what we now call the Losada League, known in olden days as the Black Pillar of Wealth."

Ernest finished with a deep breath and finally sat down. The HoloTable illuminated an enlarged, rotating 3D image of the shrouded figure showing his face. To William's surprise, it was him. The illumination then scaled down to show Nikher and Aoife immediately to his left and right, then Dieter, Nael, Bodhi, and Apollinaris. Each stood in a menacing pose. Behind them were the lines of descendants, all the way back to William, Huc, Baernt, Bligger, Hyneck, Finghin, and Eleutherios.

All the members of the company sat silently absorbing the weight of the task. Nikher, Aoife, and Dieter were not surprised, but they were eager to get started.

Cillian stood up and walked over to William and Ernest and added, "The wills that you now seek outline the

Seven-Hundred-Year War between the Ward League and Alvero line. They will lead you to Henry, the twentieth Ward, who will hand over the fortune to the twenty-first Ward. William, you will be entrusted with the protection of this wealth as twenty-first Ward, as well as have the task of destroying the Alvero line. Both leagues have survived through time by operating outside the Cradle. They have shaped the world while hidden in the shadows. Governments don't know the exist; history doesn't know they exist. The keys to intuiting the wills are hidden inside William's head, so make sure nothing happens to it. The Alvero line is responsible for the vilest of the world's atrocities. As you search through the history of the Cradle, you will see a special kind of evil weaving its way through time."

"Thank you, Cillian," said Haven. She rose gracefully, ensuring all could hear her. "After the Irish Atrocities, we lost much of our history and have since worked very hard to find evidence in order to prepare you for this task. After the Diamond War, our enemies became clearer and we realized that both leagues have honoured the original succession plan. After many years, my brother, Thijs, while touring Wassemoet Castle for inspiration, noticed a single stone, different from the rest, being used as an archway to support the great hall. Quickly we set up a foundation and donated the funds for a restoration project. Using concrete imaging technology, we found etched in the stone "The Declaration of Succession 1337," prior to any internal wars. The declaration referred to the eight factions of Interlaken and stated that the heir of each faction would follow the first line, namely the child, male or female, born nearest to the turn of each century in perpetuum.

"The disenfranchised from each line, called the 'disinherited,' are known as the Dark Seven. They believe they are the true heirs, as the Declaration of Succession, which is an amendment to the original Declaration of Interlaken, was agreed to as members of the IBC not the Ward League. In their eyes, by joining the Ward League, your lines forfeited succession, leaving them as heirs. They are hunting each one of you and will do anything to get their family wealth back. They will kill each and every one of you to get to William, whom they need at this point to find Henry, who has their money in those vaults you saw. This is why you were attacked the second your passport was scanned in Panama City." Haven paused and looked across the island.

"The Declaration of Interlaken 1328," Helios said loudly, just as Haven finished, "stated that the Interlaken Beer Company be supported by eight factions, with a single representative for each, bound by secrecy in perpetuum. Each year, the individual leaders of the factions were to meet in Interlaken to settle affairs and share funds. The IBC, as you all know, has survived to this day and runs as a well- respected, publicly traded company. Although none of the factions meet annually at the IBC anymore, our line being the last, it is still the foundation of this conflict.

"The Declaration of Interlaken 1328 and the Declaration of Succession 1337 fundamentally hold both the Ward League and Losada League together. Each league has seven leaders and a succession plan. The Alvero line, like all of ours, will have a single leader as well as a century heir—always two, each line has two," Helios stated eerily. "My Grandfather Nikolaos born 1908 was the Thess leader and single representative within the Losada League. He had three children: the first-born, Kaethe; Nereus, who is my father; and the youngest of the three, Vassilios. Nikolaos was betrayed by someone within the Losada League, and Kaethe, being first-born, renounced representation, so it fell upon my father. Vassilios saw an opportunity to move into the succession line. His son Archelaus's son, Dareios—who was born 1999—attacked our house with the intention to kill my father. But my father, being no fool, had suspicions about Nikolaos's death. Fearing that the Ward League was closing in, he made a deal: if the Ward League would keep the fortune safe and honour the succession, he would help end the Alvero line and in turn get his revenge."

"Do we know who leads the Alvero line, and who the heir is?" asked William after looking to Ernest for approval.

"Venacio Losada 1902," Helios wearily answered. "He had three children—Dael, Porfio, and Nemesio, who was the first-born, but his children are completely unknown. Mostly all members of the Losada line work outside the Cradle, so it's next to impossible to track them. As each century wore on, the Losada League grew increasingly powerful, and the remaining lines turned into shells of their former power. My grandfather would often joke about how little he actually knew; the betrayal of our line and William Ward himself shows that the Alvero line never intended to share power, and the Dark Seven are foolish to think that's the case. They are cogs in his machine, and any humanity they have is lost."

The rooftop stayed quiet as Helios recited the story of his family ripping apart, which caused a ripple effect for each line. William even felt the sadness of his father and their now-distant lives. But as they delved into their past, a sense of familiarity seeded amongst them, the beginnings of a bond as each line had a similar history. Together they could destroy the Alvero line and maybe repair some of the damage within their families.

The night crept in slowly as the sun descended over the dark blue horizon, stretching the shadows across the dimming beach. After a little quiet talk and much silence, the guests started retreating to their rooms for a night's rest. Nael, Bodhi, and Apollinaris stared at William, but no one said anything as they left the rooftop. Ernest had recommended William go to *Neveah* with him to discuss matters in private.

On *Neveah*, William had the feeling of being torn on the inside and regretting leaving San Diego. "What have I gotten myself into?" he said as he stretched out on the couch and sipped some of Cillian's whisky.

"This is your destiny, William. No matter what you chose, your path would have always led you to this task. There's too much history and too many people relying on you," said Ernest emphatically.

"I don't care; I can't do this," replied William angrily. "My dad warned me about this. He told me to read about the fallen Wards. If only I had, I wouldn't be in this mess."

"This is not a mess, William. This *is* an opportunity; this *is* what destiny looks like. You are the only person who can end this. You have a chance to become wealthy beyond measure as well as enrich some wonderful people and take down the Alvero line."

"I don't want to be any chosen one, or take down any Alvero line; I don't even know anything about them or what they've done or why the Wards have been fighting them," William replied with another gulp.

"The Alvero line is responsible for most of the world's atrocities, they have been manipulating the world for far to long, we have been fighting their wrath for seven hundred years, just secretly," Ernest said.

"The Ward League?" William replied, looking for confirmation.

"Yes, that's what we are, you included," Ernest replied.

"Why not governments, police, FBI, CIA—any of those? MI6, Russian spies, Contras, anybody?" William said loudly, still confused.

"They don't know about them or what they're doing, hence the secrecy," he replied calmly.

"If you know what they're doing, why don't you just tell them?"

"Because that would lead them to us as well, and we do not want that. Plus, it's way more complicated; you'll see it better after you go through history. What you must understand about us is that we shaped the world, the Cradle…"

"You shaped the world…" William interrupted, really confused.

"Yes, us, the Ward League! Well, us and the Alvero line, but like I said, they did most of the bad stuff. And one day, you will lead us. Listen, the wills outline the history of the Cradle. You must look past it and see our war, the one between us and the Alvero line. You must read the wills and look at the Cradle history as if somebody has designed it exactly to unfold the way it has, as if somebody is shaping it. Looking at history this way will guide you to Henry and how find the Alvero line."

"Can I renounce succession, like Kaethe? I mean, what if I just said no? Hypothetically, of course." William could see the horror in Ernest's face.

"You simply can't. You have no other siblings." Ernest shuffled to get more comfortable. He was looking incredibly concerned now. "Listen carefully, my boy. You renouncing succession would create chaos; succession is the only thing keeping order. That type of chaos will create desperation, which would risk the lives of too many people. Nobody wants a repeat of the Irish Atrocities, especially after they have finally balanced themselves again. I'm sorry, William, but this is your life now;

this is what you have been raised to do. And the others have been raised to help you. They have no other path; you simply do not have any other choice."

"Is Henry alive?" asked William abruptly, already trying to forget Ernest's last comments.

"I have no reason to believe he's not. Secrecy is the most important virtue of our world; I am only permitted to know certain things to help me keep you safe. You are a century heir, so your journey will require you to contain the world's knowledge and understand all of its truths, both inside and out of the Cradle." He finished as the colour in his face started to reappear.

"My...dad gave me this book," William said reluctantly, showing Ernest the old book. "I've had this feeling that I should keep it secret. Did you send this to me? He said it was found by hikers, and Henry's dead hand was clutching it."

"I didn't give that to your dad, but I assure you that if it's in your possession, it was meant for you, not him. You'll notice this as you search through the wills; no matter how events seem to flow, the outcome often reveals its creator, usually those who benefit the most."

"The old book only lists random events and people. My dad and his friend Ethan went looking but couldn't find anything. I don't see how these events connect either."

"Those events are our history. In your stateroom on *Neveah*, as well as at the safe houses, there are HoloTables and HoloWalls similar to the one on the rooftop to help you understand history. Henry only intends to be found by you, and the other leaders only intend to be found by their respective heirs. Always trust your gut; you are the only one capable of comprehending the whole truth. I can't, even. Like I said, my duty was to keep you safe while in the Cradle and guide you to this point, and I guarantee that I have passed very important info to you that you will later be able to make connections with, unknowingly. I've essentially been a conduit for you for these years, and it has been my pleasure to watch you grow," Ernest said proudly. "Nikher, Aoife, Dieter, and Eoghan's duty is to protect you from now to Henry. They are the toughest, smartest, and most skilled people I know, but they are not designed to comprehend what you eventually will need to know. Apollinaris, Nael, and Bodhi will also have parts to play, which I'm just not privy to. I'm guessing that each of them will have info directly related to their war for them to pass to you, but I'm not entirely sure, nor am I required to know or speculate."

"I just don't understand; for instance, why doesn't Henry just secretly contact me and tell me what I need to know, what I need to do." William was noticeably overwhelmed.

"Remember, he did give you that book...that's something. Don't underestimate how big or how secret both leagues are. I know they exist, yet they've managed to remain hidden from the world for seven hundred years while at the same time being at war with each other. The wills are a route to through time that will lead you to each century heir ending with Henry, along this route you will learn the true nature of this world. Currently, you aren't capable of understanding what they leaders are yet. You're, as they say in the Cradle, just entering your 'apprenticeship phase.' Just remember to always trust your decisions and don't feel obligated to reveal anything to the others."

"I wish my father was here. Why couldn't he have just continued on and figured it out like you did!" William cried in anger.

"Your father's heart was never truly in it. He hardly believed in the fortune and could never see anything outside of the Cradle, so we couldn't guide him. You can't guide somebody to something they can't see. You, however, were drawn to the fortune immediately. It's in your soul, and as century heir, we didn't have a choice but to show you."

"What if he did believe? Would he have been a guardian like you?"

"I'm not sure; the Ward League definitely operates mysteriously, but I'm sure Henry would have had a place for him, seeing as how important you are."

"Can we really trust everyone? Why wouldn't they just give me up to the disinherited and split the money?" William asked suspiciously, starting to question his safety.

"I'm not sure who you can trust fully, aside from Nikher. Henry knows the truth regarding the War of the Twin Bears, and she desperately wants to know, as her family has been divided for a very long time. The keys to finding Henry are in your head, so believe me, she will keep you safe. Also realize that the lines have all been split between good and evil; that's what all those wars are about, so even if you think you can't trust them, know that they are the good versions of their lines."

"But anybody can be corrupted."

"Yes, you must trust your intuition. If you feel you should keep the book secret, then do so. If there's a time when you feel drawn to share its contents, or even existence, then do so as well. It's your choice. You have many hidden secrets in your mind, and Henry would have made sure that everything you need to know to find him is in your head. I feel he did this for the sake of secrecy but also to ensure your safety. The disinherited will not dare kill you, for fear of losing access to the fortune.

"Listen, you are the most important person in the world now. The fate of the second age rests upon this task. You must destroy the Black Pillar of wealth and end the Age of Elites; the many have been ruled by the few for far to long. This is the last war, the final battle.

"Nikher Wassemoet is approaching within a hundred feet, starboard side," announced *Neveah* from directly inside William's head. William looked at Ernest confusedly and then, with sudden inspiration, walked up the stairs and entered the helm.

"*Neveah*, enable Blast Door Protocol!" William commanded.

William watched as the doors shut with the distinctive sound of pressure releasing. "*Neveah*, close Blast Door Protocol!" William also commanded, realizing his new authority.

Nikher and Ernest were talking below as William went back downstairs and approached them with a look of disdain.

"Whose yacht is this?" he asked both of them. They looked at each other with a smirk.

"You should have figured that out by now," said Nikher.

"It's mine, isn't it? I'm the owner taking possession of it in the Cayman Islands, and I'm the one taking it to Cape Verde, depending on how I feel, right?" cried William.

"Yes, well…unless there's somewhere else you'd like to go," responded Nikher, happy that William had finally figured it out.

"You're ridiculous. I thought you said I could trust her!" William said, staring at Ernest. Nikher looked flattered.

"You can, of course," answered Ernest.

"Listen, I worked very hard at keeping this boat clean for you," Nikher laughed, getting William to laugh as well, if only slightly.

"We need to go over the plan to get to Zermatt, as we're leaving in the morning," said Nikher.

William nodded approvingly, and the three of them relaxed in the main saloon as Nikher laid out her plans to get William and the others to Zermatt safely. Ernest reluctantly approved.

The next morning, *Neveah* warmed slowly as her lights brightened and her engines hummed. Coen was at the at helm again. The eight awoke wearily. Nikher, Aoife, and Dieter, who were all born outside of the Cradle and were raised for this task, were up very early and going through their training routines. William, Apollinaris, Nael, and Bodhi were still adjusting to their new life, not fully understanding the roles they were to play.

"We sail to the Turks and Caicos in thirty minutes." Nikher's voice suddenly entered all their heads.

"Did you hear that?" William asked Ernest as they ate breakfast on the deck of *Neveah*.

"Hear what?" replied Ernest.

"In my head, Nikher just said that we're leaving in thirty minutes, and last night, *Neveah* spoke directly to me *in my head*," said William.

"It's called Mind-Link. We use it to communicate with each other. There's a small set of electrodes behind your ear that pick up neuromuscular signals that are triggered when you internally verbalise and feeds them directly to *Neveah* or to another person, like Nikher just did. The device uses a bone conduction speaker that plays sound into the ear. It's quite simple, old tech really," replied Ernest.

"I don't have anything behind my ear," cried William as he franticly started rubbing the back of his head. "What? Ah, there it is. Wow, it's small; I can hardly feel it. Who the hell put it there?" William was beginning to grasp its usefulness.

"Nikher, I suspect," said Ernest. "Don't underestimate her; she's well trained and very resourceful. She will get you to the wills, so trust her."

"Yes, yes, she did. I remember her helping me with a hat," William said disappointedly, as he though she'd been fliting at the time. "How do I use it?"

"Just internally verbalize the name of the person you wish to talk to, or you can gently touch the electrodes behind your ear from bottom to top. Everybody is listed."

Neveah's voice now entered William's head. "Apollinaris, Nael, Bodhi, Nikher, Dieter, and Aoife are approaching, sir. One hundred feet, starboard side."

Sir, William thought, *sounds nice.*

"Well, son, this is where I leave you. You are in good hands," said Ernest, looking for a hug.

"I wish we had more time; I have so many more questions to ask," William sadly replied. "I've thought you were dead for so long."

"We will. My part is done for now; all you need is in the wills and your intuition."

Ernest gave William a big hug and then made his way back to Crystal Harbour. William watched sadly as he walked away and wished the rest of the company luck.

CHAPTER 5
HOLOGRAMS AND UNTRACEABLE FUNDS

Nikher and Aoife took command of the yacht and went over the safety protocols for the new members of the company. They told Coen to set sail for the Turks and Caicos. The seven heirs stood on the bow and looked into the horizon, letting the warm sun lay upon their faces. Clear, blue water sparkled as *Neveah* floated into the sea.

"So now that we've gone over the safety protocols, the other important issue we need to address is how insufficient the four of you are," Aoife said as Nikher chuckled. William, Nael, Bodhi, and Apollinaris all looked offended. "Follow me." Aoife gestured and they all followed her away from the helm and along a circuitous route to what looked like a small entrance way and a door, but it was unadorned. William had lost his sense of direction but thought they may be in the heart of the ship.

Aoife placed her glowing forearm on the adjacent wall, and suddenly a door appeared. "This is the HoloRoom." Aoife strutted through the door and pointed around the almost-pitch-black room. Only the hum of the wall gave increasing amounts of ambient light.

"For a minimum of three hours every day on this vessel, you will do physical training that will only stop once you're at your max."

The floors, ceiling, and walls lit up, showing a hologram of near-impossible terrain to navigate. Enemies walked in anger from a distance right through them.

"These are you suits. You'll feel every kick, punch, stab, shot, leap, and fall."

William stared at the suit, noticing similar markings along each forearm.

"Those are decorations," Nikher whispered to him as she rubbed her forearm and eyed him closely.

The surroundings dimmed again. "Also, for a minimum of three hour each day, you will be required to work on your memory." The wall illuminated again, and random thoughts of their journeys so far swam around them. "This will also bring you to your max. The world you are in now is a secret one and intends to stay that way." The four sat in awe as Aoife finished.

Later, while meeting in the main saloon, Nikher and Aoife started to go over the plans to get to Cape Verde safely, but they were interrupted almost immediately.

"Why are we going to Cape Verde anyway?" asked Apollinaris nervously. He was short with a narrow nose, dark hair and eyes, and tanned skin. He'd worked at an investment firm prior to receiving the will and leaving for the Cayman Islands. He was just ten years old during the Diamond War and only remembered his great Uncle Vassilios violently leaving his house.

"SkyView," said Nikher.

"What's SkyView?" asked William.

"SkyView is our next mode of transportation; it's a supersonic jet we use to reconstruct history. It has cloaking tech that allows us to stay off radars, as well as invisibility shields that mostly hide it when its grounded. This allows us travel around the world without being noticed. It was developed after the Irish Atrocities. Its database holds the accepted history of the Cradle—historical disputes and a multitude of speculations—essentially anything in the public domain. But we also have sought out non-public information and added it as well. It's interfaced with the HoloTable and the HoloWall and essentially has the same function, but it allows us to see history from the sky and gives a true sense of the world," Nikher proudly added.

"It also allows us to change history to our theories," Aoife interrupted, raising her voice slightly. She didn't like the mention of Irish Atrocities. "SkyView has a SkyDeck below with an Augmented Reality window that interacts with the earth. For example, you could watch the Battle of Poitiers 1356."

Nikher gave Aoife a leer that sliced the air in the room. Aoife impressively ignored her. "Then SkyView will hover and digitally display the battle on the ground through the AR window, exactly how history recorded it," she finished.

"Also, if you have a different theory, or if you know the truth," interrupted Nikher emphatically, giving Aoife a second slicing leer, which she ignored again, "you can view and save a new version of history."

"It's not just for battles, ladies," Dieter said sternly. "We're dealing with seven hundred years of history. It simply cannot be comprehended without visual aids. SkyView has mapped corporate structures throughout history, as well as the history of government acts and legislation, and global trade. Pretty much everything inside the Cradle. If it's commonly accepted as fact, it's in SkyView's database and can be observed and altered. We're going to need it to reconstruct history and the Seven Hundred Year War in order to find the current Alvero leader and heir."

William felt much better knowing about SkyView, as he was beginning to feel insecure about finding the current Alvero leader and heir. Immense feelings of hopelessness would crash over him like waves. If not for Nikher, who seemed so confident to him and very driven, he didn't know if he could endure his own thoughts of failure. Even Aoife, he thought, as well as Dieter, seemed so confident and full of purpose. *Maybe being outside the Cradle allows you to see things clearer*, he thought.

"But before we go to Cape Verde," Nikher added, "we're making a stop in the Turks and Caicos to meet Eoghan. From there we'll be splitting up. Dieter, Nael, and Bodhi sail with Eoghan; William, Aoife, and Apollinaris will stay with me on *Neveah*."

"And who is Eoghan?" Nael spoke reluctantly.

"He's my brother," Aoife said.

"Okay, but why are we meeting him?" Nael added.

"I was going to get to that, but was interrupted earlier. Eoghan is the captain of *Truth*—the name of the yacht, not the literal truth. We're much safer splitting up, and we need to make a few extra stops. This will make four people per yacht. Each yacht has four safe rooms, if needed, as well as facilities for more training time in the HoloRoom. Aoife and I will protect William and Apollinaris and guide them out of the Cradle, and Dieter and Eoghan will get Nael and Bodhi out."

"What extra stops? Why aren't we going?" asked Bodhi nervously

"Mainly because we don't understand enough yet. We need to find out more about the Diamond War; hopefully, William here has info in his head. We are going to see Kaethe, who will be in St Lucia on vacation. Nereus has set up a meeting for us. The only problem is that I'm sure Vassilios knows about it." replied Nikher.

"If Vassilios knows, why would we go and take the risk?" William asked. He was growing increasingly concerned with the "in his head" comments, as he was sure there was nothing in there.

"Because we need to talk to her in person; plus, I have a plan. You'll have to trust me."

William was quiet, as usual, as *Neveah* sailed past Little Cayman and Cayman Brac. Coen made some interesting comments about each island.

"Cayman Brac has a bluff running the length of the island. It's forty-five metres high and has many caves, even a bat cave. There's also a parrot reserve and a Russian warship that's a great dive site. Very small population, though. Only about two thousand people live there."

Everybody else was scattered around the yacht in their own heads. William sat on the foredeck of *Neveah* as she sailed around the southern tip of Cuba and north of Jamaica and Haiti toward the West Indies.

Neveah finally made it to the Turks and Caicos. She slowed, and Coen enabled Sunken Treasure while still out at sea. He steered through a fairly busy marina between Pine Cay and Stubbs Cay, barely entering the North Atlantic Ocean. *Neveah* docked beside a similar yacht, which William thought was likely partly submerged. Moving about the yacht and rummaging in an oversized compartment was a large, strong man with a bright ginger beard and wild ginger hair. He had a muscular build and tough sunken eyes with a hint of crazy.

Neveah notified William that Eoghan was approaching. He boarded and made his way up to the main saloon, where everybody was nervously sitting.

"Where is she?" Eoghan cheeringly questioned as he entered the room, looking for Aoife.

Aoife stepped out from behind Nael. "Right here, idiot," she responded.

Eoghan walked right up to her and gave her a big hug. "How did it go? I see everybody is here safely. Which one is William?" asked Eoghan in his thick Irish accent.

"Everything went fine, of course. That's him." Aoife pointed over to William, somewhat approvingly.

"Really? He's skinnier than I thought. What's with the dumb look on his face?" Eoghan said, half joking.

"That's his normal face," Aoife answered with a laugh.

"Hey," cried William, "that's enough. You're Eoghan, I guess. You're taking Dieter, Nael, and Bodhi to Cape Verde?"

"Yes, that is our plight, William. we need to get to SkyView and then Zermatt to get you to the wills safely. A lot of us are relying on you. Are you sure you can handle this?"

"No, not at all," William replied. "To be honest, everything is still quite vague and overwhelming."

"Well, I would love to sit here and chat all day, but we must be off. Good luck!" Eoghan grinned at William and gave Dieter, Nael, and Bodhi a wave to join him.

"Are you all set? You know the plan?" Nikher asked Eoghan mistrustfully.

"Yes, yes...of course. We'll see you in Cape Verde! I'll be on the beach waiting."

And with that, the four of them boarded *Truth* and sailed southwest. Way off in the distance William could see the yacht rise out of the ocean and speed off.

"You don't like him very much, do you? Is there something I should know?" William asked Nikher when he caught a moment alone with her on the aft deck.

"I don't like anybody," she responded. "The Finghin line has a long history of killing; I'm not sure we can really trust them."

"You mean the Irish Atrocities?" William asked. Nikher gave an eyes-wide-open nod.

"What exactly are they? What did they do that was so bad… well, atrocious?"

"That requires a long answer; this goes back to the beginning. First of all, I don't believe Kiliaen killed William or that William sold because of something the twin bears did. I think the Atrocities started during that war. The Irish Atrocities that we know of now was a killing spree that lasted sixty years from 1890 to 1950, and it involved three generations of O'Sullivans— Fynglas, Oisin, and Éibhear. Fynglas was the son of Clár…you'll remember that she and her brother, Ruairí, took over when Turlough, died. Fynglas was only fifteen at the time. When he came of age and learned that most of the wealth was gone, he started killing members of his own line that had joined the Ward League. He passed his malice and wrath to his son, Oisin, who then passed it to Éibhear. They hunted down and killed much of our kin: the Wassemoets, del Verdiers, von Steinachs, Kadaněs, O'Sullivans. All except the Thess line, because they were still part the Losada League. The Ward League hadn't got to them yet. By the end, Éibhear, who was the most vile, would kill simply for the fun of it. I can only guess that someone in the Alvero line had had enough, as the realized they were killing the only people who knew how to get to Henry."

Nikher had answered, but William could tell she wasn't finished and was just looking for the right words.

"But why did they kill everybody?" William asked, hoping to prompt Nikher along.

"Well, the Ward League has only survived this long because of secrecy; the O'Sullivans tried to kill and torture their way back to their money. Since the beginning of the Ward League, our histories have been stored in our relatives known as "conservators." Each conservator was told a small section of our time. Family trees are quite large and complex, so information could be spread literally around the world. A lot of the time, people were given a small inheritance with the job of protecting a small but important piece of history, typically a truth. If they had a loose tongue, money would disappear. Some people stayed inside the Cradle because they were of no use in this war, but we can still be used to pass information."

"Like my dad," William said, suddenly realizing the truth, in a sad sort of way.

"Yes," Nikher said reluctantly. "But that doesn't mean he hasn't played a very important part—he likely has, perhaps unknowingly, given many answers to you, although you don't know the questions yet. Those will unfold as we go." Nikher spoke reassuringly and repositioned herself on the aft deck, sinking into the white leather cushions.

"If one was pointed in the right direction and given all the pieces, they could rebuild history and be led directly to Henry, along with the rest of the Ward League. For Fynglas to know this and hunt our conservators leads us to believe that the Alvero line must operate in a similar fashion, which means we can find their leader and their heir. We tried searching for years, all through history, but found no trace of any line, or any wars. Inside the Cradle, neither league exists. Truths are a rare commodity outside the Cradle, and the keys to them are prophesied to be in your head. We only know of wars through the guardians whose task is to ensure succession."

"The wills," exclaimed William. "They are the new messengers."

"Yes, I'm sure they must be," Nikher responded promptly.

"Have you ever seen one? Do you know what's in them?" asked William, still feeling the need to keep his secret about his old book—not so much because of the events but more due to the madness of it. Plus he wanted to read about the fallen Wards before sharing it with Nikher.

"Never seen one personally, but they list historical events. Cillian also told all of us on the rooftop, remember?" Nikher then began speaking in Cillian's voice. "'The wills that you now seek outline the Seven Hundred Year War between the Ward League and Alvero line and will lead you to Henry, the twentieth Ward, who will hand over the fortune to the twenty-first Ward.' I've spent half my life learning history, same as the others who were born outside the Cradle."

"Did you just repeat that word for word…what Cillian said?" asked William, remembering Ernest saying something about memory. "Do you have…oh, what did Ernest call it, an idedict memory?" he added unsurely.

"Close," Nikher said with a laugh. "It's called an eidetic memory" Seeing William was still confused, she pronounced slowly, "Eye-DET-ik, memory—it's similar to a photographic memory, but eidetic memories are viewed as an 'out there' experience rather than being in the mind. Visual, auditory, and other sensory stimuli are externally projected. It's like having your own SkyDeck. This is what Aoife was describing in the HoloRoom."

"You have this?" William asked excitedly.

"Yes, but it's not something you're born with, or only prevalent in children, like most doctors would have you think."

"Well, how do you get it then?" William asked, hoping for an easy answer.

Just as Nikher was about to answer, Aoife walked up from the deck below.

"You develop it." Aoife took it upon herself to answer.

William wasn't sure if she'd been eavesdropping during the whole conversation, but the second she entered Nikher's sight, he could feel the tension between them immediately. *There has likely been conflict between the Finghin and Baernt line*, he immediately thought. He remembered what his father and Ethan had told him: "Finny, or the 'Bear,' as they were aptly nicknamed," and then something about them running the mercenary armies and privateers. They'd worked closely together, he realized, but the Baernt line was divided in the fourteenth century and the Finghin line in the nineteenth. William's mind was racing, trying to see history, but he quickly snapped back to the conversation.

"Okay then," he said slowly. "How do you develop it?"

"First off, belief," said Aoife adamantly. "If you believe it's possible, you will try…and, of course, at first you will fail. But if you truly believe it's possible and keep trying, it will develop. It's an advantage to being born outside of the Cradle. We don't have hang-ups or societal weight; we're free. The HoloRoom can only guide the willing."

"Well, if it's similar to a photographic memory, it's generally believed that you're born with it. I don't ever remember hearing that it's something that can be developed," said William.

"Of course not. Can you imagine if everybody had an eidetic memory? Everything would be a breeze; the world would be far more advanced. Everybody would be much more of a… threat," Aoife said, as if stating a common fact among her kind.

"What do you mean, a threat?" asked William.

"Think about it—it's quite easy to rule the world if most of the inhabitants are, well, let's just say insufficient," Aoife smugly answered. William was beginning to see why Nikher didn't like her.

"We were just talking about the wills" Nikher interrupted, "and how we wouldn't need them if the psychos Fynglas, Oisin, and Éibhear hadn't killed half the conservators."

"Really, Nikher, you're so naïve. You don't think the Kiliaen line was part of that? You think your line is so clean, so innocent." Aoife angrily looked at William. "She thinks the Kiliaen line has disappeared because there's no mention of them, but all that means is that they're more devious than she cares to admit…more evil."

"Dominican Republic, seen starboard side, with its capital of Santo Domingo, is the oldest continuously inhabited European settlement in the Americas. Founded in 1498…" William suddenly heard Coen in his head, and he remembered telling him that he loved hearing his updates.

"The Dominican Republic is the only place in the world where the turquoise semi-precious stone known as larimar is found. It's called 'larimar' because it resembles the colour of the Caribbean Sea. It's also an impressive producer of baseball players, many ending up in the big leagues. Unfortunately, many believe baseball is their only way out of poverty, so many drop out of school," Coen finished.

William, feeling he'd had enough of Aoife and Nikher for the time being, excused himself and went to join Coen at the helm. It was the only place where he had a feeling of control, as it was the safest place on the yacht. Being at the top also gave him a sense of purpose. Quietly standing beside Coen, he thought of his responsibility to lead this group, although the group was now only four. Nikher still hadn't told him why Dieter, Nael, and Bodhi had gone with Eoghan. Anyway, he had enough on his mind and was glad to not have to think about that. Nevertheless, at some point he would have to lead this group, the other four included, although maybe not Eoghan, through seven hundred years of life to two people who likely want to kill him. While doing this, he'd need to avoid at least seven other disinherited heirs who want what's in his head. *Nice*, he thought, looking uneasily at Coen and then out to the ocean.

Coen steered the yacht past the Dominican Republic toward Puerto Rico where, apparently, the pina colada was invented. It was also home to tiny tree frogs that can sing, the world's largest single-dish radio telescope, and the US Virgin Islands, which were first settled around AD 100 by the ancient Ciboneys. It later became a slavery trading post and was now home to one of the largest oil refineries in the world. William didn't have the heart to tell Coen that he wasn't in the mood, but he also didn't want to leave the helm.

They continued sailing for a few hours, with Coen talking about the British Virgin Islands, including Virgin Gorda Baths and a labyrinth of beachside boulders. He explained that Anguilla had prehistoric petroglyphs and a wildlife conservation site. Coen finally caught on to William's inattentiveness, but instead of passing the time in silence, he started to describe things in greater detail and asked him to visualise not internally but as an image outside the mind. William suddenly realized what he was doing and immediately snapped out of his heavy mood. He tried to project a labyrinth of beachside boulders with a bunch of Ciboneys playing on them.

The yacht eventually slowed, once again shifting the momentum, while the guests swayed and rebalanced. William heard the familiar Sunken Treasure command, which he'd started to love, thinking it was the coolest thing.

"ETA ten minutes, Nikher. I'll have the dinghy ready, port side," Coen said internally to everyone.

William confusedly walked through the interior deck, trying to find where the port-side dinghy was. Eventually, he felt a gust of warm air as two thick doors automatically slid open, revealing a large room filled with jet skies, larger sets of scuba equipment, and a fifty-foot power boat. The room was filling with water, allowing the vessels to float, just as the wall was hydraulically lifting, like a car trunk. Nikher, Apollinaris, and Aoife eventually made it. Only William and Apollinaris seemed impressed. Nikher and Aoife were still brooding.

"Wow!" said Apollinaris. "This is impressive."

"I know," said William, happy to be the owner of the yacht, if only temporarily.

"So why are we here? Why Nevis?" Apollinaris asked.

"Banking and privacy, Apollinaris, you should know that. Weren't you in banking?" Nikher answered.

"No, actually I worked at an investment firm underwriting companies," answered Apollinaris sharply.

"Nevis is the one of the few places where you can create completely anonymous companies. Regulators hold no information on either the ownership of the company or its assets. Since some of us don't belong in the Cradle, we can't exactly open a regular business. Recently there has been a global crackdown on offshore finance, and there are only a few left. They're often used for money laundering, tax evasion, and other schemes. We just need them to purchase things; it's quick and easy," answered Nikher calmly. William sensed Apollinaris's uneasiness and mistrust.

"Okay, makes sense, but what are we doing here now?" Apollinaris asked again, hoping for more detail.

"Well, if you must know," Nikher replied, pretending to be annoyed, "we need to get you Cradle dwellers access to some untraceable funds."

After everyone had boarded the small power boat, Coen used a joystick to enable the thrusters and exited *Neveah* sideways. Aoife sat on the stern, with Apollinaris and Nikher at the bow. William beside Coen. As the island grew closer, the stunning stratovolcano Nevis Peak grew and overshadowed the town's glistening buildings. Coen told William that when a series of earthquakes damaged most of the colonial-era stone buildings, a new style of architecture developed. Georgian stone buildings were rebuilt with a stone ground floor and wooden upper floor.

"Then there's the legend of the pirate Red Legs Greaves, who managed to escape during the tsunami of 1680 that sunk an entire town on the west coast."

William listened attentively, trying to visualise a pirate with red legs being thrown around in a giant wave, and a town at the bottom of the ocean, but the scene in his head was getting weirder and weirder, so he stopped.

After docking on the Charlestown Pier and losing the breeze, they all felt the sudden extra heat, which was almost intolerable. The island was handsomely inlaid with many two-storey buildings with balconies for enjoying the view, the sun, and the breeze.

They didn't stay long at the lawyer's, just enough time for Nikher to introduce William and Apollinaris, to a rather shady man in a small, dated office. William was shown the details of the anonymous entity that had been prepared. Nikher then led him to a private, unassuming bank, where the entity already had an international account set up.

"One hundred and eighty million," William screamed in his head as Nikher quietly laughed in his ear. "Holy effing moly!" William was in shock, as he had never seen that amount of money in a single place.

"Yes…calm down," Nikher responded, still with a laugh.

William walked out of the bank with a stiff neck and wide eyes and stared at Coen in shock.

The afternoon heat didn't ease up, so the five of them found a nice little beach bar and enjoyed lunch before heading back to *Neveah*, en route to St Lucia. William couldn't stop smiling the entire time. Nikher, Aoife, and Coen just laughed.

"You know that money's not yours, right? Not yet" Nikher said.

"It's for emergencies," Aoife added.

"I know, I know," William whispered. It was all he could do. He was still in shock.

CHAPTER 6
DEATH LISTS

Coen sailed *Neveah* south past Montserrat, where the Soufrière Hills volcano had erupted in the 1990s. It had black-sand beaches, coral reefs, cliffs, and shoreline caves. They went past Guadeloupe, which was shaped like a butterfly and was home to the highest waterfall in the Caribbean. Next came the island of Dominica, with a volcanically-heated, steam-covered Boiling Lake. Lastly, they saw the island of Martinique, an overseas region of France. Its largest town, Fort-de-France, had many narrow streets and steep hills that Coen had drunkenly fell down once or twice...and broke his ankle.

After sailing for a few hours, Aoife, Nikher, and Apollinaris were getting restless. Coen finally announced they were getting close to St. Lucia.

"The island was previously called Iyonola, the name given to it by the native Amerindians. Later it was known as Hewanorra. This volcanic island is more mountainous than most Caribbean islands. The Pitons form the island's most famous landmark, and get this—there's a drive-in volcano!

Oh, and the police are known to keep death lists and carry out extrajudicial killings of suspected criminals. This is their attempt to make St Lucia more attractive to tourists. They call it Operation Restore Confidence…just a heads up." As Coen finished, Nikher gave him a wow-too-much-info look.

They were on their way to meet Apollinaris's great aunt, Kaethe, whom Aoife and Nikher believed knew who the rest of the disinherited were, being so close to succession. Settling into the main saloon after docking *Neveah*, Aoife, Nikher, Apollinaris, and William wanted to discuss the Thess Line.

"So what do you know about Eleutherios?" Aoife asked Apollinaris.

"Not much, really, just that he was an astronomer and mathematician before he fled Greece, and that he was a founder of the Interlaken Beer Company."

"What about the Diamond War? Have you ever discussed it with Helios?"

"No, never mentioned the Diamond War, and my dad always refused to answer any questions whenever I asked about Vassilios. I was only ten when he attacked my dad.

"Think, has your dad ever said anything interesting about Eleutherios?" Aoife asked.

"My dad said his middle name is Theophilus," he replied hesitantly, "but nobody has ever been able to historically confirm it." He looked into everybody's disappointed eyes.

"Hopefully we can get some answers from Kaethe," Nikher said. "Seeing as this is the only war that hasn't been wiped from memory by the O'Sullivans." Aoife didn't appreciate the comment, but she didn't offer any defence.

Kaethe was staying at a resort on Jade Mountain, which was known for its views of the famous Pitons, two volcanic spires located on the southwestern coast of the island. The curved structure sloped up the mountain and boasted many individual bridges that all led to stunning infinity pool retreats with numerous stoned-faced columns reaching toward the sky.

Nikher rented a private mansion above the resort on the top of mountain that had commanding panoramic views of the Pitons and Caribbean Sea. The mansion was about thirty thousand square feet; it had a helicopter pad and a gigantic sundeck with an infinity pool and a majestic view. Nikher pointed out the many safety features of the mansion, including a safe room, a sea pod that could slide down the mountain, and several escape tunnels.

"The house is owned by a local criminal organization. They rarely use it, but it's perfect for us," Nikher informed the group. William and Apollinaris weren't sure what to make of it.

"What time is she supposed to be here?" Apollinaris asked eagerly.

"Any minute now," Nikher responded as she went to sit by William on the sun deck. Nikher normally worn long-sleeve shirts, which William thought was to hide her tattoo. But just before she sat down, she changed into a short-sleeve shirt to be more comfortable in the sun. William noticed that there were no markings now. William stared and wondered but thought better of asking in front of Aoife.

At that moment, Coen internally said to them all, "Kaethe is here; I'll escort her in."

"Hello, all," said Kaethe in a lovely voice as made her way to the lounge area of the sun deck, delicately escorted by Coen. She was about eighty years old but didn't look a day over sixty. She had dirty-blonde, curly hair and was wearing a classy hat to hide from the sun and a very pleasant green sundress.

"Hi," responded Apollinaris, nervously moving closer to give a hug. "It's great to see you again, although much has changed since we last spoke."

"Yes, sweetie, I'm sorry for all the secrecy, but we had to keep you safe...you know, until you were old enough," said Kaethe.

"I'm thirty!" he exclaimed. "How old did I have to be?"

"Well, it was more that we were waiting for William, actually. Ernest knew that Bill, William's father, wouldn't tell him anything, so we had to wait. I think Ernest was just giving Bill more time with William, knowing what must be done... well, you know. You're lucky your father is your guardian." Kaethe looked endearingly at Apollinaris. "And you must be William," she said before giving him a hug. "Aoife, I assume?" she said, looking at Nikher.

"No...uh...I'm Nikher."

"Oh, I'm sorry, my dear. Well, it's great to finally meet you all."

"Unfortunately, we can't stay too long," said Nikher. "We'll let you get back to your vacation, we just had a few questions if that's okay."

Kaethe happily agreed and looked at her watch. "Anything for my little Apollo," she said as they all sat on the sundeck. William and Nikher tried not to giggle.

"Your father, Nikolaos, was the Thess leader inside the Losada League, wasn't he?" Nikher gingerly asked.

Kaethe's eyes narrowed as she heard the Losada name. "Yes," she responded sharply.

"He was born in 1908, right?"

"Yes," she politely replied

"And since you were the first-born, you had to take over representation, right? But you denied it. Why?"

"There is no representation inside the Losada League, as you call it. The Thess seat stays empty until succession. But there were certain duties I would have had take over, which I didn't want to." Kaethe took a sip of tea. Noticing everyone's confused look, she added, "I was born in 1938. You know what happened in 1939?" Kaethe's wrinkly old eyes tried their best to widen.

"World War II," answered William, who was struggling to see any connection.

"When I was a little girl, my father would let me sleep in his office. He loved me dearly, and I would pretend to sleep just to hear his voice. For the first five years of my life, I knew nothing of the world other than his love and a war he was deeply involved with."

"You mean the Losada League was involved in the WWII?" Aoife asked surprisingly.

"Well, everybody was involved in that war, but I don't know for what means. It could have been anything, really."

"Did he ever tell you anything about the Losada League and what they were involved in?" Aoife politely asked.

"No, never. The only thing I remember from the times I was pretending to sleep…it was so long ago, I'll likely get this wrong…was something along the lines of him saying that the war was essential for new markets. He also mentioned a super army, or superpower, to protect the gold, and some kind of system to print unlimited money for protection. When I was around eight, I stopped sleeping in his office and was really never around his work. That's all I remember; I'm sorry. His death was quite shocking and sudden. I hadn't yet told him that I didn't want the succession." She paused, remembering his face.

William interrupted. "Even though you knew one of your grandchildren would be the next heir?"

"Yes. I didn't want this for my family. This fortune isn't about money—it's about power and control and manipulation, and I didn't want any of it. My brother, Nereus, was next in line. He was a good person and wanted to change the world, but Vassilios didn't think he was fit to lead the Thess line, so he attempted to kill him. He now has a son, Dareios, whom he feels is the rightful heir and…" Kaethe's sadness could be felt by all in the room. "And he will come after you, William. They all will; they all are extremely desperate to get you."

"I know. Thank you, Kaethe. Do you know who the other heirs are?" William calmly asked.

"I don't know any of the heirs, but during the Diamond War, Nereus and Vassilios had orders directly from someone called Nemesio. He ran the operation, and everybody else worked democratically." She started to move around as she was getting nervous.

"Do you remember any other names from the Diamond War?" William asked.

"Only Éibhear, who everybody feared, aside from Vassilios. There was also a Tamus del Verdier and Hagan von Steinach, but that's it. The other parties involved were companies or groups, but I don't really remember the exact names." Kaethe shuddered when she mentioned Éibhear. She obviously felt his wrath through Nereus.

Éibhear…that doesn't surprise me, thought William. He was starting to feel that this name would be mentioned often. He also noticed that the Wassemoet name wasn't heard much, which coincided with what Aoife had said earlier about them.

"Can you tell us anything more about the Diamond War, anything that Helios may not have known?" Aoife asked, feeling confident.

"Well, my dear, I do believe Nereus would have told you everything," Kaethe said, looking slightly annoyed.

"I'm sorry, but Nereus hasn't told us much. We're just trying to find out as much as possible about the Losada League. We need to know what they've been involved in." Aoife felt sorry that she annoyed her.

"Well, sweetie, the Diamond War ended 1999. It was a very delicate operation that you wouldn't quite understand. Aren't you supposed to find the wills?"

"Yes," answered everybody at the same time, sitting eagerly.

"Don't you think there's an evolution to the Losada League that you must see prior to unwrapping something as sophisticated as the Diamond War?" Kaethe stated in a motherly tone. "If Nereus hasn't explained the details of the Diamond War yet, it's because you wouldn't understand it. You have a path, and you must trust to things you don't understand. It's okay."

"I get it, believe me," said Nikher. "Most of my life, I've only been told pieces of this picture, and I'm sure the fundamentals of this war will be in SkyView. We're just hoping to have an idea of it so that in the future, we will be…more prepared… you know?" She sounded unconvincing.

Kaethe loved their enthusiasm but knew they would never understand the war in its entirety. She'd also been told by Nereus not to mention it, but she felt a warmth in her heart to oblige, so she tactfully responded. "Listen, I can't tell you how or why, but what I can say is that the Diamond War was resource theft…on a grand scale. Its aftermath has left over 50 per cent of the population of Sierra Leone in poverty, despite having a vast wealth of diamonds, gold, titanium, bauxite, and rutile. After becoming independent from the UK in 1961, the country experienced widespread corruption, mismanagement, electoral violence, and a collapse of the education system. By the late 1980s, almost all of its diamonds were being smuggled and traded illicitly, with revenues going directly into the hands of private investors."

"I've heard of Sierra Leone. Isn't it the most dangerous place on earth?" William sounded like Coen adding interesting tidbits. But Kaethe looked sharply at him in a fit of disappointment.

"Yes, but that's by design. Listen, if you were planning to rob a country, your first step would be to destabilize it. On that note, I've probably said too much. I must be off. It was a pleasure meeting all of you, and I wish you the best. Please get to the wills and begin your journey." Kaethe got up smiled and proceeded to give a hug to each one there, ending with Apollinaris.

"Kaethe, may I ask just one more question?" William asked boldly.

She checked her watch one last time. "Of course," she politely responded.

"What did you mean when you said earlier that my Uncle Earnest was giving my dad more time with me, knowing what must be done? And that Apollinaris was lucky to have Helios as his guardian? What must be done?" Just as William voiced the question, he realized the answer.

"I assumed Nikher would have told you by now." Kaethe gave Nikher a look of encouragement as the door closed behind her.

William and Apollinaris both looked at Nikher, expecting an explanation, while Aoife took protective position.

"Look, I'm sorry. I should have told you sooner, but it's time for both of you to di…" She tried to answer but was cut off suddenly as a spear raced passed her head like a bullet. It pierced the concrete. Then two men shot across the thick metal ropes and landed on the sun deck.

"Die? Nikher, no, no…not today. His head is much too valuable." The older man pointed at William and then at Apollinaris. "But sure, kill this one; he's of no worth. Actually, let's kill three of you. Good thing we're on a mountain; it would be a shame if you got too close to the edge." He was trying to intimidate and control the situation.

William grabbed Apollinaris and dragged him behind Nikher and Aoife, who had moved closer together while their forearms burned—one with a blueish-grey sheen and the other with a fiery-green and glowing Gaelic markings.

"I like our odds, Archelaus. How was your nap? What moron do you have with you this time?" Nikher taunted while Aoife finished squaring up to her side. "William, Apollinaris, get into the house, now!" Nikher commanded them.

"Ah, so you don't know Dareios yet," Archelaus boasted.

William remembered that Dareios was Archelaus's son, one of the seven. He knew he wanted what's in his head and would love to kill Apollinaris.

"Haven't had the pleasure, but I'm sure he's as useless as you," Nikher said sarcastically.

Four other men had repelled down from the roof and were blocking the entrances to the mansion.

"Uh...Nikher," cried William, "house is blocked now. What do we do?"

Nikher looked at her watch. "Stay close to Apollinaris."

"Apollinaris, meet Dareios," Nikher said calmly, as if the situation was under control. "He wants your money. As a matter of fact, Archelaus wants it too. You should see the necklace I got made; it's very sparkly." William couldn't believe what he was hearing.

"Mine too," Aoife added. "More of a Gaelic theme, though; you'd love it."

"That's funny. Oh, I had one made too, you know...to commemorate the Flight of the Earls," Archelaus insulted in response. He started to move closer.

That comment really angered Aoife, and her forearms were burning bright green.

"You know you have no right to those diamonds, or anything else," he continued. "You're on the wrong side; you're making a huge mistake. Beyaert and Kiliaen were lied to as well; they're innocent. Nemesio knows the truth. Hand over the Ward, and I'll tell you everything ... honest." Archelaus put on his most trustworthy face and placed his hand on his heart.

"Don't listen to him, Nikher," Aoife shouted, fearing her longing for the truth.

"You know their innocent don't you" Archelaus could sense the weakness for truth in her eyes. "Beyaert was enslaved to his wealth but Kiliaen refused so William imprisoned him, the Wards are nothing but thieves! He finished sharply.

Dareios now moved closer to both of them and said, "Last chance. There's lots to share, and there's no need for this, Apollinaris." Dareios looked over to him. "We're family, so let's end this. We give the Ward to Nemesio and it's over; we'll split everything, I promise." Dareios lacked an honest tone.

At that point, Aoife had heard enough. She lunged at Dareios, who swiftly backed up and brandished what looked like a bludgeon but with a handle. It was wrapped around his fist and extended to his elbow; each end opened up to reveal hidden, bright red, humming electrocutors. Aoife looked shockingly at Nikher, nervous about the weapon.

"You like?" Archelaus proudly asked, throwing his arms back and firing up his bludgeons. "Instant heart attack!" Archelaus swung hard at Nikher's head, but she dodged. Aoife took another shot at Dareios while he was distracted, hammering his chest. Nikher countered Archelaus by striking him in the ear.

Both men forced back slightly, and injured Archelaus's head was ringing. But with a desperate burst of energy, they both ran at the girls. Dareios blocked a defending kick from Aoife and landed a hard strike with the red electrocutor right into her glowing forearm.

"Graphene—strongest material on earth," she smirked. The green glow wrapped around her arm, weaving its way toward the strike and protecting her from the electrocutor as it sizzled.

The two men increased their anger and landed strike after strike with the electrocutor. Nikher and Aoife blocked the hits strategically, completely frustrating them. The four other men were distracted by the fight but were seemingly on orders to keep William and Apollinaris from escaping or attacking.

"You can't keep this up forever," Archelaus screamed in anger. "You're too weak and foolish."

"It's not always about strength." Nikher struggled to talk while they wrestled. "Sometimes…it…helps," she panted, "to have a little…you know, foresight."

She looked at her watch once again with a satisfied smirk on her face. Archelaus, feeling concerned, pushed off her, Aoife was still fighting Dareios, who noticed Archelaus push off and did the same.

"We have you cornered; there's nothing you can do. No way out this time," Archelaus said confidently, while William and Apollinaris were surrounded by the four men.

"I wouldn't worry about us—I'd worry about the outstanding warrant for the two of you. I heard there are two Thesses on the St. Lucia police's death list," Nikher smiled. "Hopefully no one has tipped them off about your current whereabouts."

Suddenly, there was a loud bang and the front door went flying through the foyer. Fifteen armed men, with "St. Lucia Police" across their chests, ran through the mansion, tactfully securing it with military precision. They ran onto the deck with guns brandished, steadily aiming at each target.

A detective entered the sun deck and addressed the crowd. "Archelaus Thess, Dareios Thess." Two other officers pulled out handcuffs while the others still nervously aimed directly at each target. "You both are under arrest for extortion, aiding and abetting, murder, racketeering…" The list when on and on. Once the detective was finished, he surprisingly made a motion toward William and Apollinaris.

"No! No!" Nikher screamed. "Not them." She pointed at Archelaus and Dareios. "There are the men you want. You have the wrong guys."

The officers raised their guns in warning, one of them using the butt of the gun to hit her in the face, almost knocking her out. Aoife trembled in horror as she watched the colour drain from William's and Apollinaris's faces. Two officers screamed something unintelligible back at Nikher, warning again as she continued to scream. Archelaus, Dareios, and the other men had already backed up with their hands on the back of their heads. Now they stood in shock. William, in his horror, managed to notice the electrocutor mechanically descending into the bludgeon.

The detective calmly motioned a warning to Nikher. "We have made no mistake," he said in broken English.

They all watched in horror as William and Apollinaris were escorted through the house. The remaining officers cuffed Nikher, Aoife, Archelaus, Dareios, and the rest and escorted them at gunpoint through the house and into two vehicles. One was an armoured van, which William and Apollinaris went into, and the other looked more like a bus. It housed the rest.

Archelaus was fuming as he sat in the bus with his feet and hands cuffed to the seat in front of him, where Nikher was sitting, similarly cuffed.

"What did you do, Nikher?" he asked desperately in a frightened whisper. "You know you can't involve the police. You put all of us at risk. Are you insane? They kill everybody on the death list." Nikher didn't respond but all could see the worry in her posture.

Aoife was noticeably still trembling and in shock. "We have to get out of here," she whispered. She couldn't believe Nikher's plan. Involving the police was strictly forbidden outside the Cradle, as it risked having the DNA of everyone databased. She couldn't believe Nikher had been so stupid. But just as she thought that, she released "She isn't that stupid. These police can't be real." She also noticed that there were only three officers on the bus, so she assumed the rest were escorting William and Apollinaris safely back on *Neveah*.

With hope, Aoife sprung into action. Her forearms glowed as she pried her wrist as hard as she could against the metal bar that housed the other end of the cuff. Just before it snapped, Dareios noticed what she was up to and bellowed a loud cough. One of the officers looked back. As he looked away,

Aoife urged Dareios to distract him, showing him that her cuffs were off.

"Uh…I have to use the bathroom." The officers ignored him "Officer, I really have to go." Dareios shrugged at Aoife, who gave a piercing stare. He pleaded again, but the officers still ignored him.

"Me too," Archelaus joined in, sensing the formation of a plan.

This time they got a response in very broken English. "Yu ken pease yor pents," he yelled, not looking back.

Aoife rolled her eyes and mouthed "You guys are idiots." Using all her strength, she jammed her forearms between her foot cuffs and the metal bar. The sound of metal snapping was too loud for a cough to cover up, and one of the officers immediately rose and rushed back, yelling unintelligibly and pointing the gun at her.

She rose out of her seat and rushed at him, brandishing her green, glowing forearms. He fired shot after shot, but each bullet was absorbed into the Gaelic markings. Reaching him, she knocked the gun out of his hand and swiftly hyperextended his front leg by jamming the bottom of her foot into his knee and stepping over him. The other two officers had gotten up as well and pointed their guns at Aoife, but the commotion had startled the driver. The bus suddenly swerved, putting both men off balance. Aoife took advantage of this and rushed at them. In a single motion, she punched the gun out of one of the officer's hands and kicked out the weapon of the others.

Both men, now unarmed, started throwing punches to knock her back, but she blocked and protected her face desperately.

She was finally subdued as one of the officers lunged at her legs to knock her off balance. She fell into a seat, and the other officer leapt over the seat and landed with his knees on her chest. Aoife let out a terrible cry of pain. She was now caught, and the bus driver had regained control. Both men struggled to re-cuff her closer to the front of the bus, but as they were doing this, they heard two loud snaps followed by a loud thud. Nikher had broken her cuffs and, with her heel, smashed the officer with the broken leg in the face, knocking him out. The two officers at the front of the bus struggling with Aoife looked up in panic. One of them reached for his gun and managed to fire off a few shots, which Nikher absorbed eloquently. With only one officer attending to her, Aoife easily managed to break his arm, while Nikher caved in the chest of the other. The bus driver slowed down, fearing for his life. He pulled over and put his arms up. Nikher, out of anger and in a show of no mercy, looked directly at Dareios and kicked the driver, knocking him out as well.

Both Aoife and Nikher gathered themselves, rubbing their forearms in discomfort. Archelaus and Dareios could see small marks where the bullets had hit; slowly the blueish-grey and green faded but were still noticeable.

"What do you want to do with these guys?" Aoife asked Nikher as she eyed Archelaus and Dareios. "We can't leave them here; it's not good for anybody if their DNA gets into a database."

"Ya, I know," Nikher said angrily, still panicking as her forearms glowed bright again. "I was expecting them to be executed. We can't risk them being detained and questioned, but we also need to get after William and Apollinaris." Nikher quickly looked around for a solution.

Aoife, already a step ahead of her, grabbed the bludgeons and briefly checked them over, but she was unable to open the electrocutors. She looked at Nikher for a nod of approval. Nikher kept one bludgeon and threw the other to Dareios, which he caught. Instantly, it glowed bright red and sizzled, melting the cuffs. By the time they looked back up, Aoife and Nikher had run off after William and Apollinaris.

"That…was…brilliant!" Aoife whispered while panting and grinning ear to ear as she and Nikher ran off.

"You were quite impressive as well, breaking those cuffs. And that guy's knee…ouch!" Nikher replied, proud of her plan and smiling as well. The two girls laughed and bonded, seemingly forgetting seven hundred years of Wassemoet/O'Sullivan strife.

They ran for a few miles and finally met up with Coen and William, who were on their third vehicle change, ending in an armoured white Maserati en route to *Neveah*.

"Everything good?" Coen asked Nikher as she climbed into the back seat.

"Yes…go…go," Nikher excitedly responded. "They won't be far behind."

"Did they fall for it?" Coen asked.

"Ya, they'll be searching the island for William for a while. Aoife was amazing, by the way. Nobody died, which is always good. Only a few broken bones." Aoife sat back, relishing in the compliment.

"Good, I was getting worried. It's not safe driving around and changing vehicles," Coen said.

William and Apollinaris were still confused and trying to put it all together.

"I'll explain when we get back to *Neveah*," Nikher said, noticing their confused faces. "Keep your eyes peeled for anything; stay alert," she commanded.

And with that, they drove to the marina, obeying all speed limits and stop signs. Coen drove like an old man. Coen had sent word ahead, and *Neveah* was already warmed up and ready to go. They started cruising immediately, and all felt the warm breeze as *Neveah* powered through the small inlet and out to venture across the ocean. William, facing backwards in the main saloon, enjoyed the breeze as he watched the island shrink out of focus.

After a well-deserved meal, William felt he'd waited long enough for the full account of what had happened. He reached for Cillian's whisky.

"You know, Cillian left that here for you. He thought you might need a stiff drink once in a while, and he wanted you to have something of…well, quality," Aoife informed William, sounding even more Irish.

"Well, was he ever right about that," William responded and gestured with a "cheers" to him, wherever he was.

Once all had enjoyed a stiff drink and were thoroughly relaxed in the main saloon, Nikher proceeded to regale them with the story of the bus escape, even re-enacting Aoife blocking the bullets. William was thoroughly entertained by the images of Aoife raging through the bus. He was also highly impressed by the strength of the two of them and wondered about the markings even more now, but he also had many other questions.

"I didn't realize you both had those on your forearms," William uttered. "I saw them on Nikher back when Spytihněv and Archelaus attacked us. What are they?"

"Its graphene, an incredibly strong material that's woven into our skin. Its layers of carbon are one-atom thick and can absorb strikes that would normally blow through steel. It's our weapon of choice, as it were," Nikher answered intently as she rubbed her arms.

"Why do they disappear sometimes?" William eagerly asked, excited to finally get some answers.

"It reacts to our adrenaline. It's an eloquent weapon. I prefer it because it's always with us but simply regarded as a tattoo. We can't exactly travel with conventional weapons, as we must make sure to always appear innocent, in case the real police get involved."

"Why does it matter if the police get involved?" Apollinaris asked.

"We have to make sure that we stay out of databases, both us and the other lines, even Losadas. That's why they had those electrocutor bludgeons. If they connect, it just looks like a heart attack. If there were gun shots at the mansion and a dead body were found, the police would open an investigation, and all DNA would be collected and implicated. DNA, as you know, is unique to each person, and if enough traces are left around the world, it might spur an investigation that leads to the Ward League. That's why we operate outside the Cradle. If my DNA were found, it would just lead to multiple fake people, never to a Wassemoet. I've never been in any system anywhere."

"But there were gunshots on the bus, you said. Were those police real? Weren't you afraid of getting shot?" William asked.

"Definitely afraid of being shot, but they weren't St. Lucia police officers. Aoife and I are well trained; we have been blocking bullets since we were little girls. And haven't you noticed that the clothes feel a bit different?"

"Yeah," William said as his eyes narrowed.

"They're graphene based," Nikher explained, "meaning they act as a weapon deterrent. Don't get me wrong—bullets still hurt, but they just don't pierce."

"What if they shoot you in the face?" asked William.

"That's what the forearms are for, as we can't cover our faces," Nikher responded. "I also ensured that the weapons were all single shot, which is super easy to block. We needed to convince Archelaus and Dareios. If blanks or rubber bullets were used, they would know right away. I knew Archelaus would attack but not with Kaethe around, so I made sure we seemed vulnerable on the sun deck, and he took the bait. Once Kaethe left, Coen had time to radio the thugs."

"But who were they?" William was still confused.

"Just local organized criminals," Nikher replied. "As far as they know, they were hired for two separate ransoms. I just made it look like a case of mistaken identity so that Archelaus would think William and Apollinaris might be executed…you know, being on the St Lucia police death list, or mistakenly on the death list. We paid the thugs handsomely in advance, which always limits the potential for any real violence."

"Ahh, I get it. Archelaus and Dareios will have to assume we're…dead, or at least that we might be?" William nervously responded.

"Yes, and that allows us to get one of you out of the Cradle," added Aoife, suddenly realizing the scope of the plan.

"Yes, that was the intention. Any takers? Both of your passports were just scanned when we got here. The Cradle will forever think you're here. We'll just file a missing person report in a few days. We can even blame the death lists, as they're not exactly official."

"Funny, nobody mentioned anything to me, not even Ernest," William panicked. "I can't do it this way. Is there any way I can talk to my parents one last time? I'm just not ready yet." William realized that he better read about the fallen Wards as soon as possible.

"There's no way to contact them, and I'm sure your father would have raised a stink if he were told you were executed as a St. Lucia crime lord anyway, which also would not be the best for St. Lucia tourism." Nikher smirked but quickly realized that it wasn't something to laugh at.

"I'm okay with you using me; my dad understands. He told me this would have to happen at some point," Apollinaris said.

"I'll figure it out before we get to Cape Verde. How many days until we get there?" William said, starting to calm down.

"Are you sure? We can choose one of these islands here—Barbados, St Vincent, Grenada, Trinidad and Tobago—before we cross the Atlantic Ocean," Nikher said encouragingly.

"I need to think. I can't just off myself here—I do have family inside the Cradle, you know. Why can't we just use aliases forever?" William said. "Or what did Ernest call them? Invented people? You know, to cross borders and move about. We just won't use our real IDs ever again." William was beginning to dread the whole idea of dying.

"Still too risky. As long as the Cradle thinks you're alive, every agency in the world will strive to ID you. As far as they're concerned, you're out there somewhere. If you get out before being databased, the link to your true identity is severed forever." Nikher took a deep breath and continued. "You can only leave the Cradle if your DNA isn't in any system. Once it's in, you're screwed, because any time your DNA is found after death, it proves you're alive. This will get any ambitious detective excited and likely make a career out of trying to find you, ruining his family in the process. We just can't afford to have any agency looking into us; it will make it far too difficult to operate if we're under investigation."

Nikher got up and leaned on the bar while she rubbed her forearms, almost as a reminder of the effort that was being put out. "Look, I know this is all new, but you must understand. Our fortunes…all of our fortunes…weave in and out of the Cradle; it's too big of a sum to keep in one place. We need to get you out of the Cradle soon. It's an unnecessary risk to keep you alive."

"Okay, okay, I'll think of something," William replied.

"Good, we need to be able to operate freely but still have access to the world financial system. That's why we use places like Nevis, that still allow us to seamlessly operate anonymously. There are only a few places like that left, as world governments are closing in on the offshore banking system. We need to free the fortunes and spread them across our lines before that happens. The Ward League isn't involved in anything illegal, except maybe tax evasion, which is unavoidable sometimes, but I know they pay full taxes at every opportunity. I've been involved with a few companies for them, and they're always forced by the board of directors to operate 'professionally,' as they call it, meaning abiding by all rules within its jurisdiction. Like Coen's driving." Nikher and Aoife laughed simultaneously.

"Anyway, just think of my line. We joined the Ward League in 1357. We were one of the wealthiest families in the Netherlands at that time, and we pledged to help *every* Ward. We've been working together for seven hundred years now, which means the Ward League has kept our money safe for seven hundred years."

Nikher looked exhausted but continued. "The only way to do that was to create a world outside of the Cradle. They needed an entity that could move the wealth around so that it would pass through time untouched. The Cradle is comprised of every monarch, republic, imperial system, and religion in history. It encompasses capitalism and communism, and every system that wields control. That's why we operate around it. As for the actual wealth, I don't know where it's hidden or how it's hidden. I just know why it's hidden. The where and how are in William's head."

"Okay, I only have one last question," Apollinaris said. "Please forgive me, I'm really trying to put this all together. Why couldn't we just call my Aunt Kaethe?"

Aoife, William, and Nikher all got up and laughed, trying not to hurt his feelings in case he was serious.

Suddenly, William's laughter dwindled after taking a second look at Apollinaris's expression. "Oh…um, I'm just going to guess here." He looked at Nikher oddly. "But I would assume that most networks are recorded. Data is actually bought and sold quite often; it's not really that new of a thing," William eventually sputtered out, satisfying an embarrassed Apollinaris.

William took a deep breath, feeling the weight again, but also feeling impressed with the plan Nikher put together.

He wasn't concerned anymore that he hadn't been told about it, as he realized it was better that he hadn't. She was smart enough to predict everybody's reaction, all the way to Aoife realizing that the police were fake and easy to escape from. The growing pain in his stomach came from knowing that the news of his death would get to his parents "That's what Kaethe meant by Apollinaris being lucky that his father is his guardian. My father will think I died in search; he'll think he failed and didn't do enough to stop me," William muttered to himself. He could feel a terrible rip on his insides. "My god, he's lost me and Ernest; he'll be devastated." William didn't like the feeling, and he wasn't happy over what his father and mother would have to go through, and Sarah...*especially Sarah! She will feel so guilty!* He thought, but there was no other way. But first he realized he had to read about the fallen Wards and learn how to die.

"Look, we have a long way to Cape Verde. It's about a five-day cruise, so get some rest," Nikher said politely as she headed toward her stateroom. The rest soon followed suit as *Neveah* cruised across the North Atlantic.

CHAPTER 7
FALLEN WARDS

William woke early in the morning the following day, partly from the sun beaming through his blast-proof windows. The water glistened, calming him before his mind was once again overwhelmed with confusion and intrigue. He began the day in the HoloRoom. In both of his workouts, he pushed himself mentally or physically farther than at any other point in his life. After a routine coffee, he finished stretching and headed to the galley. On the way, he heard through Mind-Link, "All completed Nikher, Bodhi, and Nael are out. You can read all about it in the Utuado news this morning. See ya in Cape Verde. Like I said, I'll be on the beach!"

The update from Eoghan seemed to awaken and interest everyone as they all met in the galley at the same time. Aoife and Apollinaris had already started breakfast.

Nikher had found the article and slowly read it aloud, first telling everyone that Utuado was a municipality of Puerto Rico:

"Two adventurers, Nael del Verdier from France and Bodhi Kadaně from the Czech Republic, went missing and are presumed dead while hiking the Tanama River Cave. Heavy rains shut down local tour companies, but the two adventurers ignored the warnings from local experts and decided to go anyway, not realizing how quickly the labyrinth of caves can fill up with rain water. Local authorities have ruled it an accidental death and also stated that it's unlikely they would be able to recover the bodies, as it's too dangerous to search the labyrinth of the caves, even in dry weather."

Once Nikher finished reading the report, they all immediately glanced over at William with a "you're next" look.

"That idiot!" cried Nikher. They were all still looking at William, who pointed to himself in confusion.

"Not you," she responded promptly. "Eoghan. He was supposed to get them out in separate countries. Nikher threw the rest of her plate of food into the garbage, having lost her appetite, and stormed out of the galley. William wanted to talk to her more and started to follow, but Aoife grabbed his arm to hold him back. He persisted.

Nikher stormed to the aft deck, her favourite place. William followed and could hear her talking to Eoghan.

"What were you thinking? That's a link, and I told you very specifically to get Nael out in Port-au-Price, Haiti and Bodhi in Utuado." Nikher screamed at Eoghan and then noticed William. She waved him onto the deck and at the same time linked him to the conversation.

"Look, Nikher, we went to the Port-au-Prince slums like planned, but it really was too dangerous to fake a death. We couldn't even enter them," Eoghan replied vehemently.

"Eoghan, I don't think you understand. Now del Verdier and Kadaně are linked to the same incident. That's not good."

"There was just no time. We had to get to the river caves before the storm, or else it would have looked like suicide. We made a quick decision; the storm was greater than forecasted and came on way too strong. What about you? Did you get Apollinaris and William out?" Eoghan was hoping to deflect the negative attention.

"Yes, we got Apollinaris out, but not William...not yet, anyway."

William cut Nikher off. "I wanted to wait."

After a short conversation with Nikher and Eoghan, William asked to be excused and went back to his master stateroom to read in private. He still didn't want to share the book with anybody, so he claimed that he wasn't feeling well. Nikher let him know that he still needed to talk with her Uncle Thijs before landing in Cape Verde. William walked briskly through the main deck and saloon and down to the mid deck, avoiding Aoife and Apollinaris.

After sinking into the lush chair in the corner of his stateroom, William peered out just before thumbing the pages to the familiar dog ear. *Dad was right*, William thought immediately as he started to read about the horrors of the fallen Wards. Each tale was enough to rot his stomach, and they may have been enough to keep him home. But he realized that if staying home had been a possibility, he never would have been given the book in the first place. He started to think it was best to be honest with himself. He'd wanted this from the moment he'd started to comprehend it. He needed to mentally move past his old safe self that was his dad and Ernest. They'd needed a safe place for William to grow up in, and they'd figured the Cradle was best. And they were right.

"With all the police and firemen, government, teachers, neighbours, I know bad stuff does happen, but much of the Cradle is really safe, especially if you have a loving family to guide you. I need to start thinking big, like Ernest said—'Don't underestimate how big this is.' I'm not unfit, like I assumed Sarah and Dad thought. I am fit; if anything, I am the only one who is fit. With no other siblings, Henry would have to completely rely on me and make sure I have everything I need to find him and Venacio, knowing every other line would do everything in their power to keep me safe so I could eventually return the fortunes. Furthermore, by putting everything in my head, Henry has been able to limit the violence from the disinherited. They too want me alive, likely to torture me in some fashion, but at least alive."

Reading about the fallen Wards, William was given a glimpse into the world outside the Cradle. This was helpful when thinking about his own death and trying to come up with something clever that would give his dad hope and limit his anguish. He was even able to decipher which deaths were from the Irish Atrocities and which were Wards simply leaving the Cradle. First of all, he noticed that many of the adventurers died as tourists. *Definitely leaving the Cradle*, he thought. He also was getting better at trying to develop his eidetic memory and could project the deaths:

> "James Ward, while on vacation with his family, died parasailing after his rope got caught in the propeller. Heavy winds carried him far from the Punta Cana coast. After a lengthy search, local authorities gave up, and his body was never found."

> "Horace Ward, an environmental scientist from Wales, was presumed dead after a failed expedition of the Marianas Trench. Recovery of his body and mini-sub was simply not feasible due to the cost."

> "Henry Ward was found dead while hiking the Matterhorn; his body was entombed in ice. The hikers who found him were unable to bring his body back. Authorities have found other hikers as glaciers begin to melt."

> "Ernest Ward died while scuba diving the 1787 *Hartwell* wreck in Cape Verde with a local tour; it was reported that he was bitten in the chest and hauled off in a pool of blood by a shark."

"Marian Ward, an amateur pilot, died on a solo fight across the English Channel. A search and rescue operation was launched but eventually suspended due to worsening weather conditions. Two seat cushions found near Surtainville in France were likely from the missing aircraft, but no body was ever recovered."

"Cyril Ward, his wife, Muriel, and their two children were trapped in a farmhouse they'd recently purchased in Chippenham, northwest Wiltshire, England after it caught fire due to a faulty electrical panel. Only the dog survived. Unfortunately, fire crews couldn't make it in time, as it was the busiest night of the year with many false alarms in the large historic market town. Nothing but bone and ash left."

"Ephraim Ward, a twenty-two-year-old volcanologist, was collecting data on the stratovolcano Tristan da Cunha, which is located in the middle of the Atlantic Ocean and fed by a magma hotspot. He unfortunately took a wrong step into a hidden hotspot and probably had the most gruesome death of them all, being swallowed by magma. His research partner only found a crispy hand and forearm, which authorities believe he must have singed off at the elbow as he slowly sank in magma, throwing it as a warning for his research partner."

"Elias, Myer, and Rees Ward were all kidnaped for ransom at different times in Bogotá, Columbia. Although they were insured and the authorities were involved, the family was disappointed to hear at the last second from the kidnappers, who said that the victims had died in a failed escape and were somewhere in the Serranía de Chiribiquete jungle."

"Clarice Ward, after a successful ascent of Oregon's Mount Hood, unfortunately died while descending the mountain's southeast face, falling deep into a crevasse on the Newton-Clark Glacier. Her body was never recovered."

The list went on and on. William's eyes leisurely skipped to the deaths in which Wards were most likely leaving the Cradle. He ignored Fynglas, Oisin and Éibhear's spree for now.

After absorbing as much as he could about the Cradle leavers, he finally started to put together an idea for himself. After much internal debate, pacing, and staring out his stateroom window, plus one change of clothes, William settled on having an equipment malfunction at the wreckage. He figured he could hide a set of mini scuba gear on the wreck ahead of time. Then he would hire a private dive instructor. During the dive, he'd have his large set get caught and damaged. He planned to take it off in a panic, which would prove that's where he was last. With the hidden mini scuba gear and hand thrusters, he could escape to *Neveah*. The private instructor would eventually find the gear and call the authorities, who would search but find nothing and assume his body was going to wash up on one of the islands.

"I'd like to go scuba diving once before I die. I heard there's still lots of silver on the 1787 *Hartwell* wreck," William told Nikher on the aft deck, where she was relaxing.

"The *Hartwell*?" Nikher looked confusedly at William.

William wasn't sure if Nikher knew how Ernest had died, so he'd thrown the name out as a test.

"Ya," he responded, "I've…uh…always wanted to go scuba diving. I read about it years ago. It was a three-decker ship that the British East India Company launched. It ran onto a reef three leagues northeast of Boa Vista in Cape Verde. It's an interesting story, actually." William was starting to talk like Coen. "A mutiny broke out after the crew attempted to seize the 200,000 troy ounces of silver. The captain changed course and headed to Cape Verde, intending to hand over the mutineers to the authorities. That's where the ship ran onto a reef. What's more interesting was that one of the shipmen aboard went on to assassinate the British Prime Minister, Spencer Perceval. Anyway, not all of the silver and artifacts have been recovered."

"Ooookaaay," Nikher responded, sensing his nervousness.

William wanted to give his dad hope. He knew it would comfort his mom to know that he would be with Ernest, at least in spirit. But William secretly thought it could ignite just enough curiosity to push Bill into searching for the wills again, hopefully this time seeing past the Cradle.

With that now settled, William had to think of exactly how he wanted to die. He didn't want to discuss too much with Nikher, in case he accidentally revealed that this was the exact wreck where Ernest died. He regretted giving her the details of the wreck now; the idea had just come to him quickly, and he'd always been a terrible liar. *But she didn't seem to know about it*, he thought. *Maybe it was a good idea after all. Maybe Nikher agrees and realizes I want to help Dad get out. Better not say anything, just in case. I'll just pretend that I thought she knew.*

After thinking about it a little longer, William realized that if Nikher knew, she wouldn't let him die there, because it would create a link—which was exactly what he wanted. This would be a big risk on his part. Would his father call the local authorities and ask them to investigate? He wondered if he would investigate it on his own. He hoped so. William was tormented on the inside about what to do but eventually felt he had to leave his dad with hope.

Unfortunately, William didn't have long to relish in his great plan. The three Irish lads had bled into his mind, and in being true to himself, William decided he needed to know. If he was to find Venacio, he couldn't hide in ignorance anymore.

So with a big stretch and a deep breath, his fingers flipped a few pages back.

"On July 30, 1930, during the inaugural Campeonato Mundial de Fútbol—the first World Cup final—long-time football fan Llewellyn Ward was enjoying watching Uruguay beat Argentina 4–2, joined by 100,000 enthusiastic fans at the newly-built Estadio Centenario in Montevideo. Unfortunately, Llewellyn was caught up in the violence of the military coup, supported by the Argentine Patriotic League, and was shot multiple times."

"Vernon Ward, while jogging early in the morning, was run off the road and left for dead in a ditch."

"Rosie Ward was found beaten to death in the alley in Temple Bar after a night of drinks with co-workers. Witnesses at the bar said she excused herself to go to the loo but never came back."

"Gwilym Ward, an executive of a large aerospace company, allegedly jumped from an office window, falling a hundred feet to his death. A week later, the company's stock plummeted due to accusations of corporate fraud. They eventually rebounded due to the unlimited demand of the World Wars."

"Enoch Ward was stabbed eighteen times in the back by an IRA fanatic."

"Clement Ward, known for his love of sailing, was found dead with a skull fracture. Authorities ruled that he fell while climbing the mast."

"Wallace Ward died with nineteen others in a train derailment caused by infamous serial killer Szilveszter Matuska, who on September 1931 used explosives to successfully derail the Vienna Express as it crossed the Biatorbágy Bridge near Budapest."

"Colin Ward was killed with six others in the town of Peñaflor, Province of Seville, Spain, by José Lopera Andrés and Aldije Monmejá, who were robbing and murdering the patrons of their illegal gambling house."

"Mary Ward was shot at her isolated Northbank Cottage near Portencross in North Ayrshire, Scotland. Three shots were fired through the living room window at night, one fatally piercing her heart.

"Ellis Ward, was in the wrong place at the wrong time, according to authorities. He was an innocent bystander during the Arnon Street killings, which took place in Belfast, Northern Ireland."

"Nicholas Ward, owner of the Eastern Palace Cinema, was robbed and killed with an axe."

"Hedley Ward was found in the River Severn, which is the longest river in Great Britain, near Haw Bridge, Tewkesbury, Gloucestershire. His torso was found first, then arms, then legs, and finally his head."

William read through five times, forcing his imagination to project externally and concentrating hard each time. He wanted desperately to develop his memory. The reality sank in with each death, and he was getting angrier and angrier. He assumed he would have seen the Wassemoet, Kadaně, von Steinach, del Verdier, and even the O'Sullivan name. But the fact that they weren't listed was a worse truth, as it meant that they each would have their own lists. This made reading his much more depressing. They had truly earned the name "Atrocities."

William had had enough of the fallen Wards and felt like putting his plan in motion. Coen agreed and volunteered to take care of the details, such as organizing the private dive and booking up all the other tours to make sure there were no unwanted witnesses. Nikher, Aoife, and Apollinaris kept to themselves for the next few days as they tried to get rest. William used the quiet to get in as many physical and mental workouts in the HoloRoom as he could. He also conducted some fourteenth century research on the HoloTable before they got to SkyView. He had come to realize that each of their guardians—or any relative, for that matter—would have told them about the content of the wills. Some of them may even have had books given to them, like his dad had given one to him. Nikher was on board with William's plan regarding the mini scuba gear and even offered to place it personally to make sure he wasn't seen in the area prior to the "accident." She also kept reminding everyone that they were almost at SkyView.

CHAPTER 8
THE FOURTEENTH CENTURY

Neveah was scheduled to land in Cape Verde in about twenty-four hours. During lunch on the last day of the cruise across the North Atlantic, Nikher suggested William, Aoife, Apollinaris as well as herself discuss what everybody knew so far regarding the wills so that they could get a head start with the SkyDeck on their way to Zermatt. They all agreed to this. William still felt like keeping the old book secret and assumed the rest would too if they had one. After lunch, the four of them settled in the main saloon and opened most of the walls to let the fresh, warm Atlantic air breeze through. The water surrounded them and glistened while *Neveah* hummed along.

Nikher poured herself a glass of Heaven Hill Distillery's twenty-seven-year-old straight bourbon whiskey, Kentucky, USA, and offered a glass to the rest, who all accepted, aside from William. He settled on a wheat beer called Hoegaarden, from Belgium. William gave a little smirk, wondering at the odds of *Neveah* stocking one of his favourite beers.

Nikher sat comfortably on a sofa and addressed the company. She was wearing her trademark long sleeves and shorts, her hair a bright mess as usual. The only thing different was that her freckles had seemed to come to life from all the sun.

"Well, we're almost at SkyView, and I thought it would be a good idea to go over what we know about the wills so far. I'm sure most of you have been informed at least somewhat."

"Not me," said Apollinaris.

"During the Dimond War, Nereus and Helios both joined the Ward League at the same time. There was no need for the wills until you," Nikher replied politely.

"As my father, Cillian, said on the rooftop…"Aoife began speaking in Cillian's voice. "The wills that you now seek outline the Seven Hundred Year War between the Ward League and Alvero line and will lead you to Henry, the twentieth Ward, who will hand over the fortune to the twenty-first Ward."

"Word for word," William muttered to Apollinaris, who looked bewildered.

"Anyway," Aoife continued, "the wills house the events of the fourteenth century. Knowing that secrecy is a top priority to both the Ward League and Losada League, we must figure out what shape they were in from the beginning so that we can find Venacio today!"

"As you know," said Nikher, "the conservators previously would have been able to point us in the right direction, but we would still need the keys to find the truth of our history. Either way, it would have been up to us to find Venacio, and they wouldn't have been able to help. In fact, I think it's a blessing…sorry, I didn't mean that. I mean that nobody has been able to find any Alvero line leader in seven hundred years, and the Ward League only caught the Thess line because of Vassilios's betrayal. I think we need to start from the beginning, the very beginning."

"I agree," said William. "William Ward was born 1296. I'd say that's the beginning."

"Yes," said Aoife quickly. "Finghin O'Sullivan 1298."

"Baernt Wassemoet 1297," Nikher included.

"Eleutherios Thess 1292," said Apollinaris.

"Bligger 1291, Huc 1288, and Hynek was 1293. I'm assuming Alvero was around the same time too," Nikher finished off.

"Well, we know 1296 was when the First War of Scottish Independence started. I do know that William didn't like the English invading Scotland, and that's why he left. He ended up sailing around Europe on a merchant ship before ending up in Interlaken," said William.

"Baernt was a Viking at heart, but a good one, I'm sure. Very old journals found in Wassemoet Castle piece together a bear of a man who loved Norse mythology and wanted to relive the Viking days by travelling. That's why he left," said Nikher.

"I don't really know much about Finghin. I've heard my Grandfather Olly mention that he left to expand the clan and look for new wealth," said Aoife. "Apollinaris already told us about Eleutherios, but we don't know why he left Greece. What about Bligger, Huc, and Hynek?"

"I don't know about Bligger and Huc, but my father told me Hynek was rumoured to have smuggled hops out of Bohemia—that's what gave the beer its great taste and started this whole thing," explained William. "Nevertheless, they all made it to Interlaken and started to work. The eight of them each brought something unique to the company. Hynek Brewed the beer, Bligger made the barrels, Baernt and Finghin protected and distributed it, Eleutherios managed the money, and Huc navigated the laws of different territories. So what events of the fourteenth century do we know of so far?" William was ready to verbally name the events listed in his old book, ready to start piecing it all together. But before he could start, Aoife's mouth opened and she rhymed them off in point form:

The First War of Scottish Independence 1296–1328

The Great Famine 1315–1317

Treaty of Edinburgh-Northampton in March 17, 1328

The Second War of Scottish Independence 1332–1357

Hundred Years' War 1337–1453

The Black Death 1347–1351

Hanseatic League 1356

Treaty of Berwick 1357

Pfaffenbreif October 7, 1370

Ciompi Revolt 1378–1382

Winchester College Founded 1382

Victual Brothers 1392

Kalmar Union 1397

The Renaissance in Italy
The Peasants' Revolt of 1381

William couldn't believe it. She'd recited it exactly as it was listed in his old book. Nikher sat quietly but looked impressed. "Who told you that?" she asked.

"My great-grandfather, Tiarnán," Aoife answered. "He believes the wills are much more important than the conservators. Personally, I think he helped design them. He told me that the conservators were needed before the seventeenth century, but what's needed now is intuition. History is generally agreed upon in the Cradle, which gives us reference to build upon."

"Yes, but they are designed for us to find the truth, not what we want to be the truth!" Nikher firmly stated.

William was starting to notice that Nikher was determined to find the truth. Aoife, not shocked by the statement, responded, "Truth isn't always available, Nikher. Sometimes you need to trust your gut without the required evidence. Anyway, I'm sure the Ward League isn't going to risk any more lives by hiding secrets in people."

"I agree," said William. "If all the wills list are the facts about the fourteenth century, there's really nothing incriminating in them. Even if the disinherited got a hold of one, they'd still have to figure out how each item connected."

"Which is why your head is so important!" Nikher stated, fully realizing why she had been told her whole life to protect what was in his head. She'd always thought he possessed the truth of Beyaert and Kiliaen, but now she realized there was much more in there. "All Henry would have to do is put the keys in your head. All our brains function the same way," Nikher continued excitedly while choking on her bourbon. "It's designed to connect things!"

"Uh…I don't quite get it," William muttered while his brain clouded over.

"Your mind is always trying to connect information, twenty-four hours a day, seven days a week."

"Yeah…so?" William replied.

"Well, all Henry, your dad, Ernest, or whoever has to do is insert a specific piece of information in your head sometime during your life. At the time it was placed you wouldn't have given it a second thought, as it would have seemed isolated and irrelevant." Nikher was cut off by Aoife before she could finish.

"But as we move forward and start to learn about the fourteenth century events in the will, *that* isolated piece of information will rush to your consciousness at the speed of light whenever your mind thinks there's a possibility it *may* be relevant."

"Thank you, Aoife," Nikher said scornfully, as she wanted to finish the same thought. "That's why your head is so valuable."

"I have to admit," Apollinaris piped up, "this is impressive. Henry, or whoever, made you almost invincible. We all need you alive, as there are no other links to Henry—unless, for some reason, they decide to reveal themselves to us, which I would think would cause more chaos than anything, seeing as trust isn't all that common here." He shrugged in an obvious sort of way. "Venacio is probably the only one that wants you dead, but that would just enrage the disinherited."

"But your dad said they are puppets to his will. They likely do most of the dirty work, so he needs them, and if William's dead and they can't get any wealth, they'll turn on Venacio," Aoife chimed in, interrupting again.

"Interesting," Nikher muttered. "Either way, Venacio will kill you the second the disinherited get their fortunes back, which means this all leads to a big war. Once we solve the wills and find Henry, William here will take over as twenty-first Ward. He will have access to the entire fortune, and then we can kill Venacio and his heir, which will free our fortunes."

"What will killing Venacio accomplish, though?" William interjected. He was getting tired of the attention. "I mean, wouldn't somebody else just take his place?"

"No," Nikher said. "Well, not likely. My Uncle Thijs and my mom told me that the only way to hide a fortune that big was to spread it across the world. It makes sense that the Nevisian company I have access to is part of it. Millions of dollars flow through it, but I have no idea where it comes from."

"From a financial standpoint," interjected Apollinaris, "a single large account would bring too much attention, and no disrespect to the Nevisian company, but it would be incredibly risky to leave it all offshore. The only way to keep it moving safely would be inside the Cradle using the current financial system. Just look at the last few financial disasters. Governments are quick to bail out the large corporations and banks at the expense of the working class. They privatise gains and socialize losses. The mega wealthy always increase their wealth during these situations, and many poor people go bankrupt. It's the safest place for the wealthy."

"This is my Uncle Thijs's theory," said Nikher. "He thinks the fortunes are spread around the world markets under thousands of different entities that only Henry knows about. He's the only one who has the access codes, bank numbers, and entity names. Once William becomes twenty-first Ward, he'll get access to everything."

Aoife rose and added. "And once we kill Venacio and his heir, William will simply hand over the numbers, codes, and names to each line, thus returning our fortunes."

"And it's highly likely that Venacio operates the same way, meaning only he and his heir have access codes, bank numbers, and entity names," added Apollinaris.

"That's it," William cried excitedly. "Markets will swallow up the wealth if they're dead, as no one other than Venacio or his heir has access to it. It's too big of an amount to leave as inheritances."

"And they wouldn't do that anyway," said Nikher. "They use this wealth for power. Remember what Kaethe said: 'If you were planning to rob a country, your first step would be to destabilize it.' I think William is right. Venacio will not have an inheritance plan aside from his heir, and I bet you anything he or she has been groomed for that power."

"How do the disinherited fit in then, aside from just wanting their wealth back?" asked William as he cracked open another Hoegaarden and misted the air.

"I would imagine…" Nikher started but then paused, her eyes darting back and forth and then narrowing. "That when each line fell, the ones who stayed with the IBC would have been left with nothing."

"Nothing but revenge and hate in their hearts," Aoife interrupted once again. Nikher didn't mind being interrupted this time, as she knew that she didn't have personal experience with this. "And would have looked to the remaining factions," Aoife finished.

Nikher, without hesitating, continued. "Which I have a feeling was always led by members of the Alvero line, who would have promised to help get their wealth back as long as they were loyal. Eventually they grew out of the IBC; it's been a few hundred years since any line was a shareholder, but the factions would have continued to meet annually and share profits to honour the Declaration of Interlaken. I mean, they still honour the Declaration of Succession, so as each line was divided, the Alvero line's wealth and power grew."

"Because there were less members to share with." William interrupted this time, finally putting it together.

"Yes," replied Nikher with a cute look of frustration. "Until all were gone. Now he controls everything as well as a small army of disinherited that have grown up under his influence."

"And, as per the Declaration of Succession, have now come of age. Most of them would be at least twenty by now, just like us," said Apollinaris. "Which brings up an interesting question. Since we need William to find the Ward League, would we need Venacio's heir to find him?"

"Not necessarily," Nikher replied politely. "I think the Ward League is only holding wealth, but Venacio—or at least his son, Nemesio—is actively growing it along with his power. Kaethe pointed that out to us. We don't want his wealth; we just want him dead."

"That's right," added Aoife. "We don't know what type of person this is, which is why it makes sense for us to follow history. We may see a pattern to the Alvero line that leads to him, whereas Henry isn't actively doing anything within the Cradle, so it would be impossible to find him!"

"Maybe, but maybe not. He did help end the Diamond War," Apollinaris said, finishing his second bourbon.

"He's right," said Nikher. "I looked into it. In 1999, shortly after Nereus switched over to the Ward League, the Lomé Peace Agreement was signed, ending the decade-long civil war in Sierra Leone. This means Venacio and the disinherited could be following history just like us; this could be just the gigantic battle between good and evil that the world doesn't know about."

"Yeah," they all responded with a deep exhale.

"Also realize that the lines have all been split between good and evil. That's what all those wars are, so even if you think you can't trust them, know that they are the good versions of their lines," William muttered.

"What? they all replied.

"Sorry, that was just something Ernest said to me," William replied, surprised that he'd said it word for word.

"The Ward League had appealed to the good in each line, and that's how we won each war," he added.

Nikher looked at him in disgust. "That's just not true," she muttered.

"But there is no good in the Alvero line," Aoife muttered, deep in thought.

They all gave Nikher a frustrated look; the denial of the Kiliaen line wasn't helping.

"Okay, so," William started, wanting to get back to the events of the fourteenth century, "what do we know about the First War of Scottish Independence, 1296–1328?"

"Well," said Nikher, "it started when England massacred most the population of Berwick in 1296. Then the Scottish were defeated at the Battle of Dunbar, and then the king abdicated. Within months, most of the country was subdued. They even removed the Stone of Destiny, but at the end of both wars of Scottish Independence, Scotland retained its status as an independent state."

"But what started the first war?" William asked, remembering that he'd read it somewhere and wishing he had a better memory.

"The King Scotland died in 1286—Alexander III," Nikher replied "This left his three-year-old niece, Margaret, as heir."

"What happened to her?" asked Apollinaris

"Uh…she died too. Got sick on the trip to back to Scotland from Norway," replied Nikher.

"There were no other heirs? Just a three-year-old niece?" he asked in surprise.

"No, he had his own children, but they were already dead. David was the oldest, and he died in 1281. Daughter Margaret died in 1283, and Alexander died one year later, in 1284. He also had a child with a second wife, Yolanda, but the child died in pregnancy in 1286."

Apollinaris never shied away from math. "So they all died within nine years, with no other heirs. So that's why England invaded? They had no king?"

"Oh…umm…no," Nikher responded. "Did none of you take history in any of your schools or universities? Never mind. When Scotland didn't have a king, the heads of state governed the country. They were known as the Guardians of Scotland, and when Margaret died, that left thirteen different claims for the crown. Fearing civil war, the Guardians wrote to the English king to arbitrate. The king agreed, but 'forced by threat of war' that the claimants acknowledge him as their Lord Paramount, which was the highest authority. And then all Scots were required to pay homage to him. In what became know as 'The Great Cause,' the claimants pleaded their cases before the English king. Eventually, John Balliol was chosen as King of Scotland, and within a month swore homage to the English King."

"I still don't get why they invaded," said Apollinaris.

"Land," said Nikher. "Back then, land was considered wealth, and nobles were promised Scottish land if they annexed it."

"Don't forget the Auld Alliance," William suddenly remembered, adding to the conversation. "Didn't the English king order the Scottish king to supply him with troops and money to invade France, but instead they sent emissaries to warn the French king and negotiated the Auld Alliance, both agreeing to support each other in case of an English invasion? That's when the English massacred everybody in Berwick."

"Yes, William, that's correct," replied Nikher.

Aoife motioned to speak. "Doesn't it seem odd to anyone that Alexander and all of his heirs died? And then the English king became Lord Paramount?"

Aoife always steered history toward conspiracies, which didn't go unnoticed. Nikher rolled her eyes, as she desired evidence and truth above all else. Apollinaris looked indifferent, but it made sense mathematically, which he loved. But something had inspired William. It struck a chord, so to speak, that vibrated in him, but he couldn't put a finger on it.

"That could be why it's in the will," William answered. He was trying to remember everything and looking for connections "Okay, so what happened after the massacre of Berwick?"

"The Battle of Dunbar," answered Aoife. "Then the King abdicated and the Scottish nobles, led by William Wallace, revolted and fought at Irvine. This was followed by a Scottish victory at Stirling Bridge."

"And after clearing the English out, Wallace wanted to open up Scotland for commercial access," said William.

"That's exactly right, William," said Aoife. "In the archives of the Hanseatic town of Lübeck, there's a Latin document dated October 1297 that tells the merchants of Lübeck and Hamburg that they now had free access to all parts of the Kingdom of Scotland, which had, by favour of God, been recovered by war from the English."

"That's crazy," cried Apollinaris. "I had no idea Wallace was a businessman. Hey, Aoife, didn't you mention Hanseatic in the list?"

"Yes, it was the Hanseatic League 1356. Merchants established the league to protect their economic interests along the trade routes within the affiliated cities and countries across northwestern and central Europe. Hanseatic cities had their own legal system and operated their own armies for mutual protection. Hansa was the old High German word for 'convoy.'"

"Okay, okay, can we go over that later!" cried Apollinaris. He was having trouble following the war they were currently discussing.

"I agree," added William. "Let's finish the first war."

"Sounds good," said Nikher. "A week after that letter was signed, Wallace invaded England, starting in Northumberland. The English army fled behind the walls of Newcastle. Wallace ran across the countryside west into Cumberland, pillaging all the way to Cockermouth. Then he led his men back to Northumberland, burning north of seven hundred villages and full of booty. Soon after, Wallace was knighted and appointed Guardian of Scotland."

"Can I just jump back to how Alexander died? I mean, he was a king, so he should have had guards around him," said Apollinaris.

"I'm glad you asked," Aoife said excitedly. "He fell from his horse. After a night of celebrating his second marriage at Edinburgh Castle, as well as advisor meetings, he left the next day to visit the queen at Kinghorn in Fife. He was advised not to make the journey due to weather conditions, but he did anyway. And here's the part I have a hard time believing. He was separated from his guides, and it's assumed that his horse lost its footing due to the darkness. He fell, maybe even off a cliff, although there are no cliffs in the area. The king was found dead on the shore the following morning with a broken neck."

"Separated from his guides?" Apollinaris questioned. "Fell off a cliff? Yeah, I'm with Aoife, that doesn't really add up."

"Yeah, well," interrupted Nikher, "that's what's written. That's what we know so far. If you can find witnesses or evidence on the contrary, I would gladly hear it. Anyway, while Wallace was being appointed Guardian, the English and French signed a truce excluding Scotland and deserting them as allies. This meant the English could attack without fear of France's involvement. The English army decimated the smaller Scottish force near Falkirk but failed to subdue the whole country. Wallace retreated to the woods and resigned his guardianship in December 1298. After a few years and a truce, the English king raided Scotland once again in 1304. All leading Scots surrendered except for Wallace, who refused to capitulate and accept his country's occupation and annexation."

"Yes, but Robert the Bruce and William Lamberton," said Aoife, "seemly paid homage to the English king but had a secret pact for the future preservation of the Scots and their independence. They were essentially waiting for the elderly English king to die."

"Thanks, Aoife," said Nikher. "Wallace was eventually captured, and the English government displayed his limbs separately in Newcastle, Berwick, Stirling, and Perth. With the capture and execution of Wallace in 1305, Scotland seemed to have been finally conquered, and the revolt calmed for a period. Aoife, do you want to tell them about the not-so-secret pact? I'll leave the conspiracy parts to you."

"Of course. The secret pact was not so secret. A gentleman named John Comyn, who once tried to negotiate terms of submission between Wallace and a few others and the English king, found out about the secret pact between Bruce and

Lamberton. Bruce and Comyn met and agreed to support each other for a future claim of the Scottish crown. However, John "Red" Comyn III revealed the conspiracy to the English king, and Robert the Bruce fled. What I find interesting is that his dad, John "Black" Comyn II, was a Scottish Guardian 1290–1292 when the English king was originally asked to arbitrate, which led to him becoming Lord Paramount, which started the whole mess."

"Thank you, Aoife," said Nikher politely. "Probably a reasonable explanation, but let's move on. So now Bruce is quite mad, as he'd paid homage to the English king but had to flee back to Scotland. He eventually approached Comyn and stabbed him for his treachery, although not fatally. Two of his attendants finished him off. Bruce's only option now was to become king or a fugitive, so he asserted his claim.

"Less than seven weeks after killing Comyn at Dumfries, Robert Bruce was crowned as King Robert I of Scotland at Scone Abbey on March 25, 1306. Trying to free his kingdom from the English, he was then defeated in battle and driven from the Scottish mainland as an outlaw. His wife, three brothers, sisters, and daughter were captured by the English. All three brothers were hanged and quartered.

"The English king finally died in 1307. The Scottish kept fighting and defeated the English in a number of battles, most notable being the Battle of Bannockburn 1314; by 1320, the Declaration of Arbroath was signed by the community of the realm of Scotland, affirming Scottish independence from

England. Later, the Treaty of Edinburgh–Northampton 1328, which was the peace treaty between England and Scotland, officially brought an end to the war."

"That's it?" asked Apollinaris.

"Yes, that's it," said Aoife. "But that was just the first war."

"It's hard to tell what this has to do with the Ward League. You said SkyView has all of this in it, right, Nikher?" asked William.

"Yes, you can zoom in on each war. We can even see Bruce stabbing Comyn. As long as it's part of history, it's been digitized and placed in the SkyDeck," she answered.

"That's pretty cool!" William said, impressed "Okay, so what was next?"

"The Great Famine of 1315–1317, caused by bad weather and crop failure. It affected Northern Europe, including the British Isles, northern France, the Low Countries, Scandinavia, Germany, western Poland, and some of the Baltic states. Millions of people died, and it led to a vast increase in crime. People would do anything to feed their families. During these years, Northern Europe took on a more violent edge. Many people also started to mistrust medieval governments' capability to deal with the crisis," said Aoife.

"Well, no need to see people starving to death in SkyView," said William. "Apollinaris, what do you think this has to do with the Ward League?"

"Well, I'd say it's simply showing us their mistrust of those in power. It's an impossible event to really be involved in, and

I'm sure the aristocracy had plenty to eat, which would have angered everybody," he answered.

"That's what I was thinking. Some of these events are likely symbolic," said William.

"Okay, so why don't we just motor through these quickly , and then we can each use SkyView to dress up some of our theories?" said Aoife. All nodded in agreement.

"Next was the Treaty of Edinburgh-Northampton March 17, 1328. After the Declaration of Arbroath 1320, which declared Scottish independence, they still had to make peace with England. The Treaty of Edinburgh-Northampton was ratified by parliament, and the terms stipulated that in exchange for £100,000 sterling, the English Crown would recognize the Kingdom of Scotland as fully independent, and Robert the Bruce and his heirs and successors as the rightful rulers. The borders were to be recognized as those in place during the reign of Alexander III. England also agreed to return the Stone of Destiny, but they didn't until 1996," Aoife's finished.

"Hey, that's the year I was born," William said. They all gave him a funny look.

"Wasn't the Declaration of Interlaken signed in 1328 as well?" questioned Apollinaris.

"Yes, as your father said, 'The Declaration of Interlaken 1328 stated that the Interlaken Beer Company (IBC) be supported by eight factions with a single representative for each, bound by secrecy in perpetuum. Each year all factions are to annually meet in Interlaken to settle affairs and share funds,'" said

Nikher. William immediately knew she'd repeated it word for word, and he was slightly jealous. It reminded him to work on projecting his memories.

"Which leads us directly to the next item on the list," Aoife said excitedly, which is the Second War of Scottish Independence 1332–1357. But here's where it gets interesting, because by 1332, the Interlaken Beer Company had been operating successfully for fourteen years!"

"So they were part of the events moving forward," Apollinaris muttered in realization.

"Exactly," said Aoife, happy to be getting to this part."

"It's true," said William. "They were too young to be involved with the first war, and the great famine was too big. They weren't powerful enough to be involved with the treaty, so these items were likely symbolic. The company would have been operating for only ten years by then. But by the Second War, they were split into eight factions. Were there any mercenary armies in the First War of Scottish independence?"

"No," answered Nikher.

"What about the Second War?"

"No mercenaries, but privateers were used."

"What started the Second War then?" asked William.

"A group of disenfranchised nobles didn't fully accept the terms of the treaty. They felt they were deprived of their rights to Scottish lands. They became known as the disinherited, believe it or not—and no, I'm not sure who started calling our enemies the disinherited. Anyway, the English disinherited, led by Edward Balliol, son of the former Scottish king, first attacked at Dupplin Moor. The decisive victory left the invaders in a great position. Supporters soon joined, which added to their ranks. On September 24, 1332, Edward was crowned King of Scots, and within two months he offered his loyalty to the English king."

"Obvious who backed the attack," said Aoife. "The English king definitely backed the war, but he would have had to do it discretely, and he needed someone to convince the disinherited that they had support. Then Balliol as King of Scotland pledged his support to the English king's future battles on penalty of all of Scotland and its isles. He then withdrew to Annan but didn't remain there long before he was driven from Scotland.

"In a Parliament held in February 1334, Balliol surrendered Berwick as an inalienable possession of the English Crown. In July of the same year, he yielded considerably more to Edward III, including Roxburgh, Edinburgh, Peebles, Dumfries, Linlithgow, and Haddington. Eventually, after several engagements and decades of war, the Second War of Scottish Independence was settled with the signing of the Treaty of Berwick in 1357. By this time, the English were preoccupied with France during what's now known as the Hundred Years' War 1337–1453. We can go over the details of the battles and strategy in SkyView. There's just too much going on to verbalize."

"How were the privateers involved?" asked William

"French privateers attacked royal ships and loaded merchantmen anchored at the Isle of Wight. This was how France entered the war under the Auld Alliance. They also sent troops and supplies," replied Nikher.

"What is a privateer?" asked Apollinaris.

Aoife was pleased to answer. "A privateer is a private ship that is commissioned to engage in war, usually given a letter of marque that empowers the person to attack foreign vessels during war time. They essentially do it to harm fleets and are allowed to take any spoils. It was essentially a business. Investors would retrofit old warships, recruit large crews, and take all the prizes they could."

"That takes us to the Hundred Years' War, which I'll just highlight for obvious reasons," said Nikher. "Essentially, five generations of kings fought for the largest kingdom in Europe. English monarchs had always held land in France, which was a major source of conflict throughout the Middle Ages. French monarchs would take every chance they could to strip land away, especially when England was at war with Scotland. As the centuries passed, English holdings were sometimes much larger than even the French royal domain. But by 1337, the English only held Gascony.

"In 1316, a principle was established denying women succession to the French throne. Essentially, it started when the French king was dying without sons or brothers, and the closest male relative was the King of England. So the throne passed to a cousin instead, Philip Count of Valois.

Disagreements between France and England over confiscated lands forced the English king to reassert his claim to the French throne. One of his advisors was a gentleman by the name of Robert Artois, who'd been exiled from the French court over an inheritance claim. He urged the English king to reclaim France by giving him extensive intelligence on the French court. The French king met with the Great Council of Paris and agreed Gascony should be reclaimed on the ground that the English were harbouring their mortal enemy, Robert Artois." Nikher paused, got up, and stretched while pouring another bourbon. She let out a yawn and continued.

"On a summer day in 1340, the English fleet set sail, arriving off the Zwin esturay. After a withdrawal and a change of wind, they decimated the French fleet in what is known as the Battle of Sluys. The war continued. The Battle of Crécy was a notable event and a complete disaster for the French due to the longbowman attacking too early. In the Battle of Neville's Cross, Scotland attempted to aid the French but lost, which greatly reduced the Scottish threat. The English drove north, capturing Calais on the English Channel and allowing them to keep troops safely in northern France."

"By 1348, the Black Death arrived in Paris," said Aoife, giving Nikher a break. She also knew that one of the theories of the War of the Twin Bears was coming, and she assumed Nikher would rather not have to describe what happened. Nikher looked over nicely at her and said thanks on Mind-Link.

"I'll go over the details of the Black Death later, but it's estimated that it killed as many as 200 million people, so there was lots of death happening, just keep that in mind. After the plague had passed and finances were back in order, the English king's son, the 'Black Prince,' led a chevauchée from Gascony into France. They pillaged Avignonet and Castelnaudary, sacked Carcassonne, and plundered Narbonne. After the violence, the Black Prince offered peace to the French king, known as John the Good, but he refused. This led to the Battle of Poitiers 1356 and the capture of the French king after a mounted unit that was hidden in the forest flanked the French retreat. After the Battle..." Aoife looked at Nikher empathetically. "France plunged into chaos. French nobles and mercenaries rampaged. I'll recite an actual report from the Cradle time from near the city of Poitiers in Aquitaine, western France," Aoife said gravely.

"'All went ill with the kingdom and the State was undone. Thieves and robbers rose up everywhere in the land. The nobles despised and hated all others and took no thought for usefulness and profit of lord and men. They subjected and despoiled the peasants and the men of the villages. In no wise did they defend their country from its enemies; rather did they trample it underfoot, robbing and pillaging the peasants' goods.' Mercenary companies hired by both sides added to the destruction, who plundered the peasants and churches," [1]Aoife finished.

---

1 From the Chronicles of Jean de Venette

"Finny and the Bear controlled mercenary armies back then, so that's why…," William spoke aloud and looked at Nikher, nervously not wanting to hurt her feelings. "Um…when was the War of the Twin Bears?"

"In 1358," Nikher coldly replied, waiting for anyone to open their mouth. "The IBC also traded lots of beer, goods and weapons. They were all over Northwestern Europe; they weren't just into mercenary armies. I'd like to look at the battle in SkyView another time. There were lots of other ways for them to benefit from the war. I know Huc was a Master of Law. Who knows what else they were into?"

"Either way, they benefited from war, right?" said Apollinaris.

"Yes," said Nikher, a little warmer this time. "The IBC benefitted from everything from the 1300s to the 1800s. Chartered and merchant companies were created and used to exploit international trading opportunities. This is why they split into eight factions; they needed a Huc in each one. Everybody brought a particular skill to their faction."

"When was the Ward League established?" William asked.

"In 1358, the same time as the War of the Twin Bears," Nikher responded. "That's when my line was split. Baernt and Beyaert formed the Ward League, Killian stayed with the IBC, and William was found dead. The Killian line was never heard from again."

"But that doesn't mean they don't exist. I'm sorry, Nikher, but we can't assume they're not involved," said Aoife sternly, getting back to her normal self.

William searched through his mind, looking for connections. After all, wasn't he supposed to have answers in his head, something to confirm these events? *They were thirty years into the IBC*, he thought. *There should be a key to confirm we're on the right track at least.* He felt that Aoife was too much into the conspiracy aspect, Nikher was too much into the truth, and Apollinaris was too mathematical. He was starting get an idea of his path. Maybe he was the one to balance them. He felt he needed Dieter, Bodhi, and Nael, but wouldn't Ernest or Henry have made sure they were together then? Maybe they weren't supposed to discuss things until they were together, or maybe it was okay to compare notes later. Either way, it felt right in his gut to move forward and discuss, but he also thought it would be much better to have the others together.

"Okay, can we stop here at the Hundred Years' War and move to what would have been next in the will?" William asked, trying to organize his thoughts.

"Sounds good," Aoife promptly replied. "The Black Death, which I touched on earlier, was one of the most devastating pandemics in history, even though it only lasted four years. Not only did the plague kill people, but various European groups were also slaughtered: lepers, Romani, Jews, friars, pilgrims, beggars, foreigners, as well as individuals with skin diseases. Infection and transmission of disease wasn't understood at the time, and people believed it was punishment from God. The Black Death wiped out a third of Europe's population, killing much of the labour force. The remaining population enjoyed wage increases because of the labour shortage and were much wealthier, better fed, and able to spend their surplus money on luxury goods, which I'm sure the IBC benefitted from.

"Guaranteed," cried William as he started to see the IBC spreading through time.

"The Hanseatic League was next," said Aoife, trying to keep the conversation going but sensing the fatigue setting in. "As mentioned before, the Hanseatic League was established to protect business interests and trade, mainly through the Baltic Sea. From 1356 onwards, the network of alliances grew to include almost 170 free cities with no ties to local nobility. The league had a monopoly on Baltic trade and waged war against pirates and privateers, mainly the Victual brothers, who were hired by the King of Sweden to break the monopoly and gain access to the maritime trade in the Baltic Sea.

"All right, what's next? Let's make this the last event for today and get some rest. We'll be at Cape Verde soon."

"The Treaty of Berwick 1357 was next," said Aoife, but we already went over it. This is what ended the Second War of Scottish Independence. The only item of note I didn't mention was that under the terms of the treaty, the Scottish king, who was captured at the Battle of Neville's Cross, was to be released. The English demanded £67,000 sterling for his release, payable over ten years. The first installment was paid, the second was late, and there was no money for the third. Taxes were raised to pay the ransom, but the king began to embezzle from his own fund. I just thought that summed up the war."

CHAPTER 9
TIME TO DIE

B etween the sixteenth and eighteenth centuries," Coen said as *Neveah* rumbled along, bringing Cape Verde into sight, "Over seventy ships have sunk off the Cape Verde coast as a result of storms, poor navigation, or treacherous reefs. The *Le Dromadaire* sunk off the coast of Sao Vicenete in 1762 during a storm; the ship was carrying gold and silver. The *Norfolk* was en route to Marseille, carrying nuts, when she sank. She had a confused captain, and stormy weather came up. Then the pump failed when it filled with the nuts it was carrying, and then it ran aground on a treacherous reef. The *Hartwell* sank off Boa Vista after running into a reef in 1784 en route to China. It was filled with 320,000 Spanish Portrait dollars. A Danish ship called the *Grev Ernst Schimmelmann*, en route from China to Copenhagen, ran aground when she hit a reef on the north coast of Maio. The cargo was Swedish coins and a cannon. The *Princess Louisa*, built in Deptford in 1733, was an impressive three-mast ship. She also hit a reef off the coast of Maio. Many of the passengers drank themselves into oblivion prior to drowning. The *Lady Burgess* was en route to Madras in

1806 when she became trapped on a reef between Boa Vista and Maio due to rough seas. Many of the other wrecks aren't accessible to divers, and there's a substantial amount of treasure left to claim." Coen finally finished with a smile.

After a really early double workout, William drank his coffee and enjoyed the commentary from Coen. He sensed his memory improving, the air was smooth and calm, and the sun rose beautifully, bringing the North Atlantic to life. He wrestled internally with how he was going to die while he searched *Hartwell*, finally settling on the most common of scuba diving fatalities—accidently running out of gas. Nikher and William had found plans of the wreck and settled on a narrow compartment to hide the gear in. William recommended a dive centre that offered private tours and asked Coen to book it. He hoped he wouldn't notice that it was the same company Ernest had hired. Fortunately, Coen didn't seem to make the connection.

Coen gave William the rundown prior to getting to the dive site. "You'll have to go through immigration using your passport and check into a hotel before going to the site to ensure the Cradle knows you're in Cape Verde. Nikher, Aoife, Apollinaris, and I are going to use aliases through customs and check into a different hotel so we don't burn our aliases. Meet us back at *Neveah* after Nikher places the mini-scuba gear."

"Burn?" William asked.

"Yeah, our aliases would be compromised if we were linked to you," Coen replied.

"Makes sense."

"I used your credit card to book hotel, so you'll have to check in with it. Use it also when you pay the dive centre. Once your passport is scanned at customs, Venacio will know you're there, and somebody will be on their way. They'll go to the hotel first and then dive site. They would have figured out by now that the police weren't real in St Lucia. I'll be your personal driver for the day. I've rented an armoured Land Rover that will be waiting at the marina."

William was starting to realize how much better Nikher's plan was. "I should have died on one of those other islands." Realistically, Cape Verde was a quick flight for a private jet, and Losada League would have lots of resources at their disposal. But he felt it was important to leave hope for his dad. He also realized that, to the Cradle, it would just look like he wanted to visit where his uncle had died. Maybe Venacio would figure it out, but the Losada League knew all the deaths were faked, including Apollinaris's.

He heard the familiar Sunken Treasure command through Mind-Link. Cape Verde was as beautiful as William imagined. The ten volcanic islands jetted out of the ocean. *Neveah* smoothly cruised through the archipelago, finally docking in an unassuming marina in Sal Rei on the desert island of Boa Vista. William split up with the rest and acted as a solo vacationer going to visit the wreck were his uncle was slain by a shark. The rest shuffled through immigration at the Sal Rei Port smoothly and entered the island. William headed immediately to his hotel and checked in, put his bags in his room, and in a brisk but respectful walk, headed back down to meet Coen.

After clearing the port captain and immigration, Nikher immediately went back to *Neveah*, grabbed two mini scuba gears, and swam unnoticed through the side hatch that housed the jet skis, gear, and power boat. She then headed out to the *Hartwell* wreck.

"Okay, so all is set," William said as he closed the door to the Land Rover.

"Yes, all is good. Nikher will let us know once the gear has been placed," said Coen. "You know where she's hiding it, right?"

"Of course, we went over it five times," William nervously answered. "How long do we have before Venacio sends someone?"

"Not long. Someone would have been sent immediately. The dive centre knows to get you to the dive site quickly. I told them you have a busy sightseeing schedule, so have a list ready in your head if they ask out of friendliness. SkyView is near the São Filipe safe house, so we have to get back to *Neveah* before being seen. Eoghan and Thijs will captain *Neveah* and *Truth* to a neutral port in the Mediterranean while we fly SkyView to Zermatt. In case something happens, we have a rendezvous at Praia da Atalanta, which is a rusted old skeleton of a ship, and the Farol Morro Negro lighthouse on the east side of the island. I'll drop you off and head back to *Neveah* and have her ready for São Filipe."

William was feeling nervous and unsure of his decision but remembered Ernest telling him to trust himself and his choices. After a short drive, Coen dropped him off and William rushed into the shop. The walls were clad with all the different dive site options. Shark Point North and South were listed at the top; they were full of elkhorn coral, scroll coral, pillar coral, brain coral, yellowtail snapper, stingray, and spotted eagle ray. The Wall Rocks site was next. It was home to black durgon, trumpet, parrots, rock beauty, angel, parrots, lobsters, yellowtail snapper, stingray, spotted eagle ray, blue tang, spotted moray, and squirrel fish. Club Reef was full of cavernous coral, encrusting stinging coral, common sea fan, deep-water gorgonia, and sea anemone. Shark Bow site was twenty-two metres in depth. At the top reef could be found tiger sharks and large rays, and in surrounding caves were sleeping large nurse sharks. Turtles were also swimming around, along with large schools of sergeant majors and tooth and perches. The shop also listed all the wrecks you could visit. The 1787 *Hartwell* wreck popped out at once, and William stared at it for few seconds before snapping out of it. Written on the wall was: "Running aground on her maiden voyage, built by Caleb Crookenden and Co. of West Itchenor, West Sussex, launched in February 1787."

"Hi, um…" William was still nervous. "I'm here for a private dive with Domingas to the *Hartwell* wreck"

"That's me," said Domingas. His smile relaxed William. "Have you dived before?"

"Yes." During the cruise, Coen and Nikher had gone over the basics of diving so that William wouldn't need any beginner lessons.

"Excellent, let's go. The gentleman I spoke to earlier did say we're on a tight timeline."

"We are; lots to see and do here. It's a beautiful island."

"How many days are you here?" asked Domingas, politely keeping up the small talk.

"Just a few days. We're trying to see as much of the islands as possible."

"What else you do have planned for Boa Vista?" Domingas asked as they stepped into the small boat. William started checking over all his gear, identifying the gas valve that was to slowly leak and trying to think of different things to do. He eventually spewed out generic vacation adventures.

"Well, it's funny. Boa Vista is known for its dive sites, but there's also the Golden Dunes of the Viana Desert. Ocean winds transport huge amounts of sand from the African continent. Between the natural dunes and volcanic rock, you see a rainbow of colours that look hypnotic because of the rapidly moving clouds. It's really quite something to see…if you have time, of course," said Domingas encouragingly.

"That does sound amazing!" William exclaimed, wishing he was actually staying for a vacation. He also started to feel bad for Domingas, who could possibly feel responsible for his death. *This poor guy is going to have to go home and tell his wife that someone died on his watch today.* Unfortunately, William didn't have the luxury of choosing what Domingas should feel, and although he might have trouble with dinner tonight, he would likely get over it in no time.

The small boat slowed just above the *Hartwell* wreck. Domingas went over the last-minute safety precautions while William put his gear on. William mentally went through the location of the mini gear and told Nikher through Mind-Link that he was at the dive site. She responded by reminding him where the gear was. "I know, I know," William nervously replied.

Amazingly, Mind-Link worked underwater, and William was able to speak with Nikher.

"I can see the wreck now. Where are you?" William asked her as he gently descended toward the wreck.

"I'm back at *Neveah*. I've also got you connected on *Neveah*'s positioning system and will be able to direct you straight to Praia da Atalanta on the north side of the Island. Just remember to swim in a northwest arc from the rear of the ship."

William sank and was blessed with views of underwater sea life. The water was warm and pleasant, almost like a swimming pool, he thought. He sank gracefully down to the first mast of the ship, which he grabbed to help in his descent. Suddenly, he heard a whisper.

"William Ward, this is…" And then it stopped. William instinctively knew it was *Neveah*'s voice, but somehow it was different. A school of colourful fish swam in the distance and distracted him. Suddenly aware of his surroundings again, he could see the corals along the reef and a stingray off in the distance. A few lobsters scurried out as he disturbed the water on the bow. He reached the first mast, where a small compartment led into the main deck. Before he entered, a small tiger shark swam out from the port side of the ship. William's heart stopped and a giant knot formed in the pit of his stomach. Getting eaten by a shark wasn't exactly a thought he'd considered.

The whisper left his mind, and slowly he sank and entered the small compartment and surveyed the area. Nikher recommended he make sure the mini scuba gear was free and accessible as he planned his escape route. She also suggested he pop his head out of the water a few times and give the tour guide a thumbs up, which he did. Once he felt comfortable, he entered the compartment. This time he had to twist around another curious shark to re-enter. William was trying to remember what it said about sharks on the wall at the shop. He eventually realized it was a tiger shark due to the stripes down its body. The stripes were distinctive, meaning it was young maybe aggressive, he thought. They also ate from a wide food spectrum and were known as garbage eaters. And they were second only to the great white in human attacks. But he also remembered reading that they were mostly nocturnal hunters and may not be hungry mid morning. He sighed in relief after sinking further.

He wrestled his mask and tank off, put the mini mask on, and thankfully breathed. He then bled the gas and wedged the strap into a bent piece of metal, making it look like he got his strap caught and ran out of gas, or maybe drowned while swimming away in panic. After he was satisfied with the evidence, he put the thrusters on his hands, manoeuvred his way to the rear of the ship that had a bid gouge out of it, and headed in a northwest arc as Nikher suggested.

"I'm moving, Nikher; let me know how my arc is. Strap is caught, and tank is empty."

"Arc looks good; just remember to avoid sharks. You're not top of the food chain down there but more like third from the top, so you'll look like a fast monk seal," Nikher answered half jokingly

"What?" William cried. "You never told me that!"

"Hey, this was your idea. You may want to hit the gym once in a while; you could have died peacefully in Barbados."

"Yes, but I didn't want to actually die," he yelled back at her.

"It will be worth it, you know." Nikher tried to make him feel better.

"What do you mean 'worth it'?" William questioned as he flew under water. He absolutely loved doing that but was too afraid to seem excited.

"You know, your dad would be proud."

William was glad Nikher approved of his plan and pleased that she wasn't upset that he didn't include her. He assumed that meant secrets were okay and maybe even preferable. It made William feel better about hiding his old book and the fallen Wards. Feeling better, William started to enjoy his swim. The thrusters were very powerful, and with slight movements of his hands, he was able to dive and shoot up and flank side to side. He felt like a dolphin. He jetted close to the coral and enjoyed the glistening sun beaming through the water, which was warm and gentle. At one point in his bliss, a killer whale dove past him, throwing him around as it gulped a tiger shark. *That's at the top of the food chain down here for sure*, he thought.

Nikher stood in the helm with Coen nervously following a slick red line on a screen, guiding William back to *Neveah*, which was floating a league away from the *Praia de Atalanta* wreck.

"Okay, William, you're almost here. Stay under water and enter through the port side dinghy hatch; Coen is opening it now," said Nikher.

After entering and climbing up the sunken stairs, William put away his mini scuba gear, grabbed a towel, and dried off. He made his way to his stateroom where he sat for a while and let the weight of the news his parents and Sarah were about to receive sink in. Although he was satisfied he got to die the way he wanted to, and also leave his father hope, it was still awful news they were about to get. Eventually he gathered his wits and headed up to meet Coen and Nikher in the main saloon.

"I'm not going to lie—that was effing scary," William said as he opted for a Yuengling beer, once again impressed that *Neveah* had it stocked. "The ocean is scary. I mean, I had sharks swim past me, schools of fish, sting rays. The coral walls also had caves, and weird fish just keep going in and out; it was eerie. But those thrusters were amazing. It felt like I was flying but through water. I can't wait to do that again—in safer waters, of course. Maybe like a really big pool." William even told them of the killer whale he narrowly escaped, exaggerating the story, naturally.

"Well," said Coen, "how does it feel to be dead?"

"Not good. I feel so bad for my parents, my friends, Sarah.

"I know it's tough. Sorry, son," Coen said empathetically. "But I'm sure your dad will find his way through. I was the one who helped Ernest die here. I wish I'd of thought of it myself for you, but you seem pretty clever. It just might be enough to get him to search again."

"Don't forget," said Nikher, "If we can get through these wills and find Henry, you'll be the twenty-first Ward. When we kill Venacio and his heir, you'll be free to do whatever you want. We can spread the money across the lines and all go our separate ways in and out of the Cradle peacefully. You can wash up on a deserted island and get rescued." Nikher leaned back and looked relaxed.

"That would be amazing," William replied. "Where are Aoife and Apollinaris?"

"They're at the other rendezvous point, Farol Morro Negro Lighthouse. Coen will go get them in the dinghy once they're back, and then we'll go to meet Eoghan at the São Filipe safe house and finally get to use SkyView!" said Nikher excitedly.

"Wait, you've never used it?" William was surprised.

"No, SkyView was built for you…well, for us…but the system is clean. This was to ensure nobody had access to manipulate any event. We'll all have access at the same time."

"Who's going to fly it then?" William asked.

"Coen, as long as you trust him."

"Of course I do," William replied, "I just assumed there would be somebody else."

"Well, my line has lots of captains of the sea and air in it. It's something we've always been entrusted with in the Ward League; it goes with protection."

"What's going to happen with *Neveah* then?" William asked. "Do we just leave her here?" William did not like the thought of that.

"No," said Nikher. "My Uncle Thijs is going to captain her closer to Europe."

"How much have you been involved with? I mean, what has the Ward League been doing since the Irish Atrocities? We do know history since then, right?"

"Well, the Ward League is involved in everything. That's all I know, but me personally? I've just been training for this…you know, physical training." She rubbed her forearms. "All the safe houses, transportation, immigration, assets, Cradle history— we are the future leaders of the Ward League. Nobody knows exactly what they were involved with through time, even since the Irish Atrocities. Those would all be secrets until we find Henry and the others."

"Both Kaethe and Ernest have made comments that I don't quite understand. Ernest eluded to an apprenticeship phase, and Kaethe also said we wouldn't be able to comprehend the Diamond War, which was why we hadn't been fully told about it," said William.

"We need to trust the wills" replied Nikher. "That's our path, our apprenticeship, as Ernest said. As for Kaethe, she also said 'Don't you think there is an evolution to the Losada League that you must see prior to unwrapping something as sophisticated as the Diamond War?' Look, all I know is that the Alvero line is responsible for so much evil through history, and it's our job to understand it so we can stop whatever they're doing now."

CHAPTER 10
SKYVIEW

Coen had met Aoife and Apollinaris at the Farol Morro Negro lighthouse and brought them back to *Neveah*. William was starting to feel clearer regarding his path. Everything led to the wills, and he had decided not to disrupt the process and worry about the Diamond War, or what had been happening since the Irish Atrocities. He was getting excited to use SkyView and had spent the last few hours going over his old book while Coen was getting Aoife and Apollinaris.

"Main saloon, five minutes," Nikher said through Mind-Link. William put his old book away in his private safe and made his way to the saloon, presumably to go over the plans to get to SkyView.

"Okay, so we're going to meet Eoghan, Nael, Dieter, and Bodhi out at the safe house in São Filipe," Nikher addressed the group. "Eoghan and my Uncle Thijs will captain *Neveah* and *Truth* back to the Mediterranean and shadow us in case needed. The safe house we're going to is just outside of São Filipe, and it's quite amazing. It's built into the near-vertical fault scarps enfacing on the north, west, and south sides of the caldera, and it hides the hangar for SkyView.

"What's a caldera?" Apollinaris asked.

"It's a large cauldron-like hollow that forms shortly after the emptying of a magma chamber in a volcanic eruption. It this case, the caldera is breached on the east and lava flows out to the coast," Coen answered.

"It ends up looking like a half crater," said Nikher. "There are also two peaks that gently slope down the inside of the caldera and above. We built a hangar between them from the outside that looks like random rocks, but they open for a vertical take off. Once we're aboard, we can review the events thus far. Each of us is set up with our own unique program with the history of the Cradle as it's currently known. We may adjust as we see fit, plus we have a team program that will automatically embed historical theories when our individual ones align. Mine and Aoife's are unlocked by the markings on our arm. If you guys wish to have graphene woven in, we can have that done after we get the wills, as the SkyDeck will adjust. For now, yours will be unlocked by trace DNA."

"Trace DNA?" asked Apollinaris excitedly.

"The SkyDeck will know who's in the room once you breathe or touch the controls," she replied.

The wind sprang to life and the warm air screamed across their faces as they headed to the Island of Fogo. *Neveah's* engines rumbled as she headed southwest, passing the island of Maio. "This was home to the Battle of Maio January 23,

1814, which was toward the end of the Napoleonic Wars. Prior to that, the English exported salt to Europe from Porto Inglês, hence the city name," Coen said.

Cruising past Maio, the wind picked up and the rain started. This didn't dampen the spirits of the passengers, though, each of them excited to get to SkyView and finally fly to the wills. William, although excited to use SkyView, really did love having his own yacht and felt connected with *Neveah*, which made him reluctant to want to leave, but he knew he had to get to the wills.

"Looking out starboard, you'll see the island of Santiago," Coen said. "In the center of the old town there's a plateau overlooking the Atlantic Ocean. It's a really beautiful view, and the town is quite lovely too."

As Neveah cruised past Santiago, William was lounging on the bow in one of the many cushiony seats. He could see the Island of Fogo and the massive, active stratovolcano enveloping his view. He could see the steam baths spewing off the coast. Thinking quickly to work on his memory, he imagined swathes of lava violently exploding all about.

"And finally, we get to see the Pico do Fogo Stratovolcano, the highest peak of Cape Verde and West Africa. The eastern side of the island collapsed into the ocean over seventy thousand years ago, leaving the fault scarps on the north, west, and south and taking the shape of an enormous half crater. It sent a tsunami 170 metres high to Santiago. Its most recent eruptions occurred in 1951, 1995, and 2014, so be careful and get out of there if you feel the earth shaking." Coen finished his third island info set relishing in the active volcano.

"All right, we're here," Nikher said over Mind-Link. "Eoghan, where are you guys at?"

"On the beach, of course," he answered.

"Put some clothes on and meet us at the safe house. Only Aoife, William, and I can unlock the tunnel leading to SkyView." Nikher responded and then looked at William. "It's the same as controlling *Neveah*; your trace DNA unlocks everything you need. Your DNA is essentially your key. I still recommend you get graphene woven to you, though."

"Really?" William replied uncomfortably.

"Yeah, it's really painful at first, but it becomes part of you, and you can't underestimate it uses." But, of course, it's up to you. You need to decide what we need to kill Venacio."

"Oooookaaay," said William slowly. He was stunned, as he hadn't considered it an option. "I'll think about it."

"Heads up, there's *Truth*," Aoife stated, excited to see her brother.

After enabling Sunken Treasure and disguising *Neveah*, Coen cruised around Fogo Island to the west side to the Porto Vale Cavaleiros, just north of São Filipe. After docking at the newly updated port, Coen, Aoife, Apollinaris, and William casually walked through immigration, once again using aliases. William felt free. it was the first time entering a new country as an officially dead person. His stomach began to turn in knots, realizing his parents must have gotten the news by now.

"Where's Thijs?" Coen questioned Nikher.

"Not sure," she replied with a concerned look on her face. "I spoke to him this morning; he was supposed to be here waiting at the port for us!"

"Thijs, where are you?" Nikher asked angrily.

"I'm headed over the Atlantic. We had strong winds here and I couldn't take off. I'll be a few hours late. Sorry."

"Late! You should have told us. We're stranded now!"

"I wasn't sure how long the delay would be. I thought I could make up the time in the air, but the cross winds have been too strong," Thijs replied.

"He should have told us ASAP if he was going to be late. Coen, tell him he's an idiot the next time you see him! We can't afford to make mistakes like these. Let's get back to *Neveah* and figure out other alternative transport," Nikher said, still fuming.

Back on *Neveah*, William was feeling confused regarding this exchange. Then he remembered that Thijs was Haven's brother, who was Nikher's guardian, the one who found the stone at Wassemoet Castle and also gave them the theory of how the wealth has been moved through time. He felt as if Thijs was quite active and wondered what his position would be, if any. He felt like he should know.

With a sudden realization, William left the helm and went to his stateroom. He closed the door and touched the back of his ear and said, "Ernest?"

"Yes, William," Ernest casually answered.

"I had no idea we were connected," said William, thoroughly relieved.

"Yes, my boy, why wouldn't we be?"

"I don't know, I just never thought of it. I'm still trying to process all of this, I guess."

"Well, son, we're always connected, as long as you want"

"This is a pleasant surprise, for sure. I just had a quick question, though, then we can chat later," said William.

"Spit it out then."

"What is Thijs's role within the Ward League? He was supposed to meet us here on the Island of Fogo and take us to SkyView, but he's late. He has also been mentioned a number of times, and I just wondered who he is."

"Well, he's a researcher and captain for the Wassemoet line. He's quite active in a few of our businesses, actually. Haven is Nikher's guardian, but she allows Thijs to help as much as possible. They're twins, you see."

"That makes sense. I feel better now. We'll chat later!"

William made his way back up to the Helm.

"What was that about?" Nikher asked.

"Sorry, but when you were talking with Thijs, it made me realize I could talk with Ernest. For some reason I hadn't thought of it until then. I just wanted to say hi and make sure."

"I'm sorry, I thought you knew," both Coen and Nikher said with a laugh.

"Don't feel bad, I should have realized. I just have a lot to think about." William suddenly realized that he just hadn't needed to speak to Ernest yet, which was why he didn't think about it. Then he understood what Nikher meant by "All our brains are designed the same way…to connect things."

"So how are we going to get to SkyView?" William asked.

"Umm, well, nobody knows we're on Fogo Island, so I don't see an issue with renting a local car. It's only a twenty-minute drive up the outer crater to the cliff face," Coen said. "Or we can wait for Thijs. William was tagged at Boa Vista early this morning; if someone left right away, it would only take few hours, at least by air."

Nikher looked concerned about the timeline. "We can't wait for Thijs. They could easily be scanning the islands, or they could have paid the locals at the port to tip them off if they see us. That can be called in, and they'd know by now we had a yacht from St. Lucia when Apollinaris and William were tagged."

"She's right," Apollinaris added, feeling nervous. "Where are we headed exactly?"

Nikher pointed up at the gigantic crater. "There's a small house up there. SkyView is through a tunnel. We'd need to make it into the house. Once inside, we'd be fine, as all the entry points are reinforced."

"What about Eoghan?" William asked, "Can't he pick us up?"

Aoife quickly connected to Eoghan on Mind-Link. "They crammed into an old truck, not enough room for everybody, he said."

Coen was frantically searching for transports using *Neveah*'s onboard computers. "Well, we have a few options," he said. "Who wants the ATVs, and who wants the Jeep?"

"There's nothing else?" Nikher asked, reluctant to use unenclosed vehicles.

"We need a 4x4 to get up the mountain in case of an emergency, and most rental companies only offer old cars," Coen replied.

"Is the Jeep a two-seater or four? Does it have a hard top?" Nikher asked.

Coen frowned and held up two fingers but said yes to the hard top.

"Okay, I'll take the Jeep with William. Apollinaris, you stay in between Coen and Aoife. We should be fine, as it's only twenty minutes up."

"There's only one problem," said Coen.

"What?" they all asked.

"The rental place in São Filipe is a five-minute drive from here."

"We could take a cab," said Apollinaris.

"No, no cabs. If they've been tipped off, they could drive us into a garage or something. We need to be in control," said Nikher convincingly.

"Yeah, right," Aoife replied.

"We could walk, stay close to the ocean. You know, jump in if we see danger, and swim back to *Neveah*," said Apollinaris.

"Too long to walk, but that gives me a better idea. Go get your swimsuits on and meet me at the dinghy. Bring a change of clothes and anything else you wanted on SkyView," said Nikher.

William rushed back to his stateroom and put his swim-suit on. He packed a change of clothes and grabbed his old book plus a few small belongings and put them into a small, waterproof bag. Then he walked through the interior deck to the port-side dinghy. Eventually he felt a gust of warm air as two thick doors automatically slid open.

"Are we taking the dinghy?" Apollinaris asked quickly as they all piled into the equipment area.

"I thought of that, but we'd still be too easy to follow if *Neveah*'s been announced," replied Nikher as she threw a waterproof bag and mini scuba gear to each of them, stopping at William because he was already carrying both. William realized they were going underwater. To him it was the safest and quickest way, a no-brainer.

Nikher led the way, flying under the ocean in a V pattern just separated enough for visibility. The team looked like an odd school of fish with jets of bubbles screaming behind them as they thrust toward the city. William and Apollinaris thor-oughly enjoyed the ride and the beautiful, colourful marine life. They were quite disappointed when Nikher signaled that they were there, and the ride was over.

They washed ashore on Fogo beach; the stunning black volcanic sand stuck to their feet as they made their way up the shimmering red and black cliffside paths. They quickly changed behind some brush just before cresting the cliff and headed directly to the rental shop. Coen paid the shop extra in advance and requested they have the three ATVs running and ready along with the Jeep. He dashed into the shop to say thanks and let them know where to pick them up, seeing as it would be a one way trip.

"Well, it's their livelihood; we can't just run off with them," he told Nikher after she gave him a dirty look.

Nikher and William started out in front and drove respectfully through the street, obeying the local traffic laws and nervously stopping at each light. William stared out the window and took in the local culture with its warm colours and wooden porches. They drove past Pipi's Bar, which had a quaint patio out front of an old stone house. They passed the Pizzeria Gelateria Adriano, which made William's stomach grumble, and the Campo de Futebol de St. Filipe. After a few minutes, they made it out of the city and could see the 4x4 roads up the mountain.

Thank goodness for the 4x4, William thought as they bumped their winding way past Lagariça. The tiny farm homes became fewer and fewer as they drove up the steep slope. Finally, they passed Cisterno, the last small town up the slope to Bordeira, a nine-kilometre-wide caldera with one-kilometre high wall with vertical fault-scarps. It completely walled the western side to the village of Chã das Caldeiras. Reaching the top of the caldera and seeing nobody in sight aside from the villagers below tending the vineyards, they each hopped off their respective vehicles and looked over the edge.

"The Plain of the Calderas, this small little village, is situated in the black crater of Pico do Fogo. That's the active volcano over there." Coen pointed across the crater. "This is the highest village in Cape Verde and produces quite a bit of wonderful wine, thanks to the volcanic soil. This village was destroyed in the 2014 eruption. People simply rebuilt their homes on the lava that covered their former land, which I found to be an amazing display of resilience. Being inspired, I recommended we anonymously help fund and rebuild the winery so that the farmers could still work. At the same time, we built the hangar for SkyView, just in case we'd need it. It turned out to be a great spot."

"Okay, let's get to the safe house; it's that small stone building," said Nikher, urging everybody to hurry up.

"That's a shed?" William questioned quickly, noticing the old truck parked nearby.

"That's the entrance. There's a set of stairs that take you down to it; it crosses the face of the caldera, carved into the vertical fault scarps, all the way to those two peaks near the Mosteiros border that runs all the way down the north side of the caldera wall."

"We're here, Eoghan, on top of this volcano cliff thing overlooking the village. Where are you?" asked Aoife over Mind-Link to everybody.

Suddenly, a shiny, red-haired, red-faced man popped out of the side of the fault-scarp below and screamed "OYE! I'm in the house thing. Get your butts down here! I want to get back to the beach and my boat. I don't like heights…or volcanos!" Three other heads popped out as well.

Eoghan turned to go back into the house and briefly looked out east at the ocean and volcano. Suddenly, at black helicopter sped up the slope of the volcano from the north side. It's nose was dipped and it looked menacing.

"OYE! OYE! Chopper! Get to the shed!" Eoghan frantically screamed and pointed and then raced to the stairs. Bodhi, Nael, and Dieter closed the tinted rock-shaped window and raced through the tunneled house toward SkyView.

William felt his heart drop; they were so close. Nikher grabbed William and threw him into the Jeep. Aoife pushed Apollinaris onto his ATV.

"Let's go! Let's go!" Nikher screamed into Mind-Link, ensuring all would hear. "Everybody get to the safe house. Eoghan, get to the door."

The Jeep sped along the caldera ridge, desperately trying to reach the shed before any attack. Coen, Aoife, and Apollinaris weren't far behind. Suddenly, William heard a searing whistle and a loud bang. The helicopters had shot some sort of a rocket at them and was trying to knock them off their vehicles. The locals could see small explosions and thought the outer crater was erupting, so they frantically began evacuating. The helicopter kept firing blast after blast.

Aoife, Coen, and Apollinaris veered down the mountain, hoping that splitting up would make for a more difficult target. The helicopter moved up the kilometre-high wall, positioning itself between the Jeep and the safe house, with a cannon pointed at the Jeep. Nikher and William made a hard left and raced down the slope. The helicopter was flying low and carrying four ATVs, which it dropped from a safe distance, swiftly followed by a rider for each vehicle. Once the ATVs were grounded and manned, they sped off down the crater slope after Coen, Aoife, and Apollinaris, who were now racing through local farms and private residences. The fourth ATV and helicopter chased down the Jeep, with Nikher and William still firing rockets; they were trying not to hit them directly but derail them.

"We're not going to make it to SkyView; there's no way we can get to the house without being blown up," Nikher said through Mind-Link, panicking as she and William raced down the slope way too fast. William had to hold on with both hands and both legs to brace himself just to stay in the Jeep.

"Coen, Aoife, and Apollinaris, you guys are going to have to split up. Aoife, you stay with Apollinaris and make sure all three ATVs follow you in order to give Coen a chance to get *Neveah* ready. If we can get there, we might be able to get out of here," said Nikher.

Coen, Aoife, and Apollinaris sped through the sloped farms, weaving in and out toward the port. Coen kept looking back for an opportunity to separate, but they were too close. Suddenly, Aoife jerked her ATV and drifted sideways. She was now directed straight at them.

"Keep going, Coen. Don't stop!" Aoife screamed.

Without hesitation, Coen darted through a half rotten barn and down a hill, launching himself off a small cliff and landing hard in a stream. In the meantime, Aoife, with Apollinaris following, drove right through the three ATVs. Aoife blocked a few strikes as her forearms glowed green. One of the men leapt off his ATV and onto hers. Aoife swiftly broke his clutching hand with a strong backhanded hammer thrust. Her plan seemed to have worked, as now only two ATV's chased the two of them back up the slope of the caldera. Aoife could see the Jeep off in the distance speeding around the north side of the caldera. Aoife, still being chased, pointed right for Apollinaris to see.

"Let's go south around this crater. We'll try to lose them in the vineyards on the Plains of the Calderas," Aoife said to Apollinaris on Mind-Link.

"That will take us too close to the volcano, and there are still hotspots!" Apollinaris said nervously.

Nikher and William were still being follow by the helicopter and one ATV, which was still firing small rockets at them and trying to cause a turnover. The Jeep now headed around to the north side of the caldera. The ATV couldn't keep up with the Jeep, but the helicopter easily could. William could see the side door of the helicopter open up and a massive turret poke out. He was frantically looking around to see how they were going to escape, but he didn't feel very optimistic. This was a very small island, and they wouldn't be able to avoid the helicopter forever.

"How much gas do we have?" William asked, panicked.

"Three quarters," Nikher replied.

"Well, we can drive around for a few hours," William said, trying to feel hopeful.

"Umm, I'm pretty sure that helicopter has a bigger tank than us. We could outlast the ATV, though," Nikher replied as they jostled around like dolls. "At least the rockets stopped."

"That's because they've switched to what looks like a turret!" William screamed.

"They wouldn't use a turret…they'd kill both of us! I need to see what this is. What side is it on?"

"There's one on each side," William replied, still shouting.

Suddenly, Nikher came to an abrupt stop. The helicopter screamed overhead and turned around. She could see the turret pointing directly at the Jeep. A cloud of smoke and a blast of fire shot out. Instinctively, the Jeep wheels spun in the slope and the projectile stuck into the roof, narrowly missing Nikher's head. It was a long black cable sprung tightly and shining in the afternoon island sun. The Jeep started to lift as they sped down the slope, seemingly hitting every bump.

Then the Jeep started to slow, being held back by the helicopter winch. The ATV was catching up. Suddenly, the cable slackened and the helicopter caught up to William's side of the Jeep. William looked up but couldn't make out either the pilot or passengers. The cable winched tightened again. The helicopter steered away and rose, lifting the jeep off the ground. Thinking fast, Nikher steered toward the helicopter. The ATV was still keeping a safe distance, like it was waiting for something, William thought.

"Nikher, if that helicopter lifts us, we can't jump. That's what the ATV is for," William said, again in a panic.

Nikher agreed and kept driving toward the helicopter, trying to keep the cable slack.

"The roof…it comes off," she suddenly realized. "You're going to unhook it; there's only a few latches," she screamed. "Hurry!"

William undid his seat belt and immediately flew across and swung wildly into Nikher, who blocked him with her glowing forearm, which felt like steel. Scrambling, he unlatched the roof and it screamed off. The helicopter made a wide turn and circled behind them as the roof flew off into the ocean. William was back in his seat and managed to get his seat belt back on. They raced around the caldera and were now on the Plains of the Calderas. They could see the volcano in the centre of the crater. The helicopter shot a spike that narrowly missed the Jeep on Nikher's side. Then it shot two more; the Jeep sped toward the volcano.

"We're sitting ducks here on the flatlands; we need to get back to the slope," William frantically shouted to Nikher.

Suddenly, they heard a loud bang as the spare tire exploded. A spike clearly shot through the rear door, lifting the Jeep again. William and Nikher looked at each other, full of concern. Without hesitating, William undid his belt again and smashed into Nikher's steel arm. He opened the rear door and the metal twisted and ripped off.

"We're going to run out of parts," William said after buckling back up. The helicopter made a wide turn again and circled behind them. William looked back in fear. "There's another ATV now, and the rider looks injured." William noticed that the Jeep was pointed straight at the volcano. "You know, it's full of hotspots here. We're going to have to turn around and go back to the other side of the caldera."

"We can't, the island is too small. There's nowhere to hide, plus there are innocent people over there I won't be able to avoid." Nikher's eyes narrowed deep in thought.

"What are we going to do then?" William asked.

"I have a plan. Undo your seat belt again and get rid of this windshield. I can't see anymore."

William once again undid his belt and bounced around. He managed to get both latches undone. Nikher slowed just enough to fold the windshield down. Just as William buckled up again, the chopper circled around them. Nikher hadn't sped up; she stayed slow and drove in a straight line.

"Move! Hit the gas!" William screamed, but Nikher ignored him and concentrated intently. William looked back and saw smoke and a blast of fire; a black spike sped toward them and pierced the open trunk area. William and Nikher both jerked back.

Nikher looked over at William and said, "When I give the signal, undo your belt."

William looked shocked. "I don't want to undo my seat belt anymore—it hurts. You're not exactly a cushion, you know!"

"Just do it!" she screamed, this time through Mind-Link.

Nikher suddenly hit the gas and started up the slope of the volcano centred in the crater. All William could see was the top of the volcano. The helicopter raced forward and rose to tighten the slack and get control of the Jeep. Nikher steered up the slope, frantically looking back at the cable. At just the right time with the Jeep wheels starting to lift, she steered off the side and went straight down, which tightened the cable and tugged the helicopter down. The jeep hovered a few feet from the down slope. The weight of the Jeep was now in full control of the helicopter, which raced toward the ocean, trying to regain its lift.

"Ready?" Nikher said with a suicidal look.

William, with no other options, shrugged and said, "Do I have a choice?"

She smiled and held out her hand. "Do you trust me?" William reluctantly nodded.

"Now!" she yelled. William did as she said and unbuckled, held on to the roll bars, and stood on the dashboard. Nikher also unbuckled, reached back, and grabbed both of their bags while holding the roll bar. She smiled at William and yelled, "Jump!" They both leapt off the dashboard, landing in the ocean.

The muffled sound of the helicopter faded as it still hovered around the area where the two dove into. William and Nikher flew underwater, following the Santiago coastline to the east side, far away from the noise. They enjoyed the schools of fish and coral reefs. William even saw a nurse shark he thought was lovely. The hatch opened and the two of them finally breached the surface of the equipment room on *Neveah*. Nikher had once again successfully escaped, although super dangerously, William thought. Immediately after feeling safe, William's thoughts moved toward Aoife and Apollinaris.

"Is everybody safe?" he asked them over Mind-Link. Coen was the only one who responded.

"Aoife, Apollinaris, are you guys okay?" William asked again, but still no answer.

"We're okay, Dieter, Bodhi, and me! We stayed in the safe house. Are you guys okay is a better question. We watched a Jeep fly off the side of a volcano," Nael stated loudly and with concern.

"Yeah, we're fine. That was Nikher and I. We had our mini scuba gear with us. We're with Coen at the rendezvous spot. Where are Eoghan, Aoife, and Apollinaris? Were you able to see them?" William was quite concerned now, as he almost felt responsible for them.

"We saw them race around the southern part of the caldera being chased by two ATVs. Eoghan managed to catch up with them, but they all disappeared behind the volcano you guys flew off of," Nael said as he peered out the tinted rock window, too afraid to open it.

"One of them is dead!" Aoife said over Mind-Link.

"Who?" Nikher cried in horror.

"One of the guys on the ATVs," Aoife said, almost out of breath.

"Eoghan and Apollinaris are okay, right?" William asked again.

"Yes," Aoife cried, "just give us second. Apollinaris is in shock, and Eoghan is hurt pretty badly."

"You guys need to get out of there. I'm sure that helicopter is still around," William screamed in panic.

"No, it's gone, but we're driving back to *Truth*. We're going to have to fly a doctor in," Aoife said

"Okay, on it," Coen said immediately.

"Isn't there a local doctor he could see? How hurt is he?" William asked.

"DNA files and too many questions. We have world class doctors always available. Doctors love money," Nikher replied.

"He's burned pretty badly," Aoife said, starting to catch her breath. "Apollinaris and I got stuck in a hotspot, and they had us cornered, so we had to fight our way out. Apollinaris fought pretty well, for an investor, I must say. Anyway, he held the guy off long enough for Eoghan to catch up and help. Eoghan tackled the guy and they ended up rolling over a hotspot. He's dead, and Eoghan only survived because of his clothes. The smell was horrifying. The guy I was fighting looked at Eoghan, who was half-burned and jumped back to his ATV and sped off."

"Who were they?" William asked.

"I didn't recognize any of the guys that chased us," said Aoife. "What about you guys?"

"I think it was Finian, Ciara's brother," said Nikher. A giant knot formed in Aoife's stomach. "But I'm not entirely sure, as I couldn't get a good enough look. If it was, they meant to separate us."

"Did you see the helicopter pilot? Was it Feargal? I know he can fly," said Aoife as she collapsed in her seat.

"No, the pilot was a younger female, tanned skin and long dark hair."

"Doctor's been alerted; get Eoghan to *Truth* and go north to Mindelo Island, where he will be waiting."

"We have a doctor here in Cape Verde?" William questioned.

"Yes, we do now, we keep a running list of private Dr's all over the world." Coen responded.

William was impressed. "What about Nael, Dieter, and Bodhi? There are still three guys on the island, and the helicopter might come back too."

"Eoghan also parked next to the shed. They might figure out that's where we were going," Coen added in concern.

"Yeah," Nikher muttered. "They also could have seen Eoghan when he popped his head out the window."

"We need to get them out of there!" said William sternly, gesturing to go back.

"That's not an option, William," Nikher said in the same stern tone. "The safest place for you right now is here on *Neveah*.

"Okay then, Aoife can go get them out and get them to *Truth*!" said William, still with a stern tone.

"She won't leave Eoghan, no way." Nikher responded calmly this time. "Nael, Bodhi, and Dieter are safe as long as they close the blast door. Besides, they want you."

"What if we get to another island and go through immigration to get tagged. They'll think we escaped"

Nikher thought this wasn't a bad plan. "But you're already dead, which is why they're here in the first place."

"Oh yeah, right," he replied, embarrassed.

"Okay, Nikher, I just landed. Where's *Neveah*?" asked Thijs over Mind-Link.

"Thijs! You could fly them out on SkyView. You're a pilot," Nikher exclaimed.

"Yes, I am. You already knew that," he responded, confused.

"There's no time to waste," she said. "Get to the safe house ASAP. Neal, Bodhi, and Dieter are there. Get them on SkyView, and we'll have to meet you at a different safe house; this one's been compromised."

"All right, on it. I'll let you know as soon as I get there!" Thijs responded excitedly.

"William is going to have to allow control and appoint Thijs as captain," Coen said in a concerned way to Nikher.

"Why?" Nikher frustratedly questioned.

"SkyView *is* William's. It uses trace DNA, remember? If he's not on it, she won't fly anywhere without his authority. They won't even get into the tunnel," Coen answered, looking at William.

"That's right," Nikher said hastily. "But there's no other way to get them out of there! Eoghan is on his way to Mindelo with Aoife and Apollinaris. We can't help...we barley escaped ourselves."

"How do I give control?" William asked Coen.

"*Neveah* can do it. She's connected to SkyView and can open everything," Coen answered proudly as captain.

"To where?" William questioned.

"It's up to you. we can meet them wherever. You have safe houses with private hangars all over the world. It depends how long you want to stay on *Neveah*." Nikher answered

"We can cruise safely all the way to Greece, like you originally wanted. We have a safe house in Thessaloniki, and Helios is there. Or we can stop in Italy and drive right up to Zermatt?" added Coen, without bias.

William thought for second. He didn't really want to leave *Neveah*, as she was beginning to feel like home. Being out at sea allowed him to think and take his time to comprehend everything. He still had so many questions. If he had time he could talk with Ernest and get some clarity. If they met SkyView at the closest airport, they'd be in Zermatt within hours, and who knew what overwhelming situation they might find themselves in.

"Umm, let's do what Coen said and stay on *Neveah* all the way to Greece," William said nervously, hoping Coen and Nikher would agree.

"Sounds good," Nikher said, giving William and Coen an approving look. "Give Thijs authority to captain SkyView to the Castle of Tarasp safe house in Switzerland. We can meet them there. Then we can all take SkyView to the Ice Palace in Zermatt, which is a short drive to the wills."

"Ice Palace?" William questioned. "Is that another safe house?"

"Yes, it was just recently built. It's a former ski resort in Zermatt. We had all the lifts removed and upgraded the chalet. It sits on the top of the mountain and is sloped on all sides. It also has a private hangar for SkyView, and in the great room of the chalet, overlooking the Alps, is a giant HoloTable that *Neveah* has interfaced the SkyDeck with. This will allow us to safely discuss our theories about the century. *Neveah* will combine our theories, and the HoloTable will display the events based on what we agree on. Oh, and the chalet has a HoloRoom built in as well, so you can continue working on your mind and body." William could sense the excitement in her voice.

"*Neveah*, please make Thijs temporary captain of SkyView, to the Castle of Tarasp safe house." William calmly spoke to Neveah as if she was a real person.

"I'm in the safe house, Nikher," Thijs said over Mind-Link to her.

Nikher linked Coen and William in. "Okay, William has made you captain of SkyView. You have authority to take her to the Castle of Tarasp. We're going to stay on *Neveah* and meet you there in about four days," Nikher said.

"Will do, Nikher," said Thijs. William could sense the excitement in his voice too.

Coen raised *Neveah* out of Sunken Treasure mode and altered her appearance by changing the panelling to a plain white, draining the pool, and enclosing the main saloon area. After about five or six hours of cruising north along the African coast, William finally started to feel they had truly escaped. The air cooled and the sun began its descent. William had a light meal and went to his stateroom to rest. He lay on his bed. Off in the distance, starboard side, he could see a faint glow. *That must be Africa*, he thought. His eyes closed and he fell asleep instantly, just as he heard Coen say, "Dakar, now there's an interesting place."

CHAPTER 11
THE PFAFFENBREIF

After a wonderful night's sleep, William awoke early and started his day in the HoloRoom, getting pushed beyond what he physical and mentally could handle. After his coffee, he wandered to the galley to make something to eat. He was famished. *Neveah* had cruised all night. William tapped the screen next to his bed and scrolled to the satellite position, which showed they were cruising past La Güera, the southernmost tip of Morocco.

"La Güera is now a ghost town and has been overblown with sand. It was founded in 1920, was part of the Western Sahara War in 1975, and abandoned in 2002," Coen said over Mind-Link, knowing William was awake.

It was still dark out and the moonlight glistened across the ocean out of every window he walked by. Smiling, he strolled *Neveah*, gently dragging his fingers along the walls, doors, and sills of the ship, extremely happy to have woken up at sea still aboard her.

The galley was empty. Yawning and still in his clothes from the previous night, he opened the fridge, which was fully stocked as usual with all his favourites. He reached for some thick-cut bacon and a carton of eggs, placing them on the counter. Yet another yawn and then he opened random cupboards and drawers, looking for bread, which he eventually found. The sea was calm, and the smell bacon first filled the galley and then blissfully floated through the rest of the ship. Coen made his way to the galley as well; he turned the coffee pot on and gave William a friendly pat on the back and said "Morning."

"Nikher at the helm again?" William asked with another yawn.

"Yeah, she couldn't sleep again. Keeps having nightmares. It takes her a while, you know, to truly feel safe. She'll be fine tonight; it takes her a day or so."

"Bacon and eggs?" William asked, lifting an eyebrow.

"You bet."

The two of them peacefully ate, sitting at the island and watching the glow of the sunrise out of the galley window. Coen told William that there had been no update on Eoghan, but Thijs, Nael, Dieter, and Bodhi had made it to the Castle of Tarasp in Switzerland safely.

"Tarasp Castle was built in the eleventh century on top of a large rock, giving way to impressive views of the Inn River Valley. The name comes from "terra aspera," or wild earth. SkyView is now vaulted in the forest hangar, awaiting your arrival," Coen added as he finished his last piece of bacon.

"Can I ask you a personal question?" said William

"Of course. Anything, son."

"About Nikher...well, both of you, I guess. Why does she believe Kiliaen is innocent? I mean, I know it was long ago, but in 1356, Finny and the Bear controlled mercenaries, and I assume we pillaged France after the Battle of Poitiers. That's well documented in the Cradle. In 1357, William died/murdered/faked his death, whichever, and in 1358 there's the War of the Twin Bears, and Baernt and Beyaert pledge to help the Wards kill Alvero."

Coen looked shocked. William had been quite reserved up until now.

"Sorry," William nervously added, "I'm not trying to insinuate he's guilty. It's just, I've heard a few times now that I should have answers in my head. I want to help, but I can't. I know she desperately wants to clear her line, but all I see is...well, I just don't want her risking her life for a truth that may not be there in the end, that's all."

"There's not a cell in her body that believes Kiliaen or Beyaert killed William or had anything to do with the pillaging after that battle; it's just not in her, and she doesn't believe anybody in her family—past or present—could be involved in anything like that. Me either," he added respectfully, knowing William wasn't accusing but just trying to figure it out.

"I don't understand. It's been seven hundred years, and hundreds of your line aren't all good. I need to be open to all sides of this." William immediately regretted his words when he saw Coen's expression.

"Well, we have different beliefs." Coen placed William's plate in the dishwasher and poured him more coffee. "Listen, I get that you've been in the Cradle your whole life, and this is all new. And I don't mean any disrespect by that. I just want you to see it from a different perspective. Our line lives outside the Cradle and has been part of the Ward League since 1358. We don't have societal weight, but we're free to believe as we wish, and we believe in our line. We can feel it."

"Where has the Kiliaen line gone then? Aoife said it disappeared, and she also alluded to Nikher being naive to believe the line wasn't involved in the Irish Atrocities."

"That's her deflecting her guilt for the actions of her line. Aoife is a wonderful, strong, brave, intelligent, resourceful woman, and we're blessed to have her on our side. Same with Eoghan, Cillian, Liadán, Tiarnán, and Olly. That's the line up to Ruairí, who divided with Clár after Turlough died. The Clár line is responsible for the Irish Atrocities alone. Aoife, Eoghan, and Cillian have embers of that anger in them, and they know it, we don't. Why do you think that guy on the ATV sped off? Imagine the look in Eoghan's eyes after rolling through fire to get at him." Coen shuddered in fear, which William mirrored. He remembered Eoghan's sunken eyes and hint of crazy when he first saw him in the Turks and Caicos.

"The O'Sullivan line lives outside the Cradle too, in both leagues. Always has. The odd time they're noted in history, but nothing of significance."

"Sorry, I'm still trying to figure things out," William said immediately, hoping he hadn't insulted Coen. He was starting to understand why Nikher believed as she did.

"Listen," Coen said, putting his hand on William's shoulder, "there's more to the Ward League than this fortune. There's a whole world out there that needs us, and you are destined to lead. We're all willing to die for you. It's about Wassemoet honour and doing what's best for the world. Your line has financially supported us for seven hundred years! The Ward League always does us quite well…I mean, I'm the captain of a yacht, Thijs is flying one of the most technologically advanced jets on the planet , Haven lives in seven different safe houses around the world, and I'm sure you've noticed that your safe houses are mansions. And Nikher? Well, she's part of all of it and has the honour of fulfilling the Wassemoet destiny and leading beside you. So if you ever feel guilty because she's protecting you, just remember that seven hundred years of Wassemoet lineage rests upon her completing her task and keeping you safe."

William and Coen cleaned the galley together and moved the discussion to a lighter subject. Coen poetically described his love for football and how he appreciated the dedication and athleticism involved. William, looking to connect, agreed with Coen and then listed all of his favourite quarterbacks. Coen pleasantly smiled, but William realized they were talking about different sports.

"Football's great, but I love hockey more," said William eagerly.

"Ah yeah, now that's a skilled sport!" Coen exclaimed, nodding in agreement with William.

"Violent too. It's one of the only professional sports that allows fighting. I can't imagine fighting on skates!" said William. Coen was again confused.

"We don't have fighting in our hockey...or skating. We play on a field"

William and Coen understood each other a lot better after breakfast, even though sports were a bit of an issue. Nonetheless, William really felt he could trust Coen and Nikher, knowing they would see this task to the end—their destiny.

Coen took over at the helm while William went back to his stateroom and freshened up before meeting Nikher in the main saloon. Coen picked up where he'd left off last, highlighting the interesting facts about Dakar.

William arrived at the main saloon to meet Nikher. "So where did we leave off?" William said, eagerly looking to get back to the fourteenth century. It was early afternoon, and William was full, well rested, and ready to get to work.

"Umm, the Pfaffenbreif, I believe," said Nikher while adjusting her shorts and sinking into the sofa.

"Pfaffenbreif," William repeated

"Yes, Pfaffenbreif. In short, it was an agreement signed October 7, 1370 between the six states of the old Swiss Confederacy, declaring themselves as a unified territory: Zürich, Lucerne, Zug, Uri, Schwyz, and Unterwalden. It essentially guaranteed peace on the road from Zürich to Gotthard Pass."

"An agreement? Like a treaty? Is it related to any war or plague or anything?"

"Nope, but Gotthard Pass was an extremely important trade route back then."

"My father mentioned Gotthard Pass before I left. He said it's a fourteen-mile journey through the Swiss Alps. They even walked it. That's where he stopped following the wills and came home," added William, trying to see the connection.

"Well, the states referred to themselves as unser Eydgnosschaft, translating to 'oath fellowship' in reference to the 'eternal pacts.' The Rütlischwur is the legendary oath taken by the three founding cantons, Uri, Schwyz, and Unterwalden, It's named for the site of the oath-taking, the Rütli, a meadow above Lake Uri near Seelisberg."

"Yeah, I remember my dad saying something about the Rütli as well. He said it symbolized me, my mother, him, and his oath to the three of us. That's when he left."

"Why would Pfaffenbreif be in the will but not the Rütlischwur?" Nikher said, starting to dig a little deeper. "I mean, the Rütlischwur was the original three cantons, the Pfaffenbreif was six, and later there were eight, including Bern and Glarus. Why only mention Pfaffenbreif? It must be referring to either the amount of states or the date, October 7, 1370."

William stood up and paced around. "Okay, bear with me," he said excitedly. "It can't be a coincidence that my father mentioned the Rütlischwur and the legendary oath. He said Gotthard Pass and the Devil's Bridge stood out to him in the will, and the view is what he imagined when he read about the Rütli."

"What are you getting at?" Nikher said hastily.

"If William faked his death, which I think he did after learning about what happened after the Battle of Poitiers, those mercenaries were part of the IBC. He wouldn't have wanted to be any part of that, and who knows what else the IBC was doing? I bet a small fortune that Baernt had the same opinion at the time. I bet William faked his death and convinced Baernt and Beyaert to create the Ward League."

"What about Kiliaen then?" said Nikher, half accepting the theory.

"I'm not sure; maybe he didn't want anything to do with either league. Anyway, let's not worry about him just yet. Let's try and build what we know." William was happy to have Nikher accept that maybe the Bear was part of the Battle of Poitiers, innocent or not about the pillaging. He thought that battle was an important event for figuring out the War of the Twin Bears and why Beyaert and Kiliaen chose different paths.

"So why the Pfaffenbreif then? The number of states or the date?"

"I think it's both," William said quickly. "I've been giving this a lot of thought. Of all the things my father said to me, his mention of the Devil's Bridge and Gotthard Pass were the only things that stood out to him. Henry could have easily made anything stand out to him, so why this?" William stood and walked around the main saloon, glaring out toward the African coast.

"The pillaging took place 1356; William faked his death in 1357, and the War of the Twin Bears was fought in 1358, which divided Baernt and Beyaert from the IBC. We'll worry about Kiliaen later. Twelve years then pass, which I would assume, since…" William opened his arms wide, gesturing to the entire yacht. "They kept working. They had wealth already and would have had powerful connections around Europe. William was an expert in trade."

"And Baernt and Beyaert were experts in protection," Nikher added excitedly.

"They had to set up trade somewhere else, establish new revenue streams if they wanted to combat the remaining factions of the IBC," William finished, quite proud of his theory.

"The Hanseatic League!" both said simultaneously. Nikher quickly added, "Aoife said, 'The Hanseatic League 1356… Merchants established the league to *protect* their economic interests along the *trade* routes within the affiliated cities and countries across northwestern and central Europe.'"

Nikher was so excited, she could hardly contain herself. The sense of beginning was beyond heartwarming for her. Slowly she composed herself and continued to repeat Aoife's words slowly, allowing William to keep up.

"Hanseatic cities had their own legal system and operated their own armies for mutual protection. From 1356 onwards, the network of alliances grew to include almost 170 free cities with no tie to local nobility. The league had a monopoly on Baltic trade and waged war against pirates and privateers, mainly from the Victual brothers, who were hired by the King of Sweden to break the monopoly and gain access to the maritime trade in the Baltic sea."

"From 1356 onwards ... Trade routes…Protection,"William said, tilting his head and wondering how they hadn't seen that before. "By the way, I love how you repeat memories word for word. That's so impressive," he added, trying to subtly let her know he trusted her.

"Thanks. You'll get there too. It takes years to master, but it's one of our greatest tools. Anyway, your very great-grandfather must have been setting up trade with the Hanseatic League during the Battle of Poitiers. When he heard about it, it must have made him so mad!"

"Hey, Baernt was probably with him, you think?" William shouted excitedly.

"Yeah, that makes sense. They would have been negotiating trade and protection," Nikher said happily. "That means Baernt wasn't involved with the pillaging."

"But Beyaert and Kiliaen were," William added nervously. "That's why it's called the War of the Twin Bears. William and Baernt would have heard about what they'd done when they returned…errr, sorry…what they may have been involved with," said William apologetically.

"You don't have to apologize, I get it. The War of the Twin Bears took place in 1358, two years later. We need to find out more about that war." Nikher looked defeated again. "It doesn't make sense for them to go such different ways."

"Yeah, I agree, it can't be as simple as evil twin theory. So by 1370, they would have been…Why are you looking so weird?"

"What's an evil twin theory?" Nikher asked, never having heard the term before.

"It's just a common myth. Don't you watch movies or TV, or read books? It's a Cradle thing. The villain in some movies ends up being an evil twin. You know, there's a good twin and an evil twin. It's quite common."

"No, I didn't know twins could be like that."

"It's not real; it's more of a myth," William said, trying to make her feel better. But he could briefly see the disadvantage of being born outside the Cradle.

"I was a twin too, you know" William reluctantly admitted. "but my twin died at birth." Nikher gave William an empathetic look, sensing his sadness.

"Anyway, let's forget about Beyaert and Kiliaen for now," said William. "I want to get back to the Pfaffenbreif. So by 1370, twelve years had passed, and by then William and Baernt would have financially established themselves within the Hanseatic League—secretly, obviously, and likely under an alias, because he'd just faked his death. How old would they have been?"

Nikher snapped out of her daze and quickly did the math, wishing Apollinaris was there so she could dwell on it a little longer. "Baernt would have been eighty-eight and William would have been seventy-four."

"Which would leave Beyaert and Peter, William's son."

"But that's only two," she said. "You're referring to six states of Pfaffenbreif?"

"I was, but you're right, that's only two," William said disappointedly.

"Wait, though, your dad said the Rütlischwur to him symbolized you, him, and your mother—three united." Nikher paused and thought of her next point. "Three more states were added in the Pfaffenbreif, so six united."

"So the six could symbolize the uniting of two threes." William said that out loud but regretted it; fortunately, Nikher understood.

"Beyaert and Peter would have each had a wife and at least one child—a first-born!"

"Beyaert was thirty-eight and Peter would have been forty-two!" Nikher said, astonished.

"Yes, exactly," said William. "I guarantee the Ward League was officially formed the day the Pfaffenbreif was signed."

"October 7, 1370," said Nikher. "But how would Peter and Beyaert know the exact day?" she added.

"They would have waited for it, knew it was coming, or been involved in it. They could have signed it, for all we know. William was using an alias all the way back then. All eight of those gentlemen were very smart, smarter than we can imagine. They've passed wealth and resources all the way to us." William once again gestured to Neveah but also adding a flying gesture with his hand, referring to SkyView.

Suddenly, the safe houses that were mansions flashed through Nikher's mind, along with businesses she knew of, and cash she'd seen flowing through them and different banks.

"After setting up the Hanseatic League, they came back to Switzerland in 1370, where it all started!" said Nikher, excitedly putting her own history together.

"I bet they came back to Switzerland to destroy the remaining factions of the IBC."

"Yeah, and used the Pfaffenbreif as an historical marker for the founding of the Ward League."

"And they kept the Declaration of Succession," William said hastily as thoughts kept darting into his head.

"That's right. That was smart—it kept the two leagues aligned through time. They must have known this was going to be a long fight. I bet something in the original Declaration of Interlaken refers to time…. centuries of time." Nikher had whispered "centuries of time," which confused William.

"They also could have actually been involved in the signing of the Pfaffenbreif too," William said, thinking a little more deeply about it and eager to verbalize the thoughts in his head.

"What do you mean?"

"Well, William would have had to use an alias all the way back then, right? That means any of the people behind the events of the wills could potentially have been part of the Ward League, just under an alias." Nikher gave an agreeing nod but was more engrossed in the thought of time. She wanted to read the original Declaration of Interlaken.

After some further discussion, Nikher and William agreed to break for lunch. William was getting hungry and wanted to let the discussion sink in before moving on to more events. Coen met up with them while *Neveah* cruised on auto captain toward the Canary Islands. At lunch, Nikher and William contacted Aoife through Mind-Link to check on Eoghan. She assured them that he was fine and elaborated with, "Let's just say he's stronger now." After being satisfied with Eoghan's safety, William decided to tell Aoife and Coen about the theory of the founding of the Ward League to see if he'd missed anything. Nikher didn't look all that impressed to involve Aoife, but she agreed, nonetheless.

"Well, the timeline fits," Coen said while thinking deeply and pressing his index finger to his upper lip.

"Yeah, it does," Aoife said, agreeing with Coen.

"We need to find out what happened to Beyaert and Kiliaen. Twins don't just part ways like that; twins are very connected," Coen added.

"William mentioned an evil twin theory," said Nikher, finishing her meal on the foredeck and letting the sun and fresh air float across her now-prominent freckles. "Have you ever heard of it?" she asked Coen firmly.

"It's a myth, Nikher," interrupted William. "Myths aren't real."

"Well, some are…or, more precisely, there are a few that we believe in," Coen said calmly as he began to once again clean the dishes up.

"You believe there's a good and evil twin? I thought you said you can feel your line?" William said, confused.

"No, not that myth. Are you familiar with the tragedy of Faust?" Coen asked William.

"Goethe's *Faust*? Yeah, I was given a copy for my birthday once." William's eyes narrowed as he stared at Coen and Nikher.

"I'm not surprised," replied Coen, looking at Nikher. He could tell she wasn't familiar with it.

"In the tale, the demon Mephistopheles bets he can lure Faust, God's favourite human, away from his righteous pursuits. Faust was a successful scholar but became bored and depressed after failing to attain unlimited knowledge. He contemplated suicide but instead called on the devil for the world's knowledge and all its pleasures. Mephistopheles appears and bargains with Faust, granting him everything he wants while he's here on earth in exchange for his soul."

"The deal with the devil myth," William stated aloud, unintentionally. "You believe in the devil?" William asked with an internal laugh.

"No, not in that sense," Coen said calmly. "But I do believe that if one commits a crime against one's own nature…say, an unnatural act in their lust for riches…the act itself enslaves one's soul, to which there is no recovery."

"Is that a common belief outside the Cradle?" William asked.

"No," said Aoife, "there aren't any common beliefs outside the Cradle. But each line has its own unique ideology."

"What's the O'Sullivan unique ideology then?" William asked, slightly annoyed another layer of unknowns were being added.

"Murder," Nikher whispered to Coen, just loud enough for William to hear. William could sense Aoife's reluctance by the length of the pause, but he didn't interrupt the awkwardness. Finally, after what seemed to be a few minutes, Aoife said, "I'm not sure how to answer. We have many different beliefs."

"What about the two we just mentioned, the evil twin or the deal with the devil myth?" William quickly asked, thinking he must have received that book for a reason. "Well, we believe if a family line goes too long out of balance, an evil twin will be born," Aoife answered, followed again by a long, awkward pause.

"What do you mean?"

"One of the twins ends up as the concentration of evil of that family line, to balance it," said Aoife reluctantly.

"That's ridiculous," Nikher said with a laugh.

William could sense the irritation from Nikher, but Coen stayed calm and didn't reply.

"And what about the deal with the devil?"

"Same as what Coen said. There's no devil to bargain with, only one's self, but we believe one's own nature is determined by one's acts, pleasing the soul not enslaving it," she finished.

"You mean choice?" asked William.

"Yes, we all have the ability within us to do good and evil," Aoife said. "Using Coen's example of lust for riches, you can attain those riches through what some would consider good or bad means. To us, good, bad, or in between would just be an extension of our soul, pleasing it. Eoghan and I choose to satisfy our lust for riches through good, by helping Ward League."

"That's interesting," William said. This time the awkward pause was indefinite. It was so long that nothing else of interest was said for the rest of the meal.

After the late lunch, Coen made his way back to the helm and cruised *Neveah* north along the African coast. William and Nikher agreed to meet on the foredeck during dinner to discuss more of the will when they reached the Canary Islands. They requested Coen to slowly cruise through the islands, deciding it would be nice to see land for a change. The weather had changed from hot to pleasantly warm, and both Nikher and William retreated to their staterooms.

Once safe in his stateroom, William reached for his old book and perused it for any other myths Henry may have highlighted. Not finding any, he decided to look up different myths through the Cradle's history. He had a polished, solid wood desk and work area in his room, and as he walked over to it, he laughed, remembering how he first thought whoever owned the desk and yacht must be very important and doing incredible work on this desk. He sat down and comfortably sank into the chair. Then he gently guided his fingers along the desk and surprisingly felt odd bumps. He looked closer. Across the desk and off to the left was written "Lignum Vitae." He paused and wondered what that could possibly mean. As he was always on the look out for clues, he decided to look it up.

As he sat down, a keyboard and five-foot wide screen seamlessly raised out of the desk. After a few mechanical clicks, *Neveah*'s computer flashed, "Lignum Vitae—Latin for the 'Tree of Life.' It's the national tree of the Bahamas and is the world's densest wood. The world's first nuclear-powered submarine, the USS *Nautilus*, has its main shaft strut bearings made out of Lignum Vitae. This wood has been used as propellers on conventional ships and hydroelectric plants dating back to 1920."

Interesting, William thought to himself before digging into *Faust* and dealing with the devil myths.

CHAPTER 12
DINNER WITH A VIEW

"The Canary Islands, also know as the Isles of the Blessed! A winterless paradise inhabited by hero's of Greek mythology. After a 1341 mapping expedition, European investors drooled over the Islands and its local inhabitants, the Guanches, who were tall, blond, and blue- eyed—a rarity. As new and easy slave-raiding grounds, the settlement of the islands signified the beginning of the Spanish Empire," Coen said through Mind-Link.

This was William's signal to meet Nikher on the foredeck for an evening dinner cruise through the islands while discussing the remaining events in the will. Nikher recommended they keep pace with the others so that when they finally got to SkyView, everybody would be on the same page, so to speak. She brought Nael, Dieter, Bodhi, Apollinaris, and Aoife up to speed via Mind-Link while William was in his stateroom.

William made his way through *Neveah*, once again marvelling at her beauty. He finally made his way up to the foredeck. Nikher had taken it upon herself to make dinner for the two of them. Coen decided it would be best to stay at the helm while they cruised through the islands, just to be safe. William sat at the head of the table of the outdoor dining area. The night was warm and pleasant, and *Neveah* slowed to enjoy the distant lights of the surrounding cities and towns. Nikher looked radiant, William thought. She was wearing a classic dress, which emitted sophistication and elegance. William also looked handsome and wore one of the well- fitted suits that lined the closet in his stateroom. The two of them had agreed earlier that it would be nice to dress up for once and enjoy the night. William stood and welcomed Nikher as she rounded the helm to the foredeck. Coen could be seen faintly through the thick glass.

"You look lovely," William said as he pulled her chair out for her.

"Thank you. And you look quite handsome too." Both smiled. "I hope your hungry."

"Yes, of course."

"I thought we'd have a traditional Dutch meal: Hollandse Nieuwe!" said Nikher.

"Sounds delicious. Would you like a drink first?" He pointed to the bar located behind them.

"Yes, please. I think I'll have a glass of wine with dinner," Nikher said blissfully.

"Any particular vintages?" William asked with an airiness in his voice.

"Yes, I'll have a glass of the Santiago 75 cl red wine, 2012," Nikher replied sounding more sophisticated.

"That sounds expensive," William replied as he picked up random bottles, looking for the wine.

"It is." Nikher laughed out loud. "It's about fifteen bucks a bottle." She snickered again.

William looked funny at her. "I think we can afford something…"

Nikher cut him off before he finished. "It's from Vinha Maria Chaves."

"Ahhh, Fogo Island. It's a volcanic wine. I think I'll have some too," William said delightfully.

He elegantly poured each of them a glass. In the meantime, Nikher had grabbed the two plates she'd previously prepared from the outdoor kitchenette, where they were keeping warm.

"You can't just dig in to the Hollandse Nieuwe; it's herring, by the way. Anyway, the way of eating it is a real Dutch tradition. In the Netherlands, new herring is eaten by lifting up the herring by its tail and then taking a bite upwards," Nikher said, proud of the tradition.

William obliged and the two simultaneously lifted the herrings' tails and took an upward bite. Nikher smiled and appreciated William's playful respect for tradition.

The two laughed and ate, fully enjoying each other's company and the beautiful view of the Canary Islands. William almost felt normal for the first time since the party. Nikher also enjoyed the evening and felt normal as well, remembering that this was her hope for herself: "A nice peaceful dinner."

After they cleaned up, it was time to get to work. William switched from the volcanic wine and reached for a Lagunitas IPA, which was brewed in Northern California, grounding him briefly. Nikher poured a Holland gin, Jenever, which was the juniper-flavoured traditional liquor in the Netherlands.

"Okay," William said, rolling up his sleeves. "That dinner was amazing, by the way; thank you." Nikher smiled again, that being the third time he'd thanked her. "Okay, so what was after the Pfaffenbreif?" William asked eagerly, taking a big gulp.

"The Ciompi Revolt 1378–1382," Nikher replied.

"The Ciompi Revolt 1378–1382," William replied in a fun way.

"Really?" Nikher looked disappointed but then gave a laugh. "Let's link everybody first."

"Definitely." Like a gentleman, William escorted her to the lounge area on the foredeck, away from the eating area.

Aoife and Apollinaris were in the main saloon on *Truth*, helping Eoghan while he recovered from his burns. Dieter, Nael, and Bodhi were staying at the Castle of Tarasp safe house enjoying the peaceful rest and sitting in the zwinger. They were blessed with the sprawling views of the Inn River Valley and endless walls of mountains.

"Do we have everybody?" William asked after touching the back of his ear. The others acknowledged their presence.

"I'm assuming Nikher discussed the Pfaffenbreif with everybody. Does anybody have anything to add?" William asked.

"Yeah, I do," said Nikher eagerly. "I think there is more to the Declaration of Interlaken 1328 than what Helios said on the rooftop in the Cayman Islands." She adjusted her dress and stared at William and then off into the lights of the Canary Islands once they made eye contact.

"What do you mean?" asked Apollinaris, remembering it was his dad who made the statement of the Declaration.

"Well, your dad said," Nikher replied. William knew she was going to repeat it word for word.

"'The Interlaken Beer Company (IBC) is supported by eight factions with a single representative for each, bound by secrecy in perpetuum. The Declaration of Interlaken 1328 and the Declaration of Succession 1337 to this day fundamentally hold both the Ward League and Losada League together. Each League has a single representative and plan of succession. The Alvero line, like all of us, will have a single leader as well as a century heir, always two. Each line has two." She finished repeating what Helios had said and then added, "I understand that the Declaration of Succession holds us together, that's easy. Heirs are determined by the turn of the century along the first-born line. But I don't understand why the Declaration of Interlaken 1328 would hold the leagues together."

"Yeah, I agree; the Ward League doesn't operate as eight factions sharing profits," Apollinaris said.

"But they do operate in secret in perpetuum!" William said loudly, eyeing Nikher intently for a reaction.

There was a quiet pause, and William and Nikher gave the group time to think of a reply while *Neveah* beautifully cruised through the islands. It was much darkener now, and the islands framed a gorgeous, glittering backdrop for them.

"There must be a reason behind the secrecy, aside from the obvious," Nikher said, realizing nobody had anything else to add. "Back then, they had to operate in secret. You couldn't just open companies like nowadays, you needed Royal Charters and special permission from monarchs and governments."

"Both leagues operate inside and out of the Cradle. That's what Helios meant by the Declaration of Interlaken holding us together—the secrecy from the authorities. Probably just to avoid taxes back then," Aoife said, finally breaking her silence.

I guess, Nikher thought. "I think there's more to it; there's an underlying motive, and ultimate plan beyond that, like a mission statement, one that would apply to both leagues. Is there a surviving copy of the Declaration?" Nikher asked in general but mainly to Apollinaris.

"Yeah, but it's not a document," Apollinaris said unsurely.

"What is it then?" William asked excitedly, as he agreed with Nikher.

"It's a painting. My grandfather described it to my dad before he died; he was the one who said it binds us all together. My dad just told me about it when we got to the Cayman Islands. Nikolaos said it was incredibly detailed." Apollinaris laughed out loud.

"What's so funny?" Aoife asked.

"My dad actually said there would be a time to share what Nikolaos had told him, and to wait for it."

"Where is the painting?" William asked without hesitating.

"Venacio's headquarters, where they met annually; it's a large fresco that wrapped the wall behind Venacio," Apollinaris replied.

"That's not good," Nael said, happy to get into the conversation.

"I bet there's a copy," William said eagerly.

"No way!" said Dieter. "A fresco is a technique of a mural painting, freshly laid allowing the pigment to merge with the plaster. The painting becomes the wall. That painting would take a very long time, and would not be scalable or easily duplicated."

William was glad to hear Dieter's opinion and wasn't surprised it was related to mass production.

"Listen, William knew he was going to fake his death. If there's something more in that mural, he would have had a copy made. If that's the case, then Henry would have known about it, and we'll be able to find it," William said. "I think Nikher is right. Each of them fled their homeland for a reason, and they all met up in Interlaken. Something bound them together then, and I bet it's in the mural."

"We need to find that copy. Did Nikolaos say anything else?" Nikher asked

"No, nothing" replied Apollinaris.

"The Declaration as described by Helios is more of an extension of something, not the principle itself," said Nael.

William quickly remembered that he'd been a lawyer in his previous life. "What do you mean extension of something?"

"Well, just thinking on the heels of the Pfaffenbreif. What if the eight gentlemen had an Oath Fellowship, or Eternal Pact, that was formed during the ten years they all worked together?" Nael replied.

"That's what Nikher was referring to," said William. "An Oath Fellowship between all eight lines that bind us all to this day."

"How do we find a copy? Any ideas?" said Aoife, disheartened.

"We can likely find out who the artist was," Dieter said, giving Aoife hope.

"How?" Aoife replied.

"Well, if we know the style and the general period in which it was painted, we could narrow it down. The fourteenth century was the beginning of the Renaissance, which is well documented in the Cradle. I guarantee this artist will be in SkyView," he added.

"I think I may have seen others from the same artist," William said excitedly. "At the IBC, there's a waiting area for the main boardroom, and in it hangs seven incredibly detailed self portraits of the IBC founders." William's mind was racing in many different directions. He really wished he had an eidetic memory so that he could describe the paintings to the others perfectly.

"There were also two other painting that somehow made it into the film about the company. Henry must have had them edited in; that's what started me on this adventure. One of the paintings was of William himself, and the other was a group painting."

"William must have taken the paintings of himself and the group or had copies made prior to faking his death," said Nikher. All could sense the excitement in her voice. "If we can find a copy of the Declaration of Interlaken 1328 and figure out the Oath Fellowship, it would make the wills much easier to understand."

"Do you remember anything about them?" asked Aoife hopefully.

"Um…" William stalled, not wanting to tell them that he took pics with his phone instead of relying on his memory. "William was around fifty in the painting and looked just like my dad." William realized that wasn't much help. "Umm, I look like my dad when he was my age, so likely William looks similar to me." He thought that was better for some reason. "In the group painting, they were all standing around barrels surrounded by mountains." William again realized that wasn't much help.

"That must be in Interlaken," Aoife said aloud. "What about the individual paintings? The ones at the company?"

William clenched his teeth in frustration at not being able to remember every detail, but he decided to fake it and act like he had good grasp of them. He gave them complete descriptions as he remembered them.

The group sat quietly and tried to imagine each of their forefathers, wondering what they would think if they saw the two leagues now.

"Dieter," William said, finally breaking the silence, "after we finish here, can you create a list of potential artists? I'm sure we can identify the technique!"

"Yes, of course" he replied.

"If it's a famous artist, it could be on display somewhere," Aoife added.

"Yes, that's my thought. A well protected public museum could be the best place to hide it," William replied.

"So the Ciompi Revolt 1378–1382 was next on the wills," said William. He wanted to get through the list now and then research artist. His first thought when he'd seen those paintings was that they must have been done by a famous artist and there must be more. Why did that pop into his head then? he wondered. This could be one of the keys in his head.

"Yeah, it was a rebellion of unrepresented workers in Florence, Italy," Nikher said, seeing that William wanted to get the discussion going and away from the unknown artist.

"Unrepresented?" Apollinaris questioned.

"Craftsmen, artisans, labourers who didn't belong to a guild," Nikher replied. "Those unrepresented were forbidden from associating with city government; they grew increasingly resentful of the oligarchy and were taxed heavily."

"There was much tension during decades before the 1378 revolt. The Arti Minori, the minor guilds, were constantly in contention with the Arti Maggiori, or the seven major guilds, reducing markets and bankrupting many wealthy houses by 1349. Labourers had no boundaries in Florence, and craftsmen could be considered elite if they were successful and wealthy enough. The oligarchy became unstable as many died from the Black Death or fled. During the instability, the gente nuove emerged, or new men. This was a class of immigrants with no aristocratic background who grew their wealth from trade. Together, the gente nuova and the Arti Minori bonded over their dislike of the oligarchy. By 1355, the miserables, those with possessions worth less than 100 lire, accounted for 22 per cent of the households in Florence. Eventually, the oligarchy and the gente nuova formed a truce, only to be broken by the oligarchy in June, the month of the revolt," Nikher said, framing the revolt.

"The interesting part of the revolt, and why I believe it's in the wills, is the mysterious group that represented the lower class," Aoife said.

"Who?" asked William, looking over at Nikher.

"The group was called the eight saints, and very little is known about the group or its members," Aoife replied.

"Do you think they're from the IBC?" asked Nael, standing up and walking around the outer courtyard of the castle.

"I don't know what to think, but by 1378, all eight of them would be dead, and there were only six factions left within the IBC. I want to look deeper into the revolt on SkyView," said Aoife.

"Yeah, we all should make a note to look into the eight saints," said William.

"Okay, so what's next?" William asked, once again smiling at Nikher and the beautiful islands behind them

"Winchester College, founded 1382," Nikher said, looking at William and hoping he wouldn't repeat it again foolishly.

"Okay," said William.

"Founded by William of Wykeham as an independent boarding school for boys, scholars had to come from families whose income was less than five marks sterling per annum," said Nikher.

"Interesting," said Apollinaris.

"What's next?" William asked.

"Victual Brothers 1392," said Aoife. "They were a guild of privateers that excelled in piracy. They pirated mainly maritime trade during the fourteenth century in the North and Baltic seas."

"Originally hired to fight against Denmark, they became the blockade runners as Denmark was besieging Stockholm for Scandinavian supremacy," said Nikher. "The name derives from the Latin word "victualia," meaning provisions, and refers to their first mission, which was to supply the besieged city. Their main naval enemy was the Hanseatic town of Lübeck, which supported Denmark in the war. The Hanseatic League, however, initially supported them, as most of the Hanseatic town had no desire for Danish victory, due to its strategic location for control of the seaways. For several years after

1392, the Victual Brothers were powerful in the Baltic Sea. They had safe harbours in the cities of Rostock, Ribnitz, Wismar, and Stralsund. In 1393, they turned to open piracy and coastal plunder, sacking the town of Bergen, conquering Malmö in 1394, and occupying parts of Frisia and Schleswig. They also plundered Turku, Vyborg, Styresholm, Korsholm, and Faxeholm Castle at Söderhamn in Hälsingland." Nikher paused for a second then continued.

"At the height of their power, the Victual Brothers occupied the island of Gotland, Sweden in 1394, and set up their headquarters in Visby. Maritime trade in the Baltic Sea virtually collapsed due to the piracy. Denmark, fed up with the piracy, chartered an English ship to combat them. Denmark also united with Norway and Sweden and formed the Kalmar Union, which is the next event on the list."

"The Kalmar Union was formed to combat the influence of the Hanseatic League," Aoife added excitedly. "The Union forced the Hanseatic League to cooperate with them, leading to its decline."

"The Hanseatic League?" William excitedly asked.

"Yes," replied Nikher. "The King of Sweden conceded Gotland Island to the allied Teutonic Order, who destroyed Visby and drove them out of Gotland Island. Eventually the remaining pirates gave themselves the name "likedeelers." The most famous leader was a German named Klaus Störtebeker, who could swallow four litres of beer without a breath."

"What happened to the Hanseatic League?" William asked.

"The merchants of Amsterdam eventually broke the Hanseatic monopoly during the Dutch–Hanseatic War 1438–41," said Nikher.

"Oh, that's into the fifteenth century," said William, realizing they were already through a hundred years. "What's left on the list?"

"The Renaissance in Italy and the Peasants' Revolt of 1381," Said Aoife

"Umm, okay, the Renaissance is quite big, so I'm going to save it for SkyView, "said William. "Is everybody okay with that?" William heard a collective "Yeah."

"Last we have the Peasants' Revolt of 1381. What do we know about it?" William asked the group.

"Well," Aoife opened, "also known as Wat Tyler's' rebellion, it was a major uprising across large parts of England, mainly due to high taxes from the ongoing Hundred Years' War with France. At Brentwood, an attempt to collect taxes ended in a violent confrontation, which spread rapidly across the southeast country. Common theories are that the revolt was led by a secret organization called the 'Great Society.' The English king was only fourteen, and he fled to the Tower of London. Most of the royal forces were abroad or in Northern England. Rebels entered London and were joined immediately by locals. They destroyed the Savoy Palace, attacked the jails, burnt law books, and killed anyone associated with the royal government."

William sat listening and suddenly remembered a piece of advice Ernest had given him: "No matter how events seem to flow, the outcome often reveals its creator, usually those who benefit the most."

"What?" everyone said. He realized that he'd said that aloud. Nikher was looking puzzled, and he could only imagine the looks on the faces of the others.

"It's something Ernest said to me before we left." He repeated it slowly and well enunciated. "What was the outcome?" he quickly asked Aoife.

"Well, Wat Tyler's head was cut off and displayed on a pole?" Aoife replied.

"No, what changed after the revolt?" William asked again.

"Well, laws changed," Nael spoke up. "The revolt deterred Parliament from raising taxes for military campaigns."

"That's what the goal was all along, I bet. The Great Society could easily be the Ward League," William said excitedly.

"Seems a stretch, William," said Aoife, which surprised even William.

"William left England because of the war; he had to leave his home, because English nobles wanted Scottish land. Once again, the English were at war, but now with France over land. There are only two ways to end a war: either kill the enemy or kill the funding."

"William's right," Nikher said immediately. "This revolt is the last event in the will, but it's 1381. The Ciompi Revolt was 1378–1382, so both happened at the same time. Both the eight saints and the Great Society are mentioned in the Cradle." Nikher gave William a nod of approval.

"Winchester College, founded 1382, Victual Brothers 1392, Kalmar Union 1397, the Renaissance in Italy fourteenth to seventeenth century—all occurred after the Peasants' Revolt 1381," Apollinaris said. "Why was the Peasants' Revolt listed last?" They all looked at each other but nothing was said. By now the yawning had started.

"Morocco," said Coen over Mind-Link. "Officially called the Kingdom of Morocco, the most popular sport being football, which is played with your feet and a round ball, not a pigskin. Morocco was the first nation to sign a treaty with the US and is home to the African continent's largest wind farm. The official currency is the Dirham. We have just passed Casablanca, and just north starboard side you will see the capital of Morocco, Rabat, not the small animal, founded in the twelfth century as a military town. The seventeenth century saw Rabat as a haven for Barbary pirates. In 1912 the French made a visit, and in 1955 Morocco became independent, with Rabat becoming the capital. Moving past Rabat is Tangiers and the Strait of Gibraltar."

The group had finished up and retired for the night. Coen was giving his update as William awoke. They were headed through the Strait of Gibraltar, a wide channel separating Morocco and Spain. William once again started his day with his two workouts and then managed to have breakfast with Nikher. They discussed briefly the events of the previous night, framing it in their heads. The weather was much colder, but the sun was still shining. *Neveah* cruised through

Spain and Algeria, and William mostly stayed in his stateroom trying to organize his thoughts. *Neveah* cruised through the Mediterranean Sea and ended the day in Tunisia. The following morning after his workouts, William had breakfast with Coen and then once again retired to his stateroom to organize his thoughts for when they got to Greece. *Neveah* cruised passed Italy and Malta, and finally rounded the southern tip of Athens, Greece. Coen enabled Sunken Treasure before docking in Thessaloniki.

CHAPTER 13
VIOLENCE AT SEA

William said farewell to *Neveah* and grabbed his light travel bag along with his book. At the safe house in Thessaloniki, they met up with Helios. The house had very exotic and expensive vehicle collection, which was soon to be William's, they all instantly thought as they entered the underground garage. William was beginning to formulate a long theory in his head for the fourteenth century but couldn't articulate it, so he was trying to avoid any discussions to throw it off. He felt he had something in his head that could connect everything, but he needed SkyView to trigger the details.

Aoife, Apollinaris, and Eoghan met them there. Eoghan docked *Truth* at Mallorca while Thijs flew one of fleet jets to pick them up.

"How do you feel?" Nikher asks Eoghan as they walked between the exotic car collection.

"On fire," Eoghan said, showing the bandages. Nikher immediately noticed the type of bandage and knew he had graphene woven on. Eoghan gave her a crazy smile and said, "I had them double it."

"Double what?" Nikher asked hesitantly

"The Graphene," he said excitedly. "I got thinner stripes that can cover more area."

Nikher was impressed, as was William, who couldn't help but overhearing.

"I was having weird visions while I was in all that pain, and when I was under, I could see them chasing Aoife," Eoghan said in a whisper.

"Who?" Nikher replied, concerned.

"Finian and Ciara. Aoife had a few nightmares as well but won't elaborate," he replied, lifting an eyebrow.

Nikher remembered hearing stories that the Irish Atrocities were felt throughout their line, specifically Liadán born 1893, who was the O'Sullivan leader in the Ward League at the time, and his son, Tiarnán.

William walked through the aisle of ridiculously expensive cars, not believing his eyes or that they were his...or might be his.

"Some of these old ones are replicas," Helios said as he walked closer to William. "We didn't want to ruin any rare originals with armour." William was eyeing an armoured 1962 Ferrari GTO.

"That's a 1962. In 2008, an original 1963 sold for $70 million...that's over there," Helios said, pointing. "That one might bring too much attention."

"What do you recommend?" William asked.

"The Gallardo. Beautiful, safe, armoured. Every professional soccer player in Europe has one."

After they all paired up, Nikher and William entered the Gallardo to test the comfort level, which was surprisingly good. Aoife and Apollinaris hopped into a white Ferrari, Coen a black Rolls Royce Phantom, and Eoghan an Astin Martin. Coen planned on following Nikher and William, while Eoghan was to follow Aoife and Apollinaris.

William chose the Gallardo and could feel the weight of the armoured door as he opened it, noticing the thick glass as well.

"Please stay for a late lunch. It's better to eat here safely than risk stopping too many times en route. William, you're sure you don't want to fly to Switzerland?" Helios said as they all sat around a massive dinning room table.

"Yeah, I'm sure," William said nervously, looking at Nikher. He wanted to take the original route his grandfather did to Interlaken, as well as formulate his theory before getting to SkyView. "Nikher has kept me safe so far; we'll be fine. Nobody knows we're in Greece."

"Nobody knew you were on Fogo Island either," Helios said skeptically, looking at Nikher. The seven of them ate a very tasty, Greek-inspired lunch. The safe house was situated on ten sprawling, well-groomed and scenic acres. It was an older house with traditional Greek architecture; the underground hidden garage was the most impressive aspect of the house, although one could say it was impressive in its entirety.

William quietly ate, enjoying the view. Nikher had a few questions for Helios, which broke the silence.

"May I ask you a few questions about your dad, Nikolaos? Apollinaris told us about the mural above Venacio, and I was wondering what your thoughts were on it. We've made it through the events of the wills at a quickly and I was hoping to have the Declaration of Interlaken figured out before we got buried in the details at SkyView."

"You mean, the eight factions meeting annually in secret in perpetuum? It's pretty self explanatory," Helios answered stoically.

"Did Nikolaos describe it to you at all?" Nikher asked, getting the attention of the whole table.

"Briefly. He was quite hesitant to at the time. But he said it was big. The top half was bright, and the bottom half dark; the middle of the bottom showed the eight men, veiled, and each holding something."

"Holding what?" Nikher cut him off eagerly.

"Well, William and Alvero weren't holding anything, but they were signing a document that just said "perpetuum" and had eight signatures. To the left of them was Huc holding a law book, Eleutherios a calculus book, and Baernt an axe. To the right was Hyneck holding some hops, Bligger a stein, and Finghin wasn't holding anything but clenched fists. They were all hunched in secret around the document."

"What about the background of the painting? William asked.

"The background was eight duplicates of the eight men, each with a different member signing the document veiled across the mural and fading into a bright scene above. The middle of the top half showed the eight men standing around barrels and surrounded by mountains, with the word "annui" engraved into each barrel, which is Latin for "annual". Stretching out from that were random borders and thrones, governments, religions, monarchs of the time, much of the world."

"Nothing else?" Nikher asked quickly.

"The bottom was too dark to tell, he said, but there were lots of small details. You'd have to see it up close."

"Thanks," said William, finishing his lunch. He was sure there was a hidden painting now. The fact that the group painting he saw was in that one proved that William had made a copy. "We need to find that artist," William said to Nikher over Mind-Link. "Lets get going."

After lunch, William and Nikher thanked Helios for his help and sped off in the Gallardo, with Coen on their heels in the Rolls Royce Phantom keeping watch. They also followed up with Dieter regarding the unknown artist. Dieter informed them that the list of potentials was longer than anticipated, due to the fact that the style of painting dated all they way back to ancient Greece.

The Gallardo sped through North Macedonia and then through Albania, only stopping at Rozafa Castle in Shkodër.

It was late in the evening; they were tired, but Coen wanted them to know about the castle.

"Built on a rocky hill 130 metres above sea and surrounded by the Buna and Drin rivers. The castle was an Illyrian stronghold before it was captured by the Romans in 167 BC. It was also the site of several sieges, including the siege of Shkodra by the Ottomans in 1478 and the siege of Shkodra by the Montenegrins in 1912."

Both Nikher and William walked around, immersed in the Ancient Roman history. The sun was starting to recede, and the sky was getting darker. The air was cold and brisk. The castle was a roofless sprawl of only stone and grass, but the sunset views were amazing. William, Coen, and Nikher sat quietly as the sun went down.

The next safe house was located in city of Shkodër. It was much smaller compared to the other safe house but elegant nonetheless. It was located a street back from many historic and beautiful buildings. Many restaurants and bars filled the area. William, Nikher, and Coen nervously found a small restaurant and had a bite to eat. Nikher longed for the days when she could go to dinner without fear. William and Coen, less fearful, enjoyed the meal before retiring for the night.

The next day they woke up fresh. Coen had breakfast ready, and the three of them ate, cleaned up, and rushed out to the Gallardo, eager to get going. By lunch they had made it to the beautiful town of Split, situated along Croatia's Dalmatian coast.

"The town is known for its beaches and Diocletian's Palace, which is a fortress-like complex at the centre of town, first erected by the Roman Emperor in the fourth century," Coen said. "Surrounded by white stone walls that once held thousands of Romans, it's now home to hundreds of shops, cafes, houses, hotels, cathedrals, and bars, which is where we are going for lunch."

Coen had secured reservations at a private restaurant near the Golden Gate, which was one of the four main entrances. The three others were the Brass Gate, the Iron Gate, and the Silver Gate.

After lunch they sped north west along the Croatian coast through Šibenik, known as a gateway to the Kornati Islands and home to the fifteenth-century Cathedral of St. James, a stone building decorated with seventy-one sculpted faces.

"We're going to stay in Zadar tonight. You have safe yacht protected in the bay; it's no *Neveah*, but they're connected, like a little sister," Nikher told William as she repeatedly checked all her mirrors and blind spots in the supercar.

"Really? Wow, that sounds great!" William replied, impressed again.

"We're going to visit the Sea Organ. There's a walking bridge that crosses the inlet from little *Neveah*," Nikher excitedly stated.

"What's the Sea Organ?" William asked, staring out the window and soaking in the coast.

"The Sea Organ plays music by way of sea waves and tubes located underneath a set of large marble steps. It's one of my favourite places. My mom took me as a little girl. Zadar suffered much damage in the Second World War. They repaired the sea front with an unbroken, monotonous concrete wall with huge steps leading to the sea. Underneath the steps are tubes and cavities that turn the sea into a musical instrument. It's awesome. I'd like to think that when this is over, we'll end up repaired and turned into something beautiful like that. From wars to music, you know?" Nikher said dreamily.

"There's also a monument to the sun, 'Pozdrav suncu,' consisting of three hundred multi-layered glass plates by the steps. It's a twenty-two-metre circle with photovoltaic solar modules underneath that at night illuminate and produce a wonderful light show. There are also similar, smaller installations representing other planets of the solar system. On the chrome ring around the sun are inscribed the names of all of the saints after which churches on the Zadar peninsula have been named."

They drove into a private garage and were greeted by a marina official who escorted them to little *Neveah*, with Coen on their heels. They settled into their staterooms. William's was a little smaller but still had the distinctive thick doors. After a quick dinner, Nikher was excited to walk over to the Sea Organ to show William. Coen was hesitant to leave the yacht but finally agreed.

"I know you love that place, but it's an unnecessary risk, that's all," Coen repeated a few times, even as they crossed the walking bridge. It was very crowded at the time, which made William feel safe but also stirred a little anxiety. The road was laid with old stone, and hundreds of boats stuffed into every possible dock, many of them looking rough. The town was nice and full of low-rise apartments. The architecture was an elegant blend of the new and the old.

After crossing the bridge, William was swept back several centuries and could see the system of Zadar's walls that were built to defend against attack. This served their purpose to the Venetian Empire from 1409 to the fall of Venice in 1797. Coen had informed them of this while walking, also mentioning that the defensive system was on UNESCO's list of world heritage sites.

William enjoyed the walk and the fresh air. He could sense Nikher's excitement as they made their way along the defensive walls and entered the old town through the Sea Gate. The narrow roads were paved with old stones, and the buildings were old and new and inspiring. After a short walk, the narrow streets opened up to an ancient cathedral and what looked like an old stone Roman forum. Nikher hurried her pace to the west side of the peninsula, which welcomed the Adriatic Sea. Now running, Nikher finally made it to the Sea Organ. First thing she did was jog up and down the steps and trying to touch each one. William was smiling and happy to see her enjoying herself, as was Coen. They left her alone to enjoy the odd sound the massive concrete structure was making. Coen took William over to the monument to the sun; it was around dusk and the light show had begun. William and Coen enjoyed the show and feeling like normal tourists.

William looked over at Nikher, whose smile radiated through the crowd. William couldn't help but admire it. Suddenly, she stopped and covered her face, and William could tell something was shockingly wrong. Nikher's smile had melted into the evil grin of an assassin.

"That's Feargal," said Nikher through Mind-Link to William and Coen.

"Where?" said William, his insides starting to turn. He frantically looked around, not knowing what Feargal looked like.

"Aoife, we need backup. Your relatives are here in Zadar at the Sea Organ. Where are you?" Nikher asked. "Coen, stay close to William." Nikher's demeaner changed from tourist to bodyguard.

"On it," said Coen

"We're about twenty-five minutes out," said Aoife. "We're on our way, but not much we can do about the traffic."

"Where is he?" asked William nervously.

"He's standing next to the cruise ship. Black coat, red beard, sunken eyes, looks like a maniac," Nikher responded.

"How are we going to get out of here, Nikher?" Coen asked. William could sense his fear.

"I don't know," she answered. "I don't think he's spotted us yet."

"How did he know we were here?" William asked as shivers ran up his spine.

"I have no idea," Nikher replied. "That must have been Finian back on Fogo; he must have tracked us somehow."

"There's no way they could have tracked us to here. We cruised for four days; they could have attacked us at any time if they were tracking us," Coen answered adamantly.

"I agree with Coen," said William. His mind was racing, trying to think of how Feargal would have known and realizing any coincidence was out of the question.

"I don't think he's spotted any of us yet; he's just calmly waiting, almost like he's guarding the cruise ship, like his post or something," said Nikher.

"Coen, where would we have docked *Neveah* had we come by sea?" William asked intuitively.

"Right along that dock where he's standing," Coen replied, not happy where William was going with this.

"Well, somebody must have known you like this place. They got that info somehow; there's no other explanation. Coen's right, they would have attacked us out at sea if they were following us, or any time we were in the Gallardo." William said, a little frustrated.

"No way," Nikher said quietly and angrily, still through Mind-Link. "We can easily escape anything on *Neveah*. She's the fastest and safest yacht in the world, and they wouldn't risk a car chase—too many bad drivers on the road."

William, slightly satisfied with the answer, didn't reply. All three were hiding their faces.

"How do we get out of here? We're surrounded by a very sophisticated system of defensive walls, remember? There are only a few gates," said William.

"Not sure. I'm hiding my face and trying to think," Nikher said in her quiet, angry voice again. "First thing we do is delay. Aoife and Eoghan are on their way. If Feargal is here, so are Finian and Ciara."

Coen calmly reminded William that Feargal was the father of Finian and Ciara, Ciara being one of the Dark Seven.

"Uh oh, he's spotted me," Nikher said, alerting Aoife, Eoghan, William, Apollinaris, and Coen on Mind-Link. Nikher could hear a collective "Who?" from four voices. "Feargal," she answered. She had also added Cillian to the conversation, who was back in Ireland. She knew Aoife would have already informed him. "He's on his way over. I can see his beard moving; he must be alerting somebody," she added, trying to be calm.

"Gates are going to be blocked," William said, feeling his blood start to boil once again in danger. "That's who he's alerting; we have to get out of here fast!" Panic had started to set it.

William could see Feargal start walking toward Nikher. He was fifty feet away, close enough to see each other's eyes. Nikher stayed a comfortable distance away, trying not to look over and give William and Coen away. Feargal, realizing what Nikher was doing, took a few paces left, which she copied. She copied him when he moved to the right, and when he took two steps forward, she took two back. Staring at each other, they both stopped. The crowd was beginning to build, as it was a local tradition to watch the sunset on the Organ steps. People were weaving in and out and passing around them, out of focus.

"Why isn't he going after her? Why is he just standing there?" William asked Coen.

"He's waiting for something too. You're right, we have to get out of here. We can't wait for Aoife and Eoghan!" Coen said, his words speeding up as he realized Feargal must have a plan. "Nikher, we have to run…NOW!" Coen said through Mind-Link. "There must be a way out of here, aside from the gates!" Coen's terror was starting to build.

Suddenly, Nikher sped right toward Feargal, jostling through the crowd. He gave a shudder and his eyes widened, which exemplified their sunken nature, and his jaw dropped.

"What are you doing?" cried Coen.

"Get into the old town and stay in the crowds. I'm going to break his jaw so he can't talk," Nikher responded as she sprinted and panted.

Coen and William ran right across the Roman relics and ducked into a busy cathedral. Nikher, true to her word, ran directly at Feargal and attacked. Feargal blocked as much as he could but was overpowered by the glowing forearms of the much younger Nikher. He absorbed three strong strikes, knocking him down. Nikher was about to dole out the final blow when she felt her arm being held back. A few people in the crowd jumped in and broke up the fight, holding Feargal down and her back.

She briefly saw his beard move again and instinctively looked up. Finian and Ciara had knocked over a table at an outdoor café and were running at her. Nikher, hovering over Feargal, felt a hand release her arm and had an easy chance to break his jaw but chose not to. Nikher saw an opportunity and sped off down the steps of the Sea Organ, jumping into the water and hoping Finian and Ciara would chase after her. Unfortunately, they didn't. By the time she realized it and breached the water, all she could see was Feargal entering the cathedral, likely following Finian and Ciara.

"They're in the cathedral, William, all three of them," Nikher yelled in panic as she panted and pulled herself up the sea wall. Soaking wet, she ran across the road toward the cathedral.

"Okay, we're headed up the tower at the back. Meet us outside; it looks like we can get outside from here and maybe land on the roof."

Entering, she found a crowd of tourists staring at her. Feargal, Finian, and Ciara were blending in and looking around for William. Nikher made it out to look like she was going after them but retreated when they weren't noticing and ran around back to help William and Coen off the roof.

"We have to get out of here," Nikher panted.

"How? They're inside, and I bet the gates are being watched," said William, panting as well after briskly walking down a narrow lane.

Coen briefly looked back and saw Finian's face in the tower window. "They saw us," he said, alerting William and Nikher.

"Aoife, are you guys here yet?" Nikher frustratingly asked over Mind-Link.

"Yeah, but the bridge is closed for some reason, and there are suspicious looking guys lurking everywhere. We're trying to stay hidden. Where are you at?"

"Behind the cathedral walking toward the Sea Gate. We have no idea how to get out of here," said Nikher.

"Wait," said William. "Didn't you say this defensive system was on UNESCO's list of world heritage sites?"

"Yeah, why?" Coen replied.

"There would be escape tunnels…there would have to be," William said excitedly.

"But how are we going to find an escape tunnel?" Nikher asked.

"It's in the Cradle, isn't it?" William smiled.

"Yeah, and you can connect to *Neveah* and ask her," Coen said, looking impressed.

"*Neveah*," William calmly spoke aloud. "I need to know if there are tunnels in Zadar. We need to find a way out of here and back to the safe house or little *Neveah*."

"William," *Neveah* said in a pleasant voice. William immediately smiled and linked Nikher and Coen. "At the bottom of the cathedral tower, hidden under a red carpet, is a hatch that gives access to an old tunnel that will take you to Queen Jelena Madijevka Park."

"That take us too far away from little *Neveah*," Coen said.

"Plus, we'd have to go back toward Finian and Ciara. We can't risk that; the three of us can't fight them," said Nikher.

"But Aoife and Eoghan can get through from the other side and help us," William said, quickly informing Aoife, Eoghan, and Cillian about the plan.

"There are four old wells with iron wheels hanging over them—that's the entrance," said William.

"Get Apollinaris to drive the Astin Martin and wait by the park. Get as close as you can to the wells," Nikher added. "We'll meet you at the Celje Castle in Slovenia; it's the closest safe house."

Aoife and Eoghan ran around the bay to Madijevka Park, and Apollinaris sped to the car. The Park was located at the feet of the Zadar walls. Each entered one of the wells. Apollinaris, not too far behind, parked the car as close as he could. Aoife and Eoghan climbed down the stone vertical steps, jumped down, and ran to the cathedral.

"We're almost at the tower," said Aoife on Mind-Link.

"Okay," William replied. "What's the plan, Nikher?"

"They're going to have to fight so that we can escape. We can't risk the gates. Are you guys okay with that?"

There was a long pause, but Cillian finally answered. "Yes, Aoife and Eohgan will fight them."

"Apollinaris, you'll have to stay in car and keep it running," Nikher said. "You guys draw them away from the cathedral long enough for me to get William and Coen into the tunnel, and then I'll help. I owe Feargal a broken jaw, she said fiercely.

"Don't bother, I'll break it for you!" said Eoghan. "You just get William out of there."

An old red carpet looked possessed as a mound grew in the middle of it. Aoife lifted the old wooden hatch, which flipped the carpet over. William, Nikher, and Coen had briskly walked back to the cathedral, taking the long way around, knowing Feargal, Finian, and Ciara were following.

"There's the cathedral!" Nikher said excitedly. "Aoife, where you at?" she asked over Mind-Link.

"In front of you," Aoife said as she poked out of the cathedral entrance.

Feargal, Finian, and Ciara had sped around the corner right on Coen's heels. Suddenly, all the O'Sullivan eyes met. William, Nikher, and Coen were caught in the middle of an Irish storm. William could feel the hatred emitting from all of them. They picked up speed and ran as fast as they could into the cathedral, leaving an Injured Eoghan and Aoife to fight the three O'Sullivans.

William, Nikher, and Coen ran as fast as they could to the tower hatch. Coen begged an old lady to cover the hatch with the carpet. They sped down the tunnel, up the wells, through the park, and into the car with Apollinaris.

"Drive!" Nikher screamed at Apollinaris, who looked shocked and scared.

CHAPTER 14
THE WILLS

Nobody heard from Aoife or Eoghan. All of them had repeatedly tried to reach the Irish siblings, but to no avail. Not a word came through Mind-Link. Cillian was currently in the sky, flying from Ireland to Zadar. It was about midnight, and they had finally reached Celje Castle in Slovenia. They all feared the worst; the mood was sullen. Coen didn't inform William about it at all during the drive, not even about the castle.

"Would they have really killed them?" William asked Nikher as he sipped an Irish whiskey while sitting by the fire in a small private study.

"Yeah, they would," she responded angrily. "It's my fault for going to Zadar. We never should have gone." She wiped a tear from her face, took a deep breath, stood up, and started to angrily pace around, not wanting to show William any emotion.

"Cillian, let me know when you land," Nikher said over Mind-Link.

"I will. Get rest, and I'll let you know as soon as I land, I promise," Cillian replied. That had been the tenth time she'd asked.

"Aoife, Eoghan, can you hear me?" she said in a broken voice for the hundredth time.

William wasn't doing much better. *Having death hang over you is incredibly toxic*, he thought to himself. He struggled to speak, feeling his throat tighten.

"Don't blame yourself, that won't do any good," William said, trying to comfort her.

"I should have known better; I never should have gone back there," she said angrily.

"But how would they have known you were going to go there?" William asked. "It doesn't make any sense."

"That was my fifth time there; they could have had somebody tracking me my whole life and seen a pattern, you know. Feargal was just standing there waiting, like he'd been there for days," Nikher replied.

"I don't know, Nikher, that seems extreme," said William.

"They know we were en route to Europe. Once you left San Diego, they knew; St. Lucia, they knew; Boa Vista, they knew. They've been preparing for this since you left your home. They've been waiting your whole life."

Nikher and William finally fell asleep halfway through the night, Nikher on the couch and William in a comfortable reading chair. With only a few hours sleep, Nikher awoke immediately as the sun first shot a ray through the window.

The fire had gone out and the stone mantle had begun to shine as the sun crossed it.

"Cillian, Cillian," Nikher yelled. "Haven't found them yet?"

He responded through Mind-Link. William looked over, concerned, but not saying anything as he awoke.

"You said you were going to contact me once you landed," she said angrily.

"I just got here in the middle of the night; it's a long flight to Zadar, plus a drive to the walls. I've been running around the old town, but everybody's asleep and I have nothing to go on," Cillian responded.

"The car," Nikher said excitedly. "Apollinaris!" Nikher screamed through Mind-Link, trying to wake him up.

"Yeah...wha..." he answered slowly.

"Where did you park the other car?" Nikher demanded.

"Umm...at the marina, in the garage by the Gallardo you drove," he answered slowly again.

"Cillian, go see if there's a white Ferrari at the marina, at our private garage," Nikher said excitedly, hoping it wouldn't be there and that Aoife and Eoghan were on their way.

"Okay, will do, Nikher. I'll keep you posted."

Nikher and William freshened up and made their way down for a quick breakfast.

"We're about a seven-hour drive to the Castle of Tarasp and SkyView. Cillian will bring all the personal belongings we had to leave and meet us there after he finds Aoife and Eoghan," Nikher said, not willing to believe that they may not be found, even though she was informed the Ferrari was still at the marina.

They piled into the Astin Martin and drove through Austria, the southern part of Germany, and then back through Austria. They finally made it to the Castle of Tarasp on the far east side of Switzerland.

"SkyView," Nikher said, pointing to a vault door after a long walk through a Medieval stone-walled tunnel under the castle grounds.

Finally, William thought. The vault door opened only as William neared. Beyond the threshold lay a fierce looking jet with slick, long, clean lines. William admired and walked around it in awe, trying to take in all in. He could plainly see the curved crease on the underside of the jet, which he assumed descended when in flight. *The SkyDeck*, he thought.

After twenty or so minutes of admiring the exterior, Nikher urged them to the entrance. "William, will you do the honours?"

William looked stunned, and his jaw was closer to the floor than to his nose. "Umm…well, let us in…SkyView?" he said unsurely. At once and silently the staircase unfolded and elegantly lowered to their feet. They all looked at each other, more impressed than they had imagined.

William entered the fuselage, touching the sleek leather seats and modern furnishings, while Coen made his way to the cockpit. William couldn't believe he had a private, undetectable jet. He tried to soak in the thought of it. The back of the jet was blocked by a curved padded wall. William intrigued neared it.

"Hi, William," he heard *Neveah*'s voice in his head. "Do you wish to use SkyDeck?"

"Yes," William said, gesturing for all to follow.

The distinctive sound of pressure releasing was heard, and a curved door rotated. Within seconds, the door reopened to a large, curved screen filling their full vision. Seven chairs mirrored the window in an opposite arc. William immediately sat in the middle chair; Nikher sat to his left. A multitude of buttons and switches surrounded each chair, but William could tell his had the override and would control what they saw. Slightly dazed, he kept getting lost in the world, briefly forgetting about Aoife and Eoghan, until that reality shot back at him.

"Where do we want to go first?" Coen asked over Mind-Link.

"We need to find Aoife and Eoghan. We go where we think they are," William said immediately.

"Italy. They're safe in Italy!" Coen screamed over Mind-Link. "There's a message here. They crossed the Adriatic Sea to the east coast of Italy, landing in Pesaro, and made it to a safe house in Florence. They had their electrodes ripped off in the fight! They're on their way to Zermatt and will meet us at the wills."

"Thank God!" William said as he perused the buttons and stared at the black window.

Coen readied SkyView, and William could hear the roof open. The engines roared, and after a minute or so, it began its vertical lift.

"We'll be in Zermatt in about twenty minutes. It will take us longer to land than fly there," Coen said with a laugh.

Everybody smiled and found a comfortable sleek chair to lounge in. Nikher looked the most relieved, finally getting to the wills, which was the first task. The next one was to keep them safe while William figured out what the wills meant and how to find Henry.

Flying over Zermatt, Coen slowly descended, landing in a hidden hangar of the recently purchased ski resort nestled in the Swiss Alps. They all piled out and right back into a large black SUV and headed directly to private vault at the foot of the mountain.

They twisted and turned down the mountain, eventually veering off the main road down a snow-covered gravel road that was slightly used, eventually steering into an unused road that only Coen must have known was there. Finally, curving around a sharp peak that spiked out of the ground, William could see a large metal door recessed into the mountain. Just to the side, two small, mailbox-looking objects protruded out from the ground, one on each side. Coen slowed between them and stopped at William's window.

"Touch it," he said to William.

William obeyed, and the garage door began to slide open. Once inside, and with the metal door closed behind them, they exited the SUV slowly and with anticipation.

"Well, this place is interesting," William said as he walked around, trying to take it all in. They were in a large, smooth metal room with comfy furnishings. Behind a large thick glass wall was an elevator door that had a red light illuminated. The elevator door opened, and a tall, thin man walked out as the large sheet of thick glass descended into the floor.

"Good afternoon, everyone, I'm Gabriel Müller, Keeper of the Wills. Please come with me," he gestured.

One by one, the elevator descended to each person's appropriate floor based on trace DNA. William, the last to go, entered by himself. The elevator descended about seven or eight floors and finally stopped. William's stomach was sinking lower and lower. When the door finally opened, William entered a well-lit room with a pedestal and parchment under glass on it. Across the walls were paintings by various artists. William's eyes strained as he searched for the Declaration painting, but it wasn't there. The one of William was, though, but this one had the title of fourteenth Ward. It hung directly behind what William was sure was the Will.

William took a few slow steps closer. On the pedestal were two large parchments, pressed under a thick slab of glass. The right one recorded the events of the fourteenth century, just as they'd been recited by Aoife as well as his book. On the left was a letter addressed to the fifteenth century Ward. It read;

> "It's with a heavy heart I write this, for your life
> is not yours until my creation has been destroyed.
> In my search for a better world, I partnered with
> an ambitious Spaniard, and we were soon joined
> by six loyal men – We became wealthy beyond

measure – hidden in the shadows through trade and commerce – The Spaniard had an insatiable lust for new markets – I thought I was moving the world away from hierarchy – from aristocracy – from boundaries – from war – I thought I was freeing my common man – I was in error – The Spaniard and the six men deceived me and drove the world toward war – toward boundaries – toward aristocracy – toward hierarchy – The Pillar of Wealth I created had blackened – The seven are being led by the Spaniard and using wealth for malice – The first stone has been laid and our Pillar begins – we have been unified – We have a new ally – We honour the two Declarations to stay aligned in perpetuum – As I write this I die – The Black Death had taken the Spaniard, but his Pillar endured and gains in strength – You are a century Ward – You are entrusted with the fifteenth century – Your destiny is to destroy the Black Pillar and undo what I unwittingly enabled – A guardian has kept you safe, and an ally heir has guided you here – Ideas are weapons – Both Pillars are well hidden from the world – A key is needed to unlock it – A single transaction will unlock your mind – The parchment accompanying this letter contains the events of the fourteenth century that each Pillar has been involved with – The necessary information to decode each event will be hidden in the conservators – It would be foolish to underestimate the malice of the Black Pillar of Wealth or its reach – It is a new foundation of evil.

"A century Ward is born with immense strength – Your soul – Your Self – Is the purest of our line – it is your gift – this is your burden."

So there it is, William thought in a deep peace. *It's true.* There was always a part of him that thought it was all fake, a big joke. But the evidence was undeniable, the options to turn back nonexistent, and the weight of it growing heavier and heavier. He realized that the letter was intended for the fifteenth Ward, and he was the twenty-first Ward. "How could one possibly topple that Pillar. The strength it must have gained in all these years is surely immeasurable."

William eyed each painting, being sure to burn each image into his mind. Nearly four hours had gone by, and he was unsure if he was going to leave. He started searching for a different way out, places to hide, even food. His spirits were at their lowest, hope was slipping, and desperation was sinking in. Throwing the weight of it off and simply ignoring it, he forced himself back into the elevator and ascended.

Nikher and Aoife greeted him first as the elevator door opened. William's heart warmed seeing Aoife alive and excited, which lifted his spirits. Even seeing crazy Eoghan gave him a much-needed shot of adrenalin. Coen, Apollinaris, Dieter, Nael, and Bodhi were all talking by the two SUVs. William noticed how happy and excited they seemed, and looked confused.

"What's wrong?" Aoife asked after being released from a large hug from William.

"Why is everybody so cheerful?" he replied

"We can finally get to work. We have the wills, and we have SkyView; there's no stopping us now!" Aoife exclaimed.

"Oh yeah, I guess," William reluctantly responded. "Let's just make sure we try and stay together from now on; we have a lot of work to do."

William was still not back to his normal self and couldn't carry the weight of it all at once. Mentally he threw away the six hundred years, deciding to focus on a century at a time. The others must have had less weight in their wills. They were almost acting like they had succeeded at something, but in reality, they all were light years away from any success.

William's voice took on a serious tone. "Coen, can we get to back SkyView? Eoghan, get back to *Truth* and get her to the west coast of Italy, near Florence. Thijs, please take *Neveah* to the Hanseatic town of Lübeck on the Baltic Sea."

They all looked shocked at William's tone but politely obeyed. Nikher and Aoife immediately fell into line, thinking that William must have received some direction in the vault. Ready and excited, Nikher, Aoife, and Coen escorted

William back up the mountain to SkyView. Eoghan drove Dieter, Nael, and Bodhi up, and then immediately left to get *Truth* near to Florence.

Coen fired up SkyView. The seven heirs were sitting comfortably in the jet and staring at William for direction.

"Nikher, Aoife, please come," William asked. Bodhi, Apollinaris, and Nael gave a confused look as the cylindrical door rotated and closed.

"I wanted to talk with you briefly before I bring the others down," William said as he nervously flicked switches and pressed buttons.

"What about?" Nikher said, looking concerned.

"I want to know what accompanied your wills. Mine had a letter addressed to the fifteenth Ward."

"Mine just had the list—you know, the one we'd already discussed," Aoife said.

"Nothing else? No additional letter?" William asked.

"No," she responded.

"I had a letter," Nikher said. "It wasn't signed, but above it was the painting of Baernt, so I assumed it was him"

"Can you tell me what it said?" William asked.

Nikher of course repeated it word for word: "Our line has been broken, and one of our kin lost – We were deceived by the Spaniard – Our wealth had blackened – But we have a new ally – In my hubris I aided a storm of deceit and death – We honour the two Declarations to stay aligned in perpetuum – As I write this I die – The Black Death had taken the Spaniard, but his Pillar endured and gains in strength – Our wealth has a new captain and a new purpose – The Black Pillar must be destroyed – You are a century Wassemoet – Entrusted with the fifteenth century – You are at the command of century Ward – Your destiny is to destroy the Black Pillar and undo what I ignorantly enabled – A guardian has kept you safe, and an ally heir has guided you here – Ideas are weapons – Both Pillars are well hidden from the world – The parchment accompanying this letter contains the events of the fourteenth century that each Pillar has been involved with – The necessary information to decode each event will be hidden in the conservators – It would be foolish to underestimate the malice of the Black Pillar of Wealth or its reach – It is a new foundation of evil.

"A century Wassemoet is the embodiment of good – You are entrusted to guide our line – it is your gift – this is your burden."

"Mine was similar," William said, deep in thought, "addressed to the fifteenth Ward. William felt he enabled the creation of the Black Pillar of Wealth."

"Ernest referred to it as well," Nikher interrupted, "on the rooftop, remember?"

"Yeah," William said. "The wealth and malice seemed daunting from what I read. It said it would be foolish to underestimate the malice of the Black Pillar of Wealth or its reach, as it's a new foundation of evil. That was seven hundred years ago, so I fear what this monster has grown into. 'Both Pillars are well hidden from the world – A key is needed to unlock it – A single transaction will unlock your mind,' William finished. "Also, it mentioned the soul. I had wondered about the unique beliefs outside the Cradle that you guys shared, and if the Wards had one," he said reluctantly.

"What about the soul?" Nikher asked, eagerly leaning away from him on her SkyDeck chair.

"'A Century Ward is born with immense strength – Your soul – Your Self – Is the purest of our line – it is your gift – this is your burden,'" William recited, looking for any reaction from them. "Have you heard anything like that before?"

"No," replied Nikher. Aoife shook her head no as well.

"This could be why the Declaration of Succession is every century," stated Aoife.

"It seems William thought the century Wards had a soul with immense strength, a gift," William said, trailing off in thought.

"Why do you seem concerned?" Aoife quickly asked.

"Well, after our last talk about Faust, I did some research about the deal with the devil myth," he replied. "Going back a thousand years, almost every century in the Cradle lists a prominent tale of somebody selling their soul to the devil. In the eleventh century, Pope Sylvester II used a book of spells stolen from an Arab philosopher and learned sorcery. He made a pact with a female demon called Meridiana, who appeared after he had been rejected by his earthly love, and with whose help he managed to ascend to the papal throne.

"In the twelfth century, scholar Sæmundur Sigfússon was credited in Icelandic folklore with having made pacts with the devil and managing by various tricks to get the better of the deal.

"In the thirteenth century, in the *Codex Gigas*, a monk with broken vows promised to create in one night a book to glorify the monastery forever by including all human knowledge in it. Realizing by midnight that this could not be done, he called upon Lucifer to help finish the book in exchange for his soul.

"In the fifteenth century we have Faust, which we all already know about. In the sixteenth century, however, we meet John Fian, who was a notorious sorcerer who confessed to having a contract with Satan during the North Berwick witch trials in Scotland.

"In the seventeenth century, Bernard Fokke, a captain for the Dutch East India Company, sailed so fast from the Dutch Republic to Java that legend grew he was in league with the devil.

"In the eighteenth century, Jonathan Moulton was alleged to have sold his soul to the devil to have his boots filled with gold coins when hung by the fireplace every month. The nineteenth century on saw a multitude of legendary deals with the devil, from artists, poets, musicians, business people, investors, and healers," William finished.

"But nothing in the fourteenth century," Aoife said, finally clueing in.

"Yeah, that's weird," Nikher said.

"I don't believe William made a deal with the devil at all. He may have believed he did, that's all," William said.

"And you're concerned there's false belief in you?" Nikher asked, standing up and walking around.

"Well, yeah, I don't feel like I have anything special about me. I mean, there may be somebody better. Maybe this succession plan wasn't very well thought out. Maybe we should pick someone else, that's all. You're way smarter and stronger than me. This could be why this fight has lasted so long, if William believed each of us had some special power, but we don't. That's why it's been seven hundred years. Look, don't tell the others yet, okay? You can mention everything else about the pillars and the keys and all that, I just don't want to share that yet."

CHAPTER 15
A VIEW FROM ABOVE

Where to, William?" They all heard the voice over Mind-Link as SkyView rumbled out of the hangar and lifted above the Swiss Alps.

"Up," William replied. "As high as she goes. I want to see all of Europe!"

SkyView's engines howled, and they could all feel an immense suction to their seat— up and up and up—until it stopped and they froze in mid air, hovering.

William gingerly caressed the buttons on the arms of his chair until he saw what he was looking for. A switch labelled "open" had a protective cover. He lifted the cover and, without hesitation, flicked the switch. Elegantly the SkyDeck descended on a forward angle, and a small joystick lifted out of a section of the arm. Suddenly, a large part of the world was in front of them, centred by Europe along with the earth's horizon. It was the most beautiful sight William had ever seen. The clouds were so far below, it was dream-like. From the blue ocean to the green desert lands, it was quite amazing. No one said a word; they just stared and soaked it all in.

"Team SkyDeck enabled – Session 1 – William, Nikher, Aoife, Apollinaris, Nael, Bodhi, Dieter." They all heard *Neveah*'s gentle voice.

"Now remember, we're going to power through the highlights for each event. We all can use SkyView later to develop any theories; *Neveah* will track what we agree on, so keep the insights to a minimum while we all absorb the century," said Nikher.

"Okay," William said, snapping out of his trance and shaking his head. "Are we in space?"

"Close. Anything above this will be augmented reality on the SkyDeck window. You won't notice the difference, though, same as when we need to get really close to the earth. We can simulate cruising around the universe. It's much safer than space travel, or dodging skyscrapers and mountains," Coen responded with a laugh.

"Awesome! Okay, I want to watch the Cradle version of what happened to King Alexander the III," William said. "Coen, can you take us close to the UK?"

SkyView's engines roared, and they were there within minutes.

"Can you take us closer to Kinghorn, Fife?"

"Sure," Coen replied, "but for short distances, when the SkyDeck is enabled and at this altitude, you can have control. Use the small joystick, just like a video game! I'll be on standby."

Nervously, William tilted the joystick forward, and the jet descended toward Europe. Borders became clearer: Spain, France, Italy, Switzerland, UK, and off to the right you could see Norway. SkyView moved closer and closer, past France and across the English Channel, past London, Cambridge, Leeds. It finally hovered over Edinburgh.

"There's the route." Nikher used an interface to highlight the route from Edinburgh Castle to Kinghorn Fife on the large window

"That's not a very far distance. Where was the body found?" William asked as he manoeuvred SkyView from Kinghorn to Edinburgh Castle and back again within minutes.

"We can watch it. There are two versions. In one he fell of a cliff, and in the other off a horse," replied Nikher

The jet didn't move but the screen raced toward Edinburgh Castle. William's heart leapt out of his chest, and he instinctively grabbed Nikher's arm.

"We're not moving, relax. We can watch the two versions at eye level." Nikher laughed at William and gently pulled her arm away.

The window illuminated the entrance to the castle, and Alexander and his guides exited. William was immediately shocked, as he didn't expect to hear an actual conversation. There was only moonlight in the sky, but visibility was satisfactory. The SkyDeck followed the riders through a forest, zooming up and around like a drone, giving the seven viewers a complete account of what transpired. Alexander, at a moderate pace, was soon separated from his guides. Visibility was satisfactory. Suddenly, after twisting through a forest path and down a steep embankment, his horse lost its footing, forcing

Alexander to flip forward. The scene ended with a hollow crack. SkyDeck stayed zoomed on the fallen king. Then time sped forward and the sun rose to a group of riders finding the body and escorting it home. SkyView rewound the scene speedily back to Edinburgh Castle.

The window illuminated the entrance to Edinburgh Castle again. Alexander and his guides exited into the moonlit sky. The SkyDeck followed the riders through a forest, zooming up and around like a drone, giving the seven viewers a complete account of what transpired. Alexander was riding at a moderate pace, was soon separated from his guides. Visibility was satisfactory. Suddenly, after twisting through a forest path and down a steep embankment, Alexander's horse elegantly trotted through. SkyDeck zoomed out for a wider view, and the seven could see Alexander racing toward a cliff. Suddenly, his horse noticed the void and tumbled forward, narrowly avoiding the edge; unfortunately, Alexander couldn't control the momentum and flew off the cliff. SkyDeck stayed zoomed on the fallen king. Then time sped forward and the sun rose to a group of riders finding the body and escorting it home.

"How does the SkyDeck know what they would have been talking about? How would we know what they were saying all the way back then?" William asked.

"There's enough dialogue chronicled in the Cradle to recreate general conversations. *Neveah*'s connected and has a sophisticated AI interface, so the SkyDeck will even recreate conversations based on any theory in order to meet up with the desired outcome. That way it will look more natural to us and be easier to comprehend," Nikher responded. William's eyes were bulging out of his head.

William directed SkyView back up, putting all of Scotland in view along with the North Sea. Scrolling through the touch screen interface, William found the enactment module that followed a timeline starting at 1286 and ending at 1400. Immediately after Alexander's death was a still image titled "Guardians of Scotland" and an arrow pointing toward SkyDeck. With the flick of a finger, the SkyDeck window illuminated. The Guardians were in a great, old, stone castle hall discussing the death of Margaret, the thirteen claimants to the crown, and the fear of civil war. The Guardians agreed to have the English king Arbitrate. The scene shifted to the English king demanding by threat of war that the claimants acknowledge him as Lord Paramount.

On the SkyDeck, Upsettlington began to flash on the window. William pressed it with a hand gesture, and SkyDeck began to move and redirect itself to the border town. It illuminated the scene where the Guardians of the Realm and the leading Scottish nobles gathered to swear allegiance to King Edward I as Lord Paramount in Upsettlington.

"After this was the Great Cause, where the thirteen claimants plead their case to the English king," Nikher said. "Balliol was eventually named king, and he immediately paid homage to the English king."

"Yes," said William. "This is where funds and troops were demanded for a French invasion, but emissaries were dispatched to warn the French instead, which led to the Auld Alliance"

Newcastle flashed on the SkyDeck. William again used a hand gesture to press it, and SkyView manoeuvred south to Newcastle. The SkyDeck illuminated gathering troops, along with a fleet that sailed up the coast to join them.

"They're headed to Berwick; it's 1296," said Nikher.

William, steering north, dragged the illuminated troops and fleet up to Berwick. He manoeuvred down, and the SkyDeck's Augmented Reality window displayed the brutal war onto the ground. The English had massacred most of the population of Berwick.

William steered SkyView and they watched the Battle of Dunbar, a re-enactment of the king's abdication, and the gathering of the Scottish nobles led by Wallace. They also saw a fight at Irvine and again at Stirling Bridge, which ended in victory. The seven sat in awe of the battle and imagery and were overjoyed after the victory. Even though they knew all about it, something about the viewpoint made it more real.

"Here's the letter to the merchants of Lübeck," Nikher said as she flicked an image on her interface screen at the SkyDeck window, which displayed it along with an arrow pointed toward Lübeck. "After Wallace had cleared the English out, he wanted to open up Scotland for commercial access. A week later, Wallace invaded England."

Nikher steered SkyView to Northumberland, and they could all see the English army retreating behind the walls of Newcastle. SkyView followed Wallace across the countryside from Cumberland to Cockermouth, pillaging all the way. Wallace then led his men back to Northumberland, burning north of seven hundred villages on their way.

Soon after Wallace was appointed Guardian of Scotland, a re-enactment Nikher skipped through. SkyView sped back up for a wider view and then zoomed in on the English and French signing a truce that excluded Scotland.

"The English could now attack without fear of French involvement, which they did near Falkirk," Nikher said.

SkyView sped north between Glasgow and Edinburgh. They all watched in horror as the Scottish army was decimated. The seven watched as the English longbowmen picked off Wallace's spearmen and cavalry. A highlighted Wallace was shown retreating to the woods, with a note displayed on the AR window saying he had resigned his guardianship by December 1298.

"A truce had been negotiated that lasted until 1304, when the English again raided Scotland," said Nikher. "All leading Scots surrendered, aside from Wallace, Fraser, and Soulis, who refused to capitulate. Here we see John Comyn negotiating the terms of the submission."

"This is when Bruce and Lamberton paid homage to the English king but had a secret pact for Scotland," said Aoife.

"Yes, they were waiting for the elderly king to die," replied Nikher.

"While a parliament was held in 1305 to establish Scottish governance by the English, Wallace was captured," Nikher said, steering toward the countryside, where Wallace's legs were shown bound beneath his horse en route to London. After a weak trial, he was executed at the Elms of Smithfield." The seven watched as Wallace was hanged and then drawn and quartered. Apollinaris and Nael and Bodhi had to look away when they put his head on a spike. The English then displayed his limbs at Newcastle, Berwick, Stirling, and Perth. The SkyDeck hovered and highlighted each spot.

The SkyDeck when on to show John "Red" Comyn revealing the Bruce conspiracy to the English king. "Here is Bruce stabbing him for it." Nikher flicked a clip over to the widow.

"It was his dad who was one of the Guardians that recommended the English king arbitrate in the first place, right?" Aoife asked.

"Yes, that's correct," replied Nikher.

SkyView followed Bruce back to Scotland, where he asserted his claim to the throne. It showed him being crowned at Scone Abbey in 1306. The seven watched as Bruce was defeated in battle and driven from the Scottish mainland. His family was captured, and all three brothers were hanged and quartered. Nael and Bodhi looked away again.

"This is when the English king had finally died in 1307; the Scottish forces grew in strength, and Bruce came out of hiding."

The seven watched as they defeated the English in a number of Battles, most significantly the Battle of Bannockburn in 1314.

"The Declaration of Arbroath was signed in 1320 by the community of the realm of Scotland, affirming Scottish independence from England. Later, the Treaty of Edinburgh–Northampton 1328, the peace treaty between England and Scotland, officially brought an end to the war."

It was getting late, and the landscape had darkened. The SkyDeck had a unique way of illuminating the Augmented Reality window so the seven could still enjoy much of the detail. William decided it was time to pack it in and requested Coen to take them back to the Ice Palace for a night's rest. William had recommended everybody get some dinner but immediately update the SkyDeck with the insights they'd gained through the journey so far.

William awoke early in the morning and enjoyed a coffee while overlooking the Swiss Alps after two invigorating workouts. After a short breakfast, the seven heirs decided to get started and use SkyView to see the devastation of the Great Famine.

SkyView soared up to frame as much of Europe as possible. The SkyDeck beautifully displayed the northern countries, and

Coen sped down to the Baltic States and then slowed. William took control, flying at low altitude to witness the extent of the death. Governments were inadequate and unable to deal with the crisis. They had no capability to plan or help.

William slowed across Northern Europe, Poland, Germany, Scandinavia, and some of the low countries and then back up to Northern France and the British Isles. The SkyDeck window displayed the death toll for each country, totalling millions. The aristocracy was also shown hoarding what food they had. William slowed country to country, and the SkyDeck displayed on the terrain the escalation of violence as Europe began to take on a more violent edge. People were becoming more desperate to feed their families and resorting to criminal behaviour.

"This is terrible," William said, looking back and forth between Nikher and Aoife.

"All because of bad weather and a bad harvest," Nikher added.

"This is ignorance; this was avoidable," Aoife said sternly.

SkyView zoomed back up, framing Europe again. "Hey, Coen, can we save this exact view?" asked William over Mind-Link. "Maybe program a default button that will take us back here, like a thinking spot."

"Of course," he responded, and a light flashed on one of his controls.

"Let's go to England," William said to Coen. "Northampton to be more precise."

SkyView sped down, slowing only to hover over Northampton. William flicked a clip that displayed the signing of the Treaty of Edinburgh-Northampton on March 17, 1328. A copy was also displayed on the side of the SkyDeck window. Under it was a point-form summary:

Terms - In exchange for £100,000 sterling, the English Crown would recognize:

The Kingdom of Scotland as fully independent;

Robert the Bruce and his heirs and successors as the rightful rulers of Scotland.

The border between Scotland and England as under the reign of Alexander III 1249–1286.

The English king is also to return the Stone of Destiny to Scotland.

"You know, that stone wasn't returned until 668 years later. It's in Edinburgh Castle now," Nikher said.

"Interesting," William replied.

"This was also when the Declaration of Interlaken was signed in 1328, right?" William asked. "Where was it signed?"

"Interlaken," replied Aoife.

"I know in Interlaken, but was there an exact spot, like a castle or something?" William asked.

"That's unknown," replied Nikher.

"Coen, take us to Interlaken please?" William asked. SkyView sped over Belgium, Luxemburg, Eastern France, and finally hovered over Interlaken. "Hopefully everybody was on the same page with what they entered last night," William said as his eyes widened and he gave a head nod. "*Neveah*, is there a signing location for the Declaration of Interlaken?"

"No, William," she responded.

"Can you display what we've agreed upon regarding the Declaration of Interlaken 1328 so far?" he asked.

The AR window illuminated the dark figure sitting at a desk in a large, poorly-lit room. Behind the man was a well-lit painting, just as Helios had described. The text, "Location Unknown" flashed at the bottom.

"Thanks, *Neveah*. Can you display anything we don't agree on regarding the Declaration of Interlaken 1328?"

The SkyDeck zoomed in on the details, but they were too faded and blurry to make anything out.

"The details are faded because we haven't described them accurately enough for the SkyDeck," said *Neveah*. "Nael, Apollinaris, and Dieter theorize that what holds both leagues together regarding the Declaration of Interlaken 1328 and aligns both Pillars is the nature of secrecy from authorities operating inside and out of the Cradle. William, Nikher, Aoife, and Bodhi agree with that but theorize that there is an overall greater meaning to the painting hidden in the detail."

SkyView zoomed back up to William's default spot. "Now, the Second War of Scottish Independence 1332–1357," William said, standing up and walking around the Skydeck, slightly off balance due to the angle. "Remember, by now the IBC was successful and likely involved in this war. They had just split into eight factions."

SkyView sped toward England, and the SkyDeck displayed the disinherited nobles, led by Edward Balliol's son, arguing about the terms of the treaty and how they were deprived of their ancestral rights to Scottish lands. The scene also showed the King of England secretly backing the invasion that divided the Scottish citizens between the current King David II and Balliol.

SkyView flew across England, following the rebels and English allies sailing form Yorkshire to Kinghorn. From there they marched to Dunfermline and then on toward Perth, finally camping at Forteviot, just south of the River Earn, en route to the first skirmish, the Battle of Dupplin Moor. William watched various accusations of treachery and incompetence, ending with archers picking off the rushing Scots as they crushed into each other piled up in a heap as high as a spear. The English surrounded the bloody heap and stabbed repeatedly, ensuring no survivors.

Nikher steered SkyView over to Roxburgh. Balloil had been crowned King of Scots, and William and Nikher watched as he offered his loyalty to the English king. Later, he withdrew to Annan, where he was soon driven from Scotland in what was known as the Camisade of Annan.

"Surprise attack," Nikher said. "Edward Balliol, along with his supporters, were in bed when they attacked."

Next came the Battle of Halidon Hill 1333. Nikher was steering SkyView. The three watched as the Scottish cavalry was forced to dismount their horses due to the boggy earth and rush uphill toward the English. They were picked off by the archers easily. Moving to a Parliament held in 1334, they watched as Balliol made good on his promises and surrendered Berwick as an inalienable right of the English Crown, and later that year gave up Roxburgh, Edinburgh, Peebles, Dumfries, Linlithgow, and Haddington. SkyView continued to move, first showing Balliol's allies deserting him, and a Scottish ship off the coast disrupting supplies sent by the English king. The king summoned an army of thirteen thousand men for a three-front invasion. The naval force, troops led by the king, and troops led by Balliol all met up in Perth, as they were met with little resistance.

William felt a strong pull as Nikher steered toward France, where the French king had prepared six thousand troops to aid the Scots. By 1336, the French king also told English ambassadors that they intended to invade. With messengers en route to warn the English king, French privateers attacked Orford as well as several Royal ships anchored at the Isle of Wight. The English king returned to England to plan a force to enter Gascony.

Nikher fast forwarded to 1343 and watched the French, English, and Scottish enter a treaty meant to last until 1346. "So now we have overlapped with the Hundred Years' War by about ten years," she said to William. Nikher showed the highlights of the Battle of Crécy that resulted in an English victory and heavy loss of life among the French, which was part of the Hundred Years' War.

"Okay, let's move on, because we're drawing to the end of the Scottish Wars of Independence," Aoife said.

Nikher steered SkyView toward England, where they watched a disastrous invasion by David II, which led to his capture. Over the next ten years, the English king made several ransom offers. By 1355, the Scottish launched a successful assault, capturing Berwick, which led to the episode known as the Burnt Candlemas. After recapturing Berwick, the English king sacked Haddington, destroying most of the buildings. He ravaged Lothian and burned Edinburgh and the shrine of the virgin at Whitekirk.

"By now the English grew distracted as they entered the Hundred Years' War with France, so after several decades of conflict, the Second War of Scottish Independence officially ended with the signing of the Treaty of Berwick 1357. The English released David II in return for 100,000 merks.

"So at the end of both wars, Scotland retained its independence," Nikher said as she got up and stretched.

"The year 1357…that's when William faked his death," William replied

By now it was early evening, and the seven had travelled all over England, Scotland, and parts of France. They headed back to the Ice Palace and settled in for an early night, deciding to start the morning off with the Hundred Years' War.

The next morning, the sun crept over the Alps, and all were waiting for Nikher, who was up late after having trouble sleeping again. She managed to grab some fruit and meet everybody as they were about to take off. William gave her a disappointed look as she flopped down beside him on the SkyDeck. Coen roared the engines and they soared up to a commanding height. The SkyDeck opened to a bright, cloudless view of Europe. After some input, the SkyDeck displayed the historic tension between the Crowns of England and France, all the way back to the origin of the Royal family itself, which was French. That was why English monarchs always held lands in France. Throughout the centuries, land was a major source of conflict, and by 1337, the English only held Gascony.

"Now we have to go back to 1316, where an odd principle was established that denied women succession to the throne," Aoife said. "This led to 1328, when the French king died without sons or brothers."

"His closest male relative was his nephew, the King of England at the time," Nikher said, interrupting and flicking an image of the new king onto the window of the SkyDeck. "This was the French king's cousin, Philip the Count of Valois. The other major player in the beginning of this war was Robert Artois." Nikher showed a clip of Robert being exiled from the French court after a falling out over an inheritance claim. The clip showed him urging the English king to start the war and reclaim France, and then going over extensive intelligence on the French court. Nikher steered SkyView to Paris, where the new French king in 1337 met with his Great Council and decided to take back Gascony on the grounds that the English sheltered the French mortal enemy, Robert Artois.

SkyView swiftly flew and followed the English fleet after a declaration by the English king to reclaim the French throne. The fleet arrived off the Zwin estuary the next day, where the French fleet had assumed a defensive formation off the port of Sluis. The SkyDeck seamlessly displayed the Battle of Sluis 1340, and the seven watched as the French fleet was completely destroyed. The imagery of the naval warfare was a nice break from the bloody Scottish wars, they all thought.

Nikher fast-forwarded to 1346, and they watched the English prepare and mount an invasion across the English-controlled channel, landing in Normandy, Cotentin, at St. Vaast, capturing Caen. French troops marched north toward the low countries, pillaging as they went. They were defeated at the Battle of Crécy by the English. SkyView followed the English army as it marched to the City of Calais in 1347, on the English Channel besieging and capturing it, and landing safely in Northern France.

SkyView zoomed up to its default position to display a break in the war due to the Black Death. Seamlessly, the Augmented Reality imagery took them much higher into space and displayed much of Northern Europe, highlighting the countries devastated by the Black Death. It also displayed the years: 1348, 1349, 1350, 1351, 1352, 1353, 1354, 1355.

Once the Black Death had passed, Nikher steered back above Paris and flicked an image of the English king's son, the Black Prince. They followed him as he led a Chevauchée from Gascony into France, during which he pillaged Avignonet and

Castelnaudary, sacked Carcassonne, and plundered Narbonne. This led to the Battle of Poitiers. The seven watched as English troops hid in a forest and led a flanking movement, cutting off the French retreat and capturing the French king. Nikher watched in horror with her teeth clenched as French nobles and mercenaries rampaged. She fast-forwarded the chaos, which actually made it worse, as thieves and robbers rose up everywhere.

Finally it was over. William followed the interface timeline and hovered over the Cathedral City, Reims. They watched as the French citizens built and reinforced the city's defences. The English besieged the city for over a month, but the defences held. William watched in awe as a freak hailstorm devastated much of the English army and forced them to negotiate.

The SkyDeck soon highlighted the signed Treaty of Brétigny 1360 and proceeded to list the land that would be transferred, as well as the English king abandoning his claim to the Crown of France. The death of the Black Prince in 1376 was followed by his father, the king, in 1377. SkyView then followed a small French professional army as it pushed back. By 1380, the English only held Calais and a few other coastal cities.

By now the seven were exhausted and mentally drained. They had travelled through almost fifty years of war. William instructed Coen to head back to the Ice Palace, where they took some much needed rest.

The next morning, six of the company woke early, while Nikher yawned her way onto the jet, making it seven. SkyView lifted to a comfortable position at the height of Europe and then drifted down to Brentwood and the beginning of the Peasants' Revolt 1381. The seven agreed to do a deep dive later, as it was last on the list in the will but part of the Hundred Years' War.

SkyView flew back to France to watch the French peasantry and urban communities in disarray. They watched many arguments between citizens unwilling to continue to pay for the war, which relied on royal taxation, mainly through the Harllee and Mailotin Revolts of 1382.

After the revolts, SkyView flew back to England and they watched the new King of England express his disinterest in the war. SkyView shifted and displayed a scene on the SkyDeck window that showed a group called the Lords Appellant in 1388 conspiring to reignite the war. The will was there, but France lacked the funding to continue, and a three year truce was signed.

Throughout the next decade, SkyView sped around the English Channel displaying repeated raids by pirates that heavily damaged trade and the navy. The French king responded, and French pirates under Scottish protection raided many English coastal towns. A short clip highlighted the evidence that the French king used state-legalized piracy as a form of warfare in the English Channel. He used such privateering campaigns to pressure enemies without risking open war.

"Were going to dive into half of the fifteenth century here, just to close off the war," Nikher advised the group.

SkyView retreated from the English Channel and flew off to Northern France. The Augmented Reality SkyDeck window displayed the natural beauty of the terrain, along with the digital Battle of Agincourt 1415. The seven were surprised as the watched an English army, made up of almost all longbowman, claim victory over the much larger French force. The seven watched as the English retook Normandy, Caen, and Rouen by 1419. They saw the assassination of John the Fearless. They witnessed the marriage between the English king and the French king's daughter, which set up the English kings as heirs to the French throne, leaving the French king's eldest son illegitimate.

SkyView sped off to Paris, where they watched the terrain as the English army, digitally displayed on the SkyDeck window, won the Battle of Verneuil 1424, and were defeated in the Battle of Baugé. By 1428, Joan of Arc appeared at the siege to Orléans, sparking a revival in the French spirit. They watched as the tide began to turn against the English and the French took several strongholds, which opened the way for the French king's eldest son to march to Reims for his coronation in 1429. SkyView tilted northwest to watch the Battle of Compiègne 1430, where Joan of Arc was captured and burned at the stake by the English in 1431. SkyView sped up to and hovered over the entire French and English countryside and displayed the financial aspect of the war. English victories excited the prospect of total triumph, which convinced the English to pour money into the war. But the greater resources of the French monarchy prevented the English kings from completing the conquest.

The SkyDeck finished off the war by hovering over both countries and illuminating the French standing army, organized in 1445, which was the first since Roman times. This was partly as a solution to marauding free companies. The mercenary companies were given a choice of either joining the Royal army as compagnies d'ordonnance on a permanent basis, or being hunted down and destroyed if they refused. The war accelerated France's transformation from a Feudal Monarchy to a centralized state, and England was left in financial trouble, which led to the War of the Roses 1455–1487.

Once again, the hour had grown late, and the seven were overwhelmed with visons of greed and blood. Their brains were on fire, trying to organize and connect the events of each war.

CHAPTER 16
THE SECOND HALF

The next day, the seven once again met early in the morning. Nikher was on time and looked fresh and excited.

"Ready to get started?" she asked William, putting her arm around him.

"Definitely," he responded. "Looks like you got some sleep."

"Like a baby!" she happily exclaimed.

Coen rolled his eyes playfully, and they entered SkyView, making their way through the seating area and down to the SkyDeck. They sat in their usual seats, and Coen flew up to the beautiful familiar view of all of Europe.

"The Black Death," Nikher said eerily. "This was one of the deadliest pandemics in human history, resulting in 75 to 200 million deaths."

"This is when Alvero died," William added "The Black Death had taken the Spaniard, but his Pillar endured and gains in strength, that's what it said in the letter that accompanied my will."

SkyView hovered as the SkyDeck window digitally displayed sickness and death. They watched as religious fever bloomed and Europeans targeted various groups, such as Jews, friars, foreigners, beggars, pilgrims, lepers, and Romani. Citizens also singled out and exterminated those with skin diseases. People were starting to believe that the plague was a punishment from God. Jewish communities were repeatedly attacked; two hundred were murdered in Strasburg. Communities in Mainz and Cologne were annihilated. All in all, 60 major and 150 smaller communities were destroyed.

Skyview followed many Jews who relocated to Poland, where they received a warm welcome from King Casimir the Great. SkyView zoomed back up to the default position and the window displayed a third of Europe dead, which resulted in a labour shortage and reduced population that was much wealthier, better fed, and had significantly more money to spend on luxury goods.

On the note of luxury goods, the SkyDeck AR window flashed "Hanseatic League 1356."

"Remember, we're back to the middle of the Hundred Years' War," William said, getting a leer from Nikher. "Coen, take us to the Baltic Sea, close to *Neveah*. Let's take a break and enjoy lunch." William looked around seeing if everybody was in agreement, which they were.

The jet made its way to the Baltic Sea, first hovering at a digital 200,000-foot view to take in all of the ocean and Northern Europe before hiding in a national park that had access to the Lübeck waterways. These led into Germany, enabling the invisibility shields in case of tourists. Thijs had a dinghy ready and met them on a public dock to take them back *Neveah*.

After a lunch, Coen made his way to the helm, along with Thijs as co-captain. William had decided to cruise the historical trade routes as they learned about the Hanseatic League. *Neveah*'s onboard system interfaced with the SkyDeck, which was able to use a digital representation of earth so that William could control the scale. Cruising through the trade routes, the seven watched the development of the Hanseatic's own legal system and military representation. The network of cities grew to include 170. *Neveah*'s interface displayed the century-long monopolization of sea navigation and trade by the Hanseatic League, which ensured that the Renaissance arrived in Northern Germany long before the rest of Europe. They made their way from west of the Baltic Sea to the east, prior to taking SkyView back home to the Ice Palace for some much-needed rest.

William began his early morning in a similar way. Once the rest awoke and ate breakfast, they eagerly took SkyView back to the Baltic Sea to watch the vigorous attacks from the Victual Brothers, privateers hired by the King of Sweden in 1392. The Hanseatic League monopoly was eventually broken in the Dutch–Hanseatic War 1438.

SkyView flew back to Scotland and displayed a re-enactment of the Treaty of Berwick in 1357, which was next on the list. The seven were starting to get used to moving forward and back through the century; their minds were starting to theorize and put the events together. After the re-enactment of the signing of the treaty, and the short clip of the King of Scotland embezzling from his own ransom fund, SkyView flew as high as she could and then digitally displayed the whole world, with Switzerland in the dead centre. SkyView first descended and showed peaceful merchants passing over the Devil's Bridge along Gothard Pass and then zoomed back up and highlighted Zürich, Lucerne, Zug, Uri, Schwyz, and Unterwalden, the six states that united at the signing of the Pfaffenbrief 1370, guaranteeing peace along Gothard Pass. SkyView then hovered over the Rütli, a meadow above Lake Uri near Seelisberg, and displayed the legendary Oath Fellowship, the Rütlischwur 1307, taken by the founding cantons, Uri, Schwyz, and Unterwalden.

The Seven didn't hover long over Switzerland, as the theory of the foundation of the Ward League was well agreed upon. The six states represented Peter Ward, his wife, and first- born uniting with Beyaert, his wife, and first-born, as well as taking an Oath Fellowship, eternal pact to topple the Black Pillar on October 7, 1370. Instead, they travelled to Florence, Italy to learn more about the Ciompi Revolts of 1378–1382. But first they landed near Florence to have lunch and stretch their legs at the Vincigliata Castle safe house.

After a short break, the SkyDeck flew back up and digitally reconstructed the beautiful city of Florence in 1339. They watched the tension grow between the Arti Minori and the Arti Maggiori, back then the labouring classes of Florence, which also had no set boundaries. An artisan could be considered an elite if he was wealthy and successful enough. The seven watched the oligarchy either die of the Black Death or flee to safe territories. During the instability, the gente nuove emerged, or "new men." They were a class of immigrants with no aristocratic background who grew their wealth from trade. Together, the gente nuova and Arti Minori bonded over their dislike of the oligarchy.

By 1355, the misérables, those with possessions worth less than 100 lire, accounted for 22 per cent of the households in Florence. The oligarchy and the gente nuova formed a truce, only to be broken by the oligarchy in June, the month of the revolt.

The SkyDeck fast-forwarded to 1378 and watched the artisans, labourers, and craftsmen not belonging to guilds lose their homes due to the heavy taxes. The labourers were growing increasingly resentful of the establish oligarchy and lack of participation within the Florentine government. The SkyDeck displayed thousands of lower-class citizens forcibly take over the government, hang the executioner, and demand three new guilds be added so every man could participate in government. Soon betrayal set in that led to a battle for the Piazza della Signoria between the Ciompi and the forces of the major and minor guilds, led by the guild of butchers. That ended in the Ciompi being slaughtered, leaving that day as one of the bloodiest in Florentine history.

Prior to heading back to the Ice Palace, the SkyDeck showed a brief speculative clip regarding the eight saints who were still an unknown group that represented the lower classes. Everybody already had suspicion regarding the group but kept the discussion to a minimum.

The morning came and once again William got both his workouts over with early. The seven companions made their way to Winchester, England and watched the Cradle's representation of the construction of the college, as well as the enrollment process of the seventy poor scholars on the SkyDeck, before jetting east to the Baltic Sea to once again view the privateer battles of the Victual Brother 1392.

The seven watched from the perspective of the guild of the Victual Brothers, from the time they were hired by the King of Sweden to when they were running the blockades and keeping Stockholm supplied. They watched as the guild turned to piracy and coastal plunder, collapsing the maritime trade, sacking the town of Bergen, and conquering Malmö in 1394. They occupied parts of Frisia and Schleswig. They also plundered Turku, Vyborg, Styresholm, Korsholm, and Faxeholm Castle at Söderhamn in Hälsingland. Eventually they occupied Gotland and set up their headquarters in Visby. The King of Sweden conceded Gotland to the allied Teutonic Order, who promptly sent an invading army to destroy Visby and removed the Victual Brothers from Gotland. After the expulsion from Gotland, the seven watched the brothers rename themselves to Likedeelers, meaning equal sharers. They expanded their attacks into the North Sea along the Atlantic coastline, raiding parts of France and as far south as Spain.

SkyView travelled back northeast to witness the Scandinavian aristocracy from the Kalmar Union who wanted to counter the influence of the Hanseatic League. SkyView flew to Denmark, Norway, and Sweden, and they all watched as the three countries united under a single monarch, keeping the countries as separate sovereign states but having domestic and foreign polices directed by a central power.

Coen recommended they stay at the Vincigliata Castle in Florence, Italy for the night prior to diving into the Italian Renaissance, which was next on the list. They all agreed to get a very highlighted view of the century so they'd have a similar structure to build upon prior to laying down the theories into SkyDeck.

"Vincigliata Castle was built in the thirteenth century on a rocky hill to the east of Fiesole in the Italian region of Tuscany. Since the eleventh century, it was an ancient stronghold of Florentine nobility, before being sold to a wealthy banking family who lost it during the banking crash of 1345 when the English king defaulted on his payments. He had borrowed money to fund the Battle of Crécy and the Battle of Poitiers in 1356," said Coen as they all walked through the courtyard, admiring its beauty and historical significance.

"What do you mean defaulted?" William asked.

"Well, the English king had borrowed 600,000 gold florins from the Peruzzi banking family, and another 900,000 from the Bardi family. In 1345, Edward III defaulted on his payments, causing both banking families to go bankrupt."

"Which caused a banking crash that led to this castle being sold to a wealthy merchant family who owned it for three hundred years before it drifted into decay, By 1941, it served as a small prisoner-of-war camp known as Castello di Vincigliata Campo. It housed some high-ranking British and Commonwealth officers," Nikher responded, continuing to walk around, enjoying the atmosphere.

"During its time as a POW camp, there were a number of escapes, naturally. An attempt over this wall here failed," Nikher pointed. "That landed the prisoner in a month of solitary confinement. A tunnel was also designed. Various prisoners took shifts digging for six months of hard, blistering work. Waiting for the right moment, they eventually escaped, although a few were caught and eventually returned." Nikher finished before retiring for the night, hoping to get a good rest.

The Vincigliata Castle shrunk early in the morning as SkyView ascended, soon framing the entire country of Italy. It was a rainy morning but the SkyDeck AR window still managed to display history beautifully. The SkyDeck first centred on Italy and highlighted the economic growth of the thirteenth century, which led to the Renaissance. A network of trades routes were displayed, linking the Italian states to established ports in the Mediterranean and eventually the Hanseatic League and northern regions of Europe for the first time since the fourth century.

The seven watched as a modern commercial infrastructure developed, with joint stock companies, double-entry book-keeping, a systematized foreign exchange market, an international banking system, insurance, and government debt. A new mercantile class emerged who had gained their position through financial skill and broken from the control of bishops and local counts. The SkyDeck moved around Italy to display the impoverish aristocracy and decline of feudalism through increased trade of the early Renaissance. The demand for luxury goods led to greater numbers of tradesmen becoming wealthy, who, in turn, demanded more luxury goods. This increase in trade gave the merchants almost complete control of the government of the Italian city-states. The seven watched as those who grew too wealthy were at risk of the monarchy confiscating their lands. Some of the northern states kept medieval laws that negatively affected commerce.

SkyView sped back to England and framed the Battle of Crécy and Battle of Poitiers 1356 banking crash, highlighting the Ottoman expansion but most notably the Black Death. These catastrophes caused the European economy to go into recession. There was more to the Bardi family crash than just the English king. The SkyDeck listed other European powerful rulers who were indebted to the Bardi family. This was one of the main reasons for the bankers' downfall, which opened the way for the Medici family to rise to power in Florence. The seven watched as wealthy businessmen looking for favourable investments could not find any in the current financial mess, so instead they chose to spend more on culture and art, fuelling the Renaissance.

SkyView sped over to Milan to witness the cruelty of Giangaleazzo Visconti, who ruled at the time. He launched a series of long wars that culminated in the siege of Florence and the death and collapse of his empire. SkyView sped back to Florence, where the people were rallied by having the war presented as one between a free republic and a tyrannical monarchy, between the ideals of the Greek and Roman Republics and those of the Roman Empire and Medieval kingdoms. SkyView zoomed around Florence, and the SkyDeck was rapidly displaying the emerging influential Renaissance figures, such as Ghiberti, Donatello, Masolino, and Brunelleschi. Author Dante appeared on the window along with his works, as did the scholar Petrach, and the first stirrings of Renaissance art were to be seen, notably in the realism of Giotto. The seven allowed SkyView to take them all the way to Leonardo da Vinci 1452–1519 before calling it a night and agreeing to start with the Peasants' Revolt of 1382, the final item on the list.

Morning came early as usual for William as he completed two especially torturous workouts. After a lengthy and nourishing breakfast, the seven were looking forward to closing out the century and beginning the task of putting things together with what they were now theorizing was happening outside the Cradle at that time.

"Ready?" Coen said over Mind-Link as they all sat comfortably on the SkyDeck. A collective and excited "Yes" was heard.

Coen promptly started up SkyView and soared into the familiar default position. All of Europe was in view, but weather was blocking some of the eastern parts. William could see flashes of lightning over England as they descended toward Brentwood. After an initial thrust, SkyView slowed as the background for the Peasants' Revolt illuminated the SkyDeck window, including the tension from the Black Death, the high taxes of the Hundred Years' War, and the instability of the local leadership in London.

At the start of the fourteenth century, the majority of the English people peacefully worked in the countryside as part of a sophisticated economy that fed the country's cities and towns and supported extensive international trade. The SkyDeck replayed images of the Black Death and its toll, killing 50 percent of the English population. It showed that land was now plentiful and labour was in short supply. Soon labourers were charging more for work, which decreased the profits of the landowners.

The seven watched as chaos ensued, forcing the authorities to enact emergency legislation to fix wages at pre-plague levels and make it a crime to refuse work. SkyView flew across northern England to witness protests and disturbances, and then across to the western towns of Shrewsbury and Bridgwater. They watched an uprising occur in York followed by tax riots in early 1381. SkyView zoomed back up and hovered above

England; the weather worsened and gave way to a digital great storm, which the window indicated the English people felt was a prophecy for future change.

A well-organized group of villagers led by Wat Tyler (the Cradle knows little of his former life), as well as Kentish rebels led by Jack Straw (who was unknown to the Cradle) advanced to Canterbury and entered without resistance. They attacked properties in the city with links to the hated Royal Council and dragged enemies out of their houses and executed them. Prisoners were freed, and then Tyler convinced a few thousand rebels to march to London the next morning.

SkyView soared back up, getting a better view of England. Movements toward London, Essex, Suffolk, and Norfolk looked coordinated from the sky for non-military action. SkyView hovered over the Tower of London, where the four-teen-year-old English king was safely hiding, because most of the Royal forces were fighting abroad or in Northern England.

SkyView soon turned to the peasantry, who were now armed with battleaxes, swords, and bows. They watched them cross from Southwark onto London Bridge, which was opened from the inside due to either fear or sympathy for the rebels. The rebels advanced into the city. On the north side they approached Smithfield and Clerkenwell Priory, which was the headquarters of the Knight's Hospitalier, an old military order. They destroyed it along with the nearby manor.

Heading west along Fleet Street, the rebels attacked the temple, a complex of legal buildings owned by the Knights.

The contents, paperwork, and books were brought out and burned in the street, and the buildings were systematically destroyed. SkyView still hovered over Fleet Street, where the rebels attacked Savoy Palace, a luxurious building belonging to John of Guant,

William flicked a clip of quotes from chronicler Henry Knighton that appeared in the interface: "such quantities of vessels and silver plate, without counting the parcel-gilt and solid gold, that five carts would hardly suffice to carry them."[2] The interior was systematically destroyed, furnishings burnt, precious metals smashed, gems crushed, and paperwork set on fire and thrown into the Thames and city drains. It was also noted that almost nothing was stolen by the rebels, as they declared themselves "zealots for truth and justice, not thieves and robbers."[3]

SkyView hovered back to the Tower of London as the SkyDeck AR window displayed the young king watching the city burn, with the rebels surrounding the tower. The AR window brightened, simulating the next morning as the seven followed the young king and small bodyguard to Mile End. SkyView hovered and the SkyDeck again displayed a re-enactment, this time of the rebels negotiating with the king for the abolishment of serfdom and free tenure, the surrender of hated officials on their list for execution, as well as amnesty for the rebels. The king agreed and issued charters announcing

---

2 According to the chronicler Henry Knighton
3 According to the chronicler Henry Knighton

the abolition of serfdom, SkyView zoomed up and they could see the news spreading around the country. The king, however, declined to hand over his officials; instead, he promised to personally hand out the required punishment.

With SkyView flying around England witnessing the glory of the news, it was suddenly forced to return to the Tower of London. Wat Tyler and the rebels had not left following the signing of the Charters, so William and the rest of the seven watched in confusion as Tyler became angry when the king asked why they hadn't left yet. Tyler responded with another demand, which led to an argument with some of the royal servants. The Mayor of London intervened, and Tyler then absurdly made a motion toward the king. Royal soldiers immediately stepped in and ordered Tyler's arrest. Tyler turned and attacked the mayor, who in self defence stabbed Tyler. A royal squire came in to finish the job and stabbed Tyler repeatedly. The seven watched in shock at the turn of events, not understanding.

Tyler's head was soon cut off and displayed on a pole. The rebel movement collapsed. SkyView sped back up to view the Royal suppression of the revolt. A summons was put out for soldiers, and around four thousand showed up in London. Expeditions were soon sent to the rest of the troubled parts of the country.

SkyView flew to Essex, where the young English king met with a group of rebels seeking confirmation of the new grants, which the king rejected, reportedly telling the rebels "peasants you were and peasants you will still be. You will remain in servitude, not as before, but incomparably harsher." The seven watched as executions followed, skewed court trials commenced, and vague laws were invoked to ensure suppression of the revolt. Fear spread across the land, and most of the rebel leaders were captured and executed. William watched the trial of John Wrawe, who in a hope for a pardon named twenty-four colleagues, but he was instead hanged, drawn and quartered.

They watched as the royal charters signed during the rising were formally revoked, and as the death toll rose to 1,500 as people were either executed or killed in battle. There was no further attempt by Parliament to reform the fiscal system or impose a poll tax. The Commons concluded that the military effort on the continent should be "quietly but significantly reduced."

SkyView zoomed back up to a commanding height, framing the whole of England. The SkyDeck concluded the Cradle's version of events and illuminated "The institution of serfdom declined after the revolt, wages increased again, and lords began to sell their serfs freedom for cash." And the SkyDeck ended with, "Unable to raise taxes, the English government was forced to curtail its foreign policy and military adventures and begin to examine options for peace."

CHAPTER 17
A TABLE OF WEAPONS

William awoke in a daze; his head was full of connections and theories. Over the following months, the seven embarked on a spirited but much slower journey through history using SkyView. Together they accumulated hundreds of flights—some combined, some personal, some short, some long—and many non-flights, but they all had many hours using the HoloTable and HoloWalls. A unique but broken theory was starting to take shape. *Neveah*'s AI had a way of intuiting the events by listening to the muttering of each party as they looked for the connections that kept slipping out of the chaos.

Williams daily routine had solidified into excessive physical and mental training in the HoloRoom before anybody else awoke. It had become his place of balance. Ideas were forming around the theories, and his mind was beginning to look past the events and toward the motivations of the founders. Everything was becoming clearer.

For the first time in weeks, he went back to SkyView as a thought grew in his mind. "Let's go back to Alexander,"

William said to Coen. This time he was only accompanied by Nikher and Aoife. "Something happened before they all met," he added

"What are you thinking?" Nikher asked.

"In the letter that accompanied my will, it said, 'Ideas are Weapons – Both Pillars are well hidden from the world – A key is needed to unlock it – A single transaction will unlock your mind' Well, Alexander's death is what preceded the First War of Scottish Independence 1296. William was born 1296. This event occurred before his time. I think the key is in here somewhere," William said.

"Ideas are weapons," Aoife repeated. "The only events that occurred prior to the founding of the IBC 1318 were the First War of Scottish Independence 1296–1328 and the Great Famine 1315–1317. Something in these events gave them an idea."

"What do they have in common?" William muttered.

"Ineptness!" Nikher stated, as if obvious. "The ineptness of those in power. Alexander being separated from his guides led to the First Scottish War, or inviting the English king to arbitrate, and the ineptness of local governments to deal with the great famine."

"Remember what Kaethe said, this fortune isn't about money. It's about power, control, and manipulation," William said. "And Ernest also said that no matter how events seem to flow, the outcome often reveals its creator, usually those who benefit the most."

"Coen, take us back up as high as possible," William said. "I want to see the world."

Suddenly, they all jerked forward and then sunk into their seats. Once the horizon was visible, William got out of his chair and neared the SkyDeck, repeating what was in his letter.

"We became wealthy beyond measure – hidden in the shadows through trade and commerce – The Spaniard had an insatiable lust for new markets – I thought I was moving the world away from hierarchy – from aristocracy – from boundaries – from war – I thought I was freeing my common man – I was in error – The Spaniard and the six men deceived me – they drove the world toward war – toward boundaries – toward aristocracy – toward hierarchy – The Pillar of Wealth I created had blackened."

"William showed Alvero!" Nikher said with a sudden inspiration "That was the transaction, the key. It's the ineptness and ability for manipulation, but he meant it for trade, free trade beyond borders, away from hierarchies, so he could grow his wealth without fear. Remember the wealthy merchants in the Italian city-states? As their wealth increased, they were increasingly at risk of the monarchy confiscating their lands and refusing to update medieval laws."

"But Alvero didn't agree with free trade or free borders; he preferred the hierarchies and played them against each other, hiding in the shadows. He was driving conflict to create and protect his wealth," William said.

"If you were planning to rob a country, the first step would be to de-stabilize it—that's what Kaethe also said," Aoife stated wearily. "The Second War of Scottish Independence 1332– 1357 started four years after the Declaration of Interlaken 1328 and was overlapped by the Hundred Years' War 1337–1453. With ten years of success at the IBC, Alvero was finally ready to make his move. While William was off in the Baltic Sea, Alvero was busy war mongering," Aoife finished what they all were thinking.

"And now we're here seven hundred years later," William said as he hung his head and moped back to his chair.

"Well, how does everybody feel?" William asked the group the following morning as they all sat on the balcony, sipping their coffee or tea and absorbing the grandiose view of the endless Swiss Alps.

"Eternally tired," Nael replied. William gave an interested look.

"Grateful," Dieter replied. "Grateful this is almost over. I can't learn anything else about the fourteenth century."

"I agree," said Aoife. "I couldn't find anything else if I tried… and I did! I literally ran out of information to process." William again gave an approving look.

"What about you, Bodhi? We haven't heard much from you," William asked.

"Well, I finished with the events long ago. I've been looking into the smaller, often overlooked details of the century, the minutiae."

"No," William laughed, "I mean how do you feel?"

"Ohh…well, I feel that I've grown as a person. Being a fairly spiritual person, I never gave our history the respect it deserves."

"Yes, that's most of the Cradle's problem. I was frankly guilty of it myself. They have no respect for history, which is why they repeat it so often. They never look at it from this vantage point; it's been quite eye-opening," admitted Nikher.

"I agree," Apollinaris said. "I feel overwhelmed, but I'm starting to get a sense of the real world. My old life feels so small now, so insignificant. That was a small, selfish world I used to live in."

"Now that we've all processed as much as we can about the wills and the events of the century," William said, but he was interrupted by Nikher.

"How do you feel?"

"Like I'm 1 per cent done. No, actually I feel it's time to go over what theories we agree on that link to the events, hopefully starting off in the right direction to find Venacio."

William finished his breakfast and made his way over to the large HoloTable in the great room overlooking the Alps.

The seven all followed and sat in a familiar pattern, with William having Nikher and Aoife directly at his side.

"*Neveah*, please display the events in order and our agreed upon theories as to what occurred outside the Cradle between the Ward and Losada League," said William.

"Of course, William," *Neveah* responded softly.

The HoloTable clouded over and turned to a solid steel. It illuminated a rotating 3D image of the First War of Scottish Independence 1296–1328 while hovering over 3D terrain of Scotland and England. The names Nikher, Aoife, William, Dieter, and Bodhi all illuminated and travelled along the perimeter of the table.

"Ah, look at that…. *Neveah*'s the best!" William exclaimed. "A few of you, me included, believe there's some connection to the Stone of Destiny, stolen in 1296, the same year William was born. The Stone was returned in 1996, the year I was born."

The HoloTable displayed a hologram of the Stone being taken to England and fitted to a wooden chair. It showed some coronations, an attempted theft in 1950, and its travel and return to Scotland.

William looked confused. "That's it?"

"Yes, aside from the dates being of interest, there are no other theories," *Neveah* said through Mind-Link in all of their heads.

"Okay then, moving on," William said. He had hoped some of the others had come up with more about the Stone.

The HoloTable illuminated again, and this time it was Alexander III's journey to Fife, where he died, but this time he was murdered. The guards were shown being paid off to get lost. The English king and one of the Scottish Guardians were then shown conspiring to have him become Lord Paramount and arbitrate the succession. Everybody's name circled around the table, indicating they all agreed on this theory. Soon Bodhi and Nael and Apollinaris dropped off and the HoloTable illuminated William and Alvero discussing and agreeing, learning that events are easily manipulated, but they just need planning and time.

"This is what I believe started William and Alvero on their path. At the time it would have seemed like an unfortunate event when the Scottish king died, but when you look at the events leading up to and after it, you can see that it could have been engineered," William said, getting nodding approvals from Nikher and Aoife.

"So you think someone killed that little girl, Margaret? She was three!" Bodhi said, unconvinced.

"It doesn't matter if it's true or not, it's the idea," William said in a friendly tone to Bodhi.

"Ideas are weapons," Aoife repeated.

"Yes," William replied. "I believe that William first thought of this. He grew up in England and despised that war, which is why he left. He probably learned as much as he could about it to try to avoid it or stop it. Anyway, he developed a theory but couldn't prove it, so he was helpless. At some point he met Alvero and told him how the event could have been engineered. That's the transaction mentioned in my will. The two of them formed the basis of a company, and the rest is history." William finished but they all laughed

"You mean unwritten history," Nikher corrected him.

Suddenly, Bodhi's, Nael's, and Apollinaris's names joined the others travelling around the HoloTable. "You know, having it framed that way makes it seem plausible," Bodhi admitted, followed by Nael and Apollinaris.

"So we all agree then!" William stood up, excited "The reason the First War of Scottish Independence 1296–1328 is in the will is because that's where William and Alvero got the idea of hidden manipulation, and they formed the IBC around that."

"Don't forget time," Nikher said. "Time is an element that helps them stay hidden. You can't manipulate events in short periods of time, or you risk being connected to it."

"Yes, exactly," William replied. "They formed the IBC, later adding the rest of the founders."

The HoloTable displayed the re-enactment. The rotating hologram depicted each of the founders laughing, agreeing, shaking hands, and signing documents. Each of the seven names were now circling the table in unity.

"This calls for a celebratory drink," William added, "and I can think of none better than Cillian's Irish whisky."

"Its 11:00 a.m.," Nikher stated, but they gave her a nasty look.

The Great famine 1315–1317 rose up on the HoloTable and began to rotate. Below the title could be seen the malnourished dead bodies. Suddenly, the whisky didn't taste so good.

"Aoife, Nikher, and I figured this is also in the will to show us the ineptness of governments and how they handled the famine. You really need to combine these two events to see the full idea. This ineptness was the door they needed, as a weak, inept government would be easy to manipulate."

William addressed the group, and everybody's name circled the HoloTable.

"Wow, two in a row," Aoife said.

"Yes, but realize we don't have to agree to move forward; we just need a basis for why these events are in the will. Then we can look for evidence," Nikher said while Aoife rolled her eyes.

"That was the easy part," said William. "Now we need to weave in what the IBC is involved in."

The HoloTable illuminated and a hologram of Europe appeared. Oversized founding members were seen leaving their homelands and en route to Interlaken. William and Alvero arrived first. They shook hands and sought out the other members, first meeting Hynek, who had smuggled hops out of Bohemia and was with Bligger.

The four were seen tasting beer, and Bligger was describing barrel making. William was laying out the trade routes, and Alvero was finding new customers. The four shook hands and agreed to find experts in law, finance, and protection. Finghin and Baernt came storming into view, larger than life, and the six started talking. Finny and the Bear nodded their heads and agree to run the protection and distribute the beer. Huc showed up next holding a law book and explaining how he had influence in the French court already, and had big ideas. He was shortly followed by Eleutherios, who convinced the seven men he was an expert in mathematics.

The hologram illuminated all of Europe again, this time showing the founders at work: Hynek busy growing the hops, Bligger making the barrels, William mapping the known trade routes and finding additional goods to trade, starting with beer and weapons, Finny and the Bear along with small armies distributing the beer and weapons, Eleutherios staying in Interlaken keeping track of all the funds, and Alvero and Huc travelling all over Europe finding new markets and navigating the laws for each territory. The hologram sped up and showed the IBC growing, profiting from the war, and adding new markets and new things to trade. The founders, although spread across Europe, migrated back to Interlaken annually until the year 1328, when suddenly the hologram froze and illuminated the next event.

"Next we have the Treaty of Edinburgh-Northampton, March 17, 1328." The HoloTable illuminated again. "We have a mixture of thoughts, some believing it's in the will because the Stone of Destiny was agreed to be returned during these negotiations, some believe it's referencing the Declarations of Interlaken, which occurred the same year, and some think it's symbolic—the end of one war and the start of another, the hidden war we're now entwined in," *Neveah* said softly through Mind-Link as the different pairs of names circled the HoloTable. The HoloTable depicted the 1328 annual meeting in Interlaken and the founders agreeing to the creation of the eight factions to spread across Europe, each faction being supported by a founding member. Each member left the meeting and travelled across Europe, adding new members as needed.

"Moving on to the Second War of Scottish Independence 1332–1357," Nikher said as she continued to sip her whiskey and enjoy the endless view of the Swiss Alps.

"Once again we have a mixture of theories, but they all weave together," Neveah said. The HoloTable illuminated, displaying the eight factions growing and profiting. Alvero and Huc were inside both the English and French courts, urging the disinherited to reclaim their ancestral lands, as well as promising that they would have the discrete backing of the English king. They saw Finghin's privateers attack the town of Orford, while Baernt captured royal ships anchored at the Isle of Wight.

"The war would have likely happened on its own, but it needed a little organization and a nudge. Everybody agrees it was Alvero and Huc," Neveah said over Mind-Link. "They also had connections in the French court and used Finghin's and Baernt's privateers. Most of the privateer ships were investor supported, and we found a few paper trails leading back to the IBC."

"These were the early stages of the eight factions. The cradle has some records, but it was during this war that they faded into the shadows," William said. "There are other records somewhere, though, financial records. My dad said that when he searched, he found some that led to this dead end too, but he did mention that there are better records somewhere. Somehow that idea was put in his head, and I don't think it was put there by accident," William said as he finished his Irish whiskey and stared out at the Alps.

"Well, we need real evidence. I barley agree with Alvero and Huc urging the disinherited," Nikher said disapprovingly

"It's not going to work that way, Nikher," Aoife said. "We're not going to find any evidence. We have to develop a theory, that's the point."

"Aoife's mostly right. We're not going to find evidence in the Cradle, but we will need evidence to prove these theories, or we could be pointed in the wrong direction. There must be markers, or truths, hidden somewhere for us to find to let us know we're on the right track. The wills are letting us know the routes they took through history; if we can prove what aspects of the events they're involved with, we can hopefully find the pattern that leads to Venacio and his heir," William said, as though trying to convince himself.

"Okay, so let's move on," Nikher said firmly. "Once we get the theories for each event on the table, we can then search to prove or disprove them."

"Yes," said Nael. "We have to prove the theory somewhat, or we could end up going in the completely wrong direction."

The HoloTable illuminated the Hundred Years' War 1337–1453 and displayed France below it. The time counted down to 1316. Aoife's and Nael's names circled the HoloTable. Huc, along with duplicates of himself, were seen among the

French nobility. They were all agreeing to establish a principle that would deny women succession to the French throne. The Holograph sped forward through time to 1328 and displayed the French king dying without sons or brothers. The image then sped over to England to show his closest male relative, who was the King of England. Five other names joined the circle, and the hologram sped back to France to see Robert Artois fleeing over an inheritance dispute. This was where Alvero and Huc came into the picture and guided him to the English king to urge a war to claim France.

"Time," Bodhi said. "Who knows if Alvero and Huc had already targeted Robert Artois? His father died when he was young, and he spent his whole life openly trying to reclaim the inheritance."

The HoloTable displayed Robert as an eleven year old hearing about his father's death and his aunt being awarded his inheritance. Robert eventually became a trusted advisor to the King of France. From there he tried to use his influence to reclaim his inheritance. When that failed in 1331, he used a forgery to attest to his father's will. This also didn't work, and once the deception was uncovered, his wife and children were imprisoned.

"This is when he fled to England and joined the English king," William said.

The HoloTable followed the war once again. It showed the men generally agreeing on the IBC trade and profits. Each year the leader of each faction was seen en route to Interlaken for the annual meeting. A large, long table centred the great hall of the castle hidden in Interlaken, with Alvero at one end and William at the other. Eleutherios was busy portioning out the earnings from each member. The eight leaders drafted and agreed to the Declaration of Succession 1337. They referred to the eight factions of Interlaken, and that the heir of each faction would follow the first line; the child, male or female, born nearest to the turn of each century in perpetuum would be the heir.

Time sped forward, following each line out and back to Interlaken, like a giant European lung. It stopped in 1356 at the Battle of Poitiers and briefly displayed the pillaging by French mercenaries, led in the shadows by Finghin and twins Kiliaen and Beyaert. Nikher's name was absent any time Kiliaen and Beyaert were in view. Bligger, William, and Baernt were shown riding back from Germany. Once again, they all met in Interlaken.

This time the HoloTable had theory of the meeting. Neveah's AI had listened to enough speculation and was able to engineer the conversation to meet up with the general outcome they theorized. The names kept moving on and off the table, making it hard to know who believed in what. William stopped watching it when he realized that he could look it up later. Instead, he just concentrated on the general theory.

Alvero was noticeably old and decrepit, and a few of the seven had estimated that he was infected with the Black Death. William knew this to be true. The eight men were much older now, and the paintings of their younger selves hung on the wall behind each of them. They sat at a large table with Alvero and William at each head, with stacks of money in front of them, each being counted and portioned out by Eleutherios. William and Baernt discussed their economic interests in the Hanseatic League and Northern Italy, as well as the wealth opportunities of free trade. Hynek presented a summary of the hops and farms that were added, while Bligger gave a report on the increased barrel production. Alvero gave his account of supplying the war effort and then asked Finghin for an update on the privateering and mercenary armies, since Finghin had come back with more money than usual.

William and Baernt watched in horror as Finghin told them of the thieving and robbery after the Battle of Poitiers, implicating Kiliaen and Beyaert. Baernt refused to believe his twin boys were involved and accused Finghin of treachery. William argued adamantly that there was much wealth in trade and condemned them for misuse of the innocent. Alvero and Huc argued that there is more money in war. The argument raged and culminated with Alvero accusing William of being ignorant of the empire that he'd designed. Alvero reminded William it was he who was the link between the disinherited and the English king, and it was Huc who schemed to have the principle established that denied women succession to the French throne and led to Alvero and Robert Artois urging on the English king. Six of the men stood up to add to the argument. William pleaded with everybody to move away from malice and threatened to leave the company if they did not. Alvero suggested they buy him out, as long as William agreed to abandon all his established trade.

Nikher's name was noticeably absent for the Finghin description of the battle, but it re-emerged for the rest of the imagery.

"So what's next then," William asked, urging *Neveah*, who was interfaced with the HoloTable, to move forward.

The hologram followed William, his wife, and Peter to Northern Italy, where William made the plan to fake his death to keep his family safe and hidden while he destroyed what he'd created. The War of the Twin Bears hovered above the table, but still no theories had been uncovered.

"Nothing," said William. "It was 1358, right here, right after William faked his own death. I would have thought somebody would have something." He looked around, hoping for a lead, something to go on. Realizing nobody had any insight, they all agreed to stop for the day and have an early dinner, seeing as they'd all skipped lunch. After eating, William went for a long mountain hike to try and settle his mind and allow a place for everything he'd learned to stay fresh before settling in for an early night's sleep.

"Ernest, are you there?" William asked through Mind-Link before falling asleep; he had a nagging question in his head.

"Yes, William, always," Ernest responded.

"Sorry I haven't checked in that much, it's just quite over-whelming going through these events. There not much room left in my head." William added with a big yawn. "My dad mentioned that there are better records somewhere. Do you have any idea where? The records he found are back home and listed transactions up to when the company started branching off and split into the eight factions."

"The only place I could think of would be where they met annually in Interlaken. Your dad never went to it; he never intuited anything beyond the Cradle, so without a theory to prove, he had no direction, which is ultimately why he went home."

"Wouldn't Venacio still control the original Interlaken Castle?" William asked.

"No, neither league has ownership anymore in the IBC; it's a public company now. But both leagues keep members inside the company to have access to history, as well as to sometimes use it for influence. Remember that video? Now it's a mutual territory, so to speak. The table in the great hall is still there and is surrounded by a row of books, ledgers, maps, and lots of interesting but un-incriminating historical markers. But it's much too dangerous for you to go. Members of the Losada League go there all the time."

Once again, William began the next day in the HoloRoom. Both of his workouts were getting significantly more intense. After a stiff routine coffee of on the balcony overlooking the Alps, William gestured everybody to gather around the HoloTable to finish off the century.

The Black Death slowly illuminated and hovered, and the HoloTable quickly identified that all agreed this was symbolic to the death of Alvero. The Hanseatic League 1356 soon replaced the Black Death, and once again they all agreed that William had been working with the league prior to returning to his last Interlaken meeting. The HoloTable clearly defined the two Pillars of Wealth, one on each side of the table, separated by the sands of time. The Black Pillar soon showed Alvero's ghost and heir, then Finghin, Hynek, Bligger, Huc, Eleutherios, and Baernt, although he was en route to the White Pillar. Behind them were wars, trade, and borders. The White Pillar was half built. William stood in front of it, and behind it were trade routes linking the Hanseatic League to Italy. Once again everybody's name circled the table, which wasn't a surprise, as this had been discussed many times. But it was nice for all to see it official, so to speak.

The room was quiet as the Treaty of Berwick 1357 floated on the HoloTable. Only William's and Aoife's names circled the general theory it symbolized, which was William leaving the IBC.

"An end to the war, and an end to the IBC," William added, trying to justify the theory.

"The Pfaffenbreif is next," Nikher said excitedly.

The Hologram showed a touching scene of the ghosts of William and Baernt overseeing Peter's and Beyaert's families uniting on the Devil's Bridge along Gotthard Pass. *Neveah* once again reconstructed the conversation. The seven watched as they took the Oath Fellowship, agreeing to eternally honour the Declaration of Succession and to use their combined wealth to destroy the Black Pillar one line at a time. In doing so, they would free the wealth for each to enjoy.

Moving forward, the Ciompi Revolt 1378–1382 hovered over the table, as did a broken theory that somehow the eight saints represented the eight founders. Names started to circle. Peter and Beyaert were seen urging the gente nuove to bond with the Arti Minori.

"The gente nuove were new immigrant class. Remember, they had no aristocratic background and grew their wealth from trade," Nikher added. Although they all were well aware. "The Arti Minori were the minor guilds."

"We know," Aoife said immediately. "We've all seen this revolt a hundred times."

"Sorry," Nikher said, "but I remembered what Ernest told William, which may fit here:

'No matter how events seem to flow, the outcome often reveals its creator, usually those who benefit the most.'"

"Who benefitted?" Aoife asked

"This revolt had a long-lasting impact on many generations to come—merchants, trades, artisans," Nikher replied.

"What if it was an investment?" said Apollinaris. "The Ward League was hidden at this time. What if Peter and Baernt used money to fund the revolt on behalf of the lower class? This ties in with the Italian Renaissance. Remember, the merchants almost had complete control of the governments of the Italian city-states in the thirteenth century, prior to the famine and the Hundred Years' War when the English king collapsed those banks by not paying his war debts. Maybe the eight saints represent eight different portions of money previously collected at Interlaken?" His eyes were noticeably wider.

Every name began to circle the HoloTable after a brief conversation.

The HoloTable glistened silver as the sun burst through the window. Winchester College 1382 had rays piercing through it. Everybody's name circled, agreeing upon an anonymous investment by the Ward League giving the poor access to education.

The Victual Brothers 1392 soon hovered over the HoloTable. Once again, a difference in opinion made the names hard to follow, but a general theory of the Alvero, Huc, and Finghin heirs using a combination of privateers and influence to break the monopoly of the Hanseatic League emerged. The Kalmar Union 1397 was the outcome of the influence on the Scandinavian aristocracy, which led to the downfall of the Hanseatic League.

"Just to be straight," Nael said, "the Victual Brothers was the privateering and piracy by Finghin's heir, and the influencing of the Kalmar Union was the Huc and Alvero heirs?"

"Yes, definitely," William said.

The Italian Renaissance swept across the HoloTable, and for such a broad event had few theories that involved both Leagues, a combination of the unknown artist they were looking for, the rise of the merchant class, and the need to hide their wealth from the monarchy. The Huc and Alvero lines appeared to be behind the urging of the monarchies to confiscate the lands of the extremely wealthy. Also, they agreed that the Ward League's spending on culture and art helped to fuel the Renaissance. There was also brief theory from Aoife and Bodhi regarding the two banks that went bankrupt.

"I still feel there's something more to that Bardi family," Aoife added.

The Peasants' Revolt of 1381, which was last on the list, finally made its way onto the HoloTable. William's theory still stood, that the Ward League was behind the mysterious 'Great Society' organizing the peasants to revolt over taxes and abolition of serfdom, eventually deterring Parliament from raising taxes to fund the Hundred Years' War.

"You know, from this height, just looking at the two leagues over the century, you can almost see them battle," William said as he walked around the great room.

"What do you mean?" Nikher asked, hoping something in his head had finally been triggered. *Finally some evidence*, she thought.

"You really have to remove the Cradle. The Cradle, the events that are all irrelevant, it makes it seem more confusing than it should be," William said, deep in thought. They all looked confused at William but listened eagerly. "Let's get to SkyView. I need to map what's in my head, to physically see what I'm thinking. It's reminding me of something."

CHAPTER 18
THE LUNGS OF WEALTH

The HoloTable turned back to a solid piece of steel, and all seven fumbled over each other as they hurried to SkyView. Once seated, William heard the engines roar, which forced everybody into their seats. William immediately opened the SkyDeck and enjoyed the view as they ascended above the mountains.

"Coen, I want to see all of Europe!" William stated firmly.

SkyView soared up; the view was as breathtaking as always, cloudier than usual but full of greens and blues.

"So imagine it's 1318, and the eight founders are en route to Interlaken," William said, trying to frame his thoughts.

Nikher used the interface to highlight their travels on the AR window.

"Okay, now let's go back down to Interlaken," William directed Coen. "So William and Alvero meet first, and then the rest of them are added one at a time. Now let's go back to the Sky. Actually, can we go to simulated space? I want to see the curve of the earth with Europe in the middle!

"Nikher, can you show the eight men through the years? Can you estimate the annual routes based on the theories we've already put in the system? You know, everything each of them were involved in?" William asked.

"Yes, definitely," Nikher said excitedly.

"Okay, estimate routes out and back to Interlaken; show a year every two to three seconds," he asked politely this time.

"Of course," she responded.

The AR window was now framed in the deep black of space. The sands of Northern Africa were in view, as were the North Sea, Black Sea, Mediterranean Sea, Baltic Sea, even as far as the Caspian Sea.

"Whoa," Nael said. "This never gets old."

With all of Europe clearly centred, in bold the number 1318 appeared in the Bay of Biscay between Spain and France. Then 1319, 1320, 1321, 1322. Every few seconds, two or three coloured lines shot out from Interlaken.

1325, 1326, 1327. Now there was eight colours: 1328, 1329, 1330. Starting at Interlaken, the coloured routes jetted out to England, Ireland, Germany, Netherlands, Greece, Spain, France, Czechia, and back like veins in a lung. "The eight factions" William stated as they watch the IBC breathe across time.,

1337, 1338, 1339. Eight routes were seen, starting in Interlaken and then making their way to France and then England.

"The Hundred Years' War!" Aoife said.

1346, 1347, 1348. Two veins break off, both to the Baltic Sea and then to Italy. "That's Alvero and William looking into new trade routes and markets," Nikher said as she scrolled through the data.

1354, 1355, 1356. "You can see the IBC change now. Seven factions are concentrating on the English and French war, and look," William pointed to the Baltic Sea. "One faction, back and forth, Interlaken to the Baltic sea. That's William."

1356, 1357, 1358 "Now there's two, but they don't go back to Interlaken."

They watched as six veins stretch from Interlaken to France and England, while two veins breathed from Northern Italy to the Baltic Sea.

"You can clearly see the two leagues now," William stated.

"Whose is the one route that's everywhere?" Apollinaris asked.

"That's Alvero; mostly he's searching or new markets, but you can see the odd time he drags Huc with him, especially to Italy," Nikher replied.

1367, 1368, 1369. Switzerland was highlighted. "The Pfaffenbreif," they all said simultaneously. "The Ward League isn't a route anymore. Nikher, can you highlight the other areas they were identified in," William asked. A white pillar was placed in Switzerland and the Baltic Sea.

"Now we're going to see them start to fight," William said, looking around at everybody.

1378, 1379, 1380. Two veins were seen in Italy more frequently, and two white pillars appeared, one in Italy and one in England.

"The revolts!" Aoife said, thinking out loud.

1390, 1391, 1392. The clear single route of Interlaken to France, changed to Interlaken to the Baltic Sea. "Finghin!" they all yelled simultaneously. "His faction and heirs led the piracy in the Baltic for the next few years."

1395, 1396, 1397. The Alvero and Huc lines' routes from Interlaken to Italy then changed to Interlaken to Denmark, Norway, and Sweden. "The Kalmar Union," Nael blurted out.

The next day William finished both his workouts early as usual. He was getting stronger both mentally and physically. Over breakfast, they had a discussion over the SkyView session the night before. everybody had a clear overview of the role of both leagues and the initial strife. William took the opportunity while everybody was at the same table to go over a pre-prepared speech he had written for when they all had agreed on an over-arching theory.

"I'd like to take a minute…if you could all just stop eating for a second. I was hoping something in my head would have clicked by now, but it hasn't…yet. For the last few months, I could sense I was getting close to something, but nothing connected. But last night on SkyView, I felt something. Seeing the war between the league develop felt like the beginning to a story that I was told years ago; it was so familiar. Now that we've developed this world, we need to find the details in it to confirm it. Each event will have something in the Cradle that proves our involvement," said William. Then he repeated William's words from his will:

"Both pillars are well hidden from the world – A key is needed to unlock it – A single transaction will unlock your mind."

"William's right," said Nikher. "The devil is in the details. There's got to be something that confirms each event, a key."

"Bodhi, didn't you say you finished with the wills long ago and have been looking into the details of the century, the minutiae?" Aoife said. "Well, have you found anything?"

"Nothing to confirm any events, but I did find something you may find interesting," Bodhi replied. He then gestured them over to the HoloTable. Bodhi's name crept on to the side of the table, and a large, illuminated schoolhouse-looking building emerged. "Its the Bethlem Royal Hospital, It means..." Bodhi was cut off by Aoife. "Chaos and confusion," she said, finishing his sentence.

"The institution for the insane was founded in 1247," Bodhi said, as similar notes appeared as the building illuminated.

"I spent a long time searching Irish At..." Aoife gave Bodhi a leer. "Umm...bad stuff," he squeaked out. "There's a fair bit, going back to the ninth century..."

"Bodhi get to the point," Aoife screamed and then reluctantly apologized.

"Anyway, hidden in a bunch of massacres and murders, one stuck out. Apparently in 1948, two Irishmen broke into the insane asylum looking for a woman. Watch," said Bodhi, pointing to the table.

The hologram illuminated a small town just south of London. Midnight, July 15, 1948. A 1936 Horch 830 BL drove to the front entrance of the hospital. Two men, possibly Oisin and Éibhear, they immediately thought, slowly crept out and forced their way into the asylum. At gunpoint, Éibhear forced security to alert a doctor, who promptly came to the scene. The two Irishmen demanded to know what room the woman they were looking for was in. With a gun to his head, the doctor finally escorted them to her. The seven watched horrified as Éibhear, the angrier one, forced the doctor to perform ridiculous experiments all night in hopes of extract info. Eventually the woman collapsed, and the doctor told them she was brain dead. The two men looked at each other in anger and killed the security guard and the doctor and fled.

"A night nurse who was hiding overheard their Irish accents and called the police." Bodhi finished with an interested grin.

"She was probably a conservator; she was probably in there trying to hide from them," William announced. "Oisin and Éibhear were trying to get info on the Ward League out of that poor woman. Maybe she has a relative, somebody she confided in before hiding."

"It's only 1948; that's pretty recent. I wonder what she knew," Nikher said "We should go find her, search out her relative. Who knows what info she had?"

"I agree," said William, who was deep in thought. "Devil is always in the details," he repeated in a whisper. "Okay, we need to get to work."

"Dieter," William pointed.

"Yes, sir," he answered. "You need to find me that artist!"

"Will do," he quickly replied, excited.

"Nael," William sputtered.

"Yes," he answered gingerly.

"Your line was involved in urging both wars, so find me proof!" William said in a commanding tone.

"Apollinaris, before I left, my dad told me he'd found the transaction of when William sold, but he also said there are better records somewhere. Find them; they must be hidden somewhere in your history. Eleutherios kept the records back then!"

"You know, those records will be at Interlaken Castle," Nikher told William over Mind-Link.

"Yes, but we can only go there as a last resort. I'm hoping the Thess line has something for us," William repeated. "Aoife, Nikher, and I are going to Bedlam to find out more about that conservator."

The lack of connections in his head was beginning to worry him, so the news of a possible link to a conservator was very encouraging. He was starting to feel like he was letting down the team; his part in this was supposed to be in his head.

Nikher, Aoife, and William piled into SkyView. This time, they enjoyed the main area in the fuselage for the short flight, taking a break from the SkyDeck. The closest safe house to Bedlam was Warwick Castle. SkyView landed in a small forest near Ethelfleda mound.

"Warwick Castle was originally a wooden fort built by William the Conqueror during 1068. It was rebuilt in stone during the twelfth century. During the Hundred Years' War, the facade opposite the town was refortified, resulting in one of the most recognizable examples of fourteenth-century military architecture. It was used as a stronghold until the early seventeenth century," Coen said after a long break, giving the seven some history.

William led them through another secret medieval tunnel to the castle after landing. Most of the Castle was open to the public, so they could all hear the chatter of impressed tourists as they searched the grounds. Warwick Castle commanded a lot of area, but they were able to find their private section of it easy enough. William immediately wanted to get to London, which was about an hour and a half away. Nikher and Aoife agreed, so they quickly toured the small portion of the castle and made their way to the private garage. They all entered a large SUV and made their way south through the English countryside.

William could see Bedlam on the horizon. By this time, they all had read the police report two or three times, but the police never released the woman's name to the public.

"I guarantee they have a file on her somewhere; institutions like that keep impeccable records," Aoife said as they mirrored the route of the two Irishmen, parking just in front of the of the entrance.

William and Nikher got out of the SUV and entered. Aoife elected to remain with Coen to avoid suspicion, Nikher and William were greeted immediately.

"Can I help you?" a well-dressed and caring elderly woman approached.

"Ahh…my wife and I have an appointment with Dr. Vernwarth. Her brother is having issues," William said with a laugh. Nikher dug her nail in his arm. The nice old lady gave them a funny look but gestured for them to follow her.

"Wait here," she said, pointing to a small waiting room that had a total of three seats.

"Can I get you anything? Coffee, water?" she asked politely.

"No, thank you," both Nikher and William replied at the same time. She then went to inform the doctor.

"You were supposed to have the brother with issues!" Nikher said slightly annoyed.

"So what's the plan? How are we going to get access to those records?" he said.

"Once we find out where they are, we can come back tonight. We'll break in, just like Éibhear," Nikher said in a serious tone.

"Hi, I'm Dr. Vernwarth." A tall, young, honest-looking man poked his head around the corner. "Please, come into my office," he said in a friendly voice.

Nikher and William followed and sat across from him. A wall of patient files filled the entire space behind him. William and Nikher gave each other a look.

"So from what I understand, your brother is having issues," Dr. Vernwarth said to William.

"Sorry, no, it's actually her brother…Éibhear…he needs help…he has a lust for violence William replied.

"Éibhear?" the Dr. repeated the name as if he'd never heard it.

"Yes, Éibhear" Nikher replied with a shutter not liking the idea of being fake related to him, but also trying to reassure the doctor that the name was real.

"Her grandmother had a brief stay here too," William said.

"Really?" the doctor said. "So mental instability runs in the family?" He started writing things down. William and Nikher gave each other a grin again.

"I bet she's on your wall here," William pointed behind the doctor.

"When was she here?" he asked.

"In 1948," they replied simultaneously. "She wouldn't be back there in that case. These only go back fifty years," he replied.

"Where then?" William asked.

"Uh…they're scanned and archived on our internal system," the doctor replied, uncertainly.

"What about physical copies?" asked Nikher.

"The physical copies are kept in storage in the basement."

"Can we get a tour? We can walk and talk. I want to make sure it's the best place for her brother." William quickly got up, already having the info he needed.

The doctor was taken aback but agreed to have a "walking tour meeting thing," as Nikher ended up calling it.

William and Nikher walked briskly and made up answer after answer about Éibhear as the doctor escorted them through the old part of the building.

"These rooms go back to the thirteenth century." As they walked, the doctor said hi to several patients.

William and Nikher walked briskly past the rooms. William kept peering in and glancing at each patient, trying not to make eye contact, but curious about their story. Nearing the corner room on the second floor, William noticed that it was empty and larger than the others. He put his hand on the doorknob to get a better look inside, and suddenly he heard a whisper: "William Ward, this is…" Shocked, he pulled his hand off, but this time he didn't panic. Ignoring the doctor and Nikher, he put his hand on the door again. "William Ward, this is…" The voice was *Neveah*'s, but it was different, just like when he faked his death at the ship wreck. He put his hand out once more and a for a third time he heard "William Ward, this is…"

In the middle of the night as planned Nikher, William, and Aoife left Warwick Castle and rose above Ethelfleda mound. After the very short flight, Coen landed SkyView in the tennis court and surrounded it with its invisibility shield. William, Nikher, and Aoife, all clad in black and looking like ninjas, walked peacefully through the already-opened back door and disabled security system. They also walked by where a security guard should have been posted, but he was currently on the third floor inspecting noises in the heating system.

"I told you, these guys are the best," Nikher said to William as she escorted him into the basement.

"Who are they?" William asked, referring to the company that she'd hired to break into the asylum for them.

"It's a company we have access to, anytime we have semi-illegal things needed inside the Cradle we use them. There prepared to get caught if need be and take the fall. It helps us stay hidden. They don't actually know who we are, to them it's just an anonymous contract. They have a drone in the vents, so the guards will be busy for a while. Plus, they already scoped out the archive room for us."

The three of them nervously walked down the stairs. Thanks to the hired help, Nikher had a steady feed of the guards' conversation in Mind-Link, in case they decided to patrol the basement. William, Nikher, and Aoife walked uninterrupted directly to the archive room, which was basically a museum of file cabinets.

"Its all organized by name, not by year," William said, obviously frustrated.

"We don't know her name," Aoife replied. William glared at her.

"Well, we have to scan them all then. William, you take A to H; Aoife, you take I to P, and I'll take the rest," Nikher said in an authoritative tone.

William, Aoife, and Nikher each began frantically opening each cabinet and speeding through each file, being sure that their digital AR glasses were recording each page.

Back on SkyView and the HoloTable, *Neveah* had begun organizing the files as per William's direction. He was hoping to have a file to read on the way back to Warwick Castle.

"The guards are headed back to their posts," Nikher said over Mind-Link.

"Don't stop," William said. "We need every file, and everything in every file."

"This is a dangerous game, William," Aoife said, not looking over at him.

"What? All we have to do is get by one guard at the back door and then run to SkyView. I'm not leaving without every file!" he said angrily.

"Everybody is back at their post now; apparently they all think it was a raccoon in the vent," Nikher updated them, still tapped into their feed.

Finally, William finished his last file in the last cabinet along his wall. Aoife had finished too, so they both helped Nikher finish hers. They walked through the hallway and up the stairs, where the security guard was now in view blocking the exit.

"What now?" said Aoife.

"Coen, get SkyView ready. Run!" William said as he booked it, running as fast as he could past the guard.

"What are you doing? Are you insane?" Nikher said, reluctantly following him.

William body checked the door and sprinted across the field. Nikher could hear the guard warn the others.

The tennis court was a short distance away and was surrounded by a fence. William entered first, followed by Aoife and then Nikher.

The one guard had followed. "Stay there! Don't move!" he yelled as he pointed his pistol at them.

William kept taking steps toward SkyView, which was hidden behind its invisibility shield.

"I said don't move," the guard commanded again, but now the three of them were only a step away from the shield.

William waved, and from the point of view of the guard, he just disappeared. SkyView rumbled and the thrusts of air knocked the guard over. He stared into an empty, loud, windy tennis court as the three escaped.

"What is your problem?" Nikher screamed at William. "He saw us. What if he reports us? I can't believe how reckless you are!"

"Reports us?" William laughed. "What? Three ninjas ran across a field and disappeared into a loud, windy tennis court. He won't want to end up as a patient, believe me."

"Well, yeah, if he reports it, it's in the Cradle now. It's searchable," she responded angrily.

"You really don't know much about reality, do you?" William said as he made his way down to the SkyDeck. "He won't be reporting anything. I guarantee it," William replied.

Aoife was also giving William a dirty look. "What, you too?" William said, dismissing their concerns. "Okay, *Neveah*, show us what you got!" said William after shaking off the attitude he was getting.

"Coen, get us to space. I want to be as far away as possible while we go through this," William commanded.

"You know that once we get to a certain height, it's a simulation?" Aoife said, looking confused

"Yes, I do." William shook his head again. Suddenly, the SkyDeck roared and they were once again forced into their seats. The world got smaller and smaller until they could see the horizon. Then they saw the whole world, and then a small green/blue ball, and out of the right side of the AR window, the yellowish-red glow of the sun.

William was feeling in control but desperate to find the file of the woman. He knew that if he found out what the conservator knew, it would unlock his mind. This was the key, he was sure of it.

"*Neveah*, show me all females who died in the asylum," said William.

Neveah displayed numerous files across the window. A small line of glowing planets and eternal space leaked through the background. William rolled his eyes, disappointed in the amount of woman who had died.

"Wow, that's a lot. Okay, ones that have Irish names in them," he added.

Neveah opened a side window and started to display all of the files that had Irish names mentioned in them, starting from 1247.

"No, no, limit it to the twentieth century and only women who have died in the asylum who have Irish names mentioned in their files," William said, being sure to emphasise *their*.

"Wait, go back," Nikher yelled. She stood up and walked toward the window of space. *Neveah* started to rewind the images of file names she had displayed. "Slower," Nikher commanded. By now she was touching the screen. William noticed an uneasiness about her. *Neveah*, frame by frame, smoothly backed up. "Stop," Nikher said with half a voice, a distinct sadness was in her eye.

"Kiliaen!" William screamed as his eyes widened. The file opened, and Nikher could barley look.

"Kiliaen Wassemoet began his stay on December 17, 1358 until 1422." William read the pages as fast as he could, noticing the tears along the side. Many of the pages had been ripped out.

"It can't be a coincidence that woman was hiding in the same place Kiliaen once stayed," Aoife said nervously. She could see that Nikher had many different emotions going through her.

"Wait, what's that?" William said, watching broken pages as they crossed the screen. "He was signed in by a W.W. Why are there dollar signs by W.W?" William said, looking nervous.

The pages slowly turned; the three of them were reading intently. Kiliaen was tormented by his soul, a bad choice, a mistake. The pages turned and the doctors' notes were becoming less and less detailed. They basically just repeated what looked like normal behaviour. The pages finally stopped at the last page. At the top was written in bold and circled: "W.W. Donor," followed by, "1358, 1359, 1360…" With increasing amounts of money beside the date, all the way to 1422.

"William was donating to the hospital the whole time Kiliaen was there. Why?" asked Aoife.

"William was keeping him there, imprisoning him," Nikher said angrily and glared over at William.

"Why would William have him committed? That doesn't make any sense," said Aoife.

"He wouldn't join the Ward League, that's why. It was the next best thing to killing him," Nikher said, "This is what Archelaus was trying to tell us back in St. Lucia! He said. 'Beyaert and Kiliaen were lied to, Beyaert was enslaved to his wealth but Kiliaen refused so William imprisoned him, and the Wards are nothing but thieves!'" He said Nemesio knows the truth."

"So William payed off the hospital to keep him in there even though he wasn't sick?" questioned Aoife. "So he never went back to the IBC."

"Doesn't seem like he was given a choice, like we were led to believe," Nikher said, giving William a dirty look again.

"Coen, take us down. I've seen enough," Nikher commanded. She was now furious with William.

"Nikher, there has to be a reasonable explanation. This doesn't seem right." William pleaded with her.

"Do not talk to me right now. Everything you say is a lie. You have no answers in your head; you're useless!!" Nikher replied, her anger growing.

"Nikher, you don't mean that," Aoife said, trying to calm the situation. She could see a glow emanating from her arms.

"This is getting out of hand," said William.

"Getting out of hand, you say? What about helping the Wards for seven hundred years based on a lie. I'd say that's getting out of hand." Nikher stormed around the SkyDeck, her arms glowing.

Coen sensing the turmoil flew back to the Ice Palace to separate Nikher from William and let her cool down. Once they landed, Coen escorted Nikher to the chalet, repeatedly reminding her to calm down and assuring her that they could discuss it in the morning .

The next day, William skipped his morning workouts in an attempt to catch up on his sleep. But all he could manage to do was stare up at the ceiling, reluctantly agreeing with Nikher. All his thoughts of how righteous the Ward League was were disappearing. Eventually, he made his way to the HoloTable, hoping Aoife had already updated everybody so he wouldn't have to.

By the time he got there, everybody was searching for the missing woman—aside from Nikher, who was apparently snowmobiling with Coen and still very mad at William.

"Found her," Bodhi said. "Hannah Evans, born in Chichester, England, 1907. She's the only female patient declared brain dead in 1948. Highlights from the police report are also in there. See, two Irishmen." Bodhi finished.

"Does she have any relatives listed?" William asked, eagerly settling into his usual chair.

"None alive; she was an only child and had no kids of her own," Bodhi answered.

"Pull up the entire file, and let's go through it," William said to *Neveah*.

The hologram displayed six individual representations of the file so each could go through it at their own pace.

Hannah Evans committed herself into Bedlam in 1935, stating she wanted to be close to an old friend. She was only twenty-eight years old. Hannah was initially diagnosed with secondary mania, a mental disorder that disturbs brain functions and causes different kinds of delusions, including grandiose delusions. Initially, these delusions would only occur randomly, and at most twice a year.

Hannah was later noted to show signs of schizophrenia, increased episodes of belief not in line with reality, hallucination, and delusions. She became obsessed with the idea that she was being followed, her food was being poisoned, and her thoughts were being listened to.

Her diagnosis was later updated to paranoid schizophrenia when the episodes became a full belief. She thought she was the secret keeper for the hidden families that ruled the world, and she believed she held the truth to Seven Secret Wars. Hannah also offered, on many occasions, millions of dollars to staff to keep her safe. She repeatedly referred to reality as "the Cradle" and said that she wasn't safe in here or out there.

"Well, looks like she actually was both; correct and suffering mentally, not just hiding from Oisin and Éibhear," Apollinaris said as he sat back feeling bad for Hannah and what she had to go through, all because the Ward League used her to keep its secrets.

"Look at her journal: Seven Secret Wars, Seven Secret Letters, etched in stone…two left to pass," William cried. "We need to find Nikher!"

"Wait, look, here's a drawing," Nael said.

"It's a castle…that's Wassemoet Castle! Remember we saw it on the rooftop HoloTable?" Apollinaris said excitedly.

"Didn't they find the Declaration of Succession etched in stone there?" Apollinaris said, still excited.

"That's correct!" William said, more excited than all of them.

William explained everything over Mind-Link to Nikher and Coen. Nikher never responded, but he was sure Coen was asking questions for her. Finally, they all agreed that the castle needed another restoration project, realizing they hadn't looked deep enough into its secrets.

Thijs was able to fast-track the project by stipulating that the anonymous donor was dying and wanted to see it finished prior to his passing.

CHAPTER 19
WHERE IT ALL STARTED

O ver the next few days, William increased the intensity of his workouts, continuing to push his mind and body to the max. His eidetic memory was improving and was now projecting some of his childhood memories with clarity.

Dieter had finally found the artist responsible for all the paintings that hung in the waiting room at the IBC.

"Giotto di Bondone 1267–January 8, 1337. He was known as the most sovereign master of painting in his time. He drew all his figures and their postures according to nature," Dieter quoted the Cradle to the group one morning as numerous paintings hovered over the HoloTable.

"Giotto's masterwork is the decoration of the Scrovegni Chapel, also known as the Arena Chapel in Padua. It is regarded as one of the supreme masterpieces of the early Renaissance. The fresco cycle depicts the life of the virgin and the life of Christ. It was completed around 1305.

Thanks to Ernest, I was able to get copies of those original paintings of the eight founders at the IBC. I went through around fifteen or so experts but managed to narrow the list down. Apparently Giotto was the only one capable of that realism at the time. He's considered the world's first celebrity painter, but what I found funny and seemingly fitting with our secret nature is the fact that almost every aspect of his life, aside from painting, is subject to controversy: his appearance, his birth date, his birthplace, his apprenticeship, his burial place, even the order in which he created his works." Dieter finally finished, very happy to have found him.

"Have you found a copy of the Declaration of Interlaken painting?" William asked hopefully.

"No, I've gone through every digital collection involving Giotto that's chronicled in the Cradle and found nothing, but I have the names of a few people who have private collections that are known to include Giotto." Dieter was disappointed but could tell William was happy with his effort.

"Anything on those two wars, Nael?" William asked.

"No, sorry, nothing," he answered.

"What about you, Apollinaris? Have you found those records anywhere?" William asked

"Unfortunately, no. I have some idea where to look, starting—where they met every year at Interlaken."

"Interlaken Castle," Aoife said.

"Yes, I was afraid you were going to say that," William said with fear in his voice.

"You know Venacio will have that place fully guarded," Aoife said, to which William nodded his head, assuring her he'd realized that long ago.

"Ernest told me it's a mutual territory now. Both leagues have members working there as employees, and it's still used by the IBC as a satellite office. I've always had a feeling we should go there, since Ernest mentioned it. There are definitely clues there; it's just really dangerous for us to go," William said

"Okay, like hidden in your head clue or just a feeling clue?" Aoife said with a confused look.

"Just...a feeling," William said quietly but angrily, as nothing had connected in his head yet. This was frustrating, considering how much progress he was making both mentally and physically with his daily workouts.

"Okay, okay, take it easy," Aoife said, turning to look away from him.

"Listen, we all agree on the century. We have the artist now. That painting has to be with a private collector, we'll soon have the Secrets of the Wars. I say we go get those records. The records my dad found are back in San Diego. These records will give proof, I guarantee it," William said, trying to convince himself and the rest.

"Let's go then," Aoife said, ready for action as always.

William once again updated Nikher through Coen. He still wasn't sure if she was going to come. He finally found her hiding in the SkyDeck, not wanting to be in the same area as him just yet.

SkyView rumbled as they headed north to Interlaken for a very short flight. Nikher still wasn't talking to William, but he was ignoring her, hoping the etching in the stone would prove

Kiliaen was in Bedlam for another reason beside William trying to imprison him.

SkyView landed beside the Interlaken safe house that was under the Harder Klum, which was the top of Interlaken's viewpoint. The old safe house was quite secure and disguised as a farm. They hopped in an old armoured truck and made their way toward Interlaken Castle. William entered and thought it was more of a stronghold than an office. The front entrance was a luxurious, stone, square wall that was once concrete armour and had two large steel doors. Both doors opened, and William, Nikher, Aoife, and Apollinaris were approached by four security guards, two on the left and two on the right. All four spoke something different into the cuffs of their suit coats.

"Mr. Ward, Mr. Thess, Miss Wassemoet, Miss O'Sullivan, please step to this side of the room." Two of the security guards spoke simultaneously; it appeared that they were getting orders from somewhere.

"Apollinaris, let's make this quick. I have a funny feeling about this. It doesn't seem like an office," Nikher said over Mind-Link.

"No, this is a vault," one of the guards said. Nobody was sure if he'd read Nikher's lips or heard her through Mind-Link.

"On the other side of this door is an open floor office. Please do not disturb anybody. They are all just going about their day as normal employees at the IBC. What you may or may not be looking for is the left door at the opposite end of the office."

One of the guards finished with his instruction, and then both of them stepped aside and blocked the other two guards.

William gingerly entered with Nikher, Aoife, and Apollinaris at his heels. Slowly they walked through the office that was now separated by a thick glass wall, with no visible open area. They walked along the glass, finally making it to the door described by the security guard. The door ended up being an elevator, which they all immediately entered. Once inside, the door closed with the distinctive sound of pressure releasing, and all the buttons went red and unresponsive.

"What's going on?" Aoife asked nervously

"This is a neutral territory. It must lead to a private area away from the employees," said Apollinaris.

"We can't stay here long," Nikher said. "No matter what's on the other side of that door."

The door opened before they could even guess what would be on the other side. William could have sworn the elevator didn't even move. He took one step forward and knew exactly where he was. Slowly he walked and dragged his hand across his very great-grandfather's chair. His eyes narrowed, and he stared down the table to Alvero's seat. The room was surrounded by a single endless row of books, and had reading areas on each side of the long historic table. The opposite end of the room had two doors; William had the feeling it was one for each league.

"That's a lot of books," Apollinaris said.

"Yeah," Aoife said in wonder as she grabbed one. "William of Ockham 1287– 1347," Aoife said, flipping the pages.

"He was a philosopher," Nikher said, still miserable. "You've never heard of Occam's Razor?"

"No," they all responded, with interest.

"It's a problem-solving principle. Simpler solutions are more likely to be correct than complex ones," Nikher said, very arrogantly.

William rolled his eyes, thinking that of course that would the first book Aoife picked up. The four of them opened numerous books but couldn't find anything relevant as far as financial records.

"Dante Alighieri 1265–1321," Aoife announced. Reading the author's name once again.

The Divine Comedy, Nikher said.

"The seven deadly sins," William interrupted. "Pride, greed, lust, envy, gluttony, wrath, and sloth." He tried not to make eye contact with Nikher as she rolled her eyes.

"Yes, it's a narrative poem, widely considered to be the pre-eminent work in Italian literature and one of the greatest works of world literature," Nikher said smugly.

"Why are they here?" William asked, looking around.

"No idea," Apollinaris said quickly.

"Look at the years," said Aoife. "Ockham 1287–1347, and Dante 1265–1321. These could have influenced any of the founders."

"This one's unfinished but it has Giotto di Bondone 1266–1337 listed in it, amongst a bunch of others," Apollinaris said excitedly. They all rushed over to have a look.

"Any copies of the Declaration painting?" William questioned eagerly.

"No, but all the controversial info about his life is here. Look, it's a sketch of his appearance, his birth date, birthplace, apprenticeship, burial place…"

"And the order of his works, but no mention of any IBC paintings," William finished disappointedly, looking over his shoulder.

"Look, Alvero's in here too!" Apollinaris said again, excitedly flipping the pages. "Oh man, this sketch must have been drawn when he was infected with the Black Death; it also mentions his burial place."

Nikher and the others were lost in the endless books about the century, forgetting her advice not to stay long. Several hours had passed before Apollinaris finally found what looked like financial records. "Here, I found something. This section is all what looks like expenses. Look, 1328, 1329, 1330, all the way to 1399. Every year!" Everybody rushed over and grabbed several books, some thicker than others, and carried them over to the lounge areas, laying them all out on the coffee table.

"I've gone through twenty years already, and these are just normal purchases and old payroll ledgers," Aoife said frustratedly. "Mine too," William said.

"Same here," announced Apollinaris. "I just don't get the random jumbled letters. Look, every month or so." Apollinaris pointed at a few line items that were just random letters.

"What year are you in?" William asked, grabbing the book and turning it over.

"It was 1347," Apollinaris replied.

"That's the year of the Black Death," William said, pacing around the couch. All four of them stopped reading and stared at William and watched him think.

"It's encrypted; those letters have meaning," William said with authority. "Think, Apollinaris, Eleutherios would have written all of these. You have the key."

Apollinaris looked stunned. He rose and paced awkwardly, avoiding William. "Go get; 1332, 33, 34, and 35." William said.

"The Second War of Scottish Independence," Nikher informed.

"As well as 1337, 38, 39, and 40."

"The beginning of the Hundred Years' War," she informed again.

For the next hour or so, they read page after page, internally highlighting the encrypted line items and desperately trying to break the code. By now fifteen different books were scattered about as everybody was looking for a clues—something, anything to bring clarity to the random letters.

"Look at this guy, Ibn Battuta 1304–1377. Apparently he travelled continuously for thirty years all over the medieval world," Aoife said, now picking up random books and abandoning the financial ledgers. "Or this guy, Juan Manuel, Prince of Villena 1282–1348. He was the richest and most powerful man of his time." Aoife read the handwritten notes on the inside cover.

"Apollinaris, I don't want to seem rude, but the key to this is in your head," William said.

"His head!" Nikher yelled.

William forgot she was ready for a fight and regretted his choice of words. "Sorry, I mean, the key to this may be in your head," he said, looking over at Nikher for approval. She rolled her eyes.

"Listen, I'm in the same boat as you. There's nothing in either of our heads," Apollinaris replied sadly.

Nikher noticed the sadness and looked at him and then back at William a few times. "Maybe you guys are trying too hard. I mean, remember William of Ockham?" Nikher, seeing that they weren't clueing in, gingerly held up the book that Aoife had found. "Simpler solutions are more likely to be correct than complex ones."

Everybody's eyes widened..

"Okay, what's something simple that can decipher these letters?" William asked. "It's too bad we can't record anything here. *Neveah* could figure this out no time."

"Not without the key, though. To *Neveah* these are just random letters," Nikher stated.

"This is a simple encryption that only needs the key. It could be a number, a name, a word, a phrase, a date, an artifact. Whatever it is, it will unlock the code."

"Do you remember anything that Nikolaos, Kaethe, Nereus, or Helios said? Something that would pass through time unnoticed? Think!" William said, berating Apollinaris again.

Nikher clenched her teeth. "Do you remember anything Ernest, Bill, James, or John said," she said, cutting off William.

"Vassilios, Archelaus, Dareios!" William shouted, trying to out-yell Nikher.

"Wait....Theophilus," Apollinaris said calmly as he stood up in thought. "That was Eleutherios's middle name, but there's nothing in the Cradle confirming it. My dad told me that a while ago."

"But it passed through time, and he wrote these ledgers," William said, thinking as well.

"How could the name Theophilus be a used as a key?" Aoife questioned.

"Well, there are ten letters in Theophilus, so each letter could represent a number? Maybe?" Apollinaris quickly answered.

"No, there are two h's in Theophilus; each letter would have to be different," William said, shaking his head.

"Wait, look…there are two different h's on every line item, and one's always larger than the other!" Nikher said excitedly as she mentally mapped out numbers along different line items. "That's it—that's the key! Eleutherios used an invented middle name to hide the money."

Suddenly the other elevator door opened. A man and a woman entered, not expecting to see anybody there. They stopped, and all six people stared at each other without a word.

"Oh my god…that's Finian," Aoife said in a whisper, remembering their recent fight.

"What is Finian doing here?" Nikher said to everybody over Mind-Link.

"I think that's the girl from the helicopter" William responded, noticing her long hair and tanned skin.

Finian and the girl looked just as surprised to see William, Nikher, Aoife, and Apollinaris. Their eyes slowly dropped to see all the books they had been looking at. They slowly made their way to a different section along the shelf. While staring at only William, they eased their way to the lounge area on the opposite side of the large table. William and the girl locked eyes for several seconds; the stare was mutually broken and the girl's eyes retreated to Alveros's empty seat and William's to his very great-grandfather's seat.

"We're in neutral territory here," Nikher said over Mind-Link.

"That's right," William said. "Let's just speak over Mind-Link and crack this code, and then we get out of here as fast as possible."

"Coen, get SkyView ready; we'll be there soon!" Nikher said

William, Nikher, Aoife, and Apollinaris put back every book but the six they were trying to decode, the whole time staring at the two newcomers.

"Okay, so we have the right side of the ledger figured out. How do we know what the left says? What is this money being spent on? We need letters now!" Aoife said, staring at her relative.

"Eleutherios Theophilus Thess…that's twenty-six letters, and look—the duplicate letters are different sizes! A letter for every letter in the alphabet," Apollinaris replied.

"Let's memorize every transaction from the beginning of these wars and then get out of here," William said. But as he grabbed one of the books, he was shocked to hear a familiar whisper: "William Ward, this is…" He dropped the book on the table, and Nikher picked it up, giving him a dirty look. William grabbed a different book but didn't hear anything this time.

The room was dead silent; it was obvious that Finian and the girl were speaking over a similar technology and looking through completely different books than the others. Nikher and Aoife's eyes sped across every page as fast as they could, soaking it all in. William and Apollinaris, who had made great strides with their memories, still weren't as skilled as the girls. It didn't take long for them to go through the eight books and get the random letters in their heads. Suddenly, all four of them rose and, feeling two sets of eyes on them, put the books back on the long row and quietly left through the far entrance. Once the door shut, they ran as fast as they could through the medieval halls, which gave way to an open area on top of a fortified path. Nikher easily directed Coen to where to meet them for a quick escape.

"Robert Artois," Nikher said as they all relaxed in the fuselage on SkyView.

"What?" William replied. He knew the comment was for him due to the attitude it came with.

"A monthly line item for an entire year—Robert Artois Inheritance Payment," Nikher said with the same attitude.

"Wow, Alvero didn't urge Robert Artois to help the English—he paid him the inheritance he was owed in France," William said, slouching more in his seat.

"A single transaction will unlock your mind," Nikher said. "Let's hope you have something else in there to unlock."

With the second Wassemoet Castle restoration underway, the team was ready to head to the Netherlands and view the concrete imaging. William had once again increased the intensity of his workouts; the evidence of Alvero paying Robert Artois his inheritance really did unlock his mind. Everything was suddenly more believable, more real. The malice was more apparent, and the Cradle had taken shape.

"It's a simple transaction that started a war," he told Nael back at the Ice Palace. "An investment."

SkyView roared over Germany and landed in a forested clearing close to Wassemoet Castle. All seven of them were very excited and nervous to finally learn the truth behind the wars that had separated their families. Aoife had begged William to allow Eoghan to join them, to which William reluctantly agreed. William wasn't feeling very optimistic about what truths were hidden in the stones, but he realized he deserved truth as much as the rest of them.

"Thijs, it's nice to see you again," William said as he was greeted at the oversized historic wooden door.

"Everything is set up; we think the etching are in the court-yard in the supporting pillars. Each pillar has exactly seven sections in them. The restoration project is limited to the towers, and the crew are all gone for the night," Thijs said as he eyed everybody walking into the castle.

It was dusk and quiet, and the castle was eerie and empty. Thijs escorted them through the enormous medieval stone halls. They walked under the large archway that housed the Declaration of Succession stone. William was the only one who noticed the odd stone, as everybody else had a different stones on their mind. Entering the courtyard, they were all presented with seven large pillars, each with different stoned sections leading up to a spire. Beyond the pillars was a scenic, arched walkway that surrounded the courtyard and allowed for sweeping views of the endless steep hillside. Instinctively, Nikher walked toward the first pillar located to her left.

"This one's mine. I bet they go in order a of when we joined the Ward League," she said, urging the others toward their pillars. Nikher grabbed the hand-held concrete scanner and pressed it to the stone, close to the base of the pillar. Small infrared images showed up on the screen but no letters or words just yet. Huc also grabbed a scanner while making his way towards his pillar, both looking at each other nervously. By this time, each member was holding a scanner and looking for stones to image—aside from William, who just looked desperate. He could feel his new world about to crumble.

Nikher was feeling her way around her pillar, slowly moving the scanner until she saw what she'd been desperately looking for most of her life: "War of the Twin Bears 1358." She forced William to look at a screen. He didn't like what he saw, so he moved the scanner aside and touched the stone, inspecting it in disbelief. All he could do was back away and try to reorganize his insides, which by now had completely turned over. Feeling more desperate than ever, he had the sudden urge to scan the Declaration of Succession stone. He grabbed a scanner and swiftly left the courtyard, making his way to the archway before anybody could question him.

"It's all here, Coen. William sacked this castle while Baernt was at the annual Interlaken meeting. He robbed them of everything, forcing Beyaert and Baernt into servitude. Kiliaen refused, and that's why William had him committed," Nikher finished with a cracking voice.

Thijs was making his way over to her. She looked up and noticed that Nael looked devastated. Apollinaris, Dieter and Bodhi sat looking confused; Aoife and Eoghan stood in shock.

"Where's William?" Nikher let out a scream that echoed through the hills.

"We've been deceived, Nikher," Thijs said, "for seven hundred years."

"What's Famke doing here?" Nikher asked, angry and confused.

Thijs's daughter ascended from the hillside and made her way over to Nikher, gently dragging her hand along a few of the pillars. "We needed you to see this for yourself. It's time we part ways with the Wards," Famke said in a calm, foreboding tone.

"What do you mean?" Nikher asked, moving from anger to confusion.

"We all need to end the manipulation of the Ward League," Famke said in a low tone. "We've all been robbed and enslaved to our wealth. We've been deceived. This isn't a war…it's theft."

Nael, Dieter, Bodhi, Aoife, Eoghan, and Apollinaris were being drawn toward the beautiful Famke, the truth of their wars sinking in. They had all been tricked and robbed. There was no other conclusion, they all thought.

"The Ward League has been using you to rob each other while keeping you enslaved to your fortunes," Famke said, having all their attention.

Suddenly, from the hillside behind the pillars, shadows were seen creeping into the courtyard.

"Finian! Ciara!" Nikher said shockingly. Aoife and Eoghan clenched their fists.

"As well as brothers Veleslav and Spytihněv Kadaně," Famke said as two more men approached. Bodhi backed up and hid behind Aoife.

"Who are you?" Dieter asked. Two other men entered and leered at him with fiery eyes.

"Adolar von Steinach, and this is Florian del Verdier—the *rightful* heirs," Adolar said as they made their way and stood beside Finnian and Ciara. Nael felt his stomach drop.

"And last but not least, Archelaus and Dareios Thess, but of course I know you've met already," Famke said again in an innocent manner.

"The disinherited," Aoife said.

"No, you can call us reality!" said Archelaus.

"We have brought you here so that you can see the truth firsthand," Famke said, addressing everybody in the courtyard again. "You all have been blinded by your own righteousness. The Wards are thieves, with only one target left, but we don't want to be any part of it. We've brought no weapons. We do not wish to fight; we only offer truth."

None of them had any response; they all just kept looking back and forth at each other, not sure what to think.

"I know this is shocking to all of you, but…."

William came running into the courtyard at that moment. "Nikher, I figured it out. I'm the key! Those stone aren't re…. whoa!" William stopped abruptly just in the entrance of the courtyard. Finian made a movement toward him, and William backed up. Aoife stepped in but wasn't sure what to do.

Famke gestured Finian to back up and for everybody else to step to either side of the courtyard, leaving William in the middle. A final shadow swept along the arched walkway and spirited past each opening. A tall, attractive woman with long hair and tanned skin slowly crept into the courtyard.

"Neiva, there's somebody here you may want to meet," Famke said with a smirk.

"Seven Secret Wars, Seven Secret Letters, etched in stone… only one left to pass." Neiva pointed at the final pillar.

"Hi, William," she said with a smile. "Interesting situation we have ourselves in."

"Listen, nobody needs to get hurt. We just want our money," Archelaus said, appealing to the crowd. "You've had it long enough, and now you're coming with us." His tone was changing.

Finian, Ciara, and Archelaus started making steps toward William; Nikher, Aoife, and Dieter didn't stop them. William turned and ran back through the great hall.

"Nikher!" William screamed through Mind-Link as he ran as fast as he could, hoping he included everybody. "The key isn't in my head. I'm the key! I thought I was hearing voices, but it was *Neveah*. When I touched the mast on the *Hartwell* wreck, when I touched the door to Kiliaen's room at Bedlam, when I touched the ledger at Interlaken Castle, and when I just touched the Declaration of Succession Stone, I heard the same thing: 'William Ward, this is…' But this time I answered, 'The

Declaration of Succession,' and *Neveah* spoke to me, telling me all about the stone!" William panted as he ran up a tower.

"William, we've seen the stones. I'm sorry," Nikher responded coldly.

William could sense the sadness in her voice. "But that's just it—I didn't hear *Neveah* when I touched that stone! They're fake! I didn't hear her when I scanned Hannah Evans' file. I scanned all the E's; she's fake! There is no Hannah Evans. The answers are in my head, but only when I'm in the right place, and only if I answer correctly. You have to believe me."

Nikher looked at Thijs and Famke. By this time, Coen was inspecting the stone and arguing with Thijs.

"What did you do?" Coen asked Thijs.

"William is coming with us!" Thijs said. "We're ending this war today."

"It's time you choose the right side," Neiva said to Coen and Nikher.

Aoife, Nael, Apollinaris, and Bodhi weren't sure what to do. Finian, Ciara, Veleslav, Spytihněv, and Adolar were chasing William up the stone stairs of the tower. William at this point was out of options; he knew he needed Nikher, Aoife, Eoghan, Coen, and Dieter.

"*Neveah*, when I touch the Declaration stone again, broadcast what you said before to everybody. I'm on the roof now. Everybody get into the great hall, together we're going to have to brawl our way out. These stones are not the truths you're looking for. Nikher and Coen, the truth to Kiliaen is back at Bedlam, the truth to the Hundred Years' War is back at Interlaken Castle, and the rest of the truths are scattered around Europe! You have to believe me!" William said to everybody over Mind-Link.

William rushed across the roof until he was over the great hall. Carefully, he hung over the edge and swung in through a window. "I'm in the great hall now. If you trust me, get in here!" he cried.

William could hear the footsteps of his pursuers on the roof, so he made his way to the archway, flipping over a table to use as a makeshift ladder while desperately trying to put his hand on the Declaration Stone. Finian, Ciara, Veleslav, Spytihněv, and Adolar all rushed through the window; they were now steps away. William stretched as far as he could; he was within inches. Finally, he leapt and was able to grab just enough of the stone to hang on.

"William Ward, this is…" *Neveah* once again whispered, but this time all members of the Ward League could hear.

"The Declaration of Succession 1337," William struggled to say, hanging over the archway. Finian and Ciara and the rest laughed, as they finally had him. Nikher, Aoife, and Eoghan entered the room, followed by Famke and Thijs, who was being held on to by Coen.

Bodhi, Nael, and Apollinaris entered, as did Florian. They all stared as William hung there, completely vulnerable.

"The Declaration of Succession 1337," *Neveah* said, "referred to the eight factions of Interlaken and the decision that the heir of each faction would follow the first line, meaning the child, male or female, born nearest to the turn of each century, in perpetuum. William Ward and Alvero Losada had proposed the succession plan at the beginning of the Hundred Years' War when the French king died without male heirs, which put the empire at risk. William and Alvero proposed a succession plan to ensure that the empire they are building would live on forever."

William couldn't hang on any longer, so he dropped about eight feet. Only Bodhi was there to help cushion his fall. For what seemed like minutes, they all stared at each other. Neiva finally yelled, "Get him!"

Finian, Ciara, Veleslav, Spytihněv, and Adolar immediately lunged at William, tackling him. Bodhi tried to wrestle them off but was easily knocked down. Nikher, whose arms were on fire, knocked Famke out of the way and took a hard swing at Finian, who stumbled back. Aoife's arms started to glow as well, and the fight was now on. Punches and kicks were being thrown all over the place. Even Bodhi had gotten into the mix, although he didn't quite believe in violence. Each heir managed to find their nemesis and pair off with each other, starting with Bodhi and Veleslav, and then Aoife and Ciara, Nael and Florian, Dieter and Adolar, Apollinaris and Dareios, Nikher and Famke, and finally William and Neiva, whose arms glowed a violent red as she skillfully hit William repeatedly with both arms and legs. She was so fast, all William could do was block the strikes to his head.

Eoghan took on Finian and Spytihněv and could barely survive. Coen easily contained his nephew, Thijs, who was enjoying the chaos at this point. He then saved Apollinaris from a sucker punch from Archelaus.

Eventually, the brawl exhausted all of them, and they funneled back into the courtyard, looking for more space. The black eyes and bloody knuckles were starting to appear, along with the broken noses and twisted ankles. Bodhi had suffered heavy damage from Veleslav but hadn't given up. Aoife and Ciara had fought their way into a tie. Nael and Florian's fight was more of a wrestling match, and Dieter and Adolar both had very swollen faces, but neither had backed down. Dareios had the upper hand on Apollinaris, who had broken his hand on a missed punch. Nikher had gotten the better of Famke but she wasn't giving up, and William was surprisingly beaten up pretty good by Neiva, although he thought he had trained enough over the last several months to do a little better.

Finian and Spytihněv had beaten Eoghan up badly, but he kept fighting, even though several bones were broken, including his jaw. He could barely see out of his eyes. Thankfully, Coen was there to help him, after knocking Archelaus out with a stiff punch.

After what seemed like an hour of fighting, full exhaustion had set in, and less and less punches were thrown, and less kicks landed. Thijs, who had not been fighting, saw an opportunity to escape. He mumbled something to Famke, who drew Nikher's attention away from him so he could drop kick her in the back. He grabbed Famke's hand, and they ran off across the courtyard, down the small cliff hills, and jumped into awaiting escape vehicle. Nikher, now free, could help Eoghan and get the upper hand in the fight with Finian and Spytihněv.

With Archelaus knocked out, Dareios stopped fighting Apollinaris and tried to wake him up. Coen held back Apollinaris as a vengeful Dareios lifted his dad up and carried him away. Finian, Spytihněv, Adolar, Ciara, and Neiva, who looked untouched, realized they were outnumbered now. One by one they scurried toward the cliff hills, but Aoife and Eoghan wanted to go another round with Finian and Ciara, now that the fight was even, but William stopped them and blocked the way to the hillside.

"What did Famke mean when she said 'brought us here?'" he asked Finian, as he was scared of the evil look in Eoghan's eye.

"They needed everybody to see the stones, see the truth," Finian said.

"We all know those are fake," Eoghan said in a rumbling voice while he spit a few teeth at him.

"What did Famke do to get us here?" Nikher asked, but Finian and Ciara refused to answer.

"Its okay, Thijs and Famke are on our side now." Neiva stressed. "We led him to the stones then to Kiliaen and Hannah, which led all of you here. They knew you'd only believe it if you found it out yourselves, so he made sure the police report on Hannah made it onto your SkyDeck. See, they believe the Wards are nothing but thieves."

"But why would they help you?" Aoife asked as her arms glowed bright green.

"Because we don't have a Wassemoet heir among us to collect their fortune when we get it back," Neiva said.

Coen's posture fell apart, and he had to lean against a pillar to stay up. "Famke was born in 1999," he scornfully stated.

"Yes, that's correct," Neiva said smugly. "We had to make an exception to the Declaration of Succession, seeing as she doesn't fall along the first-born line, but since the Wards have robbed everybody, and the Losadas are the only members left, the motion was passed unanimously. We were all quite happy to have them," Neiva laughed.

"Let's kill her right now, William. Let's end this!" Aoife said angry, her Gaelic markings fiercely glowed.

"We can't. Killing her alone won't end anything," William answered reluctantly.

"Why not?" Aoife replied

"Because we're just getting started, Aoife," Neiva said. "We're all too far from the real truth to start killing each other, and besides, you all need me alive to find Venacio, just like we need William to find Henry." Neiva gave William a sudden spin kick to his chest, knocking him over. She then ran off, eventually sliding down the cliff and speeding off on a hidden ATV.

"Well, I don't think they were expecting a brawl," Aoife said, surprised by the retreat.

"Yeah, I don't think anybody expected a brawl," William agreed, clutching at his chest and struggling to breathe.

Nikher and Coen looked the most shocked. "I guess you were right, William," Nikher said in an apologetic manner.

"Yeah, at least we know what the key is. Now we can go and confirm the rest of the century," William replied.

"No, I mean your evil twin theory. I guess Aoife was right too," she added sadly.

"Thijs...he's Haven's twin...that's right," Aoife said in a revelation.

"If a family line goes too long out of balance, an evil twin will be born," William, in shock, repeated what Aoife's line believed.

CHAPTER 20
A FAMILIAR VOICE

William was still healing from the beating he took from Neiva but was feeling strong enough to leave the Ice Palace and make his way to SkyView early in the morning, along with Coen and Nikher. Once again, they took flight toward London, landing close to Warwick Castle. Almost as if routine by now, Coen pulled up to Bedlam. William and Nikher limped their way into the hospital.

"Are you ready for this?" William asked, watching Nikher take a deep breath.

"Yes," she said as she exhaled.

Once again, they were greeted by the nice old lady and escorted to the waiting room.

"So you'd like another tour I've been told," Dr. Vernwarth said.

"Yes, if that's okay. We want to make sure this is the right place for Éibhear," Nikher replied.

"Well, if you don't have any medical questions, Lily can escort you."

William and Nikher both thanked the doctor and followed Lily around the hospital, finally making it to the large corner room where they last visited. William hesitated but then gently put his hand on the same spot as before and requested *Neveah* include Nikher with the truth.

"William Ward, this is…" *Neveah* said in a familiar tone.

"Kiliaen Wassemoet's room," William replied.

"Kiliaen Wassemoet's room from 1358 to 1422. He was committed by William Ward on request of Kiliaen himself due to an enslaved soul from his actions during the Battle of Poitiers 1356 and subsequent war with his brother over leaving the IBC. Kiliaen believed he'd committed a crime against his own nature, an unnatural act, which enslaved his soul. He thought there was no recovery. Baernt and Beyaert tried desperately to help, but Kiliaen refused. William and Peter were finally able to convince Kiliaen to visit Bedlam in the hopes of freeing his soul. William, Peter, Baernt, and Beyaert evolved into the Ward League and funded Kiliaen's recovery until 1422, the year of his death. From the years 1372 to 1422, Kiliaen only visited Bedlam one day per year as a reminder of his free soul. Kiliaen had a wife and children and enjoyed a peaceful life inside the Cradle."

Nikher smiled at William and asked Lily if she could enter the room.

"Sure, it's currently empty," she replied.

Nikher stepped in and noticed that it was more of a luxury apartment with large windows and a wonderful view of the manicured grounds.

"This room has had lots of special guests, mostly for short visits," Lily said as she noticed Nikher admiring it. "We have a lot of people who aren't necessarily sick stay here; sometimes they just need a break from reality."

"So what's next?" Nikher asked William, extremely happy that she'd trusted him and was able to learn that Kiliaen ended up living a peaceful life.

"Well, we have our theories and we have the wills," William replied with a smirk.

After a brief debate back at the Ice Palace, the seven agreed that William, Nikher, and Aoife should fly around Europe and confirm the theories they'd already developed. They were to broadcast their findings to the others back at the Ice Palace so they could view them on the HoloTable.

SkyView ascended with its familiar roar, and William, Nikher, and Aoife settled into the lounge area in the fuselage.

"First War of Scottish independence 1296–1328," Nikher said.

"Yeah, we just need the spot. Where would Henry hide the truth about that war?" William replied.

"What about the Stone of Destiny? The English took it in 1296 and returned it 1996, both of your birth years," Nikher stated excitedly.

Sure enough, William, Nikher, and Aoife made their way to Edinburgh Castle.

"William Ward, this is…" *Neveah* said.

"The Stone of Destiny," William replied.

"William Ward, this is…" *Neveah* stated again.

William looked confused. "First War of Scottish Independence 1296–1328?" William said, but there was no answer, so William repeated, "The Stone of Destiny, symbolizing the beginning of William's life."

"William Ward, this is the Stone of Destiny, symbolizing the beginning of William Ward's life and…"

William didn't know what else to add to that, so he took his hand off, realizing he didn't have much more time as Nikher and Aoife distracted the guards. He touched it again, broadcasting the feed to Nael, Bodhi, Apollinaris, Aoife, Nikher, and Dieter.

"William Ward, this is…" *Neveah* asked again.

"Where William had the idea to use time and manipulation to create his own reality and that those in power can be easily manipulated," William said boldly, still pressing his hand firmly, but Neveah didn't respond.

"This Stone is meant for something else, something we haven't thought of but has to do with the beginning of William's life," William said to Nikher and Aoife.

"So where do you think the truth to the First War of Scottish Independence is then?" Aoife questioned.

"A mile from Kinghorn, Fife," William replied, still thinking about the Stone.

"Where Alexander III fell off his horse," Nikher said.

"Yes, let's go," William said.

"The First War of Scottish independence 1296–1328," *Neveah* began as William, Nikher, and Aoife stood in the area where Alexander III's body was found. "William Ward studied this war and did not believe Alexander had died by accident. It was during this war that he developed his lifelong strategy to use time and manipulation to create his own reality while hiding in the shadows."

"Well, where do we go for the Great Famine?" Aoife asked as they walked back to SkyView.

"There's mention of it in the Apocalypse in a Biblia Pauperum," Bodhi said over Mind-Link. "It's a picture Bible written around the time of the Great Famine, illuminated at Erfurt. Death sits astride a manticore, whose long tail ends in a ball of flame (Hell). Famine points to her hungry mouth," Bodhi finished, sitting at the edge of his seat back in Switzerland.

"Then that's where we go," William said.

Sure enough, as William, Nikher, and Aoife walked into the ancient library and moved toward the old book, *Neveah* confirmed the Great Famine was included in the will as a reference to the ineptness and greed of those in power. William had soon joined with Alvero and formed the IBC, using this realization combined with hidden manipulation learned from the English king's success in being named Lord Paramount. William and Alvero sought out goods to trade, first meeting

Hynek, who had smuggled hops out of Bohemia and who was with Bligger. William laid out the trade routes and Alvero finding new customers. The four agreed to find experts in law, finance, and protection, adding Finghin, Baernt, Huc, and Eleutherios.

William, Nikher, and Aoife soon made their way to the National Archives of Scotland, in Edinburgh, where the Treaty of Edinburgh-Northampton, March 17, 1328, was located. *Neveah* confirmed that it was in the will to reference the signing of the Declaration of Interlaken 1328, which was depicted as a painting.

"The Second War of Scottish Independence 1332–1357," said Nikher.

"I have no idea where the truth to this would be hidden," William said.

"Me neither," Aoife and Nikher replied.

"Bodhi," William said over Mind-Link, "any thoughts on where we would find the truth to the Second War of Scottish Independence 1332–1357?" he asked as they hovered over Scotland.

"What about the heap?" Bodhi said

"Heap?" they all responded.

"Remember? During the first battle at Dupplin Moor, archers picked off the rushing Scots as they crushed each other and piled up in a heap as high as a spear. The English surrounded the bloody heap and stabbed repeatedly, ensuring no survivors."

"Yeah, I think I chose to forget that," William said. "Well, it's worth a shot. Coen, take us to Dupplin Moor, Perthshire."

Coen manoeuvred SkyView down to the battlefield after briefly re-watching the skirmish on the SkyDeck to get the exact location. Once landed, it took William ten minutes or so to settle on the exact spot of the heap, but once he did, *Neveah* confirmed their theory of Alvero and Huc urging the disinherited to reclaim their ancestral lands and being the link between the disinherited and the English king. *Neveah* also confirmed it was Finghin's privateers who attacked the town of Orford, and Baernt who captured Royal ships anchored at the Isle of Wight.

Once the three of them let *Neveah* finish confirming the actions of the IBC and increased trade through the war, they took SkyView back to Interlaken Castle to see if *Neveah* had anything to add to the IBC paying Robert Artois' inheritance to urge on the Hundred Years' War 1337–1453. William grabbed the same ledger, but *Neveah* only confirmed what they already knew—another war urged for manipulation and profit.

They didn't have to go far to confirm the Black Death 1347–1351, as Alvero was buried outside of Interlaken Castle. William, Nikher, and Aoife then made their way to the Hanseatic town of Lübeck to view the Latin document dated October 1297 and written by William Wallace, telling the merchants of Lübeck and Hamburg that they now had free access to all parts of the Kingdom of Scotland, which had, by favour of God, been recovered by war from the English.

Neveah didn't hesitate to confirm William's and Baernt's involvement in the trade and protection; she added William's desire to open up all borders and increase trade and get away from weapons and war.

After viewing the Treaty of Berwick 1357, which ended the Second War of Scottish Independence 1332–1357, their theory regarding its inclusion in the will was confirmed. It symbolized the end to a war and William faking his death, ending his involvement in the IBC.

"Well, where to now?" Nikher asked with a half yawn.

"The Devil's Bridge, Gotthard Pass!" William said excitedly.

"The Pfaffenbreif, October 7, 1370," Aoife added. They flew SkyView toward Switzerland and made their way to the bridge.

"My father walked this. It's around fourteen-miles long, but they found nothing. Little did they know," William said, gesturing along the road.

"William Ward, this is…" *Neveah* said.

"The Pfaffenbreif 1370, the official forming of the Ward League," William replied.

"Peter and Beyaert had formed the Ward League, honouring the Declaration of Succession 1337 and agreeing to use the wealth accumulated to destroy the IBC, which would in turn free it for future lines."

The Ciompi Revolt was next. William had the idea to go to the Piazza della Signoria, which was known in the history of the Florentine Republic and still maintained its reputation as the political focus of the city, It was an L-shaped square in front of the Palazzo Vecchio in Florence. William, Nikher, and Aoife wandered around the square, and William threw a coin into the Fontana del Nettuno. Nothing happened until he stepped near the edge.

"William Ward, this is…" *Neveah* said.

"The Ciompi Revolt 1378–1382, also the origin of the eights saints," William replied as the tourists cut through them.

"The eights saints represented the eight factions and the wealth accumulated during William and Baernt's tenure at the IBC being used to combat actions of the IBC."

"We're going to need Bodhi," Nikher said.

"Winchester College, founded 1382," Aoife said.

"Yes," replied William. "But I already told him, and he's been working on it. Apparently there's a famous painting called *The Trusty Servant* by the poet John Hoskins," William said before being interrupted by Nikher.

"Its a mythical creature with a pig's head and the body of a man. Its snout is closed with a padlock to keep secrets; it has the ears of an ass to hear its master calling, and the feet of a stag to show its swiftness. He's also holding working tools in his left hand, accompanied by allegorical verses on the virtues that pupils of the college were supposed to have," Nikher said.

"William Ward, this is…" *Neveah* repeated.

"Winchester College, founded 1382, which was an anonymous investment by the Ward League, giving the poor access to education," William replied, to which *Neveah* confirmed they were correct.

After Winchester College, the three of them made their way back up to the Baltic Sea, hoping to confirm the Victual Brothers 1392. Coen had the idea to see if they could find access to the most famous leader's, Captain Klaus Störtebeker's, sunken ship.

"He was a captain around 1394, he was the guy who was famous for chugging beer." Coen explained as they flew across Germany toward a wreck that was known to be captained by Klaus.

It didn't take long for them to find the ship, as they were able to link the investment records. *Neveah* promptly confirmed that the Alvero and Huc line invested in the privateers to break up the monopoly of the Hanseatic League in order to financially hurt the Ward League, which was in response to the eight saints' involvement in the Ciompi Revolt 1378–1382. This rolled directly into the Kalmar Union 1397. *Neveah* confirmed that the Huc and Alvero lines aligned with the Scandinavian aristocracy, who also wished to counter the influence of the Hanseatic League.

It took William, Nikher, and Aoife a while to figure out where to go regarding the Renaissance in Italy from the fourteenth to seventeenth century. William thought the truth was hidden in the Giotto painting, but since they couldn't locate it, Aoife finally convinced them to visit the Bardi family bank.

"The economic collapse was a crucial cause of the Renaissance; the wealthy had few promising investment opportunities for their earnings, so they chose to spend more on culture and art," Aoife said. "Also, did you know that the Bardi family continued to operate after the banking crash, financing some of the early voyages of discovery to America, including those by Christopher Columbus and John Cabot?"

"I did not know that," William said, his interest piqued.

"Peter and Baernt were involved in banking at the time… banking and investing," Aoife added, excited to see William and Nikher coming around to the idea of the bank. "We know the wealth had to make it to the Americas eventually. I'm thinking they invested in the original voyages. Back then, the Bardi family had lots of partners in their company, and they were very successful, even after the collapse. These were called "super-companies" by modern scholars. They assembled large amounts of capital through very diversified business networks."

"Wow," William said, "you've done some actual research on this."

"Yes, a lot!" she replied. "Of all the super-companies, back then, the Bardi family, along with its partners—those who were known and some who were secret—were 50 per cent bigger than the closest rival, the Peruzzi company. You combine that with investing in voyages to the Americas…" she added.

"Sounds like the Ward League to me," Nikher interrupted.

"Or Losada, new markets," William added.

"I think they both had an insatiable lust for new markets," Aoife said.

"Well, let's go then. Where was the original bank?" William asked.

"Back to Florence!" Nikher spoke, raising her hands in the air.

"Yeah, we left *Truth* off the coast there. I thought we'd be searching for the painting, but I guess we're going to the bank. At least we have a nice place to stay," he finished.

SkyView flew south across Europe and landed at a private airport close to Livorno, where *Truth* was docked. After a short drive, they made their way to Florence, and this time Eoghan and Coen joined them.

"This is it here, right?" William asked, looking at Aoife as he pointed at an old building at the end of the narrow cobblestone street.

"Yeah," replied Coen.

William walked up close to the building and put his hand on the old stone wall. Sure enough, he heard the familiar, "William Ward, this is…"

"Compagnia dei Bardi," William replied, looking at Aoife. She shrugged and urged him on. "A Ward League investment," he added, trying to sound confident.

"The Compagnia dei Bardi was a Ward League investment," *Neveah* replied, broadcasting to everybody.

"Well, there you have it," Aoife said. "The Compagnia dei Bardi is well documented in the Cradle for investing in voyages to America; this is where all our wealth travelled."

The big picture was becoming clear, and they had confirmed that *Neveah*, *Truth*, SkyView, the safe houses, plus endless other assets were all part of a multitude of hidden investment companies. William, Nikher, and Aoife pushed through to the Peasants' Revolt of 1381 to finish off the will.

"Any ideas regarding the revolt?" Aoife asked as they relaxed on *Truth* and floated in the Ligurian Sea.

"We still need to figure out why it's last in the will but occurred 1381," Nikher said.

"Yeah, I was thinking about that as well when we mapped the eight routes year by year and saw how the two leagues started to fight," William said. "I'm pretty sure the Ward League is behind the mysterious 'Great society' that organized the revolt."

"Maybe it's last because it should have been first," Eoghan said, looking unintentionally profound.

William, Nikher, Aoife, and Coen looked at each other in shock.

"He's right!" William said. "I remember now. When I was seven or eight, my Grandfather John's last words to me were, 'Make sure the last thing you do in life shouldn't have been the first.' He repeated it twice and then passed on. I thought it was general advice, but Eoghan's right! See, I did have something in my head!" William cried in excitement as he paced around *Truth*.

"Preventing the War was his last act, but it should have been his first," Aoife added.

"His last act was the Great Society, and it should have been his first," Nikher added, looking impressed.

"The Ward League ended up being at the end of his life what the IBC should have been at the beginning. Where do you think *Neveah* is hiding this truth? Not that this need confirming," Aoife said jokingly.

"Savoy Palace, maybe? Remember, the rebels trashed it," William said.

"Let's go," Aoife replied.

"It's since been destroyed. It served as Savoy Hospital for the poor and needy until the eighteenth century, when most of it was destroyed in a fire. By early nineteenth century, most of the remaining buildings were demolished for Waterloo Bridge," Nikher muttered.

"Should we go to the bridge then?" Aoife asked, just as confused as the rest of them looked.

"No, it's the last truth. This revolt was the Great Society hindering the war effort, remember. Parliament was unable to raise taxes, and England had to curtail its military expedition," William said.

"As well, it accelerated the decline of Serfdom. As wages increased, lords sold their serfs' freedom in exchange for cash...

another benefit of the revolt. The truth could be anywhere," Nikher said.

"Even here on *Truth*, where we are free," Eoghan said with an eyebrow lifted.

"*Neveah*, connect me to *Truth*," William said through Mind-Link.

"William Ward, this is…" *Neveah* said.

"The Peasants' Revolt of 1381, the final truth. William's Great Society," William replied.

"Make sure the last thing you do in life shouldn't have been the first," he heard his grandfather John's voice answer. "The world needed a Great Society in 1318, not an IBC. William ended his life the way he should have begun it. The truths you are hearing are meant to guide you through history, so you have the world's knowledge to live your life as William the twenty-first Ward and guide the Great Society."

A brief pause ensued and then John proceeded to list the events of the fifteenth century.

Chartered Company 1407

The settlement of the Canary Islands 1403

War of the Roses 1455–1485

The Siege of Belgrade 1456

Night Attack at Târgoviște 1462

Ōnin War 1467–1477

Sengoku period 1467–1600

Burgundy Wars 1474–1477

Pazzi conspiracy 1478

Spanish Inquisition 1481
The Treaty of Tordesillas 1494
The Italian Wars 1494–1559

The end

See you in the next century!

CPSIA information can be obtained
at www.ICGtesting.com
Printed in the USA
LVHW051129080920
665300LV00004B/566